One Last Lie

One Last Lie

Paul Doiron

MINOTAUR BOOKS
NEW YORK

First published in the United States by Minotaur Books,
an imprint of St. Martin's Publishing Group

ONE LAST LIE. Copyright © 2020 by Paul Doiron. All rights reserved.
Printed in the United States of America. For information, address
St. Martin's Publishing Group, 120 Broadway, New York, NY 10271.

www.minotaurbooks.com

The Library of Congress Cataloging-in-Publication Data
is available upon request.

ISBN 978-1-250-23507-7 (hardcover)
ISBN 978-1-250-23508-4 (ebook)

Our books may be purchased in bulk for promotional, educational, or business use. Please contact your local bookseller or the Macmillan Corporate and Premium Sales Department at 800-221-7945, extension 5442, or by email at MacmillanSpecialMarkets@macmillan.com.

First Edition: 2020

10 9 8 7 6 5 4 3 2 1

For Mat, teacher and friend

The world is full of obvious things which
nobody by any chance ever observes.

—SIR ARTHUR CONAN DOYLE,
The Hound of the Baskervilles

One Last Lie

I

Before I left for Florida, my old friend and mentor Charley Stevens gave me a puzzling piece of advice. "Never trust a man without secrets."

I thought he'd misspoken. "Don't you mean a man *with* secrets?"

But the retired game warden only winked as if to suggest he'd said exactly what he'd intended to say. It would be up to me to figure out the meaning of his cryptic remark.

I went to Miami to do a background check on an air force vet who had applied for a job with the Maine Warden Service and about whose character I had vague yet creeping doubts. On paper and in a series of face-to-face interviews, Tom Wheelwright had appeared to be the ideal candidate to become our next chief pilot. A Maine native currently residing in Key Biscayne, he was a decorated combat veteran with more than enough air hours to qualify him for the position. He was quick on his toes, clear-eyed, and a family man with a presentable wife and three presentable children. When I'd asked him why he wanted to trade the salary of a Learjet pilot for that of a Maine State employee, he said he hoped to raise his kids somewhere that "still felt like a real place."

It was a good answer.

Still, I couldn't shake the feeling that Wheelwright was not the paragon everyone swore he was.

For the past week, I had been interrogating every aspect of the man's life. I had started with the list of references he had provided. I spoke with his wife and parents, his brothers and sisters, his commanding officers in the air force, the management of the charter airline that employed him, former coworkers, neighbors, friends. I had reviewed multiple credit reports, paused over a criminal history that consisted of nothing but (frequent) speeding tickets, and found no red flags.

Everything checked out except for the familiar voice inside my head.

Never trust a man without secrets.

It was Charley's dictum that had prompted me to keep digging until I unearthed a name conspicuous by its absence from any of the files I'd been given. Captain Joe Fixico now worked part-time running airboat tours out of Shark Valley in the Everglades, but during the first Gulf War, he had flown multiple sorties over Iraq as Wheelwright's electronic warfare officer.

Captain Fixico had, coincidentally, also retired from the air force to South Florida. The two flyboys lived less than thirty miles from each other. And yet Wheelwright hadn't included on his disclosure list the one man who could best speak to his coolness at the stick and his courage under fire.

Fixico himself seemed surprised when I finally reached him by phone. "Tommy listed me as a reference?"

"As a matter of fact, he didn't."

"Well, that's understandable, I guess. We're not as close as we were during the war." He had a rough, rasping voice that made me imagine he possessed a fondness for tobacco. "I'm sorry, what did you say your name was again?"

"Mike Bowditch. Would you be available to get together tomorrow, Captain?"

"Of course," he'd said. "And please, call me Joe."

Then my new friend had invited me to his house in the outermost ring of the Miami suburbs.

The next morning, however, Fixico called back twice: the first time to push our appointment to late afternoon, the second time to change the location to a restaurant owned by the Miccosukee Tribe of Native Americans, out in the Glades.

"You can't miss it," he said in a voice that sounded even scratchier than it had the night before. "It's across the highway from the national park entrance. Look for the sign advertising fried gator tail and all-you-can-eat frogs' legs."

When I'd laughed at what I'd assumed to be hyperbole, the line went quiet.

"Do you think I'm proud of it?" he'd finally said. "That I don't know it's a caricature? Just be glad I'm willing to meet with you at all, Warden Bowditch."

I hadn't realized until that moment that Joe Fixico was himself a Miccosukee. Nor did I understand why the formerly cooperative air force captain was now playing hard to get.

The temperature was eighty-eight degrees. The relative humidity was 90 percent. The swollen canal behind my airport motel smelled rank and diseased, like a mouthful of rotten teeth.

I was overdressed in a navy linen suit, a sky-blue cotton shirt, suede chukka boots, and a SIG P239 handgun holstered on my belt. I also carried a badge identifying me as a Maine game warden investigator. When traveling on duty out of state, I was required to present myself as a law enforcement officer. People assumed I was a plainclothes police detective, which in a sense I was, the difference being that most of the crimes I investigated back home were perpetrated against wildlife.

Not having anything else to do with my unanticipated free time, I decided to play tourist. I had never visited Florida. In thirty-one years on earth, I had rarely even left the state of Maine.

I was parochial enough, for instance, to think the name of the four-lane highway that carried me across the flooded saw grass prairie had an aboriginal music to it. The Tamiami Trail. Later I learned it was just a mashup of the highway's starting and ending points: Tampa and Miami. The contraction was cooked up by a cynical developer to entice émigrés from Middle America to buy bulldozed swampland.

Florida had been built on a foundation of fraud and false promises as much as on a bedrock of limestone, riddled with holes and prone to devastating collapses.

In the lot outside the Shark Valley Visitor Center, I spotted dozens of cars and RVs, and I wondered, *What kind of fool chooses to go wildlife watching in the heat of a late-June day when every breath feels like being waterboarded?*

Then I caught sight of my sweating reflection in the glass booth where I paid my admission, and I knew what kind of fool.

The birds, though! Great and snowy egrets, blue and tricolored herons, anhingas posed cruciform in the mangroves, drying their wings, glossy and white ibises, roseate spoonbills, and purple gallinules walking across water lilies with their grotesquely oversized feet. Alligators lolled ridge-backed in the canals or sprawled in the verges between the paved walk and the stream. Enormous catfish, gar, and tilapia floated with a flutter of fins beneath the tea-colored surface. Never had I encountered nature in such glorious, riotous abundance. An eye-popping, caterwauling carnival of life.

I had probably lost ten pounds in water weight when, remembering my appointment, I returned to my rented sedan, buckled on my sidearm, pulled on my suit jacket, and drove across the street to the restaurant that served deep-fried reptiles.

When I stepped through the door, a blast of air-conditioning hit me in the face with the force of a meat freezer thrown open.

"I'm supposed to meet someone," I told the host. His skin was the color of bronze, and he wore his black hair long and parted straight down the center.

"He's not here yet."

"I'll sit down."

"I think you'd better."

The interior was festively decorated in bright colors and Native American motifs. The only customers were two white families—clearly foreign, clearly tourists—and a black man with gray hair seated at the lunch counter, reading a fishing magazine.

My waitress was so concerned that I might collapse of dehydration that she left a filled water pitcher on the table. She brought another five minutes later when I'd drained the first.

Half an hour passed. The families ate and left and were replaced by more families and an elderly couple and some college-age boys who were loud even before they ordered Budweisers all around. The man at the counter had managed to disappear without my seeing him leave. My server asked if I wanted to order some food while I could.

"We'll be closing soon. We close at four o'clock."

"Why so early?"

"We close when the park closes."

I tried Fixico's phone number but got an automated reply. I left a curt message for him to call me. As the restaurant emptied, I could feel the host watching me, willing me to get up and leave the way a cat wills you to feed it. I put down a ten-dollar bill for the water and the trouble.

2

I sat in my rented Hyundai with the air-conditioning cranked and fog inching up the windshield, trying to decide how to proceed. If I left now, I might still catch my flight home. But the hook had been set, and I wasn't breaking free without a fight.

Why had Fixico brought me all the way out into the Everglades only to stand me up? Why not just tell me over the phone that, upon further reflection, he had nothing to say about Captain Tom Wheelwright?

Because he wanted to have a look at me first.

In the rearview mirror, I noticed the man who'd seated me leaving the restaurant. He paused to tuck his white polo into his pants and put on a pair of wraparound shades before making his way toward a Chevrolet Camaro parked in the thin shade of a palm.

Careful of fire ants, I crossed the sandy lot. "Excuse me, sir!"

The bronze man lurched to a stop. "You're still here?"

"I have a question for you."

"OK?"

"When I told you I was meeting someone, you said, 'He's not here yet.' How did you know I was meeting a man?"

"You said you were."

"No, I didn't."

"I think you're confused. Look, I've got to pick up my kid."

I watched the sports car accelerate onto the cracked highway headed back toward Miami. Then I shaded my eyes with the blade of my hand and scanned the endless flatness. I hadn't seen the man at the counter leave, but I saw him now, not a hundred yards away.

Beyond the restaurant stood a second, smaller building with the same thatched roof—a tribal information center—and beyond that was a dirt lot that bordered a dull canal that might or might not have been the Shark River. The black man I'd noticed inside the restaurant stood on the bank, wearing a panama hat, smoking a cigar, and fishing with a cane pole unlike anything I'd ever seen in Maine.

"Captain Fixico?"

His back stiffened, but he spoke without turning. "I was beginning to have doubts about you as an investigator, Warden Bowditch. You didn't expect me to be black. Some of us Natives are."

"Do you want to tell me what that stunt was about?"

He tossed the cigar butt into the greenish water. A small fish came up to snap at it. A bigger fish rose from the depths to swallow the smaller fish whole. There's always someone bigger, someone hungrier.

When Fixico finally faced me, I saw that he had an indentation in his forehead that spoke of a head injury neither recent nor ancient. His nose was straight, his brow slanting, and his eyes were so heavily lidded he seemed half-asleep.

"I wanted to check you out before we talked," he said, a little smile playing in the corners of his mouth.

"And you didn't like my looks?"

"Not particularly. How did you find me?"

"It took a while."

"That's not what I meant. How did you find me in the first place? You said Tommy didn't give you my name as a character witness."

Witness. I made a mental note of the word choice.

"Maybe I'm a better investigator than I look."

He laughed at that and gestured toward an SUV that gleamed white across the lot. "Let me get this line in, and we can talk inside my Rogue so you don't melt any more than you already have, Mr. Snowman. I'll tell you the truth about the great Tom Wheelwright. The whole truth and nothing but."

The interior of the SUV smelled of his Cubanos. I observed a cigar burn in the otherwise pristine leather upholstery. He removed his straw hat and set it on the dash.

Unlike Wheelwright, who was impossibly fit in middle age, Fixico had acquired a belly since his air force days. He wore a guayabera shirt, relaxed-fit jeans, and flip-flops. A medical alert bracelet hung like a bangle from one thin wrist.

"So you're a detective?" he said. "And your bureau flew you all the way down here to run a background check on a man applying to become a *game warden*? I never would've thought that was an actual thing."

In fact, investigating applicants to the Maine Warden Service was one of my most important duties. Many people participated in the hiring process—including a psychologist and a polygraph operator—but ultimately, it was my responsibility to prevent an unfit candidate from acquiring a badge and gun.

"Do you mind if I record this?"

Fixico reached for an aluminum tube on the center console, unscrewed the end, and shook out a cigar. "I'd prefer we talk on 'deep background,' if you don't mind."

"Are you concerned about retribution from the air force?"

He had a laugh that seemed to scrape his vocal cords. "What're they going to do to me that's worse than what God dished out? You wouldn't think it to look at me, but I graduated magna cum laude from Dartmouth. I used to be brilliant. The undamaged part of my brain still is. It's new memories I can't retain."

What interested me was the old stuff. "So you and Wheelwright flew EF-111A Ravens in the war?"

"Spark Varks. That's what we called them. Technically, Tom did the flying, and my job was to fuck with Saddam's communications, an activity at which I excelled. After I came back from the Gulf, I thought I was headed for a career at a defense contracting firm. Six-figure income, big house outside the Beltway, marry a white woman. The Native American dream."

He smiled ironically through a cloud of cigar smoke. "None of that has anything to do with Tom Wheelwright. He wasn't in Las Vegas when my Corvette was T-boned or when I woke from my coma to learn I was being medically retired. Why did Tommy tell you *he* chose to leave the air force?"

"He said he couldn't resist the money he was promised to fly Learjets for the 1 Percent."

"That's partially true, I suppose. Tom's always been good at using truthful statements to mislead. Or maybe he's one of those people who passes polygraphs because they believe their own bullshit."

"I have all his military records, including his honorable discharge. There's not a blemish in his file."

"There wouldn't be. Pilots are held to different standards. Especially when it comes to reports of inappropriate conduct with the other sex."

"Why is there no mention of harassment charges?"

"It's the air force! Where have you been living for the past fifteen years? Tom was encouraged to take early retirement." Fixico rolled down his window to relieve the fug. "Now you're thinking, 'Why should I take the word of a brain-damaged Injun over the United States Air Force?' Because I can give you names is why. I can point you to the women. But I have a feeling you already believe me."

He was right on that account.

I tried to lean forward, but my shirt adhered to the upholstery as if with paste. "Last night, you said you were willing to talk about Tom Wheelwright. Today, you gave me the slip. What made you change your mind, Captain?"

"Truth be told, I don't recall our conversation all that well. As I said, I have a problem forming new memories. But back when Tommy and I were hotshots in the USAF—before my brain injury—I was as cocky as he was. It was the crash that humbled me. Do you know how often I overhear kids asking their moms about the man with the dent in his head? When the world looks at you and sees a freak, you no longer have the luxury of ignoring the truth."

He absently stroked the moon crater in his forehead.

"But I still haven't answered your question. What made me change my tune? I realized the significance of Tommy not giving you my name. He was afraid I'd acquired a conscience as a result of my misfortunes, and rightly so. People have been covering for that man his whole life—me included. I decided the time had come for someone to knock the great Wheelwright off his pedestal."

Alone again in my car, I called the first woman whose name Fixico had given me, a former air force second lieutenant now living outside Omaha, Nebraska.

"How did you find me?" she'd asked with a flutter of panic.

And with that, my job was done.

3

My flight left without me. I may even have watched the plane take off from the freeway where I was stalled in traffic.

The cause of the holdup was a fatality, the second I'd witnessed on the Florida highways. The dead man lay in the median grass with a blanket over him. His wrecked car looked like it had gone through a junkyard compactor. In addition to the usual first responders, I spotted half a dozen white-and-green Border Patrol vehicles.

Unable to do anything except crawl forward, I put in a call to the officer supervising the search for a new chief warden pilot. Major Patrick Shorey had been on the panel that had hired me eight years earlier. His had been a dissenting voice. So of course, he was an unabashed champion of Tom Wheelwright.

"You said this Seminole you interviewed suffered a brain injury?"

"Captain Fixico is Miccosukee, not Seminole."

"The point is he has memory problems."

"But the two women I spoke with don't, and they were both open about the extent of Wheelwright's sexual misconduct—*assaults* is the better word."

"Why didn't they file complaints against him with the air force?"

"They say they were dissuaded from doing so by their superiors."

"Two dozen people vouched that Captain Wheelwright

conducted himself with bravery and professionalism. Why should we take the word of these women?"

"Because they didn't know about each other. They never served together. There's no way they could have coordinated their stories."

"It's a fine world we're living in when a war hero can have his reputation destroyed by undocumented allegations."

"Captain Fixico gave me more names if you'd like—"

"Just send me the damned report."

The traffic began to inch ahead, then stopped again.

I checked my messages and found a text from the kid I'd hired to watch my dog. Logan Cronk was the son of friends who lived down the road from me on the Maine Midcoast. The boy was ten, blond, and big for his age (or any age).

> Shadow ate a turkey poult! It landed inside in his pen while he
> was sleeping under the trees and it didn't see him and he leaped
> out from the bushes and ate it in like three bites.

Legally speaking, Shadow wasn't a dog; he was a wolf dog. To be even more precise, he was a gray wolf with a smattering of domestic dog genes. His "pen" was a fenced enclosure on my wooded property, roughly one and a half acres in area.

Logan had attached several photographs so that I could rest assured he had been fulfilling his duties. One picture was of himself holding a turkey wing pinion, presumably all that was left of Shadow's lunch.

I wrote the boy back thanking him and adding that he'd better not have ventured inside the fence to retrieve those feathers. The wolf dog may have been raised in captivity, but he had spent the past few years on the run in the Maine mountains, killing deer and digging beavers out of their lodges, and I didn't trust him not to eat children.

I considered the empty hours ahead. My ex-girlfriend Stacey Stevens, the woman I had once considered the love of my life and who was not insignificantly the daughter of my mentor Charley and his wife, Ora, lived less than two hours away.

Stacey's last communication, months before, had been an email that ended with the words, "*If by some small miracle you're ever in Florida, I would love, love, love to see you.*"

Before I could slip down this dangerous slope, I called my current girlfriend back home.

"I'm afraid I'm here for one more night," I told Danielle "Dani" Tate.

"I hope the last interview was worth it."

"Let's just say that Tom Wheelwright will never be a member of the Maine Warden Service."

Dani was younger than I was, a former game warden who had transferred to the Maine State Police because she saw greater opportunities for advancement. To the world, she presented one face: snub-nosed, gruff, blond hair tied up tight, a badass cop. To me and me alone, she showed a gentler profile: soft gray eyes, dimples that only made themselves known when she smiled, a heart that was twice the size of mine.

As the sky darkened at the edges, leaving a hazy dome of light above the city, I told Dani about Fixico. She listened quietly as I recounted the day's revelations. Proud of myself, I ended the monologue with two of the women Wheelwright had coerced into having sex with him.

"Congratulations," Dani said.

I detected an undercurrent of sarcasm. "Thanks?"

"No, it's great that you nailed Wheelwright. But the odds are good that the guy you end up hiring will be a sleaze, too. He'll just be better at covering his tracks." She let that sit with me for a moment, then her tone lightened again. "So what are you going to do with your free night in Miami? Go clubbing in South Beach?"

"The last footprints I left on a dance floor were in junior high."

"That's probably for the best."

The joke was at her expense as well as mine—Trooper Tate was not remotely footloose.

"What?" I laughed. "You don't think I can dance?"

"You won't like my answer to that question."

I paused before I spoke again. "I promised Stacey I would be in touch if I ever got down this way."

Dani didn't skip a beat. "Doesn't she live over on the Gulf Coast?"

"Everglades City. That's about two hours from here, I think. Chances are she'll be busy anyway, but I will have made an effort. And her folks will be happy—which matters to me, as you know. I'll probably end up back at my motel with a pizza, watching baseball."

"You're presuming I'm jealous."

"You're not?"

"I'm not in sixth grade, Mike. You two shared a lot together. It's sad if you can't be friends. I trust you, and I hope you trust me. Give Stacey my best if you see her."

"The truth is, I could use a good night's rest."

"Me, too. I think I caught a bug."

My favorite photo of Stacey stared up from the lighted screen of my phone. I had taken the picture on a summer evening four years earlier while we were canoeing the famed Allagash Wilderness Waterway in northern Maine. Her dark hair was tousled. There was a sheen of perspiration on her cheekbones. Her eyes were the color of jade.

Stacey and I had lived together for close to two years, and everyone assumed we would get married. She was the daughter of people I already loved like parents. We shared a passion for the outdoors. She was intelligent, fearless, and capable. For a long time, I had believed she must be my soul mate.

In the end, it was the qualities we had in common that drove us apart. Where I was reckless, she was almost pathologically irresponsible. Where I was stubborn, she was unyielding to a fault. Where I was quick to anger, she stoked her rage with a red-hot poker. Our decision to separate had been no less sad for being by mutual agreement.

Stacey answered at once. "Well, howdy, stranger!"

"How did you know it was me?"

"I have you in my list of favorites. I'm looking at your picture right now. You're in your field uniform, looking all brooding and handsome."

"I don't look like that anymore. I grew my hair out for my job as an investigator."

"Just as long as it isn't a mullet. So, listen, I'd love to catch up, but you caught me as I was walking out the door."

Was it relief I felt or disappointment? "I'll let you go then."

"Not without telling me why you called. What's up?"

"I'm in Florida."

"No shit? Where?"

"West of Miami. I'm stuck in traffic on the 836. I just saw an exit for Sweetwater."

"You have to come see me! You'll regret it for the rest of your life if you pass this up."

"Pass what up?" I asked, worried.

"We're going on a wild python hunt."

4

On the flight to Miami, I had passed the hours reading a natural history guide to South Florida. The book included a section devoted to imported reptiles—notably, Burmese pythons and Nile monitor lizards—that had either escaped captivity or been released by negligent pet owners. Without natural predators, these two invasive species had taken over the wet prairies, pine hammocks, and cypress swamps south of Lake Okeechobee. Biologists had found deer fawns, raccoons, wild piglets, marsh rabbits, and even alligators inside the bellies of the pythons. Out of desperation, the state was holding derbies with cash prizes for civilian hunters who killed the most and biggest snakes.

That afternoon, a hiker had reported an enormous Burmese python near a trailhead in the Big Cypress National Preserve. Stacey was joining a biologist friend in an attempt to locate and capture the monster snake before it swallowed someone's toddler. She told me to meet her at a place called Fortymile Bend, ten minutes west of the Miccosukee Restaurant.

"It'll be like old times," she promised.

That was what worried me. We had brought out the worst in each other more often than the best. By ourselves, we were daredevils. Together, we were a pair of lunatics.

But how could I resist the adventure of hunting a serpent that reached lengths of twenty feet and could weigh as much as two hundred pounds?

The sun was setting, but I couldn't see it for the black clouds boiling out of the Gulf. As I neared Shark Valley, I saw the first blue pulses of electricity lighting up the thunderheads from within. The wind blew palm fronds and palmetto fans onto the slick blacktop. By the time the sign for Fortymile Bend appeared in my headlights, the rain was pelting my windshield like bird shot.

A Land Rover with a canoe strapped to the roof rack flicked its headlights as I turned into a circular drive outside the Tamiami Ranger Station. I pulled on my raincoat and hurried across the surface of crushed white shells that seemed to be what road builders used here in lieu of gravel. The wet air smelled of swamp plants my northern nose couldn't identify.

Inside the Rover, she pulled me close enough that the fumes from the bug dope on her skin knocked me out. She looked leaner, with the beginnings of wrinkles around her almond-shaped eyes. She placed a tanned hand on either side of my face.

"You're all grown-up!"

"I like to think I was before."

"Do you have a head net and bug suit?"

"I am an investigator. I was here doing background checks."

She always became most beautiful when she laughed. "You really have no idea what you're in for tonight. Florida mosquitoes are relentless. They make the Terminator look weak-willed."

"They can't be any worse than the blackflies back home."

"That's like saying death by hanging can't be any worse than death by firing squad." She handed me a small bottle of mosquito repellent. "You should buckle up. The drive to Gator Hook Strand is going to be wet and wild."

She put the transmission into gear and skidded onto the back road that split off the four-lane, heading southwest into what looked like real backcountry.

"I can't believe you're really here," she said, smiling again. "Stranger in a strange land."

"You seem to have adapted."

"I wouldn't be so sure. Did my mom and dad make you promise to come see me when they heard you were visiting Florida?"

"Not in so many words."

Charley and Ora Stevens had been heartbroken when Stacey and I split up. Ora had intuited that things hadn't been great for a while. But Charley had nurtured dreams of grandchildren.

"Being so far from my folks is the hardest part of living here," she said. "I keep inviting them down, but you know how my mom feels about planes."

Ora Stevens had been paralyzed below the waist in a plane crash during a flying lesson from her husband. He'd walked away from the wreckage with nothing but a broken arm and a crushing weight on his conscience.

"Of course, my dad knows South Florida like the back of his hand from the months he spent here back in the aughts."

"What?"

"The State of Florida hired him to help with an aerial survey, counting manatees."

"He never told me that!"

She twitched her nose bewitchingly. "Charley Stevens, international man of mystery."

I slathered bug dope behind my ears. It smelled like the liquid poison it was. "How is your job going?"

"Besides soul-crushing? We had forty Florida panthers killed in the state last year, up from the year before. We build fences along the highways and wildlife underpasses they can use to cross from one side to the other, but that doesn't help along all the back roads, where people speed along at night at eighty miles an hour. Meanwhile, development keeps encroaching into their habitat because what's the value of an endangered species compared to selling the next Del Boca Vista? And now we're seeing a crippling disorder in some of the cats that inhibits coordination of their rear legs. Wasn't there a crazy king who tried to fight the rising tide with a sword? That's me."

"Since when does your work involve catching pythons?"

"It doesn't, but once a biologist, always a biologist. My friend Buster is in charge of python eradication for the National Park Service. And God knows he needs the help."

"From what I read, it sounds like the snakes are here to stay."

"That depends on your frame of reference."

"What do you mean?"

"In fifty years, South Florida will be underwater and the pythons will be Georgia's problem. So you said the Warden Service is looking for a new chief warden pilot? Maybe I should apply."

"Ha ha."

"Who says I'm joking?"

I must have shown alarm.

"You should see the look on your face," she said. "Don't worry. I'm just having fun with you."

At the edge of the high beams, I saw a mud-spattered Ford Expedition with what I assumed was a snake-spotting tower bolted onto the SUV's roof.

A wide-beamed man in jeans and hip waders leaned over the tailgate, rummaging around for something. He straightened up when he heard our engine. He had long gray hair beneath a camouflage-patterned fedora, a stubble beard, and skin the color of a baked ham.

"That's Buster Lee. If anyone can find this snake, it's him." She opened her door and leaned out. "I've brought along a helper."

The man's drawl was so slow and syrupy it had to be a put-on. "The swamp's no place for amateurs, Stevens."

"This is Mike Bowditch. My game warden friend from Maine. You remember me telling you about him?"

He was wearing a safari shirt stretched tight across his belly. In one hand, he held a floppy canvas bag; in the other, a five-foot-long hooked tool. Presumably a snake-catching device. "He doesn't look like any conservation officer I ever met."

Stacey shook her head at me in mock disbelief. I couldn't remember seeing her in such high spirits.

Despite the bug dope, the mosquitoes had already begun to mob the bare skin of my face and the fleshy parts of my exposed hands.

Finally, Buster let the deadpan drop. "Hell, son, I'm just having fun with you. Any friend of Stevens is a friend of mine. So you're the warden she's always going on about."

"Stacey tells me you're Florida's champion python-catcher."

He struck a heroic pose with the hooked tool and the gunnysack. "I don't call myself that, understand? It's an honorific others have bestowed upon me. But I'm not going to say I don't deserve the title. Is this your first python hunt, Warden Mike?"

"They haven't made it to Maine yet, fortunately—except as pets."

"That's how they arrived here, too." He fastened a headlamp over his brimmed fedora and fiddled with it to get the beam properly aligned. "Florida is the world capital of unintended consequences."

The raindrops slapped the flat leaves of the palmettos. Lightning flashed to the south, but the thunder took a long time rolling across the saw grass prairie. At least we would be safe from electrocution.

"How do you plan on finding a snake in the dark?" I asked.

Buster let his drawl drop. "The man who reported it said it was 'in blue.'"

"That means its eyes were opaque," explained Stacey. "It's getting ready to shed its skin."

"Shedding snakes go inactive," Buster explained. "The little ones hide—because they're vulnerable—but these big boys and girls don't have natural enemies; they're the new apex predators in town, so they just camp out wherever. Go into temporary brumation."

"That's like hibernation," Stacey translated.

"Enough talking," said the python-catcher, recovering his false drawl. "More walking."

We began our hike, single file across a board bridge and down the wet path, illuminating both sides with our headlamps. Lush green ferns sprouted everywhere except in spots where pale limestone outcroppings poked through the humus. The trees along the trail were too scraggly to keep off the face-smacking rain. I recognized a few species from my nature guide: live oak, poisonwood, gumbo-limbo. All the trunks were crawling with big, banded snails like mobile carbuncles.

The mud sucked with real determination at my shoes, eager to steal them from my feet. The onslaught of mosquitoes continued, unabated. I wondered which disease I was most likely to contract: malaria, dengue fever, or the Zika virus.

"Don't let Buster fool you," Stacey said in a whisper. "He's not even from the South. He got a Ph.D. in herpetology from the University of Wisconsin. He just gets a kick out of playing the cracker."

"Kind of like your father, except he's a different brand of cracker."

"Touché."

Off in the darkness, not a hundred feet away, something screamed. Not called, not shrieked, but screamed. My first morbid thought was of a young girl being stabbed to death.

Stacey didn't slow or stop.

From around the next bend, Buster called to us, "Hey, lovebirds!"

We hurried in the direction of his voice and found the herpetologist huffing wind beside a bench.

He had his headlamp focused on the ground at his boots, but as we approached, he raised the beam just enough to show a pale, coiled form in the slough. If the python hadn't been shedding its skin, I never would have spotted it.

Stacey let out a whistle. "She's huge."

"How do you know it's a she?" I asked in a whisper.

"The females are usually bigger than the males."

"Here's a fun fact for you, Warden Mike," Buster Lee said, taking a tentative step down the bank. "Female pythons can produce offspring without even mating. I'm not shitting you. Look it up. The process is called *facultative parthenogenesis*. Lots of human females would sign up for that deal, I would wager."

"Do you want me to go down there with you?" Stacey asked, speaking fast in her eagerness.

"It's easier for one person to grab the head," he said. "Just be ready to pounce on her coils before she can wrap them around my neck."

I had never been content being a bystander. "What can I do?"

"Spectate."

I watched as Buster slid down the muddy embankment into the edge of the water, maybe two yards behind the snake's pale head. The ghostly creature seemed not to register the man's approach at all. I was beginning to think he moved with a certain unexpected grace for a person of his girth. Then he took a step forward, lost his footing, and fell face-first into the brown water. The splash caused the snake to awaken, and faster than seemed possible, it ducked into the undergrowth.

Buster sprang up from the drink to grab desperately at the tail. His fedora and headlamp had disappeared. Despite how wet he was, he managed to get a grip. The python—brought up short—whipped around with its pale mouth wide and bit him on the face. Buster gave a whimper, stumbled, and half disappeared beneath the surface, which the snake was now churning to a coffee froth.

I knew constrictors did this: used their backward-curving teeth to secure a hold on prey—or, also presumably, an attacker—but I hadn't expected this one to act like a monster out of a horror movie, and neither did the two biologists.

"Buster!" Stacey jumped down to help.

The python's distended jaws had fastened on his nose and chin. Gushing blood showed red in my flashlight beam. The coils wrapped around Buster's arm, chest, and throat were as thick around as my thigh.

Stacey tried to pull the snake free, but her efforts only seemed to cause the serpent to latch onto Buster all the harder. I considered shooting it, but there was no way to fire a round through the head that didn't risk hitting the man. What I would have given for a canister of pepper spray.

Then I remembered. I reached into my pocket and found the small bottle. I leaped clear off the bank and went into the water up to my chest.

Blood pumped rhythmically through Buster Lee's fingers as he gripped the triangular skull. The fight had torn tatters in the python's bluish hide. It looked like a zombie serpent.

As Buster muttered and moaned, I directed my pump dispenser of bug repellent at the snake's squeezed-shut eyes. The poisonous liquid just ran off harmlessly. Then I caught a flash of pinkish white: the corner of the python's mouth. I sprayed the exposed tissue with a shot of 100 percent diethyltoluamide: commonly known as DEET.

And just like that, Buster was free.

To his credit, the herpetologist continued to fight the thrashing, half-poisoned animal. He closed a hand around the throat below its jaws. Between the two of them, they wrestled the enormous serpent up the bank.

"Get the bag," Stacey said.

I used the overhanging vines to pull myself out of the sloshing water. Then, on hands and knees, I crawled across the soaked grass to grab the burlap sack. I couldn't imagine how a hundred pounds of serpentine muscle could fit inside it. Somehow they managed the feat.

Half-blind with blood, Buster knotted the top so the snake couldn't escape. The sack pulsed like the gullet of a waterbird that had just swallowed a living fish. The wounded man then collapsed to the ground with a hand over his face.

"I believe I may need medical assistance."

Stacey turned, blinding me with the headlamp she wore. "There's a first aid kit in my Rover, behind the passenger seat. Grab it for me."

As I took off down the trail, I remembered a similar incident years ago in which it had been Stacey who had been injured by an attacking animal. In that case, it had been a feral boar in the foothills of southwestern Maine.

It took me five minutes to return with supplies. I found Stacey clutching a handkerchief to her friend's face. He might have been wearing a red mask.

"Never had that happen before." His voice betrayed the genuine fear he was feeling. "Are you sure my nose is still attached?"

"Let's have a look."

I was struck by her calmness. Stacey had never been one to keep her cool.

In the focused light of her headlamp, I could see that Buster's nose was ragged but intact. The python's teeth had missed the major veins and arteries in his neck, fortunately, but his sun-reddened face was mangled and would require surgery to repair.

"How maimed am I?" he asked.

"Mildly," said Stacey, squeezing his hand. "You're mildly maimed."

Buster blinked at me through blood-crusted lashes. "What did you spray into her mouth, anyway?"

"DEET."

"No wonder she sounds like she swallowed a gallon of bleach."

The snake thumped in its cloth prison. The sound made my heart hurt. The loud bird—a barn owl, I now believed it to be—screamed again from the darkness of the cypresses.

5

Mist rose from the crushed clamshells and drifted through my headlights as I turned in to the lot outside the ranger station. I climbed out of the Land Rover and stood there in the unbroken heat, listening to the night noises. The frogs were making deep, resonant grunts like an orchestra consisting entirely of tiny bassoons.

A minute later, the top-heavy Ford Expedition swung in beside the Rover. Stacey opened the driver's door. Beside her sat Buster. His huge bristling face was bandaged from his lips to his hairline. The gauze was spotted with blood. But he was smoking a cigarette.

"Do you want me to follow you to the hospital?" I asked as she stepped out of the vehicle.

"There's no need for the two of us to wait around there." She waggled a key loose from her key ring. "Why don't you go clean up at my house? I don't know how long I'll be. But maybe you can catch a few winks, and I'll be home in time to take you to breakfast."

The idea of showering at my ex-girlfriend's felt like a betrayal of Dani.

Stacey noticed my hesitancy. "I won't even be there, Mike. I'm sure Danielle will understand."

At first, her use of Dani's full name seemed like a jab, but there was no mockery in her tone.

Buster called from the Expedition, "I'm still bleeding here!"

"His injuries look worse than they are," she said in a whisper.

"When did you get certified as an EMT?" I asked.

"Stevens!"

"Buster's really a sweetheart if you get to know him."

"So's my wolf dog, but I'm careful not to get too close when he shows his teeth."

She wrapped her arms around my neck and kissed me good-bye. The kiss was light but on the lips.

Forty-five minutes later, my GPS announced that I had arrived in Everglades City. Stacey's rented house stood on elevated pilings to protect it from storm surges. It had a low, pyramidal roof, designed to minimize the impact of hurricane-force winds.

At first glance, the interior also looked like Florida distilled to its essence. Rattan furniture, tile flooring, potted palms. But mementos of Maine peeked out from the shelves. I recognized a box turtle shell I had found on patrol. And there was the edition of Audubon's *Birds of America*; we had bought it from an antiquarian bookseller on a rainy afternoon Down East.

On the walls hung Stacey's framed photographs of Maine animals: a moose and her calf, a lynx on a snowy road, an osprey perched with a fish atop a snag. These same pictures had decorated the house we'd shared for close to two years. She wasn't a great photographer, but she knew how to creep up on wild animals before they spotted her.

Her finest photograph, though, was a black-and-white portrait she had taken of her father.

Charley Stevens looked sideways at the camera, his big chin raised, laugh wrinkles cutting lines in his weathered skin. His thick white hair stood up as if, seconds before, he had run one of his strong hands through it. His expression was one of faux suspicion.

No wonder she missed him. I did, too, in that moment.

I showered as fast as I could, marveling at the dozens of mosquito bites I had sustained in such a short time. Afterward, I stood before the mirror while the steam lifted from the edges of the glass. I hadn't expected these feelings.

I needed to leave.

Stacey had texted me from the hospital with an update. Buster was receiving stitches on his nose and jaw for the snakebite. The copious blood had made the wounds appear worse than they were, as she had deduced.

I texted back that I was glad for the good news. I thanked her for the use of her shower. I didn't tell her that I would be gone before she returned home.

After I'd dressed, I sat down at her kitchen table with a pen and a notepad, trying to find the right words to justify my graceless departure.

Again I thanked Stacey for her hospitality but said that I needed to head back to Miami lest unforeseen circumstances cause me to miss yet another plane. It wasn't the whole truth, nor was it a lie. After a long, silent debate with myself, I signed the note with *love*.

I had just put down the pen when my phone rang. Stacey's mother, Ora, smiled up at me from the lighted screen. She had snow-white hair, pale green eyes, and was, honestly, the most beautiful older woman I had ever seen. The coincidence of Ora calling here and now made me shiver. Then I realized it was after midnight, well past her usual bedtime, and I became even more worried.

"Ora?"

"Mike, where are you?"

"Still in Florida. I have a morning flight back to Maine. Has something happened to Charley?" It was the only reason I could imagine for her calling me that late.

"You haven't heard from him?"

"No, why?"

"He's gone off without a word of explanation."

"What do you mean?"

"He's disappeared. I have no idea where or why. Mike, I don't think he wants me to know where he went."

6

Five hours later, I boarded an Airbus A321 bound for Portland, Maine. I had sped east across the Everglades and arrived at the Miami airport as the rising sun was prying open a crack between the gray sky and the gray ocean.

I took my seat beside the window and gazed out at the acres of interlocking tarmac strips. Boat-tailed grackles glided down to peck for insects in the grass islands between the taxiways.

I texted Dani to tell her I'd made my flight. I had one hell of a story to share upon my return to Maine. "It involves a Burmese python," I wrote.

And Stacey.

After we'd taken off, I removed my briefcase from under the seat and retrieved the notes I had taken of my conversation with Ora Stevens. When you become a law enforcement officer, your academy instructors stress the importance of making careful records of important conversations, but it's a lesson you only learn for real when a defense attorney gets one of your arrests thrown out because you were sloppy with your note-taking. I spread the pages across the tray table.

⸻

"When was the last time you saw him?" I'd asked Ora.

"Yesterday morning. He woke me as he was getting dressed in the dark, but I fell back asleep."

"How many hours ago specifically was that?"

She paused to count. "Forty-one?"

To civilians, this might have seemed a long time to wait before reporting her septuagenarian husband missing. But Charley had been a game warden for decades, and long absences from home had been a part of their life together. Fatal collisions between moose and cars, search-and-rescue missions, and hunts for armed fugitives happened at all hours. But he was retired now and had been for a while, and even in his active-duty days, he wouldn't have left home without giving his wife a full explanation.

"Did he say anything about when he'd be back?"

"Not a word."

"I assume you've tried calling his phone."

"He doesn't pick up, Mike. I keep getting his voice-mail box."

I had never known Charley to forget his mobile phone or travel anywhere without it. Granted, cell coverage in Maine is worse than spotty. It is effectively nonexistent except around the larger population centers, but in extremis, we might use the GPS tracker in his phone to triangulate on his location.

"He didn't leave a note?"

"Just a short one beside my coffee. Charley makes me a cup every morning the way I like. *'I love you, Ora. I'll be back as soon as I get a puzzle sorted out.'* He only uses my name when he's deadly serious. Usually, as you know, he calls me Boss."

The nickname was a term of affection no younger man could get away with calling his partner in this day and age.

"Did you hear his plane leave the dock?"

"That's another thing. He didn't take the Skyhawk. He took his old Ford."

"Wait, he didn't fly?"

"No."

The old pilot was famous for never driving anywhere he could fly even if it was just down to Calais to pick up a chain saw blade from the hardware store. He'd park his Cessna floatplane in the St. Croix River while he ran errands. If Charley had taken his truck, a sap-green Ranger, he'd done so for one reason: because his ultimate destination was inaccessible by air.

"Ora, this next question is difficult. But have you noticed anything unusual about Charley's state of mind?"

"He's not showing signs of dementia."

"I only ask because—"

"He's getting older. We both are. But the answer to your question is *no*."

"Have you reached out to anyone else?"

"You're the closest thing he has to a son, Mike. If he didn't tell you, I don't know who he would have. Nick Francis, maybe."

Nick was the retired chief of the Passamaquoddy Nation. Before that, he'd been the tribal police chief. And before that, he'd been a game warden who'd worked alongside Charley when they were both young officers, in an era when Native Americans in Down East Maine faced harassment and violence unthinkable to modern Americans.

"Can you call Nick and ask if he's heard from Charley lately?"

"Yes, but I will have to tell him the truth, given the things they've been through together."

"Hopefully, he'll have some useful information. Let me backtrack a little. Did anything unusual happen the day before Charley left home?"

"We took the van down to Machias to catch some of the sea breeze and have pie at Helen's. We ran into lots of people we know at the Dike—you know how social Charley is, how he always makes the rounds among the booths—and then we drove home. Come to think of it, he was awfully quiet on the drive back."

The Dike was the local name for the wide Route 1 causeway that ran parallel to the Machias River and served as an embankment dam, keeping the Little River from undercutting the road. On pleasant days, antiques dealers and craftspeople set out tables along the side of the road, turning the causeway into a pop-up bazaar.

"Who did he talk to there?"

"I didn't see. My chapter of Planned Parenthood was gathering signatures, and I covered a shift at the booth while Charley made his rounds."

"But his change in mood happened after you left the Dike and were headed back to the lake?"

"I think that would be accurate."

So he either spoke with someone in Machias or saw something there that rattled him. And that event was likely the cause of his decision to drive off without telling his wife where he was going.

"Did you see him talking with anyone in particular—someone who might have set him off?"

"When we parked, he pointed out a table neither of us remembered seeing before. It looked like the dealer had some taxidermy and rusted old junk from the logging camps. You know how interested Charley is in North Woods history."

"And he didn't mention this dealer to you later? Maybe he made an offhand comment that struck you as strange."

"No, but . . ."

"Go ahead."

"I had the oddest sense he might have bought something from the man. He kept putting his hand in the pocket of his jacket."

"Could it have been a gift for you?"

"That was what I'd suspected, but he was awfully quiet and serious when we got home. After supper, he asked my permission to go out to the boathouse to tinker on his plane. I was asleep when he finally came to bed. And then, as I said, he woke me at four o'clock, putting on his clothes in the dark. That's early even for that bantam rooster."

By now, I was deeply worried about my old friend. I was also conscious that I couldn't disclose my fears to Ora when I was so far from home and in no position to take action.

"My flight to Portland leaves in five hours," I had said. "If you hear anything from Charley or he comes home before I take off, call me. I'm pretty sure the plane doesn't have Wi-Fi, but you can send me emails to read during my layover or when I return to Maine. In the meantime, I need you to make some calls and see if you can find the name of the junk dealer Charley spoke with at the Dike. I'll need to stop at my house on the way north, but with luck, I can be at your place by midafternoon."

"I'll call around town. And, Mike," she'd said. "Please don't tell Stacey about her father being missing."

7

When I landed in Maine, the flight attendant gave us the local time and temperature over the intercom. Somehow, it was hotter in Portland than it had been in Miami.

While we taxied, I turned my phone back on to receive cell signals and to submit the report I'd written on Wheelwright.

Dani had called to say she couldn't wait to hear about my encounter with the python. She asked if Stacey had seemed happy. She added that she was going to be spending the day at the firearms qualification course at the Maine Criminal Justice Academy with the rest of her troop. Dani had always been a crack shot.

Stacey had sent me a text:

> You bum! I was looking forward to catching up over breakfast.
> I was hoping to hear about you and Dani. She seems good for
> you. You seem good.

Ora had left me an email. While I had been en route, she'd been busy querying the other vendors who sold their wares along the Dike and had learned that the stranger hadn't given his name. The City of Machias didn't require sellers to obtain permits to set up their tables.

I called her now from the terminal.

She sounded brighter now that the sun was up. "Carol Boyce, who sells her paintings right next to where this man set up shop, overheard Charley arguing with him over some trinket he had for sale."

I remembered Carol: a big, flowing woman. "Did Mrs. Boyce say what it was?"

"She couldn't hear, unfortunately, but she said the argument got heated."

"I guess I'll be stopping in Machias before I head to your place. Did you happen to speak with Nick Francis?"

"He said he didn't know where Charley might be, but he didn't seem worried. He said I should be patient before I put out a Silver Alert on the best woodsman in Maine."

"That's an odd thing to say."

"You have to know Nick's sense of humor," Ora said. "But I feel better knowing that you're back in Maine. If anyone can track down that man of mine, it's you, Mike."

I appreciated her confidence, but I felt the task I'd taken on was weightier than I'd at first realized. Charley's disappearance wasn't just another investigation. It was far more important than that: potentially a matter of life and death.

I was waiting for my luggage in baggage claim when I noticed a tall, sandy-haired woman at the next carousel. She had her back to me, but I recognized her broad shoulders and the service dog sitting with preternatural stillness at her side, a tawny Belgian Malinois. The breed is a high-energy cousin to the German shepherd, and this one was wearing a red SEARCH DOG IN TRAINING vest. I happened to know this animal was well past the training stage, but the vest probably helped keep off handsy strangers.

"Kathy!"

My former sergeant, Kathy Frost, turned to me, as did Maple, her canine partner. "Grasshopper! What's shaking?"

"My world, as usual."

"I'm the last person you need to tell that to."

Kathy had one of those expressive faces that is attractive because you can see the goodness of her character in it.

She had been my field training officer, assigned to hold my hand during my rookie year, and then she had become one of my closest friends. The first woman in the history of the Maine Warden Service and its first female sergeant, she'd had her promising career cut short when she'd been ambushed outside her house by an enemy she'd never known she had. The attempted murderer fired a burst of shotgun pellets into her abdomen, and it still struck me as proof of God's existence that she had survived.

The Malinois, recognizing me as a friend and fellow pack mate, whipped her black-tipped tail back and forth. I fell down upon one knee to receive her dog kisses.

"Hey, Maple! How are you doing, girl? Have you been digging up bodies?"

"Not this time," said Kathy. "We were at Quantico teaching a program for first responders from around the country."

That explained her dappled complexion. Kathy's freckles tended to multiply the tanner she got.

Before her forced retirement, she had headed up the Warden Service's K-9 team. She now worked as a consultant for law enforcement agencies around the country and even abroad, teaching officers how to train dogs to recover corpses.

"What about you?" she asked. "Where are you coming from in your fancy linen suit?"

"Doing a background check in Florida."

"Florida! Really?" The intensity of her curiosity was such that Maple heard the excitement in her voice and pricked up her ears. "Anywhere near where a certain wildlife biologist is living?"

Kathy had been present for the beginning, middle, and end of my relationship with Stacey, including the latter's decampment for a new life in the Everglades. They had been friendly if not friends. Dani, on the other hand, was one of Kathy's beloved trainees.

I spotted my bag coming around the S-shaped conveyor belt. Considering it contained my locked sidearm, I made a dash for it, glad for the interruption.

When I returned, Kathy said, "I don't suppose you have time to grab lunch?"

"I wish I could, but I've left Shadow alone too long."

"Dani, too."

"Come on, Kathy."

"All I'm saying is you've got a good thing going for once in your life."

"I'm not unaware."

"Hey, there's my bag. We should get together soon, the three of us."

"Absolutely."

We said our goodbyes, and I began the long march to the parking lot. Almost at once, I regretted not having clued Kathy in on the mystery around Charley's disappearance. The two former wardens had worked together for years. Maybe she had an insight. But I hadn't wanted to betray Ora's confidence until I had a better sense of the situation.

I threw my bags in the back of my personal vehicle, a restored 1980 International Harvester Scout. It was only the last week of June, but the air had the heaviness of hurricane season. I had traveled two thousand miles and still hadn't escaped the hot, wet grip of the Everglades.

—

I'd been away for just a week, and yet somehow, I'd missed the end of spring and the beginning of summer. The lupines along Route 1 had faded. By contrast, the birches, maples, and beeches were fully leafed out. If anything, Maine looked even more verdant than Florida.

It was greener in more ways than one. The state had recently legalized the recreational use of marijuana. Every few miles, a new dispensary had arisen along the coastal road:

> *Ye Olde Toke Shoppe*
> *Merry Jane's*
> *Medicinal Mart*
> *Cannabis Rex*
> *Herbal Nirvana*

Like the gold rush of the nineteenth country, I suspected the dope rush of the twenty-first would end in tears and bankruptcies. The real winners would be the same transnational corporations who peddled tobacco and needed a new drug to sell.

I hadn't warned Logan Cronk that I was coming. The sight that greeted me, as I pulled into my pine-shaded dooryard, nearly made my eyes pop from my skull.

Shadow's fenced pen was littered with small bones, piles of feathers, and tatters of fur. A trio of crows perched in the high branches of the poplars within the acre-plus enclosure, waiting for a chance to pick at the gnawed carcasses without being devoured themselves.

The recumbent wolf opened one golden eye when he heard me drive up. He recognized the telltale sound of my engine but waited for me to approach the fence to rouse himself. He gave a shake that raised a cloud of hair, dander, and pollen, then trotted down to the gate to greet me.

"What have you been eating?"

He yawned, revealing two-inch-long teeth.

"Seriously, dude, what is all this crap?"

He sniffed the wire as a signal he wanted me to offer my hand. When I did, he licked my fingertips. Maybe it was a gesture of affection, but more likely he wanted to taste the residual grease from the pizza slice I'd grabbed at a convenience store.

I heard a bicycle behind me and, turning, saw Logan Cronk pedaling hard down my long drive. His blue eyes were bright with excitement; his blond hair was so long and feathery he looked like a pop star from the last days of disco. One half of his face was crimson with a rash, as vivid as a port-wine birthmark.

"Uncle Mike! How come you didn't tell me you were home?"

"Logan, what happened to your face?"

"It's them caterpillars," he said, scratching. "The ones with the poison hairs."

He was talking about the larvae of brown-tail moths, I realized. On the drive home, I had spotted some of their webs in the branches of oak trees. The caterpillars had bristles—or setae— that they shed, which caused allergic reactions, not unlike those caused by poison ivy. In recent years, the moth infestations had spread northeast along the coast. It was hard for me not to see the warmth-loving pests as harbingers of a worse future.

"What's with all the bones? You told me Shadow killed a turkey that landed inside his pen, but from the looks of things, a whole flock got in there. Plus God knows what else."

The boy's grin showed a crooked set of teeth. His parents lacked the money to have them straightened. "It's roadkill."

"What?"

"I was reading that wolves are super hungry all the time and prefer fresh meat and stuff, and I've been riding around with a trash bag picking up the dead animals along the side of the road."

"You'd better not have gone inside the fence, Logan."

"Heck no! I would never have broken the rules." He scratched an inflamed ear. "Even though I think Shadow kind of likes me."

I had only recently dared enter the animal's compound myself—and that was with a can of pepper spray that I doubted would have kept the black beast from ripping out my throat.

"That's a dangerous way of thinking," I said. "You look into his eyes, and it feels like you know what's going on inside his head. But that's just a way we fool ourselves, Logan. Even with regular dogs, we need to remember that their minds work differently from ours. People are really good at convincing themselves that the things they want to believe are true."

"Yeah, but he really likes *you*."

The kid hadn't heard a word I'd said. He was only ten. What had I expected?

"Thank you for giving him that roadkill. It added some variety to his diet. He looks big and healthy again."

The wolf had come into my care after having been shot by a crossbow bolt that had collapsed one of his lungs and permanently damaged ligaments that he needed to chase down prey. His convalescence had lasted many months.

"Do you think he'll ever live in the house with you?"

"It's tough to make predictions, Logan, especially about the future."

The wit and wisdom of Yogi Berra was lost on the ten-year-old.

"Listen," I said, "I have to take a trip north—I'm not sure for how long. Would you consider watching him a few more days? Of course, I'll pay you for the work you've already done."

"Really?"

I opened my wallet and pulled out a twenty-dollar bill for every day I had been away, 140 dollars in all. His father had said Logan was saving for his first .22 rifle, and this windfall would be more than enough to finance the purchase. The joy in his inflamed face produced an unexpected emotion in me. I became keenly aware of not having a family of my own, nor even the prospect of one. Dani had made it clear that she had no interest in becoming a mother.

After Logan had ridden off, I looked into the eyes of the wolf and said, "I missed you, pal."

And despite everything I'd just told the boy about the unknowability of animal minds, I could have sworn Shadow understood me.

8

I had made the mistake of closing all the windows before I'd left, not having anticipated that Maine would experience its first ever monsoon season. The trapped air had a damp, mildewed smell that brought to mind an antebellum mansion rotting away at the edge of some dismal swamp. When I turned on the light in the kitchen, a wolf spider the size of a half-dollar skittered across the floor and disappeared into a crack beneath the baseboard.

My plan was to clean myself up, pack a duffel with clothes appropriate to the bug-ridden month of June, and head for the North Woods. Charley and Ora lived alongside a remote, unspoiled pond in easternmost Maine where their only neighbors were black bears and moose. Maybe by the time I returned, the wolf spider would have moved on to happier hunting grounds and the wallpaper would've stopped peeling in strips from the bathroom wall.

I had accrued three days of comp time while investigating Wheelwright. The state required me to take it in lieu of cash. God forbid that I should ever be paid for the actual hours I worked. I sent messages to inform my coworkers that I would be away. I assured my supervisor, Captain Jock DeFord, that I was ready, willing, and able to return to duty should the need arise.

I put my service weapon in the gun safe and removed my personal handgun and three magazines. It was a Beretta PX4 Storm Compact. With regret, I had retired my beloved Walther

PPK/S that had seen me through so many adventures. The little .380 lacked the stopping power I needed when dealing with charging moose and charged-up men. The Beretta was harder to conceal but I rarely missed with it.

Loading the magazines with hollow-points, I gazed out my window at the leafless oaks. The nests of the invasive moths looked like spun sugar in their bare branches. In a few years, some of these trees would be dead from the defoliating infestation.

The phone rang.

It was Tom Wheelwright. I didn't want to answer but feared he would keep calling—perhaps even call Major Shorey—if I didn't pick up.

"Captain Wheelwright."

"Tom, please." Even his voice projected manly self-confidence.

"It's better that we don't communicate except through established channels."

"Totally understand. Listen, I just got a call from an air force buddy of mine, Joe Fixico. He said he spoke with you yesterday. I have to give you an A+ for thoroughness, Mike. I didn't even realize he was living in Miami-Dade."

"Captain, we can't be having this conversation."

"No, I understand. But you need to know that Fixico has mental problems. Don't get me wrong. He was a hell of an electronic warfare officer. But he was in an automobile accident a while back. It did severe damage to his brain."

He still thinks he's getting the job, the cocky SOB.

"Captain, I spoke with the women."

He didn't miss a beat. "Which women are you referring to?"

"Captain Wheelwright, I am going to hang up now. Please don't call back or attempt to contact anyone else on the search panel. We will be in touch."

Five seconds after I hung up, I had my supervisor on the phone.

"I just got your email about heading out of town," said Jock DeFord. "Is there something you forgot to add?"

"It's Wheelwright."

"I read your report," he said. "Those are serious allegations. I don't like it, but the major thinks we owe him a chance to defend his name."

"Jock, he just called me."

"What do you mean?"

"I mean I just hung up on him. He's gotten wind of the conversation I had with Fixico and is trying to control the damage. Aside from the call being completely inappropriate, there is no way in hell we can hire this guy. His application needs to be shitcanned immediately."

"He shouldn't have reached out to you. Agreed."

"Even allowing this to proceed risks blowback from the press."

"I think you're exaggerating, Mike."

"Because I understand the danger Wheelwright poses to our credibility. You need to make sure Shorey doesn't sway the hiring panel."

"I think you're selling the rest of us short. We're all on the same page about Wheelwright."

"Not Shorey."

"Pat is going to be Pat, but he doesn't have the purview to hire whoever he wants. There's nothing for you to worry about."

That was easier said than done.

When I was a teenager, the Warden Service had weathered one shit storm after another. First, an instructor at the Advanced Warden Academy had been fired for hazing cadets with his own urine. Then an undercover warden busted a well-liked fishing guide on some rinky-dink charges. The guide claimed entrapment, and the story somehow found its way into *The Wall Street Journal*. Afterward, all charges were dropped against the guide.

The bad press had reached its peak fifteen years earlier in a raid on a town along the New Brunswick border. An undercover warden investigator had disappeared somewhere around the village of St. Ignace and was presumed to have been murdered by the poaching gang he'd infiltrated. In the first hours of the house-to-house search, three residences had burned to the ground. The fire had almost certainly been set by the man who'd killed the investigator, but the media—goaded on by opportunistic politicians—had accused the Warden Service of engaging in storm trooper tactics.

Those scandals had occurred before the advent of social media and the #MeToo movement. I could guess what Twitter might do with a serial predator like Tom Wheelwright.

Before I left home, I wrote an email to Dani. I knew she wouldn't see it until she finished qualifying at the range. She would have it in her head that I would be driving over to western Maine to stay at her house. I wanted to prepare her for disappointment. And the situation with Charley was too complicated to explain via a chain of text messages.

We had been dating long-distance for more than a year now. Door to door was a two-hour drive, but the excitement of visiting her made it seem shorter. Dani was, in a word, fun. She was go-go-go. She liked racing snowmobiles across frozen lakes and speed-hiking to the tops of four-thousand-foot mountains. She had given me private lessons in Brazilian jiu-jitsu that always seemed to end in our having sex.

Less successfully, she had tried to interest me in video games we could play against each other while physically apart (*Mario Kart* was her current favorite), but I couldn't get into them. I had always been an old soul. Alone, at night, I preferred a good book. Dani's personal library consisted of her old textbooks and motivational guides by Stephen Covey and Anthony Robbins.

In my email, I laid out the meager information I had about my mentor's sudden disappearance.

"*I know you'll understand,*" I wrote. "*Charley has been the closest thing I've ever had to a real father. I owe it to Ora to track him down.*"

The old pilot had his faults. He could be reckless, scheming, secretive. He was a born actor who exaggerated his folksy Maine accent when it benefited him for a suspect to underestimate his intelligence. He had the corniest sense of humor. Nor had he handled Stacey's and my breakup with the grace for which I had hoped. And yet he remained my hero.

"*I wish he talked more about his past,*" I continued. "*It seems like everything I know about his history—from his childhood in the logging camps to his service in Vietnam—I had to pry out of him or hear secondhand. We'd known each other for years before he told me he'd been shot down and imprisoned in the Hanoi Hilton. How does someone not mention something like that? God only knows what else he's done that he's never told me about.*"

Still, in the seven years we'd known each other, Charley had conducted the equivalent of a Ph.D. program in the flora and fauna of the Maine woods. He had taught me how to do my job, enforcing the state's laws while staying true to my inner compass. Most importantly, he had instructed me in what it meant to be a man in a cultural moment when masculinity was presumed toxic until proven otherwise.

"*With luck, he'll be home by the time I get there. Probably with a bouquet of flowers and some lame excuse for Ora. Same old Charley.*"

Even while I typed these words, I felt a hollowness in my chest. I could say that he was just being himself. But in running off without any explanation, Charley had behaved like someone I didn't recognize. I was afraid, I realized. Afraid that in finding the man, I risked losing my respect for him.

At thirty-one, maybe I was too old to believe in heroes, but I needed Charley Stevens to remain what he had always been—the best man I'd ever known.

9

Driving along coastal Route 1 in the summer was one of my several visions of hell. The traffic was bumper-to-bumper where the road threaded through pedestrian-clogged villages. Then on the straightaways, tourists passed one another like maniacs, desperate to get to Acadia National Park, where they could relax among the hundreds of thousands of people just like them.

It took two hours, but I finally escaped the worst of it. Just past Ellsworth, the road opened, the speed limit rose, and soon, I was cruising through miles of rolling blueberry barrens, the bushes already in full flower. It was as if I had entered not another county but another nation.

My second patrol district had been here, in Down East Maine. The assignment had felt like exile at first. Washington County was one of the poorest counties north of the Mason-Dixon Line and an early epicenter of the opioid pandemic that later devastated so much of rural America. It had taken time, but I had warmed to the luckless region, even came to love it after a fashion, the people especially, and had settled briefly in the county before fate announced it had different plans for me.

When I crossed the bridge above Bad Little Falls and entered downtown Machias, I had the sensation of revisiting a place I'd known from a past life. Storefronts that had been vacant from my days as a patrol warden still had yellowed FOR LEASE signs in their dusty windows. Everyone was shopping at the three new dollar stores out on the strip, I'd heard.

At last, I came to the Dike. On the eastern side of the road was the salt water, still brackish from the river tumbling down the falls. On the western side were dozens of parking spaces and a guardrail separating the pavement from a well-traveled ATV trail. People in this part of the world took their four-wheelers to the convenience store to buy beer and cigarettes the way people elsewhere used their cars for the same desperate errands.

The flea market was bunched up at the north end. On this overcast afternoon, the bazaar consisted of a handful of tables and sheltered booths, plus the food truck that sold breakfast sandwiches made with apple cider doughnuts instead of english muffins. I backed my Scout into one of the many empty spaces and stepped out into the afternoon steam bath.

Ora's friend, the artist Carol Boyce, was an outsized woman in every way—large, lavish, and loud—who wore muumuus and used a paintbrush as a hair stick in her bun. She'd been an adjunct English professor at the University of Maine at Machias but had taken up painting in retirement. Her watercolors hung from the tent: blurry depictions of lighthouses and smeared lupine fields. It was hard to discern if Carol was an impressionist or just had bad eyesight.

She peered up at me when my shadow fell across her sketch pad.

"I know you," she said with an undertone of accusation. "You're our dear departed game warden."

"That makes me sound like I'm dead, Mrs. Boyce."

She smelled of rose water. "I expect you're here on account of Ora Stevens."

"How did you guess?"

"You and Charley were always as thick as thieves. She called me to ask about the strange vendor here the other day, the one who argued with her husband."

"Can you describe him?"

"He was but a ruin of a man."

"Could you be more specific?"

"'It was the careless powerful look he had, in spite of a lameness checking each step like the jerk of a chain.'"

I didn't realize she was reciting a quote until my vacant expression exposed me.

"Did you never read *Ethan Frome,* Warden?"

"In high school, I think."

She slapped closed her sketch pad. "It seemed to me that this man you're looking for had been in a pretty bad smashup, the way he dragged himself around. I would say a motorcycle was involved, based on the tattoos and the grungy affect. But you want specifics. He had a kerchief around his bald head and a scraggly beard, more gray than black; wore dungarees and a flannel shirt, no sleeves. He never removed his sunglasses, but they looked cheap, like ones you might choose from a rack at the gas station."

Her detailed description made me wish more of my witnesses were visual artists. "Did you catch his name?"

"I went over to have a look at his wares and be sociable, as I always do, but he refused to introduce himself or even say where he was from! We're a community here on the Dike. We have manners and mores. The things he had for sale seemed fishy, too. Not the usual culch."

The term is Maine lingo for the knickknacks you find in attics and basements after an aged relative passes away.

"How so?"

"It was an assortment of items you don't see for sale at souks like this. There was some taxidermy but also an electric guitar. Three mink coats. Even an espresso maker! Who sells an espresso maker at a place like this?"

"It sounds like the kinds of items you'd find in a pawn shop."

"That's exactly right! It was as if he were a pawnbroker."

"What about his vehicle?"

"One of those cheap Plymouth minivans. The ones with the flaking paint on the hoods. The color was, or had been, cerulean blue."

"I take it you didn't see the license plate."

She lifted a Japanese hand fan from the table and began to wave it vigorously in the air. "I'm a watercolorist, not a state trooper."

"Did you happen to overhear any of Charley's conversation with the stranger?"

"The only part I heard was when Ethan Frome shouted at Charley, 'You can't take that! Not without paying.'"

Finally.

"Did Charley say anything in response?"

"Yes, he said, 'I've got your number.' The look on his face when he passed my table—I've never seen Charley Stevens that mad before. Normally, I consider him to be a handsome man. Not all my female friends do. But this was the first time I remember thinking he looked ugly—ugly with anger."

"Do you know what Charley took from his table?"

She considered the question with real thoughtfulness. "Whatever it was, it was small enough to fit in his hand."

"I'm sorry to keep pressing you on this, Mrs. Boyce, but you said you looked at the items on this man's table. What did you see that might have fit in Charley's hand?"

"Earrings, watches, jackknives."

My cell phone rang at that moment. I pulled aside my coat to reach for my back pocket. When I saw whose number it was—Major Shorey's—I let the call go to voice mail and turned back to the watercolorist.

"He also had a badge," Carol Boyce said.

"Excuse me?"

"He had a badge for sale. Seeing yours made me remember."

In reaching for my phone, I had exposed the badge clipped on my belt.

"It was a game warden's," she said, "only smaller and tarnished. And it had a number on it. Don't bother asking me what the number was. I just happened to have noticed because the digits were so clumsily engraved in the metal."

"You've been extremely helpful, Mrs. Boyce, I wish there was something—"

"You could buy one of my paintings."

I waited to see if her deadpan would crack, only to realize she was completely serious.

Happily, my phone chose that moment to ring again.

It was Dani, calling presumably from the firing range.

"Sorry, but I need to take this one," I said, already backing away. "It's my girlfriend."

The artist waved her paper fan in the dead air. "A likely story!"

⁓

"You have perfect timing," I told Dani.

"I can never tell when you're being a wiseass."

"I'm serious! You rescued me from being forced to buy a painting by one of the least talented artists in Maine—and that's saying something."

Cars and trucks rumbled and roared past. I cupped my hand to my opposite ear to hear her better.

"I got that long email you sent. I was looking forward to seeing you. Of course you have to go up there to help."

"Thanks for understanding," I said.

"Where are you?"

"At the Machias Dike. I have a theory about what set Charley off the other day."

I gave her a quick rundown of everything Carol Boyce had told me.

"You think it was an old warden badge?" Dani asked.

"That's my best guess."

"It's not illegal to sell those. They come up for sale on auction sites all the time. Why would Charley get pissed off about running across one?"

"I can think of two reasons," I said. "The first is the stuff the guy was selling. It sounded like the kinds of things burglars steal from people's houses."

49

"That's a real thing," Dani said. "Thieves fencing their stolen merchandise at flea markets. It's especially bad in big cities. We're supposed to be on the lookout for anything that looks suspicious. What's the other reason?"

"Judging from how Charley responded, I believe the badge belonged to someone he knew."

"But warden badges don't have personal identification on them."

"The really old badges did. They had district numbers engraved on the front."

"So it might've been somebody Charley knew as a young man?"

"Possibly."

"What do you think Charley meant when he told the guy, 'I've got your number'? Like he knew the creep was fencing stolen property?"

"Maybe, but I'm guessing he meant something else. If you had been in Charley's shoes, what would you have done to find out his identity?"

She sighed with embarrassment. "Looked at his license plate."

"A person can't just find out who owns a vehicle by typing a license plate number into a website; you need help from a dispatcher. But that wouldn't be a problem for Charley, who still has friends in law enforcement. That's another question for Ora, I guess."

"That's where you're headed next?"

"Knowing Ora, she's going to insist I stay for dinner, which means I'll probably end up spending the night."

"I understand," she said. "I miss you, babe. It's been a long week."

Gulls chattered out on the flats, pecking for bloodworms in the acres of exposed mud.

"How did you shoot today?" I asked.

"Not my best. My head is splitting. I think it's the flu. If you're sleeping at Sixth Machias Lake tonight, who's taking care of Shadow?"

"Logan Cronk."

"This is going to end with the wolf eating him."

I would have laughed if it wasn't a real fear of mine.

She became quiet again.

"Dani?"

"You need to promise me something, Mike. You need to promise to keep in touch. I want to be your partner, not just your friend with benefits. I know you're trying to be honest and open with me, but it's not in your nature to ask for help."

It was an accusation that had the problem of being true.

"I promise."

IO

The boondocks, the williwaws, the backcountry—none of these terms properly described just how deep Charley and Ora lived in the woods. Late in life, they had built a house and a guesthouse on the shores of Sixth Machias Lake, a body of water so remote and insignificant no one had ever constructed so much as a fishing camp there. Charley's friend Nick Francis had told him that the Wabanakis, who had originally occupied all the land from Lake Champlain to Cape Breton Island, had named the lake Walcopekuhsis: "little puddle."

The Stevenses might have relocated somewhere even more isolated if not for Ora's health problems, some of which were lingering aftereffects of the plane crash that had paralyzed her; others of which were part of the normal process of aging. Her husband seemed impervious to physical decline. For Ora's sake, they had been forced to build a gated road into the lake so they could drive her wheelchair-accessible van to hospitals and pharmacies.

Charley couldn't have been more pleased with his puddle. He wanted to spend his last years living somewhere off the edge of the map. He had a floatplane and an ATV and a snowmobile—what more did he need?

It was near dark when I finally left the logging road and turned onto the unmarked jeep trail that led to their hidden pond. A mile into the uncut forest, I reached the steel gate. I had memorized the combination of the padlock but had no need of it. The gate was ajar.

In my headlights, I saw tire prints, like the tracks of two rough-bellied snakes. They belonged to a heavy vehicle: a pickup, possibly an SUV. It had entered the property but not yet exited.

The gate made a terrific bang as I swung it shut behind me, loud enough to frighten off a woodcock that had been hiding in the alders nearby. It rocketed into the shadows with a flurry of wingbeats.

The house came into view slowly, not as a structure in itself but as a row of illuminated rectangles where the first-floor windows were. As I emerged from the dense conifers surrounding the main building, I saw a black Ford Interceptor parked in the dooryard. The insignia of the Washington County Sheriff's Department reflected my high beams.

When I was the local warden, I used to know all the police vehicles by their plate numbers, but that was years ago now. The longtime sheriff had lost her bid for reelection and had been replaced by her chief deputy, and there were many new faces in the department, all of them male.

As I stepped down from the Scout, the front door opened, throwing light down the ramp Charley had built for Ora's wheelchair. The silhouette of a slight, almost delicate man appeared within the frame. He wore a chocolate-brown uniform and a duty belt laden with a gun, Taser, and all the other tools of the law enforcement trade.

I removed the badge from my belt and held it out as I advanced on the house. "Mike Bowditch. Warden Service investigator. What's going on here?"

"That's what I'm trying to ascertain, sir."

He was slender even wearing a bulky ballistic vest. He had a wisp of a mustache, like a teenager trying to grow one for the first time, and a hairline that started two inches above his eyebrows. The name on his chest was Young, which seemed so appropriate that part of me wondered if I was being pranked.

Ora wheeled her chair into the lighted room behind the cop. "Oh, Mike! The deputy says Charley assaulted a man in Houlton!"

"That's insane."

"There's a man in the hospital who swears it was Mr. Stevens," said Deputy Young.

He had a way of pushing his voice lower into his diaphragm. Rookies are so quick to play at being tough guys. I knew this from hard, personal experience.

"How long have you been on the force, Young?"

"Four months."

"Been to the academy yet?"

"I'm going next term. How are these questions relevant, sir?"

"Clearly you haven't met *Warden* Stevens. If you had, you'd know this man's accusations are bullshit."

"I'd prefer to hear that from the warden himself. You wouldn't happen to know where he is, would you?"

"Can you close the door please, dears?" said Ora. "The bugs are coming in."

Ora Stevens's green eyes were somehow even paler than those of her daughter. She had the high cheekbones of a professional model, smooth skin that might have belonged to a woman half her age, and snow-white hair pushed back from her face. She wore a mint-green blouse and a hand-knitted blanket over her legs. White tennis shoes peeked out on the footrests of her wheelchair.

"What's the name of the man who's accusing Warden Stevens of assault?" I asked.

"John Smith."

"You're sure it's not John Doe?" But the deputy didn't catch the sarcasm in my voice. "What does he say happened?"

Young removed a mobile phone from his pocket and brought up a photograph of a bruised and bandaged man. He had a shaved skull, a scraggly beard, and deeply set eyes. He looked like he'd stepped face-first into a bus.

"Mr. Smith says Warden Stevens threatened him three days

ago at his booth at the Machias Dike. Then yesterday morning, he says, he opened the door of his residence in Island Falls to find Warden Stevens waiting. In Mr. Smith's statement, he says the warden proceeded to assault him."

"That's bullshit."

"Mrs. Stevens has verified that her husband and Mr. Smith quarreled. I don't suppose you have any idea what could have provoked their argument, ma'am?"

Ora had already been too candid with the deputy, but her nature was to trust people until they proved undeserving of it.

I needed to intervene. "He was selling taxidermy mounts in violation of the U.S. Migratory Bird Treaty Act."

It was a lie, but a plausible one.

The deputy had gentle eyes for a law enforcement officer, but they were not unintelligent eyes. "Why did he pursue Mr. Smith all the way to his home in Island Falls?"

"He wanted to be certain before he called the U.S. Fish and Wildlife Service. He wanted to give the guy a chance to avoid being charged with a felony."

How easily lies came to me now.

"So you spoke with Warden Stevens?"

"I didn't need to because I know his character. Your sheriff does, too. I can't believe he dignified the accusation by sending you all the way out here, Young." I affected an air of indignation that I didn't entirely feel. "Charley Stevens is a war hero and decorated career warden. If anyone deserves the benefit of the doubt, it's him."

"Mr. Smith hired a lawyer. He's pushing us to bring charges."

"I see."

"The sheriff wanted to get Warden Stevens's side of the story before he talks to the district attorney, but Mrs. Stevens says she doesn't know where her husband is."

"He's out of cell phone range is all."

"Where?"

"Pick a spot on the map of the North Woods. Your guess is as good as mine."

He hitched his thumbs in his ballistic vest to relieve some of the weight. "So he's camping, then?"

Out of the corner of my eye, I saw Ora fidgeting. She disapproved of these falsehoods.

"Are you asking me to find him for you?" I said.

Young might have been a rookie, but he was no fool. "No, sir. I am not asking you to do anything. But if we can't locate Warden Stevens, it's a problem for us and for him. If I may speak freely, sir, no one wants to request a warrant for Warden Stevens. You really need to convince him to come forward."

"I'll see what I can do."

"I'd appreciate that, sir. I know you by reputation. People still talk about what a badass you were. I'm wondering if you can answer a question for me—unrelated to what we've been discussing?"

"If I can."

"The police academy—is it really as tough as the guys say it is?"

"Not as tough as when I was there, I've heard."

"Too bad. I was looking to test myself."

"The job will do that. It will test you every day and twice on Saturday nights. Tell the sheriff I'll find Charley Stevens. He just needs to stall the DA."

The deputy tipped his hat to Ora and shook hands with me. He was a respectful kid. I liked him, mustache and all.

But after the red taillights of his cruiser disappeared into the trees, I turned to Ora. "The way he kept calling me *sir* made me feel like someone's great-uncle."

"Aging is one of those things you can't explain to people," she said, "no matter how hard you try. They need to go through it themselves. Please, come into the living room, Mike."

The house was clean but cluttered in the fashion of many North Woods camps. Charley's three decades as a game warden meant there was an abundance of taxidermy. Deer mounts on the walls, a moose head over the fireplace, several bearskin rugs. The room resembled the Maine wing of a natural history museum. The smell of the lake drifted in through the window screens, although I couldn't see the water in the darkness.

Across the pond, a barred owl called, "*Who cooks for you?*" It made me remember the night I'd met Ora at their old camp. Charley had called in owls with his expert imitations.

"I'm scared, Mike."

I took her cold hands in mine. "That jackass Smith is just looking for a quick and easy payout. I am pretty sure he's been selling stolen merchandise at these pop-up flea markets. The DA is just going through the motions. Charley never laid a hand on the man."

She made a faint noise in the back of her throat. Her green gaze drifted from me. Then she removed her hands from mine and tucked them beneath the blanket.

From this reaction, I was fairly certain that Ora Stevens believed her husband had committed the violent act of which he stood accused.

II

Despite my protests, she insisted on making me dinner: grilled salmon with asparagus.

Ora and Charley were as far from hippies as I could imagine—I doubt that either of them could have named a song by the Grateful Dead—but they had always lived off the land. The Stevenses kept a kitchen garden and had foraged together for mushrooms, berries, and wild greens before her accident. These days, it was Charley's job to gather the free-growing groceries and pack their freezers with the moose, deer, and ducks he shot.

While Ora prepared our meal—the kitchen had been built to accommodate her wheelchair—I sampled Charley's homemade beer. Brewing was his newest hobby, and the so-called IPA was so bitter it was barely drinkable.

"Because we can't grow hops here, Charley used yarrow," Ora explained. "Or maybe mugwort. The funny thing is, he doesn't even drink beer."

It showed.

"Before we start," she said. "How is Stacey?"

"Did she tell you about what happened last night?"

"No, I haven't heard from her today."

"We had an adventure in the Everglades—a Burmese python was involved."

"Tell me."

"Right now, I think we should talk about Charley," I said. "I stopped at the Dike on my way here. Carol Boyce told me she overheard what Charley and Smith were arguing about. She said it was a badge. He took it from the table without paying. It had numbers on the bottom, Carol said."

I'd hoped the news would provoke a response, but she gazed at me with expectation, waiting for more.

"Is there any warden from Charley's past whom he had a special connection with—either a friend or a mentor—whose badge this could have been?"

"Not if it was an antique. I suppose it might have belonged to one of the old-timers who were with the bureau when he started. Charley might have recognized the number, but unless he had reason to believe it was stolen, I can't imagine why he would have reacted that way."

Everything about Charley's actions seemed out of character. The public blowup, the mysterious disappearance, the accusation leveled by Smith—I felt like we were talking about a violent stranger and not the wise, even-tempered man I considered a surrogate father.

"What about his cell phone?" I said.

"I've called the number and sent him texts and emails, but I haven't gotten a response."

"So he took it with him?"

"He always does. Why?"

"The sense I am getting is that, wherever Charley is going, he doesn't want to be tracked."

"If he left his mobile phone here, I haven't come across it. Can I pour you some more coffee, dear?"

"I'd appreciate that," I said. "I also wonder if I might use your computer."

"Charley cleared the browser search history. I already checked." More than most people their ages, the Stevenses were determined not to be left behind by new technology.

"Does he do that often?"

"Never."

Ora told me that Charley's password was *O-1BirdDog,* after the light aircraft he had flown during the Vietnam War.

Bird Dogs were small surveillance planes that often skipped just above the treetops within easy range of enemy fire. The North Vietnamese Army didn't need a shoulder-fired missile to take down a Bird Dog. The weapon that had downed Charley's plane was an AK-47.

Ora was in the kitchen, cleaning up. She had sensed that I didn't want her watching over my shoulder. The locator app probably wouldn't even function. The phone might be out of power. It might be beyond the reach of a cellular signal. Or Charley might have removed the SIM card that could be used to trace the phone's physical location.

A map of Sixth Machias Lake appeared instantly on the screen. An icon indicated the location of Charley's phone. At first, it seemed to be inside the house. Only when I zoomed in did I see that the phone was pictured at the edge of the lake.

Charley's floatplane.

In her wheelchair, Ora would have been unable to check the Cessna herself. I shut down the machine and returned to the kitchen, where she was drying the last plate with a rag. I didn't want to tell her about my discovery until I could assess the situation firsthand.

"I'm going to take a walk to clear my head."

"You'll be eaten alive. The blackflies and mosquitoes are especially bad this year on account of the wet spring we had."

"Not as bad as the Everglades, I expect."

"That's just what Stacey says!"

The mention of her daughter caused a moment of awkwardness. She asked if I needed a flashlight. I showed her the SureFire I carried in my pocket.

I hadn't taken more than two steps outside before the first mosquito jabbed her needle into my neck, but at least I could safely assume this one wasn't carrying malaria. The haze of clouds concealed the precise location of the waxing moon, but the night wasn't entirely dark. I slid my flashlight into my pocket and let my night vision guide me down the boardwalk to the lake.

Trout were rising to hatching insects. The fish made circles that rippled outward across the smooth surface. The newly emerged mayflies were *Hexagenia limbata,* and they were three inches long with greenish wings. I had worked as a fishing guide and had loved taking clients out at night for the *Hex* hatch.

Charley kept his floatplane—a red-and-white Skyhawk—tied to the dock beside the boathouse.

I pulled myself up by one of the struts and ducked to keep from knocking my head against the wing. I was correct in my assumption that he had left the door of the aircraft unlocked. As I entered the familiar cabin, the locus of so many of our adventures together, the plane rocked gently on the surface of the lake.

I shined the flashlight around the cockpit and found the phone sitting atop the pilot's seat. Beneath it was a sealed envelope with my name on it. And another, addressed to Ora.

I tore mine open.

> *Dear Mike,*
>
> *I expect this makes no sense to you, my going off like a thief in the night. You think I'm cruel for leaving Ora to wonder and worry. Trust me, I had no choice. For one, I may be a fool about my suspicions. I won't know for certain until I talk to some folks I hoped never to meet again.*
>
> *My fear is that I made the worst mistake a man can make in this life. If so, it means there's someone out there who's kept quiet all these years, waiting for me to wise up to my foolishness, a man of patience and guile. He's been expecting me, I fear, and taken precautions. I can't put Ora or the girls in danger of his retribution.*
>
> *Chances are, I'll be back before I'm missed, in which case you won't have to give Ora the other letter I've left.*
>
> *But if I'm not back, it'll mean I'm beyond anyone's ability to find, and your searching may only deliver you*

*into the grasp of the same man who killed me. Instead I
hope you will forsake revenge and destroy these notes.
Let my family remember me as the man I tried to be after
my moment of weakness.*

   *I know you well enough to reckon that you won't heed
my words of caution. Which is why I am leaving you in
the dark, too. I will cover my trail to keep you from following, but I fear I may have taught you too well.*

   I love you, son. Don't come after me.

Charley

When I'd finished, I felt an inner heaviness—like a weight
upon my soul—because I understood that this document might
effectively be my friend's last testament.

12

When I returned to the house, I found Ora parked under a standing lamp. A glass filled with amber liquid and ice cubes rested within reach on a small table. A whiskey and soda was her nightly indulgence. She looked up from the book she was reading, a biography of the photographer Margaret Bourke-White.

"You look positively bloodless," she said, peering at me above her reading glasses. "Did the mosquitoes drink you dry?"

My voice didn't want to leave my throat. "They were pretty bad."

"What did you find out there?"

"Nothing that tells me where he went."

I was using the truth to mislead her. I hoped my shame didn't show in my expression and give away the secret.

If it did, she was too polite to press the matter. Instead she smiled that incandescent smile of hers. "I hope you are staying the night."

"It's been a long day."

"I keep forgetting that you woke up this morning in Florida. It's no wonder you look exhausted. Well, your room's all made up."

My room.

She was referring to the guest cabin that Stacey had lived in years earlier, when she was newly returned to Maine and working as a wildlife biologist, back before she and I had started dating. I probably stayed there more than anyone else now, but I still felt uncomfortable when Ora called the place mine.

"There's something I want to show you before you go," she said.

I hadn't noticed the cigar box on the table beside her until she lifted it with both hands. Long ago, maybe on the occasion of the birth of one of their two daughters, someone had presented Charley with a box of White Owls. I raised the lid.

Inside was a rattling collection of medals.

I counted three Purple Hearts, two Legions of Merit, a Silver Star, a Distinguished Flying Cross, a Prisoner of War Medal, and a Distinguished Service Cross, which he had somehow never mentioned having received. It was only the second-highest award given out by the U.S. military.

"He never told me he'd won all of these!"

Ora lowered her glass of whiskey. "*Won* isn't the word Charley would have used. He keeps that box in the closet with his shoeshine kit. I can't remember the last time he took it out. While you were outside, after you'd asked me about his past, I went to fetch it. I found this inside with the medals."

From the pocket of her sweater, she produced a yellow Polaroid photograph. It showed a man who looked to be half-bear. His hair was long and black, and his beard grew high up on his cheeks. His dark eyes were narrowed, and his chapped lip was curled. The expression could only be described as murderous.

"Who is this?"

"I have no idea."

"A friend from the army?"

"No friend of Charley's could look that hateful."

"Why would he keep this picture with his military decorations?"

"I don't know," she said. "But my husband has always had conflicted feelings on the accolades he's received. I'm not sure he cares about medals and honors. But they're part of his story, and Charley doesn't believe in airbrushing history. Look on the back."

I flipped over the snapshot and saw, in Charley's familiar bold hand, these words:

In battle, in the forest, at the precipice in the mountains,
on the dark great sea, in the midst of javelins and arrows,
In sleep, in confusion, in the depths of shame, The good
deeds a man has done before defend him.

"I looked it up online," Ora said. "It's from the Bhagavad Gita."

Despite having only a junior high education, the old pilot was a secret autodidact who read widely, especially history, and liked to conceal his learning beneath his folksy affect. Nevertheless, I couldn't imagine the man quoting Sanskrit scripture.

"What do you think it means?" I asked.

"I don't know."

"Can I take this photo with me?"

"Of course." When I leaned down to kiss her cheek, she whispered, "You'll find him, won't you?"

"I will."

Afterward, I made my way down the boardwalk between the main building and the guesthouse. The entire property was connected by these raised ramps so that Ora could wheel herself to the woodshed to get kindling for the stove or even to the dock to cast White Wulff flies to those trout I had seen rising.

The cabin had electricity, provided by solar panels on the south-facing roof, but I lighted the propane lanterns mounted on the walls, in part because I preferred the smell and the white-hot intensity of their illumination.

I tossed my duffel on the bed and set the snapshot of the were-bear on the bureau.

In all likelihood, the monstrous man had nothing to do with the current crisis, but I would keep this photograph anyway in the hope of finding someone who could identify him. If nothing else, I needed to satisfy my curiosity about who he was.

It hadn't escaped my notice that, in his letter, Charley hadn't mentioned the badge that had precipitated his disappearance.

The omission had been deliberate, because he knew it was a clue that I would follow. The Warden Service had stopped stamping identification numbers on its badges long before Charley had even joined the bureau.

Whose could it have been?

Charley had never mentioned a fellow officer from that era who had been a mentor to him.

The letter, then. What could it tell me?

I turned up the gas fueling the lamp beside the bed. In the hissing white glow, I examined the text for hidden meanings.

> *I may be a fool about my suspicions. I won't know for certain until I talk to some folks I hoped never to meet again.*

As I'd suspected, whatever this was about had happened years earlier, before Charley and I had become friends.

> *My fear is that I made the worst mistake a man can make in this life.*

The "worst mistake a man can make" could mean only one thing to the Charley Stevens I knew: killing another human being.

As a reconnaissance pilot in Vietnam, he wouldn't have engaged in direct combat, but he had called in the locations of enemy forces who would then have been subjected to air strikes and other bombardments. Depending upon how susceptible he was to guilt, a Bird Dog pilot could feel as if he had the blood of thousands on his hands.

There might also have been another wartime incident of which I was unaware, something that had happened after Charley had been shot down.

He seldom spoke of the experience, but he had spent nearly a year in Hỏa Lò Prison, better known as the Hanoi Hilton, where one of his fellow inmates was a future United States senator and presidential candidate. Torture had left him with burns and rope scars. He had suffered a broken leg in the crash that had healed badly and yet rarely revealed itself. The only time he showed any sign of a limp was in bitterly cold weather after having already hiked miles across difficult terrain.

I was falling down a rabbit hole, I realized. My recent investigation of Captain Wheelwright had me focused on the sins of military men, but this mystery had all started with a game warden's badge. I needed to concentrate on Charley's life in Maine.

During the course of his long career as a law enforcement officer, he had never killed another human being. Of that I was close to certain.

Forget what you've read in novels and watched on television—in real life, cops don't respect other cops who are quick to pull a trigger. In just seven years, I had already acquired a reputation for being a gunfighter. Charley had made it abundantly clear that having a high death count was not something of which I should be proud. Just the opposite, in fact.

I returned to the letter.

> *It means there's a man out there who's kept quiet all these years, waiting for me to wise up to my foolishness, a man of patience and guile. He's been expecting me, I fear, and taken precautions. I can't put Ora or the girls in danger of his retribution.*

These sentences suggested that finding this badge had led Charley to conclude he might've been duped. The notion seemed outlandish to me. But even though I had yet to meet a criminal mastermind, it didn't mean they didn't exist. Obviously, Charley had his suspicions. He would be extra careful in confronting anyone he suspected might have gotten away with murder.

> *I know you well enough to reckon that you won't heed my words of caution.*

Damned right, there was nothing he could do to stop me.

*Which is why I am leaving you in the dark, too. I will
cover my trail to keep you from following, but I fear I
may have taught you too well.*

Charley needed my help, but he didn't want to be responsible
for placing me in danger. Why else leave a letter worded this way
if he didn't hope I would disobey his instructions? Why not give
me the name of the man or men he suspected? Wouldn't it be
more dangerous for me to wander blindly into the crosshairs of
a masterful killer?

Who are you, Charley?

What have you done?

What do you require me to do?

Lying atop the bedspread in the humid dark, smelling the lake
alive with new life, I considered these questions. My younger self
had believed fiercely in the idea that we can never truly know
another human being, that we are solipsistic creatures doomed
to brief, lonely existences. Experience had taught me that we can
only escape our private prisons by trusting and giving ourselves
to others. Now, for the first time in years, I found myself seeing
the face of someone I loved in my mind's eye and wondering
about the stranger behind the mask.

13

I awakened after dawn to the singing of a mourning warbler outside my window. Millions of Americans have heard this species of woodland bird but will never see one. The warbler's recorded song is used by television sound engineers when they need background effects suggestive of peaceful mornings and idyllic golf courses. Hear a bird singing in a commercial? Odds are it's a mourning warbler.

The lonesome bird was still singing his heart out, weeks after he should have been settling down to nest. The poor little guy hadn't found a mate.

I put on a Henley T-shirt and jeans, laced up my Bean boots, stripped the bed, and threw my duffel over my shoulder.

I stepped outside into another drowsy morning. The tree trunks were wet as if with perspiration. The earthy smell of leaf mold and crumbling stumps rose from the forest floor. Orange fungi erupted from the wounds in the bark of the rotten logs.

As I made my way up the ramp toward the house, I caught the scent of frying doughnuts coming from the kitchen. I began to salivate like my wolf back home.

I poured myself a mug of coffee and sat down at the table while Ora dusted the doughnuts with cinnamon and powdered sugar.

"Stacey called late last night," she remarked with a casualness that sounded forced. "She said you skipped out on her without saying goodbye."

"I was at her house—getting cleaned up—when you called me about Charley."

"She thought you must have had a crisis of conscience about Dani."

True enough. "Did you tell her I was here?"

"It would have meant telling her about her father, and she already sensed something was wrong. She said she was worried about him and didn't know why. I lied and told her he was off on a camping trip, but I know she didn't believe me."

Despite having been raised in a Catholic household, I had always been a skeptic when it came to paranormal matters. Then I'd met Ora and Stacey Stevens. Their "feelings" about distant events had often turned out to be true, far more frequently than could have been predicted by random chance.

"Stacey shares her mother's ESP."

"You make it sound supernatural that we're emotionally connected."

"I'm not sure it isn't."

While she prepared the rest of our breakfast—strawberries and home-baked granola—I thought of the other envelope Charley had left me, the letter to his wife. I would keep it secret for the time being. He intended it to be shared only in the event of his death. I hated myself for not telling her about it.

"What is your plan?" she asked.

"I think I'll pay a visit to John Smith and find out how he really got his injuries."

"Are you sure that's a wise idea?"

"Of course it isn't."

"Stop in to see Nick Francis on your way north. You'll be passing through the reservation anyway. Maybe he knows more than he's saying."

"You told me you'd already spoken with Nick."

"But I'm not Mike Bowditch."

It was the first time since I'd arrived that I'd seen playfulness in those beautiful eyes. The good humor lasted only an instant.

—

Half an hour later, I was driving northeast along the Stud Mill Road, a gravel-strewn highway for logging trucks that cuts through the heart of the woods from the border crossing at Calais to the outskirts of Bangor. Eighteen-wheelers, loaded with un-skinned tree trunks, barreled along at terrific speeds, heedless of deer, moose, or other motorists. I emerged into the little hamlet of Grand Lake Stream with my Scout plastered with mud kicked up by their massive wheels.

I had made my home in this village once, during a hiatus in my service as a game warden. I had worked briefly as a commer-cial fishing guide, taking "sports" out onto Big Lake and the St. Croix River to catch salmon, trout, and smallmouth bass. I had not been unhappy. It was in Grand Lake Stream that I had asked Stacey out on our first date. And she had said yes.

But the general store had changed owners twice since I had been away, old-time residents had died, houses had been sold to people whose names I didn't recognize.

I kept driving until I had entered Indian Township. According to the most recent census, just six hundred or so people lived there now. They and three thousand of their relatives, scattered about the state, were all that was left of the great Passama-quoddy Nation.

The Passamaquoddy were one of five Native American tribes in Maine, the others being the Penobscots, the Maliseets, the Abenaki, and the Micmacs. Like American Indians elsewhere, they had not prospered during the centuries since Europeans built their first blockhouses on the continent. I couldn't help but think of my visit to the Miccosukee restaurant. In a single day, I had left one pocket of Indian country for another.

Peter Dana Point, named for one of their most venerated lead-ers, jutted into the narrows between Long and Big Lakes. The road passed through unbroken forest for a half mile before it transformed into a strip of identical houses. These were all brick, all one-story, and most had cluttered yards. Near the tip of the point was a ball field and a school and some buildings designed by architects who specialize in post offices and other nondescript governmental structures.

Every person I passed—every child playing in a yard, every middle-aged man riding a bicycle, every group of women smoking on a porch—watched me drive past with interest. The reservation drew few non-Indian sightseers. What was there to see?

Nick Francis lived on Pit Row, a road named for its defining feature: a gravel excavation at the terminus. I pulled into his dooryard and turned off the engine. The home boasted a fantastic flower garden, bright with still-blooming purple lupines, orange poppies, pink azaleas, and white peonies. Someone in the Francis household had a wicked green thumb.

Nick's property also had its share of "yard art": the term Mainers use for the random items that can accumulate outside houses. In addition to the usual ATVs, snowmobiles, and old appliances, there were half a dozen canoes, including several made by the owner of the house. Nick's birchbark designs were not works of art or faithful renditions of his people's historic watercraft, but they were impressive canoes, nonetheless.

I didn't know Francis well. Our only interactions had been through Charley, but I knew that Nick had been a tribal game warden during the same period when my friend had patrolled the forests around the rez. Later, he had become police chief and, later still, tribal governor before some sort of scandal— there had been the suggestion of self-dealing—had led to crushing electoral defeat.

"If Nick Francis was padding his pocket, then I am the Queen of Sheba," Charley had remarked when the news broke.

The two men were what Wheelwright and Fixico should have been, it occurred to me. Men from different cultures who had walked through fire for each other and would do so again. There was something infinitely hopeful in their unbreakable friendship.

That said, I was unsure how I would be received by the retired tribal governor. White people rarely drove out to the point, and not all who did came with friendly intentions. Like the rest of Down East Maine, the reservation was in the grip of the opioid epidemic. Most of the worst dealers were whites, or at least they had been when I was stationed in the area.

The front door opened as I mounted the stairs.

A girl stood before me. Nick's granddaughter? He was a long-time widower who had lost his wife when she was young and had never remarried. Charley told me he had raised his son and daughters himself.

I guessed the girl to be around thirteen, although I am a poor judge of children's ages. She was pencil thin with a round face, wide-set eyes, and hair shaved on one side of her head and long on the other. She was wearing a hoodie, denim cutoffs, and flip-flops.

"Good morning," I said.

"Yeah?" she said, forming the word around a mouthful of chewing gum.

"I'm hoping to speak with Governor Francis. Is he at home?"

"Governor! He ain't been that in a while. What you want him for?"

"I'm a friend of a friend—Charley Stevens. My name's Mike Bowditch."

"I'm Molly." Her mobile eyes narrowed in recognition. "Wait a second! I know you. You used to be the warden out on the lake. You checked our boat for life vests once—wrote my pa a ticket. He tore it up and spat in your face."

The man in question was Nick's son and namesake, a troubled soul whose temper only worsened with every alcoholic beverage he consumed, and it wasn't unusual for him to drink a dozen Twisted Teas a day. He had claimed not to recognize my authority to write him a citation, even though I had stopped his pontoon party boat in Musquash Bay, outside Passamaquoddy waters.

"I remember that day well."

She cracked her gum. "My pa's an asshole. I'm surprised you

didn't shoot him when he ripped up that ticket and threw it into the lake."

"We try to avoid using lethal force in littering cases."

She smiled wide enough for me to identify the color of her gum as purple. "It would have saved us some trouble. He ran off on us a few years back. Met a Maliseet girl at the powwow on Indian Island. That's where my gramp is—up north, trying to get money out of my dad."

"North where?"

"Houlton. The Maliseet ain't got a rez of their own. They got screwed out of one by you people."

I absorbed the blow, because what was there to say? "White people haven't treated the Passamaquoddies very well either."

She scratched the stubble side of her hairdo. She moved her gum around the inside of her mouth. I had scored zero points with that one.

I offered my best smile. "You wouldn't have a number for your grandfather?"

Molly Francis sighed and fished a bedazzled phone out of the kangaroo pocket of her hoodie. She asked for my number and sent me her grandfather's contact information.

"He might not be in a good mood," she said. "Gramp's a good man, but my pa brings out the beast in him. By the way, it ain't *Passamaquoddies*. It's *Passamaquoddy*. Plural. The *s* is something you whites added for us."

14

From Indian Township, I followed US Route 1 north. The road paralleled the international boundary with Canada, and at certain crossroads, there were signs pointing east toward official crossings. I passed more than one white-and-green Border Patrol vehicle.

I wondered if any of the agents had come from the neon streets of Miami. Did they consider their Maine assignments exiles or escapes from the front lines of the immigration wars?

After a while, the pine woods gave way to hardscrabble farms that had never been prosperous. The thin glacial soil was too poor for crops to thrive. Most of the pastures hadn't been grazed in ages. In the abandoned apple orchards, the blossoms had fallen, and the trees looked like they had piles of snow beneath them.

In the flyspeck town of Orient, I passed a trailer with a NO TRESPASSING sign and a Confederate flag flying from a jutting broomstick repurposed as a flagpole. The property itself seemed to consist of nothing but the ancient mobile home and a yard land-mined with dog piles. Why were the owners of shitholes the most belligerent about keeping strangers off their precious land?

Sadly, the sight of the Stars and Bars flying proudly in Maine, the heart of the Union, had ceased to shock me.

John Smith had an unlisted address, of course. Luckily, a dispatcher at the Regional Communications Center in Houlton owed me a favor. I had cut her teenage son some slack on a poaching charge; he was a good kid who had fallen in with backwoods delinquents.

I typed the address the dispatcher gave me into my GPS and was surprised to discover that John Smith owned waterfront property. Given the description I'd gotten of the two-bit fence, I had assumed he dwelled on some dirty, dead-end road. Not that Hook Lake was considered a posh body of water. But lakeside houses in Maine don't come cheap, and even the ones that have been passed down over generations are freighted with crushing tax burdens, requiring income streams rarely achievable by men who dealt antiques at flea markets.

From Houlton, I sped west through a picturesque countryside utterly unlike the croft land I had just left. Here were great, prosperous farms, grand old homesteads with majestic oaks and elms shading the front yards. Many of them had signs advertising their produce and meat as organically raised and free of genetically modified organisms.

How quickly one Maine could become another.

After a few minutes, I found the lake road. The clouds remained unbroken, with no chinks of sunlight between them, and I had the feeling the drizzle might begin any second. I caught sight of water shimmering like hammered tin through the leaves of the maples. I eased my foot off the gas.

The house was the second of three cottages built on lots that were longer than they were wide. The developer had marked out the property lines to maximize access to the water. In the paved drive of Smith's residence was parked a dented van that matched Carol Boyce's description. I pulled in behind it so our bumpers kissed.

In the neighboring cottage, a white-haired man peeked out of his garage. He had the physique of someone who swam two miles every morning. He was wearing white short shorts and a lemon tank top. His deeply tanned skin shone with old-fashioned suntan oil, not the UV-blocking kind.

"Good morning," I said.

He chuckled mysteriously and made his way down the hill to his dock.

I strode up the front steps and pushed the glowing doorbell. I heard a muted chime inside the house but no footfalls. I pushed the button again and waited, this time for a full thirty seconds.

Smith could be passed out in there, drugged or drunk.

A warm breeze stirred the leaves of the aspens planted around the property. Another low-pressure front moving in from the south, the threat of afternoon thunderstorms.

I backed away from the doorstep to see if I was being watched from one of the windows, but there were no signs of life.

The old neighbor had returned to the garage for a life vest. He still wore the same expression of ironical amusement.

"Did you come here to kick the crap out of him, too?" he asked in an accent I associated with Martin Scorsese movies.

"No."

"Shame."

Just then, I thought I heard a screen door closing in the back of the house. It wasn't a sharp bang. More like a metallic tap. Then thudding noises that sounded like a man with a wooden leg running down a wooden dock.

"That's him, getting away," said the tanned old man.

Moments later, I heard the unmistakable noise of someone pulling the cord on an outboard motor.

I took off down the hill, rounding the corner of the building just as the engine sparked to life. Smith was seated in the stern of a battered, square-bowed aluminum boat. His hairy face was bruised and bandaged. He was wearing a flapping bathrobe over board trunks. His chest and lanky arms were mottled with tattoos.

He turned the throttle, gunning the engine, but in his haste, he had forgotten to untie the stern line from the cleat. The sudden acceleration brought the boat up short. The bow rose almost vertically from the water, but the rope didn't snap.

By now, I had reached the dock. "Police! Stop!"

As the boat swung around like a dog testing the length of its lead, Smith lifted the prop from the water. The screw continued to spin. The rope stretched in a straight line to the transom of the boat. Gas fumes boiled blue in the air.

"Police! Cut the engine!"

Panicked, Smith glanced around the boat in search of some edged tool to cut the line. In doing so, he let go of the outboard. The weight of the engine dropped the propeller back into the lake. The spinning screw threw up a rooster tail.

"Mr. Smith, I just want to talk!"

The last thing I expected was for him to pull a handgun. He must've had it hidden in the pocket of his robe. He pointed the barrel at me from a distance of five yards. I heard the shot just before I dove into the lake.

15

I am not sure how long I was underwater. Long enough to draw my Beretta from the holster inside my waistband.

I surfaced with the dock between Smith and myself, hearing the outboard revving and the dock creaking ominously as the nylon rope strained at the cleat. My mouth, full of lake water, tasted like I'd been sucking on a bullfrog.

What I thought was a second shot turned out to be the snap of the stern line as it finally gave way.

Treading water, I watched John Smith's newly freed boat accelerate down the lake. I hadn't been this pissed off in a long time. I tossed my handgun onto the wet planks and pulled myself up from the lake in one motion.

Because I had water in my ears, I had trouble hearing the old man calling to me. Finally, I saw him motioning from his own dock. A blue-and-white runabout rocked in the wake Smith had left behind.

"We can catch him!" he shouted.

Dripping, I stooped to grab my Beretta. When I straightened up, I saw that the tanned man was already idling toward me in his motorboat. His was a superior craft to Smith's in every respect. It had a windscreen and a cockpit with two seats and a steering wheel. Most importantly, it had a muscular four-stroke Mercury engine.

As he swung alongside the dock, I leaped aboard. "What's your name?"

"Max Glassman."

"I'm Mike Bowditch. I'm a game warden."

His shiny brown skin smelled strongly of coconut. "I figured you for a cop. The Mook's criminal associates travel in packs. That's what my partner and I call him."

Smith was heading south at a good clip, but the aluminum boat's squared-off bow slowed his speed. The boat bounced off every wave. Nor did its captain seem to realize he was being pursued.

"Thank you for helping me, Max." I holstered my wet weapon. "Your neighbor is more dangerous than I'd realized."

"I would say so!"

I glanced around the boat and located a personal flotation device. "Could you put this on for me, please?"

"You're kidding!"

"I'll hold the wheel."

When he saw I wasn't joking, he took the vest and pulled it over his wiry shoulders.

"What about you? Don't you have to put one on, too?"

"I should," I said, taking the opportunity to slow the engine to the faintest crawl. "You're a good swimmer, Mr. Glassman. I can tell. If you weren't, I wouldn't do this to you."

His eyes widened as the meaning of my words hit home. By then, it was too late. I had grabbed him firmly by the biceps and with a twist of my hips flipped him over the side. The vest kept his head from going under, but he managed to swallow some of the lake.

"I can't have you in the boat if he's shooting at me!" I shouted. "I'll be back to get you as soon as I can."

"You can't just—"

"The state will reimburse you for any damage to your boat. You have my word on that."

"Damage?"

He had floated far enough away that I felt safe to give the engine some gas. I turned the wheel to keep the prop from splashing him. Even above the roar of the outboard, I heard the native New York obscenities he lobbed after me.

By this time, Smith had realized he was being chased. He had opened up his two-stroke engine, heading for the narrows between the upper and lower lake. I was unfamiliar with this body of water beyond the vague memory of seeing it in a dog-eared atlas.

I gave a guilty glance back at Glassman and was relieved to see that he was already crawling toward the near shore, swimming with well-practiced strokes. Exigent circumstances had come to define my life.

The runabout was a pure pleasure to drive. If the engine wasn't new, it had been perfectly maintained. I didn't crash into the waves the way Smith did but skipped over them, feeling the bounce as ripples up my spinal column.

As I closed the distance, I began to worry that Smith was stupid enough to open fire again. I had no interest in engaging in an aquatic gunfight with this weirdo, especially when a Jet Ski might show up at any second. I had more than enough deaths on my conscience.

Fortunately, the ominous weather was keeping other boaters off the lake.

Off to my right, I saw the wetlands where the river entered the lake and, up ahead, more of the same emergent vegetation—arrowhead, pickerelweed, and cattails—hemming the narrows.

I plotted an intercept course. I gunned the engine and shot forward at forty miles an hour. My acceleration was so sudden I had to grab the windscreen to keep from sliding.

My burst of speed caught Smith off guard. He must have dropped the pistol, trying to draw a bead on me, because I saw him glancing desperately around the bottom of the boat. As I roared up on his port side, he lifted his head, realized he was heading into the thick of the marsh, and gave the outboard a jerk back toward the thoroughfare.

What he'd failed to see was the half-submerged log in front of his bow.

The boat struck the dead tree with a terrific noise—the same metallic shriek you hear during a car crash—and slammed to a stop. The collision caused Smith to tumble forward and over the gunwale nearest to me. He must have struck his skull on one of the aluminum seats, because he went down like a lead weight.

I backed off the bowrider to a safe distance, tossed out the mushroom anchor, and dived headfirst into the lake. In the shallows, the water was as warm as a baby's bath.

Unidentifiable clumps of vegetation, torn loose by the roots, floated before my eyes along with sand stirred up from the bottom. I kicked hard toward the spot where I'd seen Smith go under, hearing the *thwack-thwack-thwack* of his still-spinning propeller. If he had been using a dead man's switch, the engine would have gone off the second he fell overboard.

I stayed down as long as I could, trying to peer through the shimmering sand, feeling that incomparable sensation when you begin to run out of oxygen and your brain becomes a circus balloon expanding inside your skull. Finally, I popped up to fill my lungs. I scanned the surface for a floating body. Seeing none, I dived down again, disturbing a musk turtle that had been trying to pass unnoticed along the bottom. I saw sunken beer bottles but no Smith.

If I didn't find the unconscious man soon—assuming he was unconscious—he would drown.

The third time I rose to the surface, I realized that I'd been played.

I began swimming at top speed toward Max Glassman's runabout. Sure enough, Smith had already pulled himself into the bobbing craft. However bad a tumble he had taken, he hadn't been knocked cold. He had a fresh cut on his head. Blood streamed along his jawbone and dyed his salt-and-pepper beard pink.

He was pulling up the anchor, hand over hand, as I came up on him. Maybe he thought he could hurl the toadstool-shaped weight at me, but I was too close. He threw himself forward into the cockpit, desperate to restart the engine before I could gain a handhold on the swimming ladder.

"Hey!" I said. "Asshole!"

Distracted, desperate to flee, he ignored me.

"You're not going anywhere! Not without these!"

I raised my right arm out of the water like Excalibur from the mere. My middle finger protruded through the steel ring that held the keys to Glassman's boat.

16

I drew my Beretta from its Kydex holster and trained the sights at him while treading water.

"Don't think it can't fire because it's wet. Now raise your hands above your head."

As he followed my instructions, his robe parted, revealing a belly emblazoned with offbeat motorcycle tats. DON'T WORRY BE HORNY. ADVENTURE BEFORE DEMENTIA. LOUD WIVES LOSE LIVES. He'd even had blood-red bullet holes tattooed across his abdomen.

"Back up to the bow while I climb up," I said. "I will shoot you if you so much as flinch. That's a promise, not a threat."

Clutching the keys tightly in my palm, I used that hand to pull myself up until my waterlogged boots found the bottom rung of the swimming ladder. Then I stood up carefully. If Smith had thought to rock the boat, I might have lost my balance and fallen back into the lake. But he had come to terms with the reality of his predicament.

John Smith stood in the bow with hands raised. There were bits of plant matter—torn rushes and pondweed—in his bloody beard.

It was my first real look at the man in the flesh. Underwater, he had lost all but one of the bandages from Charley's alleged assault. The exposed wounds were ugly in the extreme. There was a laceration, stitched with black sutures, under his right eye and a blue-green bruise under the left. There was yet another contusion on his bald temple.

"Turn away from me," I said in my most commanding voice. "And kneel down."

Not that I needed to fake the anger.

"I can't kneel. I'm disabled."

I understood now what Carol Boyce had meant about Smith being "but a ruin of a man." His body was all out of kilter. One rounded shoulder rose higher than the other. That knee didn't bend. I wondered how many months he'd spent in the hospital after the motorcycle crash that (I guessed) had rearranged his skeleton.

I ordered him to lift his hand while I cuffed one of his wrists. He didn't fight me, but he didn't help either. I dragged him to the cockpit. I pushed him down in the passenger seat—his bad leg extended out straight—and cuffed his wrists together behind the seat back.

"You and I are going to have a conversation," I said, "but first, I need to make sure your neighbor isn't adrift out there."

"Fuck that Jew," he said.

I swatted him on the side of his shaved head. He glared at me.

I stuck the key into the ignition and restarted the engine, then turned the runabout around and began cruising north toward the spot where I'd jettisoned Max.

Halfway up the lake, I slowed and surveyed both shores. There was no trace of Glassman, but I sighted his orange life vest hanging from a piling at the end of someone's dock. I had been correct in my judgment that the lean man was a daily swimmer.

Still, I faced a difficult explanation at best and a potential lawsuit at worst.

"What are you doing now?" Smith asked.

"What does it look like I'm doing? I'm dropping anchor."

"What the fuck for?"

"You're going to answer my questions before I bring you back to shore."

"Who are you?"

"A friend of Charley Stevens."

At the mention of the pilot's name, Smith's mouth trembled.

There could be no question that my friend had inflicted the lop-sided man's injuries. I could scarcely believe it.

"You said you were police," he said. "You could have been anyone."

"We're not in an interrogation room, Mr. Smith. No one is recording us. The sooner you tell me the truth, the sooner we can get off this lake. I want to know about the badge."

"What badge?"

"The one my friend took from you in Machias."

"He stalked me, that motherfucker. Stalked me all the way up here. And then, he forced his way inside my house and beat me to a pulp. It was embarrassing! A guy that old."

"You must have provoked him."

"He's got Alzheimer's or something. He should be locked up in a nursing home."

"Describe the badge."

"It was brass, tarnished, and said STATE OF MAINE WARDEN on it."

"Was there an identifying number?"

"Maybe. I don't remember. Look, I'm going to catch hypo-thermia if we stay out here."

I grabbed his rigid knee to turn him toward me. "By now, you've probably realized that I can be a pretty violent guy my-self. What was the number on the badge?"

"One thirteen."

The digits meant nothing to me, but clearly they had mattered to Charley.

"And where did you acquire it? I want the truth."

"People bring me things. I give them cash up front if I think I can make some scratch. It's just normal, everyday business."

"Which people?"

"People who have stuff they don't know what to do with."

I sat down across from him in the driver's seat. "What hap-pened to you, Smith?"

"What do you mean?"

"You crashed your bike, right?"

86

"Hit a moose. I should be dead."

"Where?"

"Route 11 north of Ashland. That road is fucking moose alley."

"I believe you," I said. "Hearing you tell the truth is helpful because it makes me appreciate what a talented liar you are."

"Fuck you!"

I put my hand on his knee as if to wrench it but restrained myself.

"What is it with you game wardens? Can't you see I'm hand-icapped? This is more police brutality."

"You just tried to murder me, asshole."

"I didn't know who you were or what you wanted. You looked dangerous. You *are* dangerous!"

"That's a common problem for you? Having dangerous men show up at your door?"

"When you live in the sticks—"

"Here's the deal. The police are going to be waiting for us when we get back to shore. I don't know how your other neighbors respond when they hear a gunshot on the lake, but I'm pretty sure Mr. Glassman has called the cops."

"I was in fear for my life. And when I saw you chasing me in Max's boat—"

"How long have you been selling stolen merchandise?"

His lip began to tremble again, but not from the cold.

"That's a big part of your business," I said, "selling items brought to you by burglars. Heroin and meth addicts need quick cash for drugs. The problem is that pawn shops are pretty well policed. And the cops keep an eye on Craigslist and eBay. It's not so easy for nonprofessional thieves to find fences."

"That's a bogus accusation."

"We'll see what turns up in your house."

"You have no grounds for a warrant."

"Judges tend to be permissive when a person opens fire on a law enforcement officer. But I'm not sure your biggest worry is what the cops are going to find inside your garage. I'd be more concerned about my criminal associates hearing you were spilling their names as part of a plea deal."

He jerked his head up. "I would never—"

"But how can they be sure?"

"You'd lie and put my life in danger?" Fear had made his voice into a thin squeak.

"You tried to *shoot* me, asshole."

Back at the northeast side of the lake, I saw blue lights pulsing amid the trees. At least one state trooper had arrived.

"Have it your way," I said.

"I bought the badge at a yard sale!" Smith said. "I bought it from a college girl up in Presque Isle who didn't know what it was."

17

Smith didn't remember the address of the yard sale where he'd purchased the badge, but he knew the street in Presque Isle, which was something.

Less helpful was his description of the woman who'd sold it to him.

"Great tits and she liked showing them off. She kept leaning over the table. And she was wearing those basketball shorts with the stripes up the side. Nice ass, too."

"What about her face?" I asked. "I'm assuming she had one."

"You wouldn't have needed to put a bag over her head or anything."

I resisted the urge to swat him again. "What color were her eyes?"

"Brown."

"And her hair?"

"Dark."

Smith hadn't caught her name, but she had a roommate or roommates. They were college students, clearing out a rented house before they scattered for the summer.

"How much did you pay for the badge?"

"Twenty bucks. I tried talking her down, but she wouldn't budge, the little bitch. She was hard-nosed. I think she must've been French."

By *French,* he meant Franco American. Many of the people living this close to the New Brunswick border were descended from Acadians who had hid in the forests when the British decided to round up the first settlers and "transport" the ones who surrendered. Thousands perished on the ship voyages. *Le Grand Dérangement*, as this wretched episode came to be called, was an act of genocide, noteworthy only in that it had been committed by Europeans against Europeans. Some of those Acadians, or Cajuns, ended up in Louisiana, where they would end up inventing zydeco music, crawfish étouffée, and one of the most colorful dialects in the English language. I was of Acadian descent on my mother's side.

"Did she have an accent?" I asked.

"No."

"Then what makes you say she seemed French?"

"She was wearing makeup. The women up in the St. John Valley are all into cosmetics and dyeing their hair. Like the chicks in the bars in Québec City. You ever been there?"

"I doubt you and I frequent the same drinking establishments. Did you tell Charley Stevens about this woman?"

"Yeah, but he didn't believe me. He was sure I'd stolen that badge or gotten it from someone who'd stolen it. Please, dude, my balls are turning into ice cubes here."

This, I believed. I started the engine and turned us toward shore.

—

A dozen or so units, local, county, and state, had responded to the report of the shooting. Smith was on his way to the jail in Houlton, handcuffed to the D ring on the floor of a deputy's cruiser. Other deputies were engaged in executing a search warrant that had been granted before I could even change my socks. The district warden had been dispatched to the south end of the lake to tow back Smith's boat, provided the aluminum hull hadn't been pierced by the log it had struck.

The officer in charge was a state police detective named Zanadakis, and he had some questions for me.

He was a trim man with a tanning-booth tan who wore cologne purchased somewhere other than a drugstore. Beneath a navy trench coat, he wore a gray sharkskin suit that shone like silver and a tie with a houndstooth pattern. Forget about northern Maine, Nico Zanadakis would have been considered a dandy if he'd worked out of a precinct in Lower Manhattan's Financial District.

We stood beside his unmarked cruiser while I towel-dried my hair. I'd had a few minutes to change into a fresh set of clothes before Zanadakis arrived. We knew each other from a case long ago: Two drug dealers had gotten lost in the woods in a blizzard. Then things turned violent. Since we'd first met, I'd been promoted, and he'd been transferred. But our shared history didn't mean he held warm feelings for me.

"Why are you here exactly?"

A yellow paste of wet pollen covered the top and hood of the cruiser. My hand came away looking like it was smeared with mustard. "I got a report that Smith was dealing illegal taxidermy—migratory birds."

"Isn't that a matter for the feds?"

"I didn't want to bother the Fish and Wildlife Service agents with it until I could scope him out myself."

The lie had worked with Deputy Young, so why not again?

He jotted something in his reporter's notebook. "So your visit here was unofficial, then?"

"Insofar as I'm not on the clock."

"So he took off out the back when you knocked on his door. But if you never spoke to him, how did he know you were law enforcement?"

"Mr. Smith seems to fear individuals on both sides of the law."

"But you are 100 percent certain that he fired at you *after* you identified yourself as police."

"One hundred percent."

"That's the key thing here. You understand that, right? The attorney general's office won't go for an attempted homicide charge if there's any wiggle room."

"The neighbor, Glassman, heard the whole thing."

"Speaking of which, Mr. Glassman said you pushed him out of his own boat."

"Exigent circumstances required me to pursue Mr. Smith. I didn't know his state of mind, and I realized I couldn't put a bystander in harm's way. Between you and me, how much trouble am I in with him?"

"My guess is that the satisfaction of losing Mr. Smith as a neighbor will prevail over Mr. Glassman's hurt pride. But if he talks to a lawyer, all bets are off."

One of the troopers on the scene called to Zanadakis. "Nico, you'll want to have a look at what's inside the garage. Remember the woman who reported all those fur coats stolen?"

If this had happened in southern Maine, Trooper Dani Tate might have been the one to discover Smith's loot. I had sent her an email that morning but hadn't heard from her yet. Her range qualification was a two-day commitment, though. Maybe she'd been pressed for time and hadn't had a moment to respond.

The first rumble of thunder rolled up the lake. The clouds to the south looked oily, they were so black.

Detective Zanadakis snapped his notebook shut. "Keep your phone on."

"I can't promise I'll have a signal where I'm headed."

"You wardens always use that as an excuse."

⁓

East of Houlton, Interstate 95 crosses the border into New Brunswick and joins the Trans-Canada Highway system that connects St. John's, Newfoundland, with Victoria, British Columbia. The crossing is one of the busiest land-based ports of entry in the United States. Hundreds of eighteen-wheelers, carrying thousands of tons of cargo, pass back and forth between the two countries every week.

In a torrential downpour I left the interstate at the last exit and followed the cloverleaf down to a cluster of truck stops and fast-food franchises along Route 1.

I figured I would have better cell service here—across the

street from a Walmart—than in the woods of Island Falls, and I was right.

"Grasshopper!" said Kathy Frost. "I didn't expect to hear from you so soon, but I bet I know why you're calling. It's Dani, right? You're calling for advice to the lovelorn."

"What's wrong with Dani?"

"There it is, right there—she misses you, man. You couldn't have made time to see her since you've been home?"

"She told me not to. She said she was busy."

"Oh, Mike. You're so hopeless. Sometimes I think your wolf will be easier to domesticate than you."

"What am I missing?"

"She was going to stay over at my house last night, since I live close to the practice range, but she didn't want me to catch her bug. Your girl is seriously sick."

"Do you think it's bad?"

"When was the last time you remember that little badass admitting she was ill?"

I couldn't recall a single instance.

Rain drummed on the roof. The windows began to steam.

"So if it's not Dani," Kathy asked, "what do you need?"

"Who says I need something?"

"It's the only time you ever call me, my friend."

Kathy's last days as a Maine game warden, after she had been shot and nearly killed, were spent sitting in a cubicle in our Augusta headquarters compiling an official history of the Maine Warden Service. The higher-ups would not permit her to return to the field due to the severity of her injuries, and for once, I had been in agreement with my so-called superiors.

It had taken two weeks for everyone to realize that Kathy Frost was not cut out for office life. And the history remained unfinished. I had no idea how far she'd gotten, but I was hoping.

"I found an old warden badge from an antiques dealer, and I want to know whose it was."

I hated lying to her, but it didn't stop me. I was committed to protecting Charley at all costs to my other relationships.

"How old?" she asked.

"Not sure, but it's shaped like the current badges. Smaller, with the district number stamped on the bottom. The number is 113."

"Offhand, that doesn't ring a bell. If you want to hang on a minute, I can look it up in my files."

"Weren't you supposed to leave those files behind when you retired?"

She gave one of her hearty laughs. "Everyone takes something when they leave. I'll call you back in five minutes with what I've found."

While I waited, I struggled with whether to come clean with Kathy. She had saved my career when I was set on blowing it to pieces, and I trusted her with my life. If my investigation had involved anyone else but Charley, I would have already spilled my guts to her.

"A few guys had that number over the years," she said when she called back. "But I'm guessing the badge you found belonged to a warden named Duke Dupree. That was his actual first name, before you ask. He worked out of Clayton Lake and Churchill Depot during the Depression."

"Never heard of him."

"That's no surprise. His service was, shall we say, abbreviated."

"Did he die in the line of duty?"

"You've been to the memorial enough times. Do you remember seeing his name on it?" She meant the granite monument in Augusta on which were carved the names of every Maine police officer who had perished while carrying out his or her job. "Dupree fell asleep at the wheel and plowed his cruiser into a couple of sweethearts outside Ashland. Lucky for him, he lived in a time before social media. The Warden Service hushed it up. But Dupree lost his job. They must have let him keep his badge as a memento—policies weren't so strict back then. I'm not surprised it ended up at a yard sale. Where did you find it?"

I had to take a breath before I could lie again. "Presque Isle."

"What are you doing there?"

"I thought I'd do some fishing up in the Debouille reserve. I figured it would be cooler in the County. My mistake."

"Because there's no more enjoyable time to land a few arctic char than peak blackfly season. Are you sure you want to stick with that story, Grasshopper?"

"No, but I'm going to."

"Give my best to Chasse while you're up there."

"Who?"

"Remember Chasse Lamontaine? He's the warden up that way. It's a shame he's such a Boy Scout. My God, what a handsome hunk he is. Good luck with the 'fishing'!"

Kathy knew me too well. We are always more transparent to our friends than we are to ourselves.

18

The summer solstice had just passed, the days were as long as they would ever be, but the thunderheads had brought a premature dusk with them. The pole lights outside the truck stop blazed brightly enough to illuminate a stadium. I decided to grab a meal at the diner before calling Ora with an update. She had been good about not messaging, but the silence on her end was ominous, too. It meant that she hadn't heard anything from her missing husband.

My phone rang as I crossed the puddled parking lot. I didn't recognize the number, but the location of the caller was given as Indian Township.

"Mike, it's Nick Francis."

"Thanks for calling back."

"My granddaughter said you stopped by the house looking for me." His Passamaquoddy accent was incredibly faint: noticeable in the dropping of g's at the end of his present participles.

"She said you were headed up to Houlton."

"Yeah, I've been dealing with my boy. Probably will be for a couple of days."

"Really? I'm in Houlton now. I am at the truck stop near the I-95 exit. Have you had supper?"

"It's four o'clock. I may be old, but I ain't one of them early birds."

"I'll pick up the tab."

"Whatever you want from me must be expensive."

"Just some background information about a personal case I'm working."

"Ain't nothing more expensive than information." His tone was light, but I could sense that he was debating accepting my invitation. "Look, I know you're looking for Charley. I already told Ora to give the man some time. He'll show up eventually—he always does."

"Then why not get a free meal out of me?"

I heard him suck on a cigarette while he considered the offer.

"I guess I could use a diversion from the family problems I been dealing with. I'm down at the hospital now. Should take me fifteen minutes to get there."

"The hospital? Are you all right?"

He replied with a laugh tinged with sadness. "I'll see you in fifteen."

When they were young men, Nick and Charley had worked investigations together, on and around Down East tribal lands, including several cases that Charley refused to discuss with me. One involved the notorious gang rape and murder of a Passamaquoddy girl at Pleasant Point. The five alleged perpetrators—local white men—were never arrested or brought to trial, but I gathered that their identities had been all but confirmed.

"It was a different era," Charley had said. "There were different standards of law for whites and Indians in Washington County."

He refused to say more—which had only increased my interest.

Researching the case, I had learned that both the gang's ringleader and his sidekick had died when their fishing boat had sunk in Cobscook Bay. The Coast Guard and Maine law enforcement agencies had conducted an investigation that had lasted months—just about every Indian in Pleasant Point seemed to have been interrogated—but had come up empty.

Charley wouldn't have been a party to murder, but Nick Francis? I wasn't so sure.

I was on the verge of ordering supper when in through the diner door came a squat but handsome man in his seventies. Despite his age, his full head of hair was still a dark, blackish brown, and he had a face that must have been boyish before wrinkles and weathered skin had finally given it gravitas. His hair and shoulders were wet. It must have started raining again.

He wore a loose linen shirt—probably to conceal a gun tucked inside his waistband—chinos, and loafers. The only item that hinted at his tribal identity was a bead bracelet worn on the same wrist as a battered old Timex. On his forehead, a hemophilic bandage covered what, I guessed, were no less than a dozen new stitches.

Everyone I met these days had been battered, one way or another.

"Nick."

"Mike."

The hand I shook was hard with calluses. The fingertips were stained yellow from nicotine. He settled into the booth across from me, hands hidden beneath the tabletop.

I had always felt uncomfortable around Nick Francis. He seemed to blink less than normal people, seemed always to be staring. But it was his perpetual smile that weirded me out. When his face was at rest, the corners of his broad mouth remained upturned, giving him a catlike expression.

More than other Native Americans I had met, he made me aware of the vast distance between our life experiences.

Don't presume to know me, those hard black eyes seemed to state.

I tried to affect more ease than I felt. "I have to ask about the bandage."

"The boy and me had a difference of opinion. I shouldn't have let it escalate."

"Your son did that?"

The waitress appeared with coffee, which I eagerly accepted. Nick ordered a Pepsi, no ice.

"I'll cut to the chase," I said. "I'm concerned about Charley."

"Have you contacted the FAA?"

"He didn't take his plane."

"That ain't good."

"It gets worse. He left me a note telling me not to come looking for him."

"Seems like maybe you should honor his wishes. Charley has reasons for the things he does. They don't always make sense to anyone but him, but you need to respect his choices."

"I would if not for Ora—"

"Charley understood the worry it would cause her. Maybe he reckoned she'd be even more worried if she knew where he was going. It ain't your business in any case, and you're smart enough to know that, kid."

Two Border Patrol agents came in and whispered to the hostess. She guided them to seats in a corner booth. They sat beside each other so each had a clear view of the room. Cops of all stripes have an aversion to sitting with their backs to doors. When I was younger, I had sat against plenty of walls. But after so many close encounters with death, I knew I wasn't going to die like Wild Bill Hickok, shot by some loser coming through a door with a pistol blasting.

I returned my attention to Nick Francis. "Have you ever heard of a game warden named Duke Dupree? He was a warden back during the Depression."

"I'm old, kid, but not that old."

"This Dupree's badge showed up at the pop-up flea market at the Machias Dike. I'm positive it's the reason for Charley's strange behavior, that badge."

He rested his left hand on the laminated menu before him. Only then did I see he was missing the ring finger. "You're going to keep working it no matter what I say."

"You know I will."

I half expected him to get up and leave. Instead he cracked the first real smile he'd shown me since he'd sat down. "Then we'd better order food so you can start telling the story."

—

"You going to talk to that college girl tomorrow?" he asked when I'd finished.

"If I can find her."

"What street did you say she lives on?"

I told him. I thought he might offer his assistance, but he didn't.

"You've known Charley a long time," I said. "In his note to me, he mentioned the 'worst mistake a man can make.' What do you think he meant by that?"

"Killing someone," he said matter-of-factly.

"That was my thought, too."

Suddenly, Nick tilted his head back and looked at the ceiling.

"What?" I asked.

"Killing the wrong someone."

"That's the worst mistake a man can make?"

"For Charley it would be."

"But he never killed anyone—not after Vietnam, I mean."

Nick's reaction was to glance at the corner booth where the two Border Patrol agents were finishing their meals with strawberry shortcake and cups of coffee.

"Is that what he told you?" he asked.

"You're saying he lied to me?"

"I'm not sure why you think Charley owed you the story of his life."

A thought occurred to me; I couldn't have explained why. I reached into my pocket and brought out the snapshot Ora had found in Charley's cigar box, the picture of the bear-faced man. I pushed it across the glass-topped table.

"Where did you get that?" Nick asked.

It was my turn to be the one slowly doling out information. "Do you know who this is?"

"Of course."

"Well?"

"That's Pierre Michaud."

"Who's Pierre Michaud?"

"The man Charley killed."

"What?"

Nick reached into the chest pocket of his shirt, removed a crushed pack of cigarettes, and set it on the table. The brand was Natural American Spirit. The illustration on the package showed an Indian in eagle-feather headdress inhaling tobacco from a long pipe.

"You mind continuing this conversation outside? I could use a smoke."

But I sensed his real motive. He didn't want to be overheard.

19

The rain had stopped, and a mist was rising from the ashphalt. We wandered off past the chugging eighteen wheelers, past the arc lights, past the drop-off where the asphalt crumbled. We entered a field of wildflowers and weeds. It was too early in the summer for crickets, but I heard other unknown insects clicking from the shadowed ground, and a few fireflies flickered farther out in the tall grass.

"People listen better in the dark, I've found," he said.

"I was listening to you inside."

He chuckled. "You weren't listening. You were letting your eyes rest on me while you thought about yourself."

He had me there.

"You ever hear what happened at St. Ignace?" he said in the brief glow of the Zippo he used to light his cigarette.

"Up in the St. John Valley?" I said. "An undercover game warden disappeared. He was presumed murdered by the group of poachers he had infiltrated. The Warden Service tore apart the town looking for him. A few buildings burned to the ground in the raid. Politically, it was a shit show for the department. The colonel at the time was forced to resign."

"That's one version," Nick said, exhaling smoke I could taste on the tip of my tongue. "Everyone who was there that night tells a different story. Keep in mind I only know what I heard. I was the police chief in Indian Township at that time and had enough shit to handle with my own people."

"You're saying that Charley was the one who shot and killed the ringleader? This Michaud guy?"

"That's right."

"How is it possible that I never heard about this?"

"The exchange of gunfire happened at night on Beau Lac. That's almost as far north in Maine as you can go. The international border runs right down the center of the lake. Charley only winged the man, but the shot knocked him out of his canoe. Michaud drowned trying to swim to the Canadian shore."

In the darkness of the rain-soaked field, I was half hypnotized by the orange glow of his cigarette as it danced through the air like yet another firefly.

"You didn't answer my question. How have I never heard about this?"

"The Warden Service got raked over the coals pretty good, like you said. Both the U.S. attorney and the Maine attorney general found Charley was justified in his actions. Michaud was a cop killer. Everyone had an interest in putting the scandal to bed."

"But they never found the undercover warden."

"No matter how hard they searched."

I closed my eyes and tried to see the granite memorial in Augusta devoted to law enforcement officers who had died in the line of duty.

"Scott Pellerin," I said. "That was his name?"

"Smart kid. Too cocky for his own good, though. Charley said it must've been how he blew his cover—overconfidence."

The occasional rumble of big rigs passing along the highway made me think the storms were returning.

"How does the badge fit into this?"

"Both *Pellerin* and *Dupree* are French names. You should check out if they were related. There might be a connection."

"You seem to be working on a theory," I said.

"Am I?"

"That Charley always regretted Michaud's death because it kept him from finding Pellerin. That's why he kept that picture in a box with his other 'trophies.' For some reason, the reappearance of Duke Dupree's badge has made him rethink the events of fifteen years ago. He realized he had been misled."

"Is that my theory?" said Nick. "I'm smarter than I thought."

"It explains why Charley would want to check things out on his own—in case the man who murdered Pellerin has been preparing for the day when he was finally found out."

Nick tossed the orange ember of his cigarette into the weeds. "It also explains why he took his truck instead of his plane. He might have had a bunch of stops to make, people to talk with along the way. That old Ford Ranger of his is distinctive. Folks might remember it if you ask."

"It sounds like you're encouraging me to go after him."

"You're going to do what you're going to do. That's your MO, I've heard."

"So if Michaud didn't kill Pellerin, who did?"

"One of his confederates."

"In his letter, Charley said he didn't want to put his family or me in danger. From whom, though? Some poacher who wasn't caught in the raid? Sure, a guy who thinks he got away with killing a game warden is going to be dangerous. But you did this job, too, Nick. We've all dealt with scarier people than some toothless old night hunter."

"A toothless man can put a bullet in you just as fast as one with a mouthful of choppers. Fifteen years ain't that long ago, either. This mystery man might not be that old."

"I was speaking metaphorically."

"Seems like Scott Pellerin got killed for underestimating the men he was infiltrating. That's a mistake Charley isn't going to make. You'd best follow his example and keep your guard up."

I listened to a toad trilling across the field. "So where do you think Charley is now?"

"Your guess is as good as mine."

"He'll want to talk with the girl who sold Smith the badge," I said.

"That would be my assumption, but he can't risk giving himself away. He's the man who shot Pierre Michaud, remember. People in the Valley have long memories, even if the rest of the world has forgotten what happened up there."

"I hadn't thought of that."

"So you're determined to pursue this?"

"In the morning."

"I can recommend the motel across the parking lot."

"Is that where you're staying?"

"I have a lady friend up in Mars Hill."

Nick Francis had lots of lady friends, from what I'd heard.

"I don't suppose you want to come with me tomorrow—play investigator again."

He had a chain-smoker's laugh. "Old men shouldn't be running around, chasing after thrills. They should be content in the arms of their family. Besides, I have to stick around Houlton until Tuesday."

"What happens Tuesday?"

"My son is being arraigned. And he's going to need me to pay his bail again."

—

Following Nick's recommendation, I took a room at the motel across from the truck stop. A sign on the dresser threatened anyone caught smoking with a $250 fine. Based on the odor baked into the rug, the penalty hadn't deterred a prior occupant.

It could have been that I was smelling the residue of Nick Francis's cigarettes. My clothing reeked of American Spirits. I hung them from the shower rod with the window open to air out.

I was curious about Nick's son, Molly's dad. The fact of the younger man being in jail might have explained the bandage on the father's forehead.

One of Charley's favorite sayings came to mind: "Some people are more than they appear. And some people are less than they appear. But nobody is the way they appear."

But surely, he couldn't have fooled me, not after all the adventures we'd lived through.

The decision before me—choosing to believe in Charley's essential goodness—seemed to have momentous importance, as if in making it, I wasn't just defending my friend but also somehow defining myself.

Because I had been betrayed before by trusting in the character of a person I'd thought I'd understood, I had vowed never to be fooled again, no matter the circumstances. But I couldn't live my life distrusting the people closest to me.

I made my decision. I trusted Charley.

Kathy had been true to her word. When I opened my email, there was a message with the subject line: DUKE DUPREE!

> He killed himself after his draft board refused his application to join the army after Pearl Harbor. His wife found him in the outhouse with a shotgun at his feet and half his head blown off. That's the legend in Millinocket anyhow.
>
> Of course, you won't see this message since you're deep in the woods at Debouille Pond with no signal. I hope the char are biting!
>
> PS: Call Dani.

Dupree having committed suicide explained why his badge had held no particular value to his next of kin. The shield symbolized his dishonor. Dupree might even have pawned the badge before his death. Who could say how many hands it had passed through over the decades?

As intriguing as this information was, it brought me no closer to understanding why Charley had reacted the way he had when he saw the badge on Smith's table. What connection did he have to a failed game warden who'd died before he was born? If anything, I felt myself to be at a greater loss than I'd been before I read Kathy's message.

Meanwhile, Ora was waiting. I could picture her in the camp, in her wheelchair with the green blanket over her knees, Vivaldi playing on the old cassette stereo. I owed her the truth, I realized.

I couldn't have it both ways. In order to trust, I needed also to be trustworthy.

"Where are you?" was her first question.

"I'm at a motel in Houlton."

"Did you find Mr. Smith?"

As if the jackass deserved to be called *mister,* I thought.

But that was Ora Stevens. She would grant the devil the dignity of being addressed with an honorific.

She listened to my account of the day without interruption until I came to the part of the story where I'd met Nick Francis and he'd brought up the bungled undercover investigation fifteen years earlier.

"This has to do with that man Michaud," she said, her voice rising as the truth became clear to her. "He is the one in the picture in Charley's cigar box!"

"Yes."

"I should have recognized him, but when it happened, I couldn't bring myself to read the papers. The grief was too much for me. And I could tell how greatly Charley was suffering. Of course this is all about Scott. It's the only explanation that makes sense."

"What connection did Scott Pellerin have with Charley?"

"Oh, Mike," she said. "Scott Pellerin was once you."

20

While we talked, I opened the browser on my phone and brought up the Warden Service website. I found the page dedicated to fallen officers.

In his commemorative photo, Scott Pellerin was wearing the same dress uniform—red coat and short-brimmed green Stetson—that I had worn the day I was sworn into service.

His eyes were an unremarkable brown. His hair was an unremarkable brown. Perhaps it was the anonymity of his features that had made his superiors think him suitable for undercover work. Scott Pellerin had a face you could easily forget.

"They were like father and son," Ora said. "Scott's own father was a merchant mariner and alcoholic. His mother was one of those enablers. Scott never had a male role model until he met Charley."

The resemblance to my own life story wasn't exact—but close enough to be unsettling.

"Of course, you and Scott had different personalities," Ora continued, "and there wasn't anything between him and Stacey. She was just a teenager when he died, busy with her friends."

Still, I was surprised Stacey had never mentioned this Pellerin to me. Maybe she hadn't realized the extent of her father's connection to the young man. She had been a rebellious teen, uninterested in her parents' lives. A typical adolescent in other words.

"When you say we had different personalities, what do you mean?"

"Scott wasn't as well educated as you, but he was extremely intelligent. He was quiet, but not shy. Strangers seemed to warm to him easily. Maybe because he seemed so interested in people."

Unlike me.

"What else?"

"You were both brave to the point of being foolhardy. Scott loved taking risks. He probably would have grown out of it, as you have. Charley had been teaching him to fly, and he was close to getting his pilot's license when—you know what happened."

"Not really," I said. "All I know is that he was working undercover in St. Ignace, infiltrating a group of poachers, and that someone must have gotten suspicious because he didn't make his scheduled rendezvous with his handler."

"Stanley Kellam. The lieutenant was Scott's handler."

I had met Stan "the Man" Kellam a dozen times before his retirement. He used to run Division E, which included the entirety of Aroostook County: roughly the size of Connecticut and Rhode Island combined.

"Did they have a starting point for the search?"

"Scott mentioned that the poachers kept an illegal camp near Tornado Path on the Allagash River, so that was where they focused initially. They dredged Round Pond, which is just above the path."

"I've been there," I said. "Remember when Stacey and I paddled the Allagash?"

"Oh, yes. I had forgotten." I heard the tinkling sound of ice in a glass: her nightcap. "The search expanded to include the entire waterway, south to Chamberlain Lake and east to Ashland and then west to the Québec border and north to Estcourt Station."

She was describing a search area of a thousand square miles.

"Tell me about this Pierre Michaud."

"I only know what Charley told me. That he was a horrible man. He shot people's cats with an air gun for sport. He had two sons, just as bad. They were all poachers. There were other men involved, too. I don't remember the names. I couldn't bear to read or watch the news then—I was so heartbroken."

"What did the Michauds say when they were confronted with Pellerin's disappearance?"

"They said they had no idea where he'd gone. They pretended not to know he was a warden. That was how Charley knew there was a conspiracy to murder Scott, because they all told the same exact story. Normally, the details of their accounts would have differed."

"So Michaud and the others were interrogated?"

"The detectives held the poachers as long as they could. Scott had recorded evidence to charge a few of them with crimes, but they had to let the father go after forty-eight hours. Pierre had been careful around Scott and never broke the law in his presence."

"Ora, this is difficult, but I need to know what Charley told you about how Pierre Michaud died."

"The police and wardens went back to St. Ignace a few nights later. They had new evidence against Michaud. They used flash-bang grenades when they stormed his house, but he must have rigged it with explosives or incendiaries, because it went up in flames and took two other houses with it. Charley says it was a diversion to cover Michaud's escape.

"They searched for him for days. Charley did aerial surveillance, of course. By sheer luck, he spotted a canoe crossing Beau Lac late at night. The moon had broken through the clouds. Charley landed the plane on the water—you know how difficult that is at night—and Michaud fired at him, and he fired back. The man would have lived if he hadn't tried to swim in that cold water. Some people, including the press, called it an act of revenge, but Michaud was the only one who knew where Scott's body was hidden. They never did find it."

Secretly, I understood the reluctance of people in the St. John Valley to accept this story as the truth. Hundreds of men had been searching thousands of miles of dense forest for the fugitive. What were the odds of Charley Stevens flying over Beau Lac at the exact hour Michaud had chosen to cross the border?

"You need to go see Stanley Kellam," Ora said. "Stanley used to go out on his own time for years afterward, looking for clues that would lead him to the truth. Charley said he was guilt-ridden for sending Scott to his death."

"Do you have a phone number for Lieutenant Kellam?"

"I remember Charley saying that Stanley left the state after he retired. It sounds crazy, but I thought he said the man was going back to college!"

"Do you have any idea where?"

"I'll check the Rolodex and give you a call back. Oh, Mike, I'm sure this is the explanation for why Charley is acting so strangely. Something about this badge has made him think he can find Scott."

"Let's hope so," I said. "And you're certain you've never heard the name *Duke Dupree*?"

"I'm sure I haven't."

I put the phone down beside me on the bedspread. Then I found the complimentary pen and notepaper from the motel desk and began scribbling down as much information as I could recall from my conversations that evening.

The idea of Stan Kellam going back to college after his retirement wasn't as far-fetched as Ora thought. He had been one of those larger-than-life characters who often rise to positions of power. We hadn't crossed paths in years, but I found I could see him clearly in my memory. A massive brute of a man. Gray eyes, dirty-blond hair, a perpetual pink sunburn. And one of the most brilliant minds in the history of the Maine Warden Service.

While many of the old-school wardens boasted twelfth-grade educations at best, Kellam had graduated from Rutgers, and he had not abandoned his studies over the course of his long career. While overseeing Division E—a job that must have consumed sixty hours a week—he had quietly obtained a master's degree in criminology from the University of Maine. At his retirement roast, he'd joked about getting a Ph.D. next.

I also recalled that Kellam had come into a considerable bit of life insurance money when his most recent wife died in a car crash. There was some gossip that Stan might have played a role in her convenient demise. Not all the gossip was kidding.

There were no messages from Dani: no voice mails, no emails, no texts.

This was unusual for her. *Unheard of* would be the more accurate phrase. Charley had already dropped off the radar. I didn't need my girlfriend following suit.

Ora phoned me back before I could call Dani.

"All I could find for Stanley was a post office box in Portage," she said. "I thought the address must be out of date, so I made a call to Tim Malcomb."

She was referring to the head of the Warden Service. "What did the colonel tell you?"

"Stanley's back in Maine!"

"I hadn't heard that."

"He purchased an old sporting camp west of Portage and turned it into his own private compound. It's over on Moccasin Pond."

"I think I know the old camp Kellam bought."

I remembered seeing it advertised in *The Maine Sportsman* and the *Northwoods Sporting Journal*. It had been on the market for $1 million.

"I just wish Charley would let me know he's OK," said Ora.

"He is."

"How can you be certain?"

"Because of you."

"Me?"

"If something had happened to Charley, you would have sensed it."

"I'm not clairvoyant, Mike. I just get feelings."

"Those are called *premonitions*. Have you had any about your husband?"

"No."

"Then you need to trust yourself."

"Since when have you started believing in premonitions, Mike Bowditch?"

"I've seen too many things I can't explain," I said. "Human mysteries are nothing compared to the mysteries of the universe."

The air coming through the window screens was so saturated with moisture that it formed dew on the sills. I tried closing the windows and running the AC, but the unit made a sick, rattling sound that I feared would keep me up all night.

I sat down on the bed and found the mattress unforgiving. Then I made the call.

"Hi," Dani said.

"I expected to hear from you. How was your day on the shooting range?"

"I qualified, but just barely. I think it was the heat. My face was brick red, the guys said."

Dani was a natural marksman. Some people have to train and train, but her skills were as close to God-given as I had seen. It was as if she'd been born with the muscle memory of having fired thousands of shots: Annie Oakley reincarnated.

"Maybe it was heat stroke."

"I just had a bad day."

"You might want to take a cool bath—not too cold."

"I don't have heat stroke," she said. "To top it all off, I picked up a tick somewhere. I found it attached to my thigh, full of blood, like it had been there awhile."

"Was it a deer tick or a dog tick?" The question mattered because the former carried Lyme disease while the latter did not.

"Deer tick."

"You need to get that checked out."

"I will if I see a bullseye rash."

"It wouldn't hurt to get your doctor to prescribe some antibiotics anyway. Lyme isn't something you can blow off."

"Mike, I told you I'll keep an eye on it. How many ticks did you used to find on yourself when you were a patrol warden? No offense, but I'm tired of talking about my sucky day. Has Charley reappeared?"

"No, but I think I am beginning to understand what this is about."

"Let's hear it."

She listened quietly to my monologue. That, too, was atypical. Usually, Dani interrupted me with questions or theories whenever I told her about a case I was working on. She had the mind of a detective and couldn't help herself.

When I had finished, she said, "Be careful of Stan Kellam."

"What do you mean?"

"Kathy never told you about him? Stan the Man was her lieutenant when she was a rookie."

"Please don't tell me he sexually harassed her," I said, thinking of Tom Wheelwright.

"Worse. He tried to persuade her to quit after her husband died in that car crash. He badgered her about it for weeks after she came back from bereavement leave. Like, because she was a woman, she must be suffering so bad she couldn't do the job. He put her on a desk until she forced him to let her return to patrol."

"Kathy never told me any of this."

"That's because you're a man," Dani said. "She's your friend and all, but this is the kind of thing women have trouble sharing except with other women. She never came as close to quitting as during that stretch of time."

"I'll ask her about him."

"If she even wants to talk—sorry, I'm not being the best listener tonight. I've got a wicked headache. I'm glad that son of a bitch Smith didn't shoot you."

"That makes two of us."

"I'll hit you back in morning," she said. "I just need to get some sleep."

"If you're still not feeling well—"

"Good night, Mike. Love you."

"Good night."

21

The next morning dawned as hot as sunrise in the Congo. I stepped outside with a cup of coffee I had brewed in the little machine atop the bureau. The rhythmic thumping of truck tires on the bridge over Route 1 carried across the parking lot: the sound of commerce. House sparrows were picking dead bugs out of the grilles of the semis in the parking lot.

Logan Cronk, up early, had sent along pictures of Shadow to assure me my captive canine was alive and well. The black wolf must have slept beneath an evergreen because his fur had become coated with saffron pollen. The big animal appeared nearly phosphorescent. My very own Hound of the Baskervilles.

I ate breakfast in the diner—scrambled eggs, bacon, and a molasses doughnut—and gassed up my truck, knowing the length of the drive ahead of me. In the County, it paid to fill your tank whenever you could since opportunities could be few and far between. I was eager to get started.

Presque Isle is what passes for a big city in Aroostook County. I do not mean that as a slight. Nine thousand residents is significant anywhere in a state as rural as Maine. Presque Isle is home to three institutions of higher learning. It has an actual airport with commercial flights—only two a day, but it's something. The first successful transatlantic balloon launched from Presque Isle and landed safely outside Paris in 1978.

But if you ask anyone up north about the city, they'll say its real claim to fame is potatoes.

Prized above all others for making french fries, the Kennebec variety are harvested by tons in the fall, processed by factories that perfume the air with a pleasantly starchy aroma, and then trucked and shipped around the world.

I approached the city through vast fields of potatoes. Being June, there wasn't much to see—just endless furrows of dirt stretching to distant tree lines. In a few weeks, however, the plants would begin to blossom until the city of Presque Isle was adrift in a sea of flowers. On windy summer days, petals would tumble along the ground: purple, pink, and white.

The sun was showing through the clouds, a blurred disk, when I turned onto a street of ranch homes with mowed yards and gardens bright with peonies and hydrangeas. Not having an address, a name, or even a description of the young woman (beyond her shapely breasts), it made no sense to guess which house might be hers. I was looking instead for a certain type of person that you will find in any neat residential neighborhood.

The busybody.

I found her soon enough. Noting the slowness of my vehicle, she opened her curtains to have a better look at me. When I reached the end of the street and doubled back, moving even more slowly now, she emerged onto her front porch.

I stopped the Scout when I'd drawn even with her tidy house and rolled down the window and hung my arm out. I shut off the engine.

"Hello! I'm wondering if you can help me."

She was a short wisp of a woman with rosy cheeks and a long gray braid. I doubt if she weighed ninety pounds. She wore a purple smock, linen pants, Birkenstocks, and reading glasses propped atop her head. A wedding ring hung on a chain around her neck. "Are you lost, then?"

"Not exactly. I'm trying to find a young woman who lives on this street. Mrs. . . . ?"

"And what would her name be?"

"I'm afraid I don't know."

"Maybe you should put an ad in the newspaper, under Missed Connections."

She had the accent I had come to associate with natives of northern Maine: flat vowels and hard *r*'s.

First-time visitors to Aroostook County often remark on how midwestern it feels. They don't just mean the enormous blue skies and rolling farmland. They're also taken aback by pronunciations, which don't remotely resemble the Down East stereotype. The Aroostook accent sounds like something you might hear in a Milwaukee beerhouse or at a Nebraska Grange hall.

I produced my badge and identification card. She took her time bringing her reading glasses into position to read them. After a thorough review, she lifted the glasses off her nose and stared into my eyes with fierce intention.

"If she's a poacher, you're looking in the wrong neighborhood."

"Actually, I think she's a student at one of the colleges, living with a couple of other girls. They had a yard sale not too long ago. The girl I need to talk to has dark hair and is, um, buxom."

Her eyes twinkled. "Buxom! Haven't heard that expression since Jane Russell was on TV selling brassieres. That would be Angie Bouchard."

"Can you point me to her house?"

"Only if you tell me why you need to talk to her."

"Ms. Bouchard sold something at her yard sale. I'd like to ask where she got it."

"Was it that badge?"

"You saw it?"

"Course I did. I was there with the other early birds before she opened up. Is she in trouble for selling that thing?"

"No."

"Yah, well. Wouldn't surprise me if she were. She and her friends threw the kinds of parties that attract men on motorcycles. I can't say I'm sad she's moving out. Blue house, white trim. Number eighty-four."

"Thank you, Mrs.—"

"That badge of yours is real, I hope. You're not one of those police impersonators."

"The badge is real."

I found a dog-eared business card in my wallet and handed it to her. She took it without a word. When I restarted my truck, she was standing on the front steps, trying to get a clear view down the street of what was about to happen.

There were no motorcycles parked outside the blue house, but there was a muddy pickup pulled up to the curb, someone's old beater. More notable was the flashy Volkswagen Golf GTI in the open garage. The white hatchback still had the temporary cardboard plate the dealer gives you before you drive off the lot.

The new car might mean something or it might mean nothing. It might not even belong to Angie Bouchard.

I rang the bell, positioned the badge on my belt so that it was in plain sight, and stepped back from the door so I could be viewed from head to foot through the peephole.

The young woman who answered the door had hazel eyes and a rat's nest of brownish-black hair. She was as voluptuous as Smith had claimed. She wore a T-shirt with the EarthMother logo, jeans with holes in the knees, and a fringe of loose threads at her bare ankles. I judged her to be older than most college students, midtwenties. She held an unlighted, hand-rolled cigarette pinched between two fingers.

"Angie Bouchard?"

"Yeah?"

I produced my badge for her. "I'm Mike Bowditch. I'm a warden investigator for the State of Maine."

Her untrimmed eyebrows tightened. "What's that?"

She had an entirely different accent from her busybody neighbor. The inflection was faint but undeniably French. *What's tat?*

"I'm a detective who works for the Maine Warden Service, but still a police officer. Can I come in?"

"Fuck no. I don't let strange men in my house. Cops included."

"You had a yard sale here last month?"

"Yeah?"

She kept her voice neutral and face free of surprise, but she knew exactly why I had appeared at her door. The effect of my words was immediate. She stepped out onto the concrete stoop and closed the door behind her.

"Did you sell a badge like mine at your sale? It would have been smaller, older?"

"No."

"A man in the county jail swears he bought a vintage game warden badge at a yard sale at this address."

She produced a Bic lighter from her pocket and brought the cigarette up to her full lips. "My roommate had stuff for sale, too. Could have belonged to her."

"Is she home?"

Angie Bouchard exhaled smoke from the corner of her mouth. Only then did I realize the cigarette was an expertly rolled joint. I made a coughing noise that brought an amused light into her eyes.

"Meg's spending the summer back home in Connecticut."

"Would you mind putting that thing out until we're done?"

"It's legal, and it's my house," she said. "If you don't approve, you can leave."

Her attitude told me she had dealt with cops before. People who seldom come into contact with the police are rarely so defiant.

Was she a bad girl? Or was she just pretending to be one?

I brought out my notebook. "What's Meg's full name?"

She told me. I pretended to write it down.

"What brought her all the way to Presque Isle?"

"Her family is from here originally. They moved to Connecticut after the base closed at Limestone. Went to work for one of the defense firms. Lots of people did. Meg wouldn't have known it was illegal to sell a police badge."

"It isn't illegal. Unless it was stolen property. What about you, Angie? Where are you from?"

"Madawaska."

It was an industrial town two hours north of Presque Isle in the St. John Valley. Madawaska was noteworthy for having a paper mill with a foot in two nations. The U.S. plant sent liquid wood pulp through a pipeline above the river to the New Brunswick factory to be made into toilet tissue, among other things.

"Does your father work at the mill?"

She exhaled marijuana smoke in my face. "How'd you guess?"

"There aren't too many other jobs in Madawaska other than papermaking."

"That depends on what side you're on," she said. "There are more opportunities on the Canadian side."

"Which side are you on?"

"My mom was American. My dad is Canadian. I have dual citizenship."

"Your mom is dead?"

The past tense had given her away, and she only now realized it. "She died over the winter. Breast cancer."

"I'm sorry for your loss. Mine died of ovarian cancer. Your mother left you some money?"

"How did you—?"

"The car. Those GTIs are sweet. What was your mom's name?"

"Emmeline," she said. "My mom's name was Emmeline Bouchard."

"Was she from Madawaska, too?"

"Fort Kent."

The town was twenty miles down the river from St. Ignace where Scott Pellerin had vanished.

"The badge you—excuse me, Meg—sold at the yard sale belonged to a man named Duke Dupree. I'm having trouble understanding how a college student from Connecticut got her hands on the badge of a Maine game warden who has been dead for decades."

There was a touch of cruelty in her smile. "Too bad she's not here."

"You're lying to me about the badge, Angie. I know it was yours."

The door flew open behind her. A big, bearded man stood there, wearing jeans and nothing else. He had the heavy brow and the powerful chest of a cartoon caveman. Unusual for a man his age in a place like this, he had no tattoos. He did, however, possess what looked like a cattle brand on one muscular shoulder. Raised scar tissue made a circular pattern. He appeared to be late thirties, older than I was, and significantly older than Angie.

"Who the fuck is this?" he said in the same faintly French accent.

"No one, baby."

His eyes were like those of a nocturnal animal, dark brown, alert. A creature that preys upon weaker creatures.

"I know a cop when I see one."

"I'm a game warden, actually. And you are?"

"A friend of mine," said Angie quickly.

The man took the joint from her but was more careful about the direction he blew smoke. He looked so familiar, and yet I was positive we had never met before.

"What do you want?" he said.

"I was asking for tips on having a successful yard sale."

The man angled himself in front of his girlfriend, assuming that's who she was. I kept my eyes locked on his but used my peripheral vision in case he pulled out a weapon.

"I think it's time for you to knock on someone else's door, Warden."

A realization took hold of me. Why had it taken so long for me to see the resemblance? From my back pocket, I removed the snapshot Ora had found in Charley's cigar box and held it out for them to see.

The bearded man reacted as if I'd shown him a picture of his own gravestone. The question came out as a snarl. "What the fuck?"

My intuition had been proven correct. "I assume you know who this is, then."

"Where did you get that?"

I put the photograph away before he could snatch it from me. "It doesn't matter. So which of Pierre Michaud's sons are you?"

"Who the fuck are you?"

"I already told Ms. Bouchard."

Angie put her hand on Michaud's muscled arm but directed her words at me. "I answered all your questions."

That wasn't anywhere near the truth. I had dozens more for Angie Bouchard and the son of Pierre Michaud.

"Get the fuck out of here," he said.

"And if I don't?"

He couldn't speak the threat out loud, but I had seen murder in enough eyes to recognize a warning. "Don't come here again."

Tough guys always need to have the last word.

22

Fifteen miles west of Presque Isle, I nearly drove off the road. I was passing through green fields planted with what looked like broccoli when I spotted an enormous black shape, grazing with its head down among the plants. A horse that had escaped his corral? No, it was too tall and ungainly.

Slowing down, I spotted another, then another, then another. Moose don't travel in herds, but that was what I saw: twelve moose, ranging in size from new calves to enormous bulls, all happily dining on some hapless farmer's crop.

Take that, Everglades, I thought. *You don't have a monopoly on natural wonders.*

I stopped the Scout and got out with my iPhone to get pictures of the moose herd. My photographic skills were adequate for the purposes of recording evidence at crime scenes, but I lacked Stacey's eye for composition and light.

The big animals didn't seem to notice my presence. Moose have notoriously poor vision (I once avoided a charging bull by simply stepping behind a tree trunk and kept it between us until he calmed down), but their hearing is keen, as is their sense of smell, so they knew I was there. They just didn't care.

Each of the animals was surrounded by a swarm of blackflies. The insect clouds were visible from fifty yards away. And soon the heat-seeking bugs had homed in on me, too. I retreated back inside my vehicle.

I needed to make a phone call anyway.

I reached Nick Francis's voice mail.

"Nick, it's Mike. I found the young woman who sold the badge to John Smith. Her name is Angie Bouchard, and I'm pretty sure she's from St. Ignace. Her mother's name was Emmeline Bouchard. I had expected Charley to have found her before I did, but she didn't react like an angry geezer had recently knocked on her door. The big surprise was her boyfriend. He's one of Pierre Michaud's sons. He overheard me asking Angie about the badge, and I got the feeling he didn't know she'd sold it and was ripshit to learn what she'd done. That worries me for her sake."

I had hoped Nick was screening his calls. I watched the moose for ten more minutes until they drifted one by one into the trees across the field. The phone didn't ring. I started off again.

Past Haystack Mountain, the landscape changed from farm fields to hills bristling with timber. A visitor might mistake these forests for wilderness, but they were just another cropland. The trees comprised plantations of softwoods—spruces and firs, mostly—that grew fast and could be harvested at the earliest opportunity to turn into paper for magazines and toilet tissue.

During the era of the river drives, when cut logs were transported on highways of water during the spring floods, the Maine North Woods had been largely unbroken by roads. The practices of the old-time loggers had caused many environmental problems, but they had left the boreal forest more or less intact. Bigfoot could have been hiding here, and no one would've been the wiser.

Now you could drive the length and breadth of Aroostook County on dirt and gravel roads. From the air, the North Woods was crisscrossed with innumerable scars.

"This used to be good country once," Charley would sometimes grumble when we were airborne, "but now it's nothing but a bunch of damned tree farms, owned by New York bankers who wouldn't know a maple from a magnolia."

"And you accused me of being a young old fart! What does that make you?"

"Somebody who's lived past his expiration date."

"I won't tell Ora you said that."

"Thank you."

I had noticed that my friend had gotten crankier and more backward-looking since Stacey had left for Florida. His favorite daughter had shared some of her youthful energy with the old man and kept him focused on the future. Without her, Charley had begun to drift, like so many people his age, into reveries of lost days.

No wonder Duke Dupree's badge had affected him so profoundly.

Knowing that Angie Bouchard had been responsible for the shield resurfacing was interesting but unhelpful without context. What was her connection to Scott Pellerin? She would have been a child when he disappeared.

I was banking on Stan Kellam filling in some of the missing puzzle pieces. He had been Pellerin's commanding officer and handler, and Ora made it sound as if he'd taken the young investigator's death as hard as Charley had. But when I thought of Kellam—commanding, conniving, brilliant—I was reminded of the specific language in that letter to me:

> There's a man out there who's kept quiet all these years, waiting for me to wise up to my foolishness, a man of patience and guile. He's been expecting me, I fear, and taken precautions.

I didn't associate patience with Stan Kellam. The man had had a reputation for routinely exploding at his subordinates in red-faced rage. But guile? Absolutely. The way he'd tried to maneuver Kathy Frost into leaving the service after her husband's death.

Ora had told me that the former lieutenant had purchased an old sporting camp on Moccasin Pond in a vast swatch of Maine referred to as the Unorganized Territories. A few minutes with *The Maine Atlas and Gazetteer* located the pond by latitude and longitude, but the map was less helpful in plotting a course. The dotted lines indicating roads might be passable or not, and forget about GPS in that untraveled tract of woods. Kellam had chosen to retreat from the world in a place where no one actually lived. Population: zero.

These unincorporated townships were so remote, they didn't even have true names but were marked on the atlas by letters and numbers: T13 R17, T12 R9, and so on. Not all the dotted lines leading to Moccasin Pond on the map even had names. I would be lucky to find Kellam's compound and luckier to find my way out of the woods if darkness fell before it was time to leave.

The Rocky Brook Road headed west from Portage through the heart of the state's commercial timberland to the Québec border outside Saint-Pamphile. Instead of asphalt, or even sand, it had been surfaced with shards of granite. The sharp stones were famously fond of slicing tires to shreds. I never traveled the North Woods logging roads without at least two spares.

I drove at a good clip, knowing that poking along wouldn't spare me from getting a flat. Nevertheless, a speedster in a silver Jeep Wrangler came racing up behind me, then swerved past before I could give him room. The license plate was so mud-plastered the digits were unreadable.

In the old days, when I had worked as a patrol warden, I would have chased down the Jeep to write the driver a citation. There was no law against being an asshole, but he had cut in front of me so aggressively he'd nearly forced me off the road. But I was trying to control my temper.

I half hoped I would catch Speed Racer at the Fish River Checkpoint, where recreational visitors to the North Woods were required to stop, register, and pay an entrance fee. By the time I came upon the little gatehouse, however, my friend in the Jeep had already blown past the stop sign and continued through.

The checkpoint belonged to a nonprofit organization that acted as the de facto watchmen for the private owners of large tracts of land in northern Maine. The little building was more vertical than horizontal, painted a soft mint green, and steepled with two antennas.

The ironic thing was that, as a state game warden, I had carte blanche to pass through the gate without explanation, but my visit would have been captured on hidden cameras, and might have set into motion a chain of events whose outcome I couldn't predict. If at all possible, I didn't want the higher-ups in the Warden Service asking questions about what I was up to.

A buzzer sounded as I entered the cabin. I crossed to a counter and waited, then called into the room beyond. Instead a telephone rang. It was an old-fashioned Bakelite model with a dial and curly cord. I picked up the receiver.

"Hello?"

"Good afternoon," said a female voice. "That's a honey of a Scout you're driving! What year is it?"

I looked up to see a camera winking at me from the corner. There must have been another aimed at the lot where I'd parked.

"It's a 1980."

"Wicked cool. Where are you headed today?"

I had decided not to mention Kellam, lest he have standing orders refusing all uninvited visitors.

"I thought I'd do a little small-stream fishing."

"Where?"

"Anyplace that looks promising."

I might have imagined the note of suspicion that crept into the voice of my watcher. "We don't get many anglers coming in to fish the brooks here with the Fish River and the Allagash so close. What time are you coming out?"

"I figured I'd fish until dusk, then drive out after twilight."

"You need to fill out the sheet in front of you. Put it in an envelope with seven dollars and slide it through the slot in the box to your right."

Clipped to a clipboard was a form no less comprehensive than an application for United States citizenship. I didn't lie but fudged the details—used my middle name, John, instead of my first. Anyone looking to identify me could do so, but I didn't want to make it child's play.

As I was about to leave, the phone rang again. This time it was a different woman's voice. "Any problems with the form?"

"No."

"Make sure you're out by dark. We'd rather not have to send someone looking for you."

"You don't have to worry about me."

"Do you know how many times we've heard that before?"

23

The forest along the Rocky Brook Road had been logged so hard there was hardly a tree left standing taller than a telephone pole. The state had outlawed wholesale clear-cutting years ago, but you never would've known it from the wanton devastation stretching as far as the eye could see.

Vast fields, consisting of stumps and deadfalls, tangled pucker-brush, and a few worthless cedars, extended for miles along both sides of the thoroughfare. Poplars and willows were so splattered with mud from the logging trucks that they seemed nearly sculptural. If you had told me brutal battles had been fought here with mortars and rocket-propelled grenades, I would have believed you.

Following the highlighted route I'd drawn on the map, I eventually left the gravel road for a series of poorly maintained jeep trails that delved into the as yet uncut forest. The farther I went, the narrower and rockier these roads became. Raspberry bushes scraped paint from the sides of my vehicle with their scratching fingers.

Someone had come through ahead of me, and recently, too. Tire marks showed in the muddy dips between the ups and downs. The prints belonged to a Jeep. It had to be Speed Racer, I thought. There was only a single set, meaning that my lead-footed friend hadn't yet departed, at least by this route. It seemed an odd coincidence, to say the least, that the two of us would have followed the same twists and turns in the maze.

The Jeep had finally turned down a trail so narrow a moose would have caught his antlers in the branches on both sides. So he hadn't come here to visit Kellam, it seemed. I wondered what lay down the secret path he had taken.

It began to rain again, just enough to require that I turn on my wipers.

The lieutenant's land was protected by a steel gate, which I was startled to find standing open—as if I were expected. I looked in the treetops for a security camera but saw nothing but the roughly rectangular holes made by pileated woodpeckers. Kellam guarded his privacy; I took it as a testament to his bushcraft that he could hide a spy cam from me.

Descending the hill, I caught the first dull flashes of the lake, metallic gray beneath the heavy overcast. I swung around a curve, pulled as much by gravity as by the engine.

And nearly ran over a man in the road.

He was black-skinned. He had a shaved head. His limbs were long and thin, and the ranginess gave him a misleading appearance of being tall when he was only lanky. He wore a red kerchief knotted around his neck, a rain-dappled shirt unbuttoned to his sternum, and baggy jeans rolled above bare ankles. His shoes were dirty brogues.

In his hand, he held a long tree-pruning tool with a curved, serrated blade at the end. At first glance I mistook it for a medieval polearm.

I unrolled my window. "I'm sorry! I almost hit you."

"*Bon apre-midi.* I took you by surprise, yes?"

"I was going too fast."

"You did not expect me, too."

The accent spoke of some island blown by the trade winds. Based on the French greeting, my first guess was Haiti. But for all I knew, he could have been a resident of New Orleans's Fifth Ward or even a visitor from Montreal.

And I had thought Presque Isle felt foreign.

"Is this Stan Kellam's place?"

"You are his friend, no?"

"We know each other, but I wouldn't call myself his friend."

"No? He told me to open the gate because he was expecting a visitor."

"That wouldn't be me."

"You are just here by hazard, then?" As he approached, I saw that his skin was welted with insect bites. A cloud of mosquitoes, blackflies, and deerflies hung over his shining head, but he seemed unbothered by this personal plague.

"*Coincidence* would be a better word," I said. "Did he tell you the name of the person he's expecting?"

"Michael, he said."

"That's my name. But I prefer Mike."

"I am called Edouard. But he knew you were coming, no?"

I couldn't fathom how, but I put on a smile for the benefit of the man at my window. "Where are you from, Edouard?"

"Port-au-Prince. You know Haiti?"

"I know the name."

"You have no need to know more! It is a long way from here. A long way from Maine."

I couldn't argue the point, least of all at that moment. "Do you work for Stan, Edouard?"

"For two years, I am his—how you say?—his handyman." Then he broke into a broader grin. "He is a generous personality. My sister never asked him to give me a job. But Stan is *tres généreux.*"

"Your sister?"

"Vaneese. You will meet her next." He beckoned me forward. "Drive that way, and you will see the big house. If you see Ferox, stay in the truck unless you want to get bitten. He killed a bear, that dog! *Bon chance.*"

Edouard continued up the hill with that cruel-edged tool over his shoulder.

Whatever I had expected from Kellam, it hadn't been this. Where had he acquired a Haitian factotum? Edouard had mentioned a sister. Was she the cook?

Before me, Moccasin Pond spread out into the hazy distance.

Its surface was stippled by light rain. To my left stood several outbuildings. There was a barn for construction equipment and a garage for snowmobiles, a humming structure that seemed to contain the generator that powered the compound, and assorted toolsheds. Down at the water's edge, a long dock extended from a boathouse into the lake.

To my right was the "big house." The design, more hotel than home, showed the property's history as a sporting camp. It had the long porch of an inn, complete with rocking chairs, larger plate glass windows on the first floor, and a row of smaller windows on the second story that suggested multiple bedrooms.

But the cream siding looked new, and the green trim had just been painted, as had the doors, and the roof was fashioned of bright steel for the snow to slide off.

I stepped out of the Scout and heard the breeze sighing in the tall pines and water spilling from the gutters. I breathed deeply to fill my lungs with the wet, balsam-scented air. Then I turned toward the house and saw something that made my heart seize up like a stuck motor.

Bounding toward me came a charcoal-black dog with a square head, a muscular chest, ears clipped to points, and bared fangs. It hadn't uttered a sound until it saw me turn toward it. Then it let loose with a series of barking growls that made me dive toward my vehicle. My hand reflexively found the grip of my handgun under the hem of my shirt.

Fortunately, a woman's voice intervened. "Ferox! *Pfui! Was machst du!*"

The effect on the coal-colored dog—some sort of mastiff seemingly—was immediate. The huge animal slid to a stop as if it had reached the end of a chain. We were less than fifteen feet apart; a single leap would have bowled me over. Spittle flew from its black lips.

I was terrified to look away or remove my hand from my gun, but out of the corner of one eye, I saw the shape of a woman rushing toward us.

"Schlecht hund!"

If the language wasn't German, I didn't know what it was.

"I am so, so sorry!" she said in an accent that wasn't remotely Teutonic. "He got past me when he heard your vehicle. He wasn't supposed to be loose. He could have killed you!"

Still focused on the dog's eyes, I watched a slender brown hand take hold of his collar. Then the woman was kneeling beside the animal, fastening a muzzle over his still snarling jowls.

Only then did I really see her. She was, by any standard, one of the most striking people I had ever come across—in part because of the contrast between her mocha-toned skin and her caramel-colored eyes.

I would have put her age in her late twenties, maybe her early thirties. She was dressed as if on a modeling shoot for the L.L.Bean catalog: gingham shirt, canvas pants, and boat shoes that exposed her slender ankles.

"Don't apologize. Your brother warned me about the dog."

"You met Edouard?"

Her own speech bore a much fainter Creole accent than her brother's. It made me think she'd spent significantly more time in the United States than he had, even though she appeared to be at least a decade younger.

"We spoke on the way in," I said. "What kind of dog is this?"

"A Cane Corso. Have you heard of them?"

"They were the war dogs the Roman legions brought with them on campaigns."

Her imperfectly aligned teeth somehow only made her prettier. "I only know they come from Italy."

I estimated that the mastiff weighed somewhere around 120 pounds—20 odd pounds less than Shadow—but he was far more muscular than the wolf hybrid. In a fight to the death, I wasn't sure which would prevail. The most likely outcome would be that the two canines would tear each other to bloody shreds.

"Why were you speaking to him in German?"

"Stan says it's to avoid the dog hearing a word in English that he associates with commands."

"You must be Vaneese."

"Vaneese Delhomme."

A voice boomed from the direction of the house. "There he is! Maine's second-most famous game warden."

Stan Kellam descended the porch stairs with arms extended.

He was in his sixties, but he had a vitality about him you don't often see in men his age. He had acquired a considerable belly, but his chest and shoulders were as burly as I remembered, and he had the narrow hips of a former athlete. He wore his sandy hair barbered in the same flattop he'd sported as a young warden. His jaw was square, resolute. His mouth was small and thin lipped.

"How are you, Mike? I hope my monster here didn't give you too bad a scare."

Kellam was dressed in a maroon Florida State T-shirt, cargo shorts, and leather sandals. I'm six two, and we were eye to eye when we shook hands. As a younger man, he must have stood even taller.

"I'm fine, Lieutenant."

"Please don't call me that. I've spent the past six years trying to forget my checkered career. I see you've met Vaneese. And Ferox, the bloodthirsty bastard." He said these last words with affection while kneeling beside the dog and, to my dismay, removing the muzzle. The animal continued to glare at me with demonic auburn eyes.

"You seem to have been expecting me," I said.

He responded with a merry twinkle. "Yes and no."

Again, I paused.

"I'll explain over lunch," he said. "Vee and I were just sitting down when Ferox heard your vehicle. That's a sweet-looking Scout, by the way. Let's get out of this damned drizzle. It's like God has been taking the world's longest piss on us. When was the last time I saw you, Mike? Was it at my retirement party? I know it was a hell of a bash because I barely remember it!"

He clapped me so hard between the shoulder blades that I almost lost my balance.

24

We sat down in a dining room with hardwood furniture and a view of the gray lake. A serving bowl filled with some sort of orange stew steamed between two place settings, perfuming the air with squash, onion, spices, and meat: the smell of the West Indies, as I imagined it.

Kellam motioned for me to sit across from him while Vaneese disappeared into the kitchen. It gave me an opportunity to study his face up close. He looked decidedly older than the last time I'd seen him. His pink skin bore the divot scars of many dermatological surgeries.

"You ever have Haitian food before, Mike? I'm guessing not. This is *joumou*. Pumpkin soup, basically. It usually has beef in it, but Vaneese makes it with moose meat. I shot a big bull last fall, half a ton, dressed. How's that for fusion cuisine? Port-au-Prince meets Presque Isle."

The remark about the hunting trip made me realize that the décor of the former sporting camp was utterly devoid of taxidermy. I couldn't remember the last time I'd ventured into one of these historic lodges and not confronted a dusty moose head staring down with glass eyeballs from over the fireplace. Instead, bright paintings of turquoise seas and multicolor shanty towns decorated the walls.

The woman reappeared with a bottle of Corona and a glass for me. Kellam already had a beer in hand.

Ferox, meanwhile, curled up on the floor beside his master. I couldn't see the war dog from where I was seated—the table was between us—but I was very aware that he had an unobstructed line of attack should he choose to bite me in the crotch.

"I can see from your expression that you don't know which question to start with," said Kellam, dishing me up a bowl of stew. "I'll make it easy for you. It was Nick Francis who told me you were coming."

I came very close to spitting out my beer. "He did?"

"Said you wanted to talk with me about the St. Ignace shit show. I was pretty damned surprised to hear from him. That Indian never made an effort to hide the fact he hated my guts. I admired his forthrightness in that regard. Backstabbers are the worst."

Stunned that Nick had given me away, I felt a need to play my cards even closer now. "I didn't get that impression, that he hates you."

"There's no need to sugarcoat things with me, Mike. I'll tell you whatever you want to know—and I won't even ask why you're digging this up. All I ask is that you respect me enough to shoot straight in return."

"Deal."

He wiped beer foam from his faint lips. "How's that *joumou*?"

Vaneese had reappeared with her place setting. She arranged herself beside Kellam and sat down. Somewhere in her travels back and forth between the dining room and the kitchen, she had acquired a pair of glasses that made her look bookish but no less attractive.

"It's delicious," I said to Vaneese. "What are the spices I'm tasting?"

"Clove and allspice, mainly," she said. "*Joumou* is our national dish. Before the revolution, the slave masters forbade us from eating it. I am speaking about my ancestors, you understand."

"I take it you've already talked with Charley about what happened in St. Ignace," Kellam said, oblivious to our culinary conversation. "He was as much in the loop as anyone."

"You know details about the operation that he doesn't."

"That's true. How are Charley and Ora?"

I had thought that Charley must have visited Kellam ahead of me, but from the sounds of things, it didn't seem as if they had spoken in ages.

"Good."

"Weren't you engaged to one of their daughters?" the lieutenant asked.

"Not quite."

"Show Mike your ring, Vaneese."

She extended an elegant arm across the table to show me the diamond.

"Congratulations," I said. "When's the wedding?"

"This fall," said Kellam. "My belief is that when you find a good woman, marry her. Of course, this will be my third trip down the aisle. One of my sons has already threatened not to show, the ungrateful prick, which means three of my grandkids won't be there either. Families!"

"But you think he will relent, yes?" said Vaneese.

"He damn well better if he wants to stay in my will," Kellam said. "I can't think of a sadder discovery than to learn a boy of yours has become a bigot."

"I don't think that's the reason, *cher.*"

"It's *one* reason. That and his being older than you. And you also being a world-class fox."

The stew was in fact delicious, and I looked up from my empty bowl. "How did you two meet, if you don't mind my asking?"

He leaned his heavy forearms on the table. The hair on them was so blond it reminded me of down on a baby's head. "I'm sure there's a rumor going around the Warden Service. Stan 'the Man' Kellam bought himself a mail-order Nubian princess. We actually met in college, Vaneese and I."

The war-painted Indian logo on his T-shirt suddenly made sense. "I'd heard that you'd gone back to school."

"You stop learning, you die. That's my motto. After I retired, I decided to go get my Ph.D. I've always been interested in criminology—the hard science behind policing—and FSU has an excellent program. Plus, of course, I would be in Tallahassee and could spend my off-hours bass fishing. The university must have a quota requiring it to admit one ornery old redneck from Maine each year. God love affirmative action."

"What does *ornery* mean?" Vaneese asked in her charming accent.

"It means I'm a grouchy son of a bitch who thinks he knows more than he does. Mike will vouch for that as an apt description of me. Wouldn't you, Mike?"

"I don't know you well enough, Stan."

"Ha!"

"But based on what I've heard—"

"Good! You're shooting straight with me. Vaneese, would you mind fetching us another beer?"

I tapped the bottle. "I'm still working on mine."

"Like hell you are. Get him another Corona, Vee."

She hadn't made much progress with her own dinner but seemed not to mind being at Kellam's beck and call.

He watched her girlish hips with appreciation.

"I don't understand it either," he said, lowering his voice. "A young girl like that, falling for a lunk like me. She was getting a master's in agronomy. Had been admitted to the U.S. on a student visa before the government clamped down on those. When I told her that I was renovating a lodge in the North Woods—she couldn't even imagine this place. I finally showed it to her on a map. That was a mistake! She saw that Fish River Checkpoint is located in Garfield *Plantation*. You should have seen the fear in her eyes. I had to explain that a Maine township doesn't bear the slightest resemblance to the cane fields back in Haiti."

It hadn't passed my notice that, having begun our lunch with a proclamation that he would answer my questions about St. Ignace, he hadn't once returned to the topic.

But as I learned from Joe Fixico—had it only been two days since my visit to the Everglades?—when someone gets talking, the best thing to do is keep quiet and let them tell their stories. People often reveal themselves in their digressions.

"What about her brother, Edouard?"

Kellam gave me a wink. "Don't report me to ICE, OK?"

"He's in the country illegally?"

"Oh yeah. He's basically confined to the property through no fault of his own. He can't risk being spotted by some nosy parker. Don't get me wrong. He's not my indentured servant. I pay him well, and he has a good life. Does a lot of fishing on the lake."

Ferox noisily repositioned himself under the table, as sleeping dogs will do.

Kellam continued, "Sometimes I consider bringing Edouard to Presque Isle for a Big Mac, but it would be a stupid risk. When was the last time you visited the County? You must have noticed that our roads are crawling with Border Patrol trucks."

"I noticed."

"When I was first assigned here—this was before 9/11—you could cross back and forth to Canada three or four times a day. The customs agents in the booth would just wave you across. These days, it's like climbing the fucking Berlin Wall. But the new laws keep us safe, the politicians claim. Safe from old French ladies in Edmundston who want to get their hair done in Madawaska."

"I never would have guessed that Edouard and Vaneese were sister and brother."

He leaned across the table, his breath grainy with beer. "You ever hear of the Tonton Macoute? The Duvaliers kept the people in line with their own personal death and rape squads. Edouard's father—"

The door between the kitchen and the dining room swung open. Vaneese appeared with two more bottles. If she'd heard Kellam discussing the violent circumstances surrounding her brother's conception, she didn't show it.

"I was telling Mike about your field of study, Vee," he said.

She showed off her marvelous, imperfect teeth again. "Potatoes."

"I told her that Aroostook County was the best place to learn about potato farming—that she could write her master's thesis on it here. I'd introduce her to a dozen spud experts, I promised."

"I didn't believe him about Maine," she said. "To me, it seemed as foreign as Haiti must seem to you."

Kellam slurped the foaming head off his beer. "You ever been to the Caribbean, Mike?"

"No, but I did get to Florida recently."

Vaneese flashed that lovely smile of hers again. "Were you in Gainesville?"

"I never made it north of Fort Lauderdale." I turned back to Kellam. "I was doing a background check on someone who'd applied for a job with the Warden Service."

"I heard. You shot him down, so to speak."

Kellam had been so convincing about having detached himself from the politics of the bureau, the announcement made me sit up.

"Pat Shorey told me," he explained. "We still talk, Pat and I. He comes up here every fall to hunt. He was my sub-permittee when I shot that moose we just ate. He's no fan of yours, but I expect you know that."

Kellam missed his calling as a politician; the man had a rare gift for filibustering.

"About St. Ignace," I began.

"How'd you like to go fishing, Mike? We could talk about it on the water."

"You want to go fishing?"

"Vaneese will appreciate having us out of her hair. You have reading to do, don't you, Vee?"

"Yes, but—"

Kellam stood up. "We've got a good *Hex* hatch on this pond. The bottom is nice and silty. They won't be rising until dusk—although on dark days, you never know. I've had good luck fishing Maple Syrups on sinking lines. If you didn't pack a rod, I have about three dozen for you to choose from."

I was having trouble viewing the high-spirited chatterbox across the table as the "man of patience and guile" my friend had warned me against. But that might be a testament to Kellam's cunning. Should I go out alone with him on a boat on a remote lake, though?

But you only live once. And I had never been afraid of taking risks. Then again, neither had Scott Pellerin.

"How about it?" Kellam said. "You want to pick out a rod from my collection? I've got everything from vintage bamboo to the latest graphite."

"That won't be necessary," I said. "What kind of warden would I be if I didn't pack a fly rod?"

25

In addition to his extensive fly rod collection, Kellam owned a bunch of boats of all shapes and sizes. The one he chose for us was a Crestliner 1756 Bass Hawk. It had a V-shaped aluminum hull, casting decks in the bow and stern, an overpowered Mercury V-8 outboard, and, in my opinion, didn't belong on a hundred-acre trout pond. This was a boat built for Bassmaster competitions on Lake Okeechobee, where the contestants dressed like NASCAR drivers, in coveralls festooned with the logos of their corporate sponsors.

The drizzle had picked up while we were eating, and we both put on waterproof jackets and pants for our excursion. Kellam's rainwear didn't have any patches from Abu Garcia or Rapala, but the fabric was redder than a fire engine. Soon his face was red, too, from the rain.

Edouard helped us load and launch the boat. He didn't have on a hat or a jacket. The water just streamed off his bald head and made dark stains on his shoulders and along the tops of his thighs.

How does Vaneese feel about him acting as Stan's houseboy?

The retired warden took a seat at the wheel. He turned the key, and the outboard growled like a big cat that had been asleep and didn't appreciate having been awakened. The next thing I knew, we had exploded forward from the dock. The g-force pushed the hood off my head, causing it to flap along my neck.

"I'm sure you're wondering where I got my money!" Kellam shouted above the engine.

I wished I'd paused long enough to grab my earplugs. Most of the old wardens and guides I knew suffered from hearing loss to the point of near deafness. It was the inevitable outcome of a life running outboards, riding snowmobiles, and firing long guns inches from your unprotected ears.

"My second wife believed I was going to get killed on the job, and she saw it as her road to riches. The year before we split, she took out life insurance on me. Ten million bucks! And I said, 'What about you? What do I get if you croak, babe?' She thought that was hilarious, but we changed the policy. Six months later, she was run off the road by a logging truck. The insurance company wouldn't pay at first. An adjuster actually investigated me! He thought I'd set it up somehow. But the truck driver was a Québécois from Daaquam, a good Catholic kid. He thought he was going to hell for accidentally killing my wife, so he took the blame. I wanted to kiss that fucking frog."

By the time he'd shouted out his story, we'd sped across the pond to a cove that looked promising for trout. Kellam cut the engine, but the Bass Hawk continued its forward momentum until he pushed the button that released the anchor. The weight caught in the muddy bottom, and the boat stopped with a jerk.

My ears were still ringing from the engine noise. My head was wreathed with gasoline fumes. I felt a persistent vibration in the walls of my heart.

"I want you to use one my flies," Kellam said, still speaking loudly. "I want the credit when you catch a monster."

I stood in the bow, and he stood in the stern. I could tell it needled him that I could cast all ninety feet of my fly line and into the backing. He kept trying to muscle his line out farther and farther, which is the surest way to sabotage your casts.

He'd brought a six-pack of beer, as well as a ziplock bag of moose jerky Edouard had made. I passed on both the Coronas and the dried meat.

"Edouard uses Haitian spices. I guarantee you haven't had anything like it before."

"I'm still full from lunch."

He drained half his bottle in one gulp, then let loose with a belch. "I know you've been waiting for me to get around to telling you what happened with Scott Pellerin. Truth is, I don't like to go back to St. Ignace. Neither mentally nor physically. I haven't set foot in that town since Charley and I agreed we were never going to find Scott. What did he tell you about the disaster?"

"I'd prefer to hear your version."

"Spoken like a true investigator. I blame myself, obviously. Chasse had told me how hot the situation was, and still I sent in Pellerin, undercover."

"Chasse Lamontaine?" I remembered Kathy having mentioned the warden's name.

"He was just a deputy warden at the time, not even an anointed law enforcement officer. The warden who'd brought him on as a helper was retiring, which meant that Chasse was losing his job, too, unless he could distinguish himself somehow. It's kind of a miracle he managed it. Most deputy wardens never go on to have careers with the service. You must know him."

Chasse Lamontaine was the closest thing the Maine Warden Service had to a heartthrob. He had a cleft chin and piercing eyes. He was pushing fifty now, but in his younger years, he could have played Captain America with that cartoonishly masculine face.

"I'm surprised Chasse even wanted a job with the Warden Service," I said. "It sounds like the whole Valley was up in arms after what happened in St. Ignace."

"Given how hot emotions were running, I highly recommended to Chasse that he take his talents elsewhere, but he said people knew him and trusted him because he'd grown up there. That was how he won over the hiring panel—through his bold naiveté."

In my own limited interactions with the man, I had found

him to be earnest to the point of humorlessness, prone to self-righteous speeches, a teetotaler who made everyone in his orbit uncomfortable holding a beer. His nickname among his fellow wardens was Dudley Do-Right.

I jigged my line, raising the weighted chenille nymph up in the water column and then letting it settle again into the silt.

"It was because of Chasse that I sent in an investigator to begin with," said Kellam. "I think it was a clumsy ploy to get a full-time job, his complaining about how the Valley wardens were overwhelmed. But it was true that the locals were poaching everything that moved and smuggling drugs back and forth into New Brunswick. From St. Ignace you can throw a baseball across the river into Canada. Have you ever been there?"

"I must have driven through with my girlfriend after we'd finished paddling the Allagash, but I don't remember it."

"You wouldn't. Is that the same girlfriend who's Charley's daughter?"

"Stacey, yes."

"I remember when she was working on that moose survey out of Clayton Lake. We saw each other in the Ashland IGA. She was a spitfire, everyone said. Beautiful eyes, though. Smart, too. I don't know if you were a damned fool for letting her get away or the luckiest man alive."

I had once asked myself the same question, but since Dani and I had gotten serious, it had become moot. As Kathy had recently reminded me, I had a good thing going for once in my life.

"Anyway, Michaud and his crew—I'm talking about Pierre Michaud, not his jackass sons—they were running circles around my wardens. It made us look like the Keystone Kops. In those situations, all you can do is send in an investigator. Has DeFord had you work undercover yet?"

"He says my profile is too high."

Kellam grunted his agreement. "It was my decision to try young Pellerin. He'd infiltrated a poaching ring down in Dresden, on Merrymeeting Bay, and secured convictions across the board. Also did good work in coordination with the Rhode Island

Department of Fish and Wildlife on an interstate case, involving some guys who used to come up here from Providence to poach. That being said, I had doubts about him. You want a beer?"

"No, thanks. What kind of doubts?"

"He was too damned cocksure, in my estimation. To give you an example, he made hundred-dollar bets with guys in my division that he'd complete his investigation and secure indictments in a month. This was before he'd even met the Michauds."

I thought I felt a tug on my line, but it was only a submerged branch.

"His cover name was Scott Paradis," said Kellam. "You always want to use your real first name to avoid slipping up when you're tired or distracted. And then you choose a last name that's close to but not the same as your real one. You already know this. I can tell I'm boring you."

"No."

"His cover story was supposed to be that he lived in Rhode Island, because he'd spent time there when we'd worked that interstate case. Plus he had a sister in Providence. He claimed to be a commercial fisherman who'd been 'injured' on the job and was collecting fraudulent disability checks. When he was getting to know the Michauds, he gave them some frozen stripers he said he'd caught off Block Island to help back up his story. He said he was interested in shooting a black bear even though the season wasn't open. He asked around if there was a guide in town who might bend the rules. Pierre Michaud thought for sure he was an undercover warden and tested him, but damn if Pellerin didn't win over the SOB."

"What kind of test?"

"Oh, you know. They all went out together at night, drinking and driving along the logging roads behind the gates, and when they happened on a deer, they jacklighted it. The doe was mesmerized by the spotlight. Pierre Michaud gave Pellerin a rifle and told him to shoot the deer to prove he wasn't really a warden. Of course, Pellerin had been pretending to be drunk all night. He'd been pouring out beers when they weren't looking. So he deliberately missed by a mile, and they thought it was because he was shit-faced."

I had begun to sweat under my rainjacket. Despite the occasional storms, the humidity seemed to be ever building, never breaking.

"Do you remember the names of the guys in Michaud's crew?"

"Pierre's twin sons, Roland and Zacharie. We pinched Roland on some misdemeanors the night of the raid. He did thirty days in jail. Zacharie, though, was a felon prohibited by law from owning a firearm. Zach hanged himself in county lockup while awaiting trial."

"He committed suicide in jail?"

Kellam's smile lasted the briefest instant. "That was the state's official finding."

A law enforcement officer had disappeared and was presumed to have been murdered, and one of the suspected cop killers had taken his own life—it hadn't taken a spoonful of sugar for the public to swallow that story.

But at least it cleared up which of Pierre's sons Angie was dating. It could only be Roland.

"The fourth member of the ring was a guy named Egan," said Kellam. "Little guy. Reminded me of a red squirrel. You know how chattery they are and absolutely unafraid of anything. He was a felon, too. Sex criminal. Afterward, he did a stint in the Maine State Prison for the evidence Pellerin gathered. Drug stuff, in his case. Selling to teenagers. But like Roland, he stonewalled us and got away with it."

"And Pierre escaped," I said.

"Would have escaped if not for Charley."

Just then, I felt a jerk on the line, and the reel—my sturdy old Hardy—let out a series of clicks as the fish I'd hooked took off away from the boat. I lifted the rod tip to keep tension on the tippet and watched yard after yard of my line disappear beneath the pewter surface of the pond.

"What test leader have you got on?" Kellam asked, growing red with excitement.

"It's 4X."

"He's going to break you off."

"Like hell he will."

"I'll bet you twenty bucks he does."

There are techniques to playing a big fish, but ultimately, it all comes down to what the fish decides to do. If it dives deep, it can snap your leader or tippet at its weakest point—usually the knot. If it circles and charges back toward the boat, it can create slack that allows the fly to work free. If it jumps into the air, it can shake the hook from its jaws in dramatic fashion.

This one tried all three strategies.

It dove hard, which made me think it was a lake trout (or *togue*, in local parlance).

Then it swung around with such speed that it had me thinking it was a landlocked salmon: the fastest fish in Maine waters.

It was only when it leaped clear of the surface and I caught a flash of orange along the belly that I realized it was my favorite of all species: a native brook trout. This one just happened to be the size and shape of a football. It fell back into the pond with a tremendous splash but still attached to my hook and line.

"That's got to be a four pounder!" Kellam exclaimed.

"Closer to five."

My blood was up, my forearms were burning, and my vision had darkened along the peripheries.

I had no idea what made me look up.

For some reason, I raised my head and glimpsed the un-mistakable outline of a man on the shore of the lake. He was half-hidden in the alders. The low mist made him impossible to identify, but the silhouette removed any doubt that I might be mistaking a stump for a human being. He seemed to be wearing a brimmed hat.

In the same instant, the trout made one final effort to escape. He used all his remaining energy to give one last leap. If luck had been on my side, he might have plopped into Kellam's outstretched landing net. Instead he fell sideways into the water and spit out the fly.

"Damn it!" said Kellam.

I reeled in the line while I sought out the spot where the man had been standing. There was no sign of him.

"You owe me twenty dollars, Bowditch."

"What?"

"We bet you wouldn't get that trout onto the boat. I said you wouldn't. You said you would. Time to pay up."

26

We stayed on the lake for two more hours until the drizzle turned to rain and the rain turned into a torrent. My allegedly waterproof gear was no match for the cloudburst. Although he talked constantly, not once did Kellam mention St. Ignace. We caught a few fish, brookies mostly, but nothing close to that first lunker, also a three-pound lake trout, which Kellam killed by whacking its head with the spine of his knife. The togue gave a visible shiver and went still.

"Those lake trout are loaded with toxins," I said.

"Edouard doesn't care. To him, they're the best-eating fish in Maine."

"Have you explained about acid rain? How mercury builds up in their livers? How the oldest fish are the most poisonous?"

"The man grew up in *Haiti,* Mike. In Cité Soleil in Port-au-Prince. That's the poorest neighborhood in the poorest city in the poorest country in the Western Hemisphere. He assesses risk differently from people like us."

People like us.

I had almost forgotten that Stan was using Edouard Delhomme's shaky immigration status to rationalize near total control of the man's life. Just when I came close to liking the retired lieutenant, he would say something to repulse me.

Kellam was a complicated man, to say the least. A woodsman who also happened to be an intellectual. A career cop who thought nothing of breaking laws for no other reason than they personally inconvenienced him. Somehow this old crank had managed to romance a beautiful, intelligent woman half his age and persuade her to relocate to the geographic middle of nowhere.

I didn't trust him, and so I deliberately failed to mention the shadowy man I had seen along the shore.

Had it been Edouard? If so, he had acquired a hat since we'd left the dock. And why would he have been spying on us from the woods?

Unless he'd been armed with a sniper's rifle and told by his employer to take me out on cue.

But that was paranoid thinking.

There was a good chance the man I saw had been the driver of the silver Jeep. People did fish and hike in the Maine woods. Most did so without malevolent intentions. But Moccasin Pond was not known as a destination fishery. Maybe if word got out that it held five-pound trout, it would become one.

Could that mystery man have been Charley? My first thought was no. My friend was too bushcrafty to give his presence away in such a clumsy fashion. There is a line from a book I like that could just as well apply to my friend: "You will not see a tiger that does not choose to be seen."

Charley Stevens was a tiger.

A hatless, water-logged Edouard waited for us to motor up to the dock. "Anything?" he called.

"Togue!"

The Haitian rubbed his palms together in excited anticipation.

As I clambered with my fishing gear onto the slick dock, Kellam said, "You're staying here tonight."

"I can't."

"Why not? Do you have a room booked at the Madawaska Four Seasons?"

"I have people I need to speak with. I've been off the map all day."

"Use my signal."

"You have service here?"

He pointed to a forested ridge overlooking the pond. "See that odd spruce up there that's taller than the others? That's actually a cell tower. We've got line-of-sight access to it from the house."

Kellam had been nothing but welcoming, but I had an itching sensation that it would be wise to leave before the sun went down on Moccasin Pond.

"I told the gatekeeper I was coming out at dusk."

He sniffed. "If you don't want my hospitality, I won't force it on you, but I thought you might like to review my files on the St. Ignace operation."

"You have the documents here?"

"My own personal copies of the files. At one juncture, I'd considered using the botched operation as the jumping-off point for my dissertation. Maybe even write a book. You always learn more from failures than successes. That's a life principle that law enforcement rejects more than any other profession—the media excepted."

Kellam knew I couldn't pass up the opportunity to review the original reports. Despite what he'd told me at lunch, I had only the vaguest concept of the undercover operation he and Pellerin had conducted, its scope and duration, as well as the circumstances around the blown warden's disappearance. About the aftermath—the burning of St. Ignace, Pierre Michaud's escape into the woods, Charley's shooting of the fugitive cop killer—my information was sketchy at best.

As Kellam and I regarded each other from beneath our rain hoods, it occurred to me that his seeming lack of curiosity about my investigation had been a ruse. He was desperately curious to know what I knew. Offering me the files was the opening gambit of a game he intended to play to checkmate.

"In that case, I'll accept your offer."

Of course you will, his smug expression seemed to say.

Vaneese showed me how to get online. Evidently, the construction of the tree-shaped cell tower had been a precondition of hers before she agreed to join Stan Kellam in his North Woods redoubt. She showed me to my guest room—already prepared—and gave me the WiFi password.

"Can I ask you a question?" I asked.

"You want to know if I get lonely here?"

"That wasn't the question, but I can't deny it's been on my mind. I'm a loner by nature, but even I need people from time to time."

"I have Edouard."

"True, but—"

"You're not married, I can see from your finger. Do you have a girlfriend?"

"She's the first person I need to call."

"And you love her? No, I shouldn't ask that question. Let me ask instead. Would you be lonely in this beautiful place if you were together with the woman you loved?"

"It would depend."

"On what?"

"On whether my dog was here, too."

I decided not to mention the wolf's complicated genealogy to avoid having to answer twenty more questions.

She laughed. "Is he a big dog like Ferox?"

"Bigger."

Her eyes widened. "Really? Is he dangerous, too?"

There was something about this woman that compelled me to be utterly truthful with her. "Yes."

"What is his name?"

"Shadow."

"He is black, then?"

"I wasn't the one who gave him that name," I blurted out.

Her smile became one of amusement at my expense. She and I were close in age, but I couldn't help feeling that her life experience had made her wiser than I would ever be.

"*Fantôme*. That would be his French name."

"I like it better."

"I prefer Shadow."

She left me alone to change out of my wet clothes.

⎯

As was always the case when my phone had been off, I was greeted by a series of bell chimes as message after message announced itself in my queue.

Major Shorey had left me a summons to appear in Augusta in two days to present my report to the full hiring panel. My written summary of the covered-up assaults committed by Wheelwright had not proven sufficient to torpedo the pilot's application. I wouldn't have put it past the disgraced pilot to have appealed his case directly to Shorey.

Logan Cronk had provided me with another serving of *Fantôme* in the form of a picture showing the wolf pressing his dark muzzle against the steel fence. His eyes—as yellow as powdered sulfur—revealed nothing about his canine intentions. I worried what treat the boy might've offered to draw the animal in close for photographic purposes.

Stacey had left me a text message:

> I know this is going to sound insane, but I've been thinking about the chief pilot position. Yeah, yeah, the department fired me. I have no law enforcement background, but neither did Wheelwright. What do I have to lose by applying? Talk me out of this, please.

The prospect of Stacey Stevens returning to Maine awakened so many conflicting emotions I had to perform a deep-breathing exercise I used at the shooting range to calm myself.

There were no inquiries from Ora. As worried as she might be, she would wait for me to contact her, because she trusted that I would share whatever news I had. How I loved that dear woman.

Most worryingly, there was still nothing from Dani—not a text, not an email, not a voice message.

She didn't pick up the first time I called. I left a message telling her where I was and that I had a signal and she should call me back as soon as possible. A minute later, she did so.

"Sorry, I was asleep."

I glanced at my watch. After having worked the overnight for a year, she had been transferred to the day shift. "You're not at work?"

"They sent me home."

So much for my internal steadiness. "Why?"

"I fell down in the parking lot."

"What?"

"It was just dizziness. If I were a man, they wouldn't have made a big deal about it, but a woman trips and the guys get all protective and condescending. They wanted to drive me back to the house because they were 'concerned.' It's fucking bullshit."

The sentiments were familiar—Dani had legitimate grievances against the men with whom she worked—but her voice sounded weird, almost as if she were stoned.

"How do you feel now?" I asked cautiously.

"Tired."

"Maybe I should drive down there."

"Do you ever listen? I just said how pissed off I was about how those men treated me. I'm not some helpless girl, Mike."

Who is this person?

"I never said you were, Dani."

"But you're acting like I am." There was, no doubt, a slight slur in her voice. "I don't mean to be a bitch, but can we change the subject, please? Have you found Charley?"

"No, I haven't. I'm sorry, but I need to know you're all right. Have you taken your temperature?"

"This is pointless."

And with that, she hung up.

I sat on the bed looking blankly at the phone. Earlier that day, she had fainted or nearly fainted. She was irritable and combative in a way I had never observed before. Anxiety began to bubble in my stomach.

It would take me close to six hours to drive from Kellam's

place to her rented house in the town of New Gloucester. It would be dark soon, and I'd have to dodge moose for the first hours. John Smith had run his motorcycle into one near here. But I felt the tug of conscience telling me to go.

I was still deciding when Kellam shouted up the stairs that cocktail hour had begun.

27

Knowing his perverse sense of humor, I thought Kellam might serve me lake trout. Instead Vaneese had prepared another Haitian-inspired dish. My plate was piled high with what looked like spanish rice, sautéed onions, and some unidentifiable deep-fried disks.

"They're lobster mushrooms," Kellam explained as he cracked open another Corona. Except for a rosy flush that pushed upward along his neck and blossomed in his cheeks, he displayed no outward signs of intoxication. "Edouard picked them last fall and dried them in the cellar."

Vaneese took a seat beside her fiancé. "My *manman* would die if she heard me call this *diri ak adjon djon*."

"The real thing has wild rice, but Vee indulges me with the boxed stuff. The funny thing is I have to twist her arm to make this dish for me. She prefers American food."

"Is pasta American?" she asked.

I had noticed there were only three place settings. "Edouard's not joining us?"

"He prefers to eat in his room. He watches soccer on the computer. The man's a fanatic for the game."

"He was a good player when he was young," Vaneese said.

"What position?"

"Striker!"

"You're not having a beer, Mike?" Kellam asked.

I had already refused one during his so-called cocktail hour in favor of an iced coffee. "It'll just knock me out. And I'd like to have a look at those files you mentioned. Pellerin's reports."

"I'll dig them up after we eat," he said. "Not to change the subject, but I'm hoping you can answer a question that's been on my mind."

"If I can."

"How do the wardens talk about me these days, now that I'm gone?"

"You're a living legend."

His frown told me he didn't appreciate my attempt at humor. "What about St. Ignace? I know it cast a pall over my career. They must have taught you about it in warden school—how undercover operations can go bad."

"Not really," I said.

"Swept it under the rug, did they?"

"You yourself said that law enforcement isn't given to self-criticism."

He pointed the tines of his fork at my chest. "For the record, there's not a single day that goes by that I don't blame myself for what happened to Scott Pellerin. My intuition was screaming at me, but I wanted Michaud's head on my wall. I sent that poor kid to his death."

"*Cher*," Vaneese said, reaching for his brawny hand.

He shook her off. "Don't *cher* me. Well, I can't say I didn't pay a price for it. I was on track to be the next colonel. I was the heir apparent. Not after St. Ignace, though. I would have been a hell of a colonel, too! I would've dragged the Warden Service kicking and screaming into the modern age. I would've purged the malcontents."

"People like me, you mean?"

In the quiet room, the tapping of rain on the porch roof became suddenly loud.

"What is this really about?" Kellam asked at last. He had barely touched his plate but had wrenched the cap off yet another beer. "Why are you sniffing around this case? Who sent you? It sure as hell wasn't Charley."

"Why do you say that?"

"If there's anyone who has more of an interest in putting what happened in the past, it's Stevens."

I took a breath. "How so?"

"Ask him yourself. I thought you were his handpicked protégé. Don't tell me the Legendary Game Warden is keeping secrets from you."

Stan was referring to an honor, presented by the Maine Warden Service, which he himself had never received and probably never would.

"Stan," said Vaneese with a sternness I hadn't heard from her before.

"What? We're all being honest here. Cards on the table." He shoved his plate away, spilling rice onto the place mat. "There's something off with these mushrooms. They taste funny. Your brother's probably poisoned us all, picking death caps."

He lurched up from the table. His roseate face gleamed with perspiration.

"I need to take a piss."

Five minutes passed, then ten, then fifteen, and Kellam didn't return. After a few awkward attempts at conversation—how I conducted a background check, what she had learned about potato cultivation in Aroostook County, our shared concerns about climate change—Vaneese and I finished our meals in mutually agreed upon silence.

"I'll help you clean up," I offered.

"Thank you, but that wouldn't be so wise, I think."

"Will you be all right?"

I will never forget the look she gave me—as if I were a teenage boy whose ignorance was painful to her.

Someone had been in my room. I had left my cell on the bureau when I'd gone to dinner, and as always, I had left it screen side up. Now it was facedown. Who else could it have been but Kellam? The phone was pass code protected, but the thought of the man rifling through my things angered me. I was glad I had kept my

Beretta under my shirt through dinner. I was beginning to worry I might yet need it.

Still nothing from Dani.

What to do?

She had sounded resolute in not wanting me to leave on her account. I began to wonder again if I should ignore her wishes.

There was a knock at my door. I opened it to find Edouard in the hall with an expression that gave away nothing of his inner state. He carried two cardboard bankers boxes that were heavy enough to reveal the corded muscles in his arms.

"Stan told me to bring you these," he said.

"Thank you. Here, I'll take them."

He ignored my offer and set his burden down on the floorboards beside the bed. He seemed angry with me; his body seemed to be giving off an electric charge. I felt as if I should say something more, but he avoided eye contact. When he left, he closed the door with such force a painting of palm trees tilted on the wall.

The absence of dust on the boxes told me they hadn't been sitting in some back room for the past fifteen years. Stan Kellam had dragged them out from time to time. He had lied to me about wanting the Pellerin case to fade from memory.

The very first document had a green cover sheet bearing the watermark of the Maine Department of Inland Fisheries & Wildlife, the Special Investigations Unit case number, the surname of the target (MICHAUD), as well at the undercover officer (PELLERIN), both in big capital letters, and the initial dates of contact between the two.

The next page began with the usual predisposition probe information. The nature of the investigation: "Illegal Night Hunting / Possession of Deer, Moose, and Bear. Illegal Sale of Game." It gave the specific address of the subjects targeted.

PIERRE P. MICHAUD
D.O.B._____

223 Allagash Road
St. Ignace, ME 04778

ROLAND J. MICHAUD
D.O.B._____
225 Allagash Road
St. Ignace, ME 04778

Seeing two names there surprised me. My understanding was that Pierre Michaud had been the sole focus of Pellerin's investigation. I hadn't realized that his son Roland had been viewed as anything more than an accessory.

Angie Bouchard's boyfriend had been one of the prime targets.

Not only that, but father and son had been next-door neighbors. The way I understood it, the fire that had consumed several buildings in St. Ignace had started because Pierre had rigged his house to explode when the state police tossed flash-bang grenades through the windows. It was a planned diversion to facilitate his escape into the woods.

The grenades, used by police to startle and scare, were not meant to be incendiary devices, but they had somehow ignited a ferocious blaze. Roland's house, being adjacent to his father's, must also have burned to the ground in the conflagration.

The father might be dead, but the son was very much alive, and that was good news for my investigation. I had no information about where Roland Michaud was currently living, but it wouldn't have surprised me if he'd returned to the St. Ignace area. His father had been the poacher king of the St. John Valley, and he was the heir apparent. Bullies, in my experience, almost never left the safety of their home turfs.

I wondered if Charley had found Roland yet. So far, my friend hadn't followed the pattern I might have predicted. He hadn't sought out Angie Bouchard. Nor had he been in touch with Kellam. What was the old man even doing?

I pictured the figure I'd spotted along the lakeshore. If it had been Charley, what purpose could he have had in spying on us? Let alone in revealing himself to me.

I searched deeper into my memories and recalled the silver Jeep as it had passed me on the Rocky Brook Road. The license plate had been so muddy it was unreadable. It had been far dirtier than the rear bumper itself.

The realization took hold: The plate had been deliberately obscured.

Someone was following me.

Again, my thoughts ran to Charley. I had been on the lookout for a green Ford Ranger. Where might he have obtained the Jeep?

I picked up my cell and typed a text to Molly Francis.

Her phone must have been cybernetically attached to her body because her response was instantaneous:

How did u no my gramp drives a silvr jeep?

Either Nick Francis had tailed me into the woods from Presque Isle or he had loaned Charley his vehicle so my friend could pass unnoticed through the County.

To my knowledge, Nick Francis hadn't been involved in the raid on St. Ignace. He had been the Passamaquoddy police chief at the time, focused on tribal problems in distant Washington County.

And yet he had withheld information from me about lending his Jeep to Charley. He had alerted Kellam to my arrival for reasons I still didn't understand. No doubt he had fed me lies back at the truck stop, too. Nick Francis might well be a friend of Charley's, but I would be a fool to trust the man.

———

I sat up past midnight, reading the files.

Kellam had let Ferox out to guard the house. From time to time, I would hear the clicking of the Cane Corso's nails in the hall. The massive dog would approach my door and sniff at the crack. Having it roaming the sleeping house made me wish my room included a bedpan.

I performed an internet search to satisfy my curiosity.

Ferox was Latin for *savage*. And the basis for the English word *ferocious*. Why was I not surprised?

The lengthy document began with a synopsis written by Scott Pellerin. Law enforcement officers are taught to write in a blunt style devoid of personality or affectation, but Pellerin had managed to smuggle some of himself into the summary.

<u>SYNOPSIS:</u>

In August 20__, I, Inv. SCOTT M. PELLERIN, was assigned to conduct a Special Investigation Probe on a father and son, PIERRE P. MICHAUD and ROLAND J. MICHAUD, both of St. Ignace, ME. The men have significant criminal histories and are suspected of currently engaging in serious class D illegal hunting crimes (SEE CRIMINAL HISTORY AND WCID REQUEST SUBMITTED BY DEP. WDN CHASSE LAMONTAINE). Another son, ZACHARIE P. MICHAUD, is a convicted felon and is suspected, in addition to illegally hunting, of committing the class C felony of possessing a firearm. Family and associates of the MICHAUDS are also suspected of violating serious wildlife hunting laws and nonhunting crimes, including class B felonies related to the import and sale of drugs, as well as multiple violations of the federal Lacey Act for transportation of illegally killed wildlife across international boundaries. Under the direct order of LT. STANLEY GALE KELLAM, I was instructed to contact the MICHAUDS as an operative in a covert capacity to determine if the suspected illegal activity was presently occurring and ongoing.

On 08/28/20__ through 09/01/20__, I met and spent time with PIERRE P. MICHAUD DOB ___, ROLAND J. MICHAUD DOB___, ZACHERIE P. MICHAUD DOB___, EMMELINE T. BOUCHARD DOB___, and JON J. EGAN DOB ___, and other associates. During these interactions, the MICHAUDS told me several stories regarding their having committed serious class D illegal hunting crimes. These crimes included acts of night hunting deer, illegally killing bear, killing moose in closed season, hunting under the influence of intoxicating liquors. Discussions regarding other non–fish and wildlife crimes included growing large amounts of marijuana, smuggling marijuana across the international border into New Brunswick, Province of Canada. On the evening of 08/31/20__, ROLAND J. MICHAUD invited me to shoot a ruffed grouse (illegal to hunt except from Oct. 1st through Dec. 31st). The MICHAUDS thereby indicated to this investigator that their illegal hunting behavior is current and ongoing and that they are indubitably predisposed to commit many crimes.

I could see Pellerin grinning as he had typed these words. He had referred to the local warden, Chasse Lamontaine, as "DEP(UTY) WDN": a playful jab at the status of the latter. "Under the direct order of LT. STANLEY GALE KELLAM" was a commentary on Kellam's authoritarian style and an excuse to use his full name in print. Everyone knew how much Kellam hated his middle name.

For the first time, I began to see Scott Pellerin as a kindred spirit rather than as a ghostly rival for Charley's fatherly affections.

But there was more in these two paragraphs than the investigator's private jokes, starting with the inclusion of Angie Bouchard's mother in the official synopsis. Pellerin had named her as an accessory to the crimes he was charged with investigating. I had begun to theorize—admittedly without evidence—that Angie had found Duke Dupree's badge in her deceased mother's personal effects. Suddenly, Emmeline Bouchard's possession of an item that had belonged to the dead investigator went from curious to noteworthy.

Two other individuals were named in the synopsis. The first was Pierre's other son, Zacherie, who had killed himself in jail. The other notable person mentioned was this Jon Egan, whom Kellam had described as a "red squirrel." He was older than the others, more likely a friend of Pierre's than of his sons. Everything I'd heard about Egan so far made me envision him as the archetypal sidekick. Gangsters of all kinds have a predilection for yes-men.

As I settled down to read, I had a notion of sneaking downstairs to brew myself a cup of coffee. Then I heard the *click, click, click* of sharp claws outside my door, and I reconsidered.

28

Even before he'd disappeared without a trace in the wilds of the Allagash, Pellerin had one hell of a story to tell.

As Rhode Island fisherman and insurance fraudster Scott Paradis, he had taken a room at the Valley View Motel. Emmeline Bouchard's establishment in St. Ignace consisted of six separate cabins, each no bigger than a shipping cargo container. It overlooked a broad, braided expanse of the St. John River and the hardscrabble hills of New Brunswick beyond.

Pellerin's official report didn't include photographs, but he had sent Kellam a bunch of candids for his case file. I was struck by Emmeline's appearance. She was as curvy and coal-eyed as her daughter, but her hair was tinted magenta and chopped short. There was a hardness to the woman that came through in pictures: the constant presence of a cigarette in her sensuous lips, the tattooed tiger that sometimes peeked above her open-throated blouse, the almost masculine way she stood: booted feet apart.

There was something about the photo—taken with the subject's consent—that made me believe Pellerin had found Emmeline sexually desirable. She had certainly been flirting with the man behind the camera.

Was that how the investigator had given himself away? By letting his guard down in her bed? It would explain why the keepsake badge had fallen into Emmeline's possession. What it didn't explain was why she'd retained the incriminating item for all these years, knowing that its reappearance might precipitate a felony murder charge against her.

The fact that Emmeline was dating (or at least sleeping with) Pierre Michaud, a man old enough to be her father, must have complicated Pellerin's sexual aspirations.

Evidently, her daughter shared the same taste in older men.

Once, I would have found the idea of mother and daughter sleeping with father and son shocking, but it wasn't the first instance of pseudo-incestuous behavior I'd come across in my career in the Maine woods—nor even the most extreme. Remote places attract people with forbidden desires.

And few places were more remote than St. Ignace.

Pellerin had affected his entrée into the circle of the Michauds with one of the oldest plays in the investigator's book. He sabotaged his own truck. He then had it towed to the repair shop father and son ran as one of their several businesses. He struck up a conversation with Roland while the latter labored to diagnose the electrical problem.

He'd come to St. Ignace, Scott told the Michauds, in the hopes of shooting a "monster bear," but he hadn't realized the legal window for killing one over bait (the most effective method) had almost swung shut. Roland Michaud held a commercial hunting guide's license. He offered to take the Rhode Island rube out for the last days of the season.

The next morning, before dawn, Roland swung by the motel to pick up his client. Pellerin appeared with a rifle that must have given the poacher an erection. The investigator had brought with him a brand-new GA Precision Gladius chambered for .308 Winchester cartridges. This scoped, camo-colored rifle retailed for more than $8,000. Pellerin claimed he'd bought it after reading the autobiography of famed "American Sniper" Chris Kyle.

Pellerin and Kellam had obtained the weapon knowing it would prove irresistible to the Michauds and their associates—that they would fall over each other to use it—and that was indeed what happened.

(It must have been agony for them not to steal it when they'd killed Scott, but they'd rightly realized the risks were too great. Kellam had found the Gladius at the Valley View awaiting the return of its missing "owner.")

By the end of his initial stay in St. Ignace, Pellerin hadn't shot a bear, but he was regularly riding the gated roads with Roland and Zach Michaud with the sniper's gun and a case of beer, shooting whatever could be shot. One afternoon, Roland used the scoped rifle to pulverize a ruffed grouse at a distance of one hundred yards. The bird, Pellerin wrote, "exploded into a puff of feathers."

His characterizations of the three poachers were highly detailed: Both Roland and Zach Michaud were clones of their father. Dark, handsome, bearish men. All the Michauds had extensive rap sheets: misdemeanor assaults, vehicular offenses, multiple violations of Maine's fish and game laws. Zach was the lone felon among them. He had served a year and a half in the Maine State Prison for a drunk driving crash that had resulted in his female companion breaking her back.

The outsider of the group was Jon Egan. He, too, was a felon. Under the influence, he'd exposed himself to a troop of Girl Scouts cleaning up litter along the St. John River.

The one man whom Pellerin had failed to ingratiate himself with was the primary target, Pierre Michaud. From the start, the ringleader seemed intent on keeping his distance. During his first visit to St. Ignace, the undercover officer didn't have so much as a conversation with the poacher king.

When Pellerin returned to town two weeks later, he came bearing gifts. One was a massive cooler stuffed with striped bass on ice. The other was a case of Aguardente de Medronho, a high-octane fruit brandy of Portuguese extraction, popular among commercial fishermen. The choice of the colorless alcohol was smart; it allowed the warden investigator to travel with his own bottle containing water instead of eighty-proof liquor. And it was obscure enough to defuse suspicions. What Maine game warden would show up with six bottles of hard-to-obtain, harder-to-pronounce alcohol from *Portugal*?

The first night the Michaud boys tried the Aguardente, they got roaringly drunk—and revealed to Pellerin the full extent of their criminal activities.

It would not be an exaggeration to say that the Michaud gang had broken half the fish and game laws in the state, but those infractions were only the beginning. They also maintained acres of cultivated marijuana in the forests west of the Allagash Wilderness Waterway and smuggled pounds of it across the St. John River—along with moose and deer meat—into Canada. From the other shore, they brought back prescription narcotics, principally Oxycodone burgled from the homes of cancer patients by their *frères criminels* across the border.

The day after the drinking party, Pellerin received a visit from the poacher king himself. He returned to his motel from gassing up his truck to find Pierre Michaud waiting in his room. A Desert Eagle handgun lay on the table within easy reach. He was drinking from a mug of King Cole Orange Pekoe. The elder Michaud never drank alcohol in Pellerin's presence.

In French, he told Paradis to have a seat on the bed. He then began with a series of personal questions about Pellerin's life, starting with his childhood and leading to the moment when he'd first appeared in St. Ignace.

He was a mountain of a man, larger even than his sons. His most noteworthy features were the severe burns on his hands. Pierre had been trained as a blacksmith and kept a smithy behind his house. At some distant time in his past, he had thrust his hands into a fire (or had them thrust in by some other man). The skin had melted like beef tallow.

"I want to try out this fancy rifle of yours," Michaud said in the nasal French of the St. John Valley. "We will take your truck."

The thought occurred to Pellerin that he was headed to his own execution.

Before they could leave the Valley View, however, they were interrupted by the arrival at the motel of the local game warden.

Deputy Warden Chasse Lamontaine had been summoned by

Emmeline Bouchard to deal with a (fictional) rabid raccoon. Pellerin realized Pierre Michaud's stratagem. Deputy Chasse had a reputation as the worst poker player at every table: a man incapable of bluffing. If "Scott Paradis" was an undercover warden, as Pierre suspected, Chasse would be unable to conceal his knowledge of the stranger's identity.

To the surprise of both Pellerin and Michaud, Chasse didn't so much as blink when he was "introduced" to Scott Paradis. His handsome, guileless face revealed nothing except an eagerness to get on with locating the rabid raccoon.

Reading between the lines, I could sense Pellerin's disbelief at what had happened:

How did he not recognize me?

Granted, the two wardens barely knew each other. Chasse Lamontaine was still just a deputy, back when that position was close to a civilian job: a helper to a district warden who needed another set of hands and eyes. Being a warden's assistant had paid peanuts and rarely led to a career in law enforcement. Plus, Pellerin was based out of Division A in the southern part of the state. He had also grown out his hair and beard for the assignment.

By some miracle, Pellerin managed to avoid the first pitfall Pierre Michaud had dug for him. But there proved to be more traps set in his path.

Next, Pierre had challenged him to shoot that jacklighted doe Kellam had mentioned. Even then, though, Scott had had the presence of mind to allow himself to be hit in the face by the butt of the rifle as the recoil drove it backward. Pellerin ended up with a bruise on his cheek—and a little more of the Michauds' trust.

Reading the investigator's account of his actions made me like him even more. He was quick-witted, confident, and gifted with natural situational awareness. No wonder Charley had loved him like a son.

In his report, there were occasional mentions of Emmeline Bouchard, often in the company of Pierre Michaud, and while Pellerin documented crimes committed by the Michaud boys and

Jon Egan, he seemed never to have witnessed the motel owner breaking any law worse than possession of a controlled substance.

Once again, I began to wonder if Emmeline Bouchard had been the one who'd discovered Pellerin's secret and revealed his true identity to Pierre. Maybe the poacher king had used his girlfriend as bait to gather information from the stranger who had been so quick to ingratiate himself with his sons and so persistent with his questions.

Pellerin's report remained unfinished.

When I reached the final page—the place where a warden would have included his summary of the investigation—there was only this:

Friday, September 27, _____, Phone Call from Unknown Cell Phone

At approximately 2100 hours I received a call from a number I didn't recognize but had reason to believe was one used by the Michauds. The caller did not leave a message. I called the number back and heard an automated tone indicate a voice mail prompt. I did not leave a message.

He was never seen or heard from again.

29

I awoke the next morning to fierce barking. I had fallen asleep rereading Pellerin's report. Instinctively, I reached for the handgun I had concealed beneath the covers. In the process, I managed to send loose pages flying everywhere.

I crossed to the window and pulled back the blind. The sun hadn't yet risen. The trees near the house were filled with a gray light that had the diffuse quality of cannon smoke.

From what I could gather from his barking, Ferox was still housebound, but something had happened to send him into a state of agitation. Kathy Frost, who had spent decades as a K-9 handler, had tried to instruct me in the subtleties of dog barks. "They use different sounds to communicate aggressiveness, defensiveness, fear, general excitement," she'd said.

To my half-educated ears, Ferox sounded less like he wanted to chase a squirrel and more like he'd detected an intruder and wanted to feast on the stranger's beating heart.

I pulled the blind wider and saw a sight that made my eyes pop.

Edouard was running, naked except for his white underwear, across the clearing between the house and the forest. While I watched, he cast a glance over his shoulder in the direction of the darkened driveway. Then he disappeared from my field of vision into the pines.

I dressed, laced up my boots, and tucked my Beretta into its holster under the hem of my shirt.

Kellam shouted for the Cane Corso to shut up.

I'd never heard a dog go so quiet so fast.

Next came a door slam. I dearly hoped it was Kellam locking up his monstrous mastiff.

I descended the stairs with caution and followed the natural predawn light through the rooms until I reached one of the plate glass windows, looking out at the dooryard draped in shadows.

A game warden's patrol truck had rolled to a stop beside my Scout. It was one of the older F-150s, so scratched and muddied it was hard to imagine what it looked like washed.

The driver stepped out, a tall, straight-backed man, dressed in a fatigue-green uniform, a black ball cap, and neoprene boots. The ballistic vests patrol wardens wear make even skinny men look fat in the belly. But even wearing body armor, this guy had the physique of a decathlete.

Chasse Lamontaine.

His district lay fifty miles to the north, hard against the New Brunswick border. What was he doing at Moccasin Pond at this hour of the morning?

The lieutenant, when he appeared in a T-shirt and pajama bottoms, seemed as surprised as I was.

"What the hell, Lamontaine?" I heard Kellam say through the glass.

"I got a message you called."

"Why would I have called for you?"

Chasse was well into middle age, but like some blond men, his hair hadn't changed color, and his wrinkles only served to make his features more ruggedly handsome. His natural gaze was a blue squint. Deputy Do-Right could have served as a stunt double for a midcareer Clint Eastwood.

I chose that moment to step outside. Chasse didn't so much as blink at seeing me.

"Lamontaine, what are you doing here?"

"It's a mystery to all of us," muttered Kellam. "I didn't call your house, Chasse."

"Are you sure?"

"What do you mean *am I sure?*"

"The guy who spoke with C. J. said he was you. He said, 'Can you tell your dad Stan Kellam needs to see him down at Moccasin Pond?'"

Kellam ran a hand across his flattop. "Let's go inside and have coffee and figure this out like civilized men."

In the kitchen, Kellam made us individual cups with one of those pod machines. Chasse asked for french vanilla decaf. Stan and I exchanged bemused glances.

"I want to talk to your son," said Kellam.

"He'll be asleep."

"Then wake him the fuck up, Chasse! I want to know who's pranking us."

Both Charley Stevens and Kathy Frost had given me the same advice when I was a rookie. I thought it was hard-won wisdom they'd acquired on the job until I happened to read a particular Sherlock Holmes story. There on the page was the idea my mentors had been trying to hammer into my skull: "It is a capital mistake to theorize before one has data. Insensibly one begins to twist facts to suit theories, instead of theories to suit facts."

So while I wanted to believe that Charley, the dramaturge, was behind Chasse's appearance onstage, I knew not to jump to that conclusion.

Vaneese didn't show herself. Edouard would likely remain in hiding all day.

Kellam and I listened as Chasse, speaking French, woke up his wife. My grasp of the language was limited, but she didn't appreciate being awakened. Nor did she appreciate being asked to wake their son.

"Give me the phone," barked the lieutenant. "Michelle, this is Stan Kellam. I'm sorry to get you up, but I need to speak with your oldest boy. Yes, it's urgent." While he waited, he addressed Lamontaine, looming in the middle of the kitchen. "How old is Chasse Jr. now?"

"Twenty-one."

"What's he doing for work?"

"Security at the mill."

The just-awakened son came on the line.

"C. J., this is Lieutenant Kellam. Your father is here at my place and said you took a call from someone claiming to be me. No, it wasn't. Can you remember what this man said exactly? His precise words? No, that's fine. What about his voice? Can you be more specific? Great. Thanks for your help."

"What did he say?" Chasse asked.

"That's one observant boy you've got there," Kellam said. "Tell me something, Lamontaine. You didn't think it was out of the ordinary that I summoned you here without explanation? Or that I called your landline instead of your cell to do so?"

"I assumed you had your reasons."

Kellam sat down heavily at the breakfast table. He cupped both hands around his mug. Finally, he looked up with a scowl in my direction. "Was it you?"

"You think I called Chasse?"

"You were reading those files all night. I saw a sliver of light under your door."

"Hell no it wasn't me," I said. "Why would I even want him here?"

"Because you're a fucking enigma, Bowditch. You always have been. Maybe you read something in the report and decided to pull some mischief to expose us. The little Belgian detective gathers the suspects together . . ."

"What report?" asked Chasse, showing an actual flicker of interest.

"Bowditch has decided to reopen the Scott Pellerin investigation for reasons he refuses to share."

"Did someone find something new?"

"I've been reviewing some cold cases," I said. "And St. Ignace is the Great White Whale."

Chasse cocked his head the way a baffled dog does. "What's left to solve? Pierre Michaud killed Pellerin. Charley Stevens shot

Pierre as he was trying to get across Beau Lac to New Brunswick. Open and shut."

"There's the small matter of Pellerin's body never having been found," I said.

Chasse leaned against the counter. "I always figured Pierre cut him up and burned the pieces in his forge."

The blunt brutality of the statement stunned me.

Kellam didn't seem surprised or bothered by the callousness of his former subordinate. "If that's what's happened, we'll never know, Pierre's property having burned to the ground."

"I hope you're not planning on poking around St. Ignace," said Chasse.

Poking?

"Why not?"

"There are still people in the Valley who are angry about what happened. Game wardens aren't exactly popular. It could be dangerous."

"You're still there," I said. "It can't be that dangerous."

"I grew up in Frenchville. Everyone knows me. They understand I had nothing to do with what happened. I never even knew about the investigation."

"It was my decision to bring in Pellerin," said the lieutenant. "And my decision not to inform Chasse."

Because he was afraid of Dudley Do-Right blowing his cover.

I remembered that section in the report where Emmeline lured Chasse to the motel to see how he reacted when he met the mysterious Scott "Paradis." It had been one of Pierre's tests.

"In his account, Pellerin said that you two met," I said to Chasse. "He was baffled that you failed to recognize him. Care to explain that for me?"

He didn't seem put off by the veiled accusation but gave a self-deprecating smile and shrugged his wide shoulders. "Honestly, I don't know. I've wondered about it. C. J. was in trouble a lot back then at school. Pellerin had a beard and long hair. I've always been better with names and dates than with faces. Do you mind if I use your bathroom, Lieutenant?"

"You know where it is."

Out on the lake, a loon began to yodel. Another answered. Two males. Destined for a fight.

I waited until I heard the bathroom door close and lowered my voice. "I saw Edouard bolt when Lamontaine came down the hill. The poor guy was in his underwear."

"He hears a strange noise and assumes it's ICE coming to get him." Kellam lifted the mug and hefted it, almost as if preparing to throw it at me. "There's something you're not telling me about why you're really here. I can't figure out what it is, but I know it's not in my best interest."

Chasse returned to the kitchen looking as guileless as ever.

"Can you think of anyone who might've gotten their kicks sending you on a wild-goose chase?" Kellam asked him.

Before Chasse could respond, his phone rang. He looked at the screen. "It's Michelle again."

"*Allo?*" he said. "*Quoi? Calme-tu. Respire. Où? Et la police est sûre que c'est elle? Oh, mon Dieu, c'est horrible. Si le bureau du shérif appelle à nouveau, dis-leur que je me rendrai directement au motel. J'taime.*"

My mother hadn't taught me French, but I had spent enough time with my late grandparents that I could follow the thrust of what he was saying.

"What motel?" I asked.

"The Valley View."

"Oh, Christ," I said. "Is it Angie Bouchard?"

Chasse Lamontaine didn't ask how I knew the name, but his eyes widened from their usual squint. He nodded in the affirmative.

"A person driving by the motel this morning found her car parked behind the building, out of sight of the road. He recognized it as Angie's. She was inside, dead. Somebody strangled her."

30

Stan Kellam erupted at me this time. "You know Emmeline Bouchard's daughter? And you didn't say anything?"

"I stopped at her house in Presque Isle before I came here."

Chasse seemed focused and alert. No longer laid-back, he was taking in every word.

"Enough bullshit," said Kellam loudly enough that the dog barked at the far end of the house. "What are you really doing here? It has to do with Stevens, doesn't it? He sent you to spy on me."

"Charley has nothing to do with me being here."

"That's a lie."

I bobbed and weaved. "He didn't send me."

"I earned my master's in the interpretation of body language to detect lying. You're indicating deception all over the place, Bowditch."

"Then you know how poor even experts are at catching lies." I turned to the sink to rinse my coffee mug. "Thank you for the hospitality and the help, but I need to get up to St. Ignace."

"Not before you answer my questions."

"The state police will want to hear what I have to say."

"So use the goddamn phone."

At that moment, the Cane Corso came bounding into the kitchen. The charcoal dog moved into an attack position between his master and me. There was no question in his mind about the enemy in the room. Chasse seemed unruffled by the beast's sudden appearance.

"I need to meet with the detective in charge," I said with as much calmness as I could manage. "I would hope you can understand that."

The lieutenant's chair toppled as he pushed himself to his feet. The dog showed me his teeth when he growled—always the last thing you want to see.

"Where is Stevens?" Kellam demanded. "What is he up to?"

A single word from his master might have sent the amber-eyed mastiff leaping at my throat.

"I honestly don't know."

"But he sent you here?"

"Not directly."

"What does Charley Stevens have to do with Angie being murdered?" said Chasse. I'd been so distracted by the dog, I'd momentarily forgotten the warden was still in the room.

"Charley thinks I lied about what happened fifteen years ago," said Kellam. "He thinks there might have been some sort of cover-up. So he sent Dr. Watson here to wheedle information out of me. Isn't that right, *Mike*?"

"Stan?"

Vaneese stood in the hall between the kitchen and the rest of the house. She was dressed in a linen blouse and denim cutoffs that made her legs look a mile long. I didn't know how long she'd been lurking within earshot, but my gut told she'd heard everything.

"Go upstairs, Vee," said Kellam.

"I told you he would get out if you didn't lock his door."

For an instant, I didn't realize she meant the dog.

"Go upstairs."

"Why? What's going to happen?"

"Mike is going to explain what game he's been playing with us."

"Or what, you're going to sic Ferox on him? *Mon dieu*." She dropped her voice. "Ferox, *hier*!"

The Cane Corso cast a glance back at Kellam, then clicked across the pine floor to Vaneese's side.

"*Platz,*" she said.

The dog settled down beside her bare feet. He still looked like he wanted a chance to chew on my esophagus, but I was finally able to draw a breath.

"I owe you an explanation, Stan," I said. "And you'll get one. I promise. But right now, I have to go."

"What do you think happened, Bowditch?" Chasse asked, but there was no menace in his tone. He seemed merely curious.

Before I could answer, Kellam said, "He knows Pellerin and I didn't see eye to eye over how to handle the Michauds and wanted to go over my head. He thinks I might have ratted Scott out to Pierre."

The most startling aspect of this confession was that I'd had no such suspicions.

"You think the lieutenant was the one who blew Pellerin's cover?" Chasse asked, then added a disbelieving smile.

"No."

But Kellam hadn't heard me. He glowed with such heat now he looked like he might suffer a heart attack. "The thought that I sold out one of my wardens to the Michauds is obscene."

"Stan, you need to take it down a notch," I said.

"Don't tell me how to behave in my own house!"

Ferox snapped again. Vaneese hissed at the animal: "*Beruhigen.*"

"So what else do you suspect me of doing?" said Kellam. "You think I drove up to St. Ignace last night, killed Emmeline's daughter for no reason, and booked it back before dawn?"

"Nobody had a reason to kill her!" said Chasse Lamontaine with surprising passion. "She went to high school with my boys. Angie was an innocent girl."

Could the man possibly be that naive?

"The state police need to hear what I have to say, Stan."

"I should get back to the Valley, too," said Chasse.

"So get the hell out of here then, the both of you," said Kellam.

"You have five minutes, Bowditch, or I swear to Christ, I'm putting the dog on you."

Kellam disappeared as I went upstairs to pack my things. I wished I could have taken those two boxes of files with me, but I was already pushing my luck. And the clock was running.

Vaneese, having locked Ferox in what I hoped was a secure room, hung in the doorway. Perhaps her fiancé had told her to watch me in case I tried to steal any documents. The hardness in her eyes made me believe she, too, felt I had betrayed their trust.

"I'm sorry to leave so abruptly—"

"It gives you an excuse to leave without having to explain, no?"

I kept my mouth shut.

"Stan is not a criminal."

I tried zipping my duffel, but the teeth caught on a shirt I'd stuffed inside. "Would you call him a good man, though?"

She straightened her neck as if I'd touched a nerve. "Better than you, I think."

"That's a low bar. Tell him I wasn't lying when I said I would explain everything later."

She folded her arms below her breasts. "And we should believe you why?"

"Maybe you shouldn't—but it's the truth."

Then she escorted me through the house and outside into the humid morning. I crossed a spongy patch of stair-step moss that gave beneath my boots. Heard the burr of browsing bees. Breathed in the good smell of the lake.

Chasse had already left.

As I loaded my Scout, I looked back at the lodge and saw Kellam standing rigid behind the plate glass window. He had a Corona in his hand, and the Cane Corso was beside him.

I drove up the hill until the lake disappeared behind the maples and the spruces and the firs. No doubt Kellam would be on the phone with his old buddies in law enforcement, asking to be updated on the homicide in St. Ignace. He would spend the next hours swilling Coronas and wondering what treason Charley and I suspected he committed that had caused Scott Pellerin's death.

When I reached the gate, I found Edouard—now somehow fully dressed—standing at attention beside the steel post like a guardsman. Deerflies buzzed about his sweating skull.

I rolled down my window. "Nice meeting you, Edouard."

His mouth became a hard line. It was as if he'd overheard the argument in the kitchen and had chosen to side with his savior, Kellam. When he swung the massive gate shut behind me, the clang of metal on metal echoed inside my skull.

Chasse Lamontaine had a five-minute head start on me. I checked my cell, but now that I was out of sight of Kellam's tower, I had no service.

I was praying that whichever state police detective had caught the Bouchard case was someone I knew personally. After my promotion, I'd done meet and greets with detectives around the state: anyone I might consult on future cases. But shaking hands with someone isn't the same as working side by side to solve a crime. As it was, I was going to have a hard-enough time explaining the circumstances that had led me to knock on Angie Bouchard's door.

Why had she run back to her mother's motel?

Who had she gone there to meet?

What had she told him?

Strangulation is one of the most intimate methods of murder. The perpetrator, except in cases where the victim is a child, is almost always male. Females constitute the overwhelming majority of victims. There is frequently a sexual component. Many rapists strangle their victims so as not to leave behind a witness.

Evidence or no, I was willing to go out on a limb and surmise that Angie hadn't crossed paths with a stranger who also happened to be a sexual predator. She had known the man who'd killed her. Maybe she had even sought him out. She'd trusted her killer enough to let him get close.

In my memory, I saw Roland Michaud's ursine eyes.

Did he kill her for selling the badge and jeopardizing the secrets he'd been keeping for the past fifteen years?

Lost in thought, I'd failed to notice that I was no longer following Chasse Lamontaine's tire prints. He must have taken a detour. As a native of the county and a patrol warden, he would have known all the backwoods shortcuts.

I couldn't afford to attempt a similar maneuver. The dotted squiggles on the map, leading to the St. John Valley, might be navigable roads in reality. They might also be abandoned skidder trails, overgrown with alders and popples, blocked by deadfalls, and impassable to all but the skinniest of deer. I stuck to the same route I had taken into the woods.

This time, there was an attendant at the Fish River Checkpoint. He was a burly man with a bulbous nose and a gauzy white strip tucked into the back of his Red Sox cap. It hung down his neck like the sun protectors on the hats worn by the French Foreign Legion.

He came around to my window with a clipboard.

A chemical odor emanated from him, like an industrial perfume. "Says here you were supposed to be out yesterday," he told me in a booming voice. "You got lost, I expect."

"Lost? No. I got turned around pretty good, though."

"Ha! I ain't gonna charge you for the extra night. Let me open this sucker up for you."

"Do you mind my asking a question?"

"You're wondering about these?" He flicked the gauze dangling from his baseball cap. "Dryer sheets! The bugs hate them. I got them stuffed all in my clothes. Tonight, I won't have a single bite. Try them sometime. You'll thank me for the tip."

A moment later, I was headed back toward civilization. Blackflies that had flown in through the window assaulted me behind my ears like tiny heat-seeking missiles. I wondered if there was a Laundromat in Portage where I could purchase some dryer sheets.

Outside the village, my cell phone exploded with computer-generated musical notes. It was a symphony of buzzing voice mails, dinging texts, and trilling messages. Three of the most recent had come from Stacey.

"My mom told me about my dad," she said in her voice mail. "And now she can't reach you either. I'm coming up there as soon as I can get a flight. Don't try to argue me out of this, Mike. You know you can't stop me."

31

My first call wasn't to Stacey; it was to Dani. She hadn't left me so much as a text message while I'd been in the woods. My hope was that she had slept the whole time. She surprised me by answering.

"Ugh," she said. "What time is it?"

"Almost nine o'clock."

"Ugh."

"I wanted to see how you were feeling."

"Like shit," she said in the same loopy voice she had used the last time. "Hopefully, I'll feel better this afternoon. I want to put in a half day."

"You're not planning on going to work?"

"Mike," was all she said.

"Do you want to switch over to FaceTime?"

"So you can tell me how sick I look?" She actually managed a laugh. "No, thanks."

Instead of harping on her, I said, "A lot's happened since yesterday. The woman who sold that badge to John Smith was murdered last night. Her name was Angie Bouchard. I'd met with her only hours earlier. And I still have no idea where Charley is."

She paused a long time before she spoke again. "How old was she?"

"Twenty-four, twenty-five."

"Shit."

I brought her up to speed as I turned onto the northbound lane of Route 11, headed for Fort Kent and the Canadian border. I deliberately avoided any mention of the message I'd gotten from Stacey, alerting me of her imminent return to Maine. Given Dani's current state, it seemed a sticky subject. Once again, she listened with uncharacteristic silence.

Past Winterville, I swerved, unsuccessfully, to avoid a pool of still-tacky blood. An eighteen-wheeler must have hit a moose in the night. Afterward, my tires sounded different from the gore stuck to them.

"Dani?"

"Hmmm?"

"I was wondering if you were still there. So I'm headed to St. Ignace now and need to call the state police. I don't know who's caught the case yet, but I need to tell him what I know."

"Maybe it was Shithead."

"Who?"

"Shithead. Shit for Brains. Maybe he killed her."

"John Smith is in jail, Dani. I arrested him for attempted murder. Remember?"

"Yeah, right." She paused again, and I heard her take several breaths. "I'm going to get up and take some ibuprofen. Send me a text if something happens."

"When was the last time you took your temperature?"

Her reaction caught me off guard. "Will you lay off me?"

"I'm worried is all. You said you were bitten by a tick?"

"It's just the flu."

"I'd feel better if someone looked in on you."

What she did next almost made me veer into oncoming traffic. She hung up.

I pulled into the overgrown lot of an auto repair shop that had closed about a hundred years ago and made another call. The Scout shuddered every time a big truck whipped past. The phone rang and rang.

Please don't go to voice mail.

"I didn't expect to hear from you so soon," said Kathy Frost.

"I thought you'd still be 'fishing.' Did the bugs drive you out of the woods?"

"Kathy, I need you to do something for me. It's important."

— ·—

Route 11 between Portage and Fort Kent is one of Maine's officially designated scenic byways, but I couldn't have described the views that day to save my life. There were lakes with cottages. Green hills maybe. Rolling fields.

My head felt as if it had been shaken like a snow globe.

Kathy volunteered to drive out to Dani's house to check on her. After some debate, we agreed against summoning an ambulance, knowing what a proud person my girlfriend was. They lived two hours apart, so I wouldn't hear from Kathy soon.

"Maybe you want to cut your fishing trip short," she offered.

"I'm not fishing."

"I know that, Mike. Whatever you're up to, I hope you can justify it."

"Dani understands."

"She also sounds out of her head."

Next, I called Ora.

"I had to tell her the truth," she said, meaning Stacey. "She knew something was wrong. She senses things like I do."

"What did she sense?"

"That her father was in danger."

"We don't know that, Ora."

She treated my response as not requiring a rebuttal. "This woman they found dead this morning in St. Ignace—she was involved in this matter Charley's investigating?"

For a moment, I'd thought Ora's vague premonitions had graduated to witch-level clairvoyance.

"How did you know about it?"

The truth was less sensational. "The story's been all over public radio this morning."

· *Of course it would be.*

"The truth is, I don't know if Angie Bouchard's death is connected to this thing with the badge or not. I suspect it is."

I told her about my brief encounter with the murdered woman and her boyfriend. Then I provided an account of my hours in the company of the inscrutable Stan Kellam.

"I never liked him," Ora said with uncharacteristic tartness. "Charley used to say that Stanley's virtues outweighed his vices, but only by a pennyweight. That arrogant man knows something about Scott's death that he's not admitting. And no, it's not one of my 'intuitions' that makes me say that. It comes from having known Stanley Kellam for three decades."

"About Stacey," I said.

"She's arriving in Bangor tonight. She's going to rent a car and drive here. Tomorrow, she's planning on taking Charley's plane and flying up to the Valley."

"That's not a good idea."

"Stacey's not the way she used to be, Mike."

"Her rash decision to come up here suggests otherwise."

"Her father is in trouble. I don't have to ask what you would do in that situation, because you already know."

She was referring to my rash, juvenile behavior when my father had been accused of murder and fled into the forest. It seemed an age ago now. And of course, I had no answer for her. How do you rebut the cold, hard truth?

Nor could I forget how Stacey had handled the situation in the Big Cypress National Preserve when Buster Lee was bitten by that snake. It wasn't the competence she'd shown, treating the man's gory wound. Stacey had always been proficient at more skills than I could count. It was the steady calmness with which she'd handled her terrified patient.

If I was no longer the human powder keg I had been at age twenty-four, then how could I say that Stacey Stevens was incapable of personal growth?

"I remembered something else," Ora said. "Scott Pellerin was from Millinocket."

"What?"

"He grew up in Port Clyde, before his mother passed, but he was born at the old Millinocket Community Hospital. His mom had family up in the Katahdin region. I don't know if it means anything to you or not."

"More than you can possibly know. Do you happen to have a number for Scott Pellerin's sister in Providence?"

"Yes, I believe so. I'm not sure if it's still current."

"Can you call her and ask what their mother's maiden name was? The question will be easier coming from you than a stranger."

Ora, as sharp as her husband, deduced what I was after. "It's the badge!"

"I think so, yes."

For the first time, I thought I understood what the name *Duke Dupree* meant to Charley and why finding his badge on Smith's table had set him off on his heretofore inexplicable quest.

32

Every morning, as I prepared myself for the day ahead, I would take from my bedside a set of dog tags.

At home I kept them within easy reach, strung from a deer antler I'd found in the leaf litter near a cabin on Rum Pond. When I'd first started wearing the tags, I had felt intense emotions every time I put them on—often anger, sometimes sadness, occasionally an affectionate nostalgia for an alternate life I'd never lived. The dog tags only weighed four grams, but on bad days, they felt as heavy as an anchor chain. Now I wore them out of habit more than anything else. Just a week earlier, leaving for Florida, I had set off the metal detector at the Portland airport because I'd forgotten I was wearing them, let alone why.

Now I pulled the tags from beneath my T-shirt and, keeping one hand on the wheel, raised the two medallions to a place before my eyes where I could read the name stamped in the stainless steel.

BOWDITCH, JOHN M.

My father had been a man whose conscience had atrophied over the course of his life to the point where you doubted he'd ever possessed one. He had been a hard-drinker and a womanizer, a poacher and a scofflaw, and in the end, he'd become a cold-blooded killer.

Jack Bowditch had also been my father. Blood of my blood.

We looked so much alike you might even say I had been made in his image. The analogy might have been blasphemous, but I wore the dog tags he had brought back from two tours in Vietnam the way that certain religious people wear medallions devoted to their name saints: less in the hope of receiving divine intercessions than out of a sense of spiritual identity. I would never, could never, escape my patrimony.

Similarly, the tarnished badge of Duke Dupree had been an icon to his grandson.

Scott Pellerin.

His sister confirmed to Ora that Dupree was the maiden name of their mother. She verified that his grandfather's badge had been her little brother's most prized possession.

When Ora had told me that Pellerin was "me," I hadn't appreciated the full extent of our similarities. I understood that Charley had looked upon him as a troubled young man in need of a surrogate father. What I hadn't realized was that my precursor had been compelled to join the Warden Service for reasons not unlike those that had driven me to the same decision.

I had become a game warden to win my estranged father's respect. I had imagined he would be impressed when I announced my career choice. Instead he had mocked me for a fool.

Scott Pellerin had signed up for similarly misguided reasons. He had wanted to redeem the stained legacy of his maternal grandfather. And so he had carried Duke Dupree's battered badge with him, stashed away in secret, as a personal talisman.

It wouldn't be the first relic that got a man killed.

—

Fort Kent is the literal end of the road. It is mile zero of Route 1. There is even a marker to commemorate the designation. You have to search hard for the plaque, tucked away in a motel parking lot. I have read there is a similar monument, 2,369 miles south, in Key West, Florida, making the same claim to be the start of Route 1.

Two mile zeros. Like most things in life, where you are standing is all a matter of perspective.

As I descended the hill above town, I saw the St. John River, broad and blue, and the verdant hills of Canada beyond. In every significant way, the north shore of the river was indistinguishable from the south, and yet in 1842, an American and a British statesman had decided to draw an invisible line down the middle of the channel, severing a close-knit French-speaking community that had occupied the Valley for half a century beforehand.

Even now, as I turned onto Main Street, I couldn't help but watch the ring-billed gulls flying carelessly back and forth across the St. John, and I thought about how every border on earth is a man-made fiction. The birds are never fooled.

I made a call to the state police barracks in Houlton and spoke with a trooper working a desk.

"Who caught the Angie Bouchard case?"

"Lieutenant Zanadakis."

"Great."

The dapper detective was also looking into my run-in with John Smith. I had prayed that the investigator in charge would be someone I knew. Not someone who knew me too well.

"Is there anything I can help you with?" asked the trooper in Houlton.

"I have some information about the dead woman Lieutenant Zanadakis needs to hear. Where can I find him?"

"In St. Ignace, at the Valley View Motel. That's the crime scene. He'll be there until the medical examiner arrives and the evidence techs finish up."

I cruised down a tidy main street that ran parallel to the river: a downtown of brick shop fronts and well-kept clapboard buildings. Instead of following the traffic headed to the customs station at the foot of the bridge to Canada, I left Route 1 and turned onto a road that clung to the south bank of the river.

Most people conceive of northernmost Maine as a howling wilderness, but even I, who had visited the Valley before, found myself taken aback by the handsome prosperity of Fort Kent.

The views were spectacular. The St. John had its headwaters

across the border at Lac Frontière in Québec and drained thousands of square miles on its journey to the tidal tumult of the Bay of Fundy. Here, on the border between Maine and New Brunswick, it was a broad, sandy stream with brushy islands in the middle that inevitably would be submerged the following spring when ice floes jammed the river and the streets of lower Fort Kent began to flood.

I passed through two villages named for Catholic saints—John and Francis—before I reached a crossroads. It was T-shaped intersection where a logging road angled away from Route 161 and plunged south into the vast commercial timberland that extended to Moccasin Pond and another five hundred miles beyond that. My atlas gave the name of this hamlet as St. Ignatius, but to the French speakers of the Valley, it had always been St. Ignace.

Now it was mostly just ruins. Along the riverside, a row of charred foundations were all that remained of the houses and business that had burned the night the Maine State Police and the Maine Warden Service had come looking for Scott Pellerin. Sumacs, poplars, and assorted small bushes had grown up from the rubble, but all that fresh green life couldn't hide the violence that had happened fifteen years before. The fact that the fire that had claimed half the village had been the fault of Pierre Michaud, covering his tracks, wasn't visible in the devastation.

I came to a stop. The first drops of yet another rain shower fell upon my windshield. The hot engine hissed.

Across the road from the ruins stood a general store, closed and for sale; a Grange hall that didn't appear to have hosted a meeting in decades; and a clapboard house with a sunken roof that looked to be one good blizzard away from collapsing. Two trucks, three ATVs, and a dooryard walled with stacked firewood told me the dwelling was occupied.

I dug out the snapshot of Pierre Michaud and held it at arm's length with the overgrown ruins of his former home in the background.

Who was this man? What had he been thinking when he rigged his house with gasoline-drenched blankets, propane tanks, and canisters of acetylene? How did he imagine he could escape with a hundred police officers on both sides of the border searching for him by land, water, and air?

He must have known that Beau Lac, twenty miles north, along a tributary river, was a soft spot in the invisible fence. The wardens found a dirt bike he had ridden there and dumped into the water. Locals said Pierre had kept a canoe chained to a tree on the lake. He had family on the other side; a Canadian relative might have been waiting to pick him up.

But he never made it across.

My imagination easily conjured the scene. A full moon appearing and disappearing behind ragged clouds, a man paddling for his life across water black as spilled ink. And then, out of nowhere, a floatplane. The pilot spots the fugitive. The plane descends. It skates on its pontoons across the surface until it is within thirty yards of the canoe. Gunshots follow. The fugitive leaps into the forty-degree lake, believing he can outswim death. He miscalculates.

My friend had kept the picture of this evil, bear-faced man in the same box as his war medals. Charley disdained trophies. I thought I understood the meaning of the snapshot now. It was a reminder of a failure he wouldn't allow himself to forget. And the Hindu inscription on the back? A spell to ward off the furies who assailed his conscience by night.

As I put away Pierre's picture, I saw through the rain the shape of a person in a lighted window in the house across the road. Then the curtain fell. I could have knocked and asked to know what happened here fifteen years earlier, but I already knew the answer I'd receive.

Silence.

I engaged my wipers to clear the glass. I pushed the transmission into first gear and began creeping forward again.

Less than a mile down the road, I came to the Valley View

Motel. The sign rising from the side of the road was a charming patois:

BIENVENUE!
VALLEY VIEW MOTEL
CHAMBRES RENOVE
WELCOM SLEDDERS

Snowmobile season had ended three months earlier, but from the boarded windows of the cabins, it was obvious the motel had been closed a lot longer than that.

This morning, the parking lot overflowed with visitors. The state police, the Aroostook County Sheriff's Office, even the Fort Kent Police Department had sent representatives, as had the U.S. Border Patrol. The proximity to Canada—just a rifle shot across the river—must have engaged the interest of the feds.

I parked along the roadside, grabbed my raincoat and warden cap, and made my way up the string of vehicles. I passed Chasse Lamontaine's warden truck. It was even muddier than before. The bastard had taken a shortcut and beaten me here.

A deputy, charged with shooing away nosy neighbors and blocking reporters when they arrived, tried to stop me until I showed him my badge.

A crowd of officers milled outside the tape barrier. Standing off to one side was Chasse Lamontaine. He had his back to me, but his height and wingspan made him impossible to misidentify. The warden was on his phone, speaking to someone in French. It sounded like an argument. I slipped past before he recognized me.

I found Nico Zanadakis in conversation with a man in blue coveralls: one of his evidence technicians. This morning, the dapper detective was wearing a black trench coat. Beneath it was a charcoal blazer with a gray shirt, a black satin tie, and a silver pocket square. Also nitrile gloves to keep from contaminating evidence. He smelled of eau de cologne and DEET.

"Bowditch?" His tone was not welcoming.

"I have information about Angie Bouchard you need to hear."

"Of course you do."

"It would be best if we speak in private."

He dismissed the technician and extended an arm toward the motel dumpster. Someone had deposited the carcass of a road-killed deer inside it, and the air was alive with the buzzing of flies and the stomach-turning stench of rotting flesh. We retreated to a safe distance.

—

Zanadakis was neither the best nor the worst detective in the state police. He could connect puzzle pieces when he had a pattern to work from.

"This has something to do with what happened at Hook Lake. Your confrontation with Smith."

For the first time, I had an unimpeded view of the back lot. Angie's Volkswagen, dirty with pollen paste, was parked in the far corner. Evidence techs had opened the doors to shoot videos and photographs.

"I met with Bouchard yesterday at the house she was renting in Presque Isle."

Zanadakis raised an eyebrow. "Go on."

"Her boyfriend was there. Roland Michaud, son of Pierre Michaud. I'm sure that name rings a bell. You need to start with Roland."

"No, I need to start with you. What the fuck have you been doing up here? First you visit an amateur fence who tries to kill you. Then you drop in on a girl who turns up dead."

"I wasn't entirely forthcoming when you and I spoke at Hook Lake."

"You lied, you mean."

"By omission."

"I'm not your fucking priest, man. I don't care about categories of sin. I care about being misled by an officer who swore an oath to uphold the law. Did you think I wouldn't find out it was Charley Stevens who beat the piss out of Smith? How is the old man mixed up in this?"

"Smith had a warden badge for sale along with his other stolen stuff at the Machias Dike."

He raised the collar of his trench coat against the piss-warm rain. "And Stevens took offense?"

"The badge belonged to a warden named Duke Dupree."

"I don't know him."

"He died a long time ago. His grandson was Scott Pellerin."

His response was terse but to the point. "Fuck me. This is all connected to that clusterfuck in St. Ignace?"

"The reason I didn't tell you at Hook Lake was because I didn't know who Dupree was or that the badge had anything to do with Pellerin's disappearance. For all I knew, Charley had just gone off on Smith because he was a scumbag."

The pomade in his wavy hair caused the water to bead up. "So where did Smith say he came by the thing?"

"He bought it from Angie Bouchard at a yard sale. Scott Pellerin stayed at this motel when he was undercover. Angie's mother, Emmeline, owned and ran the place then. My guess is that Pellerin had his grandfather's badge with him—maybe as a good-luck charm—and Emmeline discovered it. She was divorced and dating Pierre Michaud at the time. No one knows how Pellerin's cover was blown, but my current thinking is the badge might've played a part."

"Was any of this confirmed by Angie Bouchard?"

"No, but the fact that she had it in her possession suggests a connection."

"How did she react when you confronted her with this theory of yours?"

"I didn't confront her with anything. I just asked where she'd gotten the badge. She lied and said it belonged to her roommate, but I am pretty sure she found it among her late mother's belongings and didn't know what it was."

"Did she say anything about coming back up here?"

"No."

"So you might have spooked her?"

The possibility had occurred to me. "Yes."

Zanadakis didn't have to state the obvious: that if I had never shown up on her doorstep, she might still be alive.

"Do you have the badge?"

Rain pattered off the brim of my cap. "No."

He seemed taken aback by this. "Where is it?"

"Charley has it."

"And where's Charley?"

"That's the million-dollar question." Before he could press me on the point, I decided the time had come to shift the discussion. "You need to bring in the state police detectives who worked the Pellerin case. I think Angie's death is connected to what happened to Scott. I think you're looking for the same killer or killers. At the very least, the Pellerin case needs to be reassigned to the Unsolved Homicide Unit."

Zanadakis raised a gloved finger under my nose. "Bowditch, you might think I don't recall the circumstances of how we met, but I do. Those drug dealers whose car got stuck in the woods during a snowstorm? You had a theory then, I remember. It was wrong, wasn't it?"

"Not entirely."

"Right now, I need to focus on the physical evidence. Conspiracy theories can wait."

"It's not a conspiracy theory," I said. "Not in the paranoid sense, I mean. There *are* actual conspiracies."

"Do you practice being such a—?"

"Bring in Roland Michaud, at least," I said.

"Why?"

"I saw Angie and him together at her house. He was half-dressed. Strangulation is an intimate way to kill someone. And he has connections to Pellerin's disappearance."

The detective took a moment to chew on this. "Maybe she cheated on him. Or he cheated on her. Things got violent. It makes more sense than her being murdered over some old badge."

"I'd like to see her," I said.

"I'm sure you would."

"I saw her alive less than twenty-four hours ago. I don't know how many witnesses you have who can speak to that period of time. I might notice some detail that helps your investigation. What does it hurt to let me look?"

Arrogant he might be, but Nico Zanadakis was no fool. As long as he got credit for clearing the case, he would exploit anyone and anything that might serve his purpose.

He brushed water off his greased hair. "All right, but you'd better not vomit on my crime scene."

We started in the direction of the Volkswagen, but the detective came to a quick stop and spun around. Chasse Lamontaine was following us. How long had he been standing within earshot?

"Where are you going?" asked Zanadakis.

His statuesque head was unprotected from the elements. The rain just slid down his nose and cheeks. "I knew Angie, too. I thought I could be helpful."

"Did you see her in the past day?"

"No."

"Then you can leave. Get back to checking fishing licenses or whatever. I'll call you when I require your expert assistance."

Chasse nodded. "I'll keep my phone on."

"You do that."

As the warden walked off, he patted his pockets until he found his cell. I kept an eye on him. Soon he was arguing with a person on the other end again. I wondered who could have made him so mad.

33

She was slumped forward against the steering wheel, her hair a loose mess, arms straight down at her sides. I had found drunks sleeping that way in their cars, with their heads on the horns. Sometimes you needed to jab their shoulders for them to wake up. But none of them had had purple bruises around their throats.

"Can I see her face?"

With gloved hands, Zanadakis reached forward and gently took a handful of hair and lifted her head. The neck didn't want to bend. Her shoulders came up, too.

"That's her," I said. "That's Angie."

"Evangeline, actually. Her full name is Evangeline Bouchard."

"Who found her?"

"A guy who used to plow the lot for the mother. He lives down the road in Allagash and still looks in on the place. He's worried kids might be breaking in and doing drugs, as if they don't have their pick of empty buildings around here."

"Was the window rolled down like this?"

"Yes."

"Keys in the ignition?"

"On the floor, as if she'd dropped them. Is this what she was wearing when you saw her in Presque Isle?"

I peered down at the mat, sprinkled with cookie crumbs and the clear plastic film used these days instead of cellophane to wrap cigarette packs. "It's the same outfit. She must have come up right after I left her house."

"Rigor was still present when Mr. Plow tried to shake her awake. He said it was like trying to move a mannequin. Rigor mortis passes off quickly in the heat so she had to have died during the night."

"What's Mr. Plow's real name?"

"Egan."

I met his eyes. "You're shitting me."

"No, why?" He waved at the fog of blackflies around his head. Maybe they liked his cologne more than they disliked the bug repellent.

"Jon Egan was part of Michaud's poaching ring. He was a suspect in Pellerin's disappearance. The cops pinched him when they stormed St. Ignace."

"One of the local guys should have filled me in on that," he said, glancing around for someone to blame.

"Is Egan still here?"

"We sent him home. I figured we'd reinterview him later. Now I'm thinking I'll pull him in this afternoon. This raid you mentioned—"

"You saw the burned buildings a mile back at the intersection."

"That's right. Half the village burned to the ground, I heard."

"You need to bring Stan Kellam in. He was the lieutenant who headed up the undercover operation and the rescue operation that followed. He's retired now but lives an hour from here in the middle of nowhere. I can give you his number."

He let out a sigh. "You weren't listening when I said you should avoid telling me what to do."

A trooper came up to tell him that the medical examiner had arrived.

"Don't leave town," Zanadakis told me. "You and I need to have a long discussion about how you came to be involved here. It wouldn't hurt if you chased down Stevens for me while you're at it."

"I'm trying."

"Try harder."

—

I retreated to the safety of my Scout and chucked my soaked cap into the backseat. The windows steamed up within seconds of my climbing inside the vehicle.

It didn't necessarily mean anything that Egan had been the one to report finding Angie's body. On the other hand, killers were sometimes the ones who called the cops—if they were confident that they hadn't left behind physical evidence.

I sat there in the dim light that seeped in through the rain-streaked windows. A hazy curtain hung between me and the past. I could glimpse movement and color through it. But details remained opaque.

The abandoned motel was a dark shape through the fogged glass. The Valley View was just a ghost of its old self. At least it had survived the conflagration that consumed the village center.

Emmeline Bouchard had escaped prosecution as an accessory to her boyfriend's crimes and continued her career as an innkeeper. She had died without facing judgment for her role in Pellerin's demise. Instead it had been her luckless daughter who had suffered for her mother's misdeeds.

I checked my watch. By now, Kathy had to have arrived at Dani's house. I tried her number.

"I was just about to call you," she said.

"Is Dani OK?"

"I'm taking her to the ER."

My back stiffened. "What?"

"She's delirious and pugnacious. She barely let me take her temperature. It's 103 degrees, Mike."

"She was bitten by a tick the other day."

"Was there a rash?"

"She said no. Can you look for one?"

"I'm getting her dressed now. I'm taking her to Maine Med. Can I call you back after I've gotten her to the hospital? Maybe you can catch a flight from Presque Isle to Portland. I know Charley would be happy to come fetch you."

I hadn't told her about the old man's disappearance, and that lack of trust had come back to hurt me, but I couldn't fill her in now. She had a crisis on her hands.

"I'm in St. Ignace, Kathy."

"What the hell are you doing there?" She knew full well the dark history of the place.

"A woman has been murdered."

"I heard the news, but how does it involve *you*?"

"I can't explain over the phone; it's too long of a story. But I think there's a chance that the person who killed Scott Pellerin is still alive and has been hiding in plain sight for the past fifteen years. And I think he knows we're after him."

"'We'? You're talking about Charley, right? The two of you are up to some stunt."

"It's not a stunt."

"For fuck's sake, Mike." Then I thought I heard a thump in the background. "I think Dani's fallen in the bathroom. I need to check she's OK. I don't care that you're in the middle of an investigation. Get your ass down here. What's happening to your girlfriend is scaring the shit out of me. She needs you. I need you, too."

Kathy had been my sergeant once. She used to give me commands. But this was an appeal to my conscience. It was a reminder that I would need to live with the consequences of whatever I decided to do next.

Dani needed me.

I pushed down the brake and the clutch and turned the key in the ignition.

—

I sped back through the rain toward Fort Kent.

To the best of my knowledge, there were only two commercial flights a day out of Presque Isle's vest-pocket airport, and they both went to Newark, of all places. I would need to hit up a friend with a plane to take me south. Otherwise, I was facing a six-hour drive to Maine Medical Center. Portland is closer to New York City than it is to Fort Kent.

I slowed as I passed through the charred crossroads of St. Ignace.

After the conflagration, investigators from the fire marshal's office had picked through the rubble looking for any sign of Pellerin. One theory was that Pierre Michaud had cut up his corpse and burned the pieces in the forge he kept in his black-smith shop. Forensics technicians around the world had re-covered DNA from the most hellish of fires, but the Maine investigators never found a trace of Scott Pellerin in the remains of Pierre's smithy.

In the hamlet of St. John, the road drew close to the river again. There was just a steel guardrail and some sapling birches as wide around as broomsticks, and then there was thin air. The cliff wasn't sheer—although it looked precipitous through my wet windshield—but the drop must have been considerable.

A logging truck passed me in the westbound lane, heading into the woods for a fresh load of timber. It splashed my Scout with enough water to fill a bathtub. For fifteen seconds, I was driving blind. Then the wipers cleared just enough glass for me to swerve back into my lane. I had nearly careened into the guardrail. I blew out a breath I didn't realize I had been holding.

My mind was busy searching for a friend with a plane. I had always depended on Charley for impromptu flights.

Who else, then?

Maybe one of the fishing guides I knew in Grand Lake Stream? A lot of them owned Cessnas and Cherokees. I thought of Stacey, on her way here from Florida. Ora had told me she was borrow-ing her dad's floatplane for the last leg. Wouldn't that have been ironic.

The rain had become a downpour. I focused on the road ahead. I failed to glance in the rearview mirror. If I had looked behind me, I would have seen the truck racing up in pursuit.

The impact and the sound—a horrible metal-on-metal crunch—were simultaneous. The jolt pushed my chest forward against my seat belt. My chin bounced off my chest. One hand lost its grip on the steering wheel.

Then came the shriek of the guardrail scraping paint off my left fender as I crossed the westbound lane. I reflexively jerked the wheel in the opposite direction. I might have ended up in the field of ferns that served as a buffer between the road and the forest, but my pursuer had come up beside me now. I caught a quick glimpse of him in my side mirror.

It was a pickup. A big one. Probably riding atop a raised suspension and oversized tires.

Then he dropped back a few feet.

Hiding in my blind spot, he bumped the tail of my Scout to send me toward the cliff. He was forcing me into the opposite lane, keeping me pinned there. My muscles had tensed from the prior contact. My hands now gripped the wheel as if they'd been superglued to it.

My left headlight exploded into shards as the front end sideswiped the steel rail again. Once again, I jerked the wheel away from the precipice.

And once again, my pursuer rammed me back toward the river. He was a hell of a driver, whoever he was. He'd practiced these sorts of maneuvers at speeds that would have left most people vomiting all over their pants.

But I had practiced, too. My reflexes reacted before my brain could transmit signals through my neural network. I pressed the gas pedal to the floor, trying to outrace him, but his engine was more powerful than mine.

Another crunch and another groan as the side of my poor Scout caused the rail to crumple. If I had struck it at another angle, I would have been shooting through space toward the river far below.

There was a bend in the road up ahead. I recognized I was on a collision course with the guardrail. I understood that I was out of chances.

I couldn't see my pursuer in my side mirror. I gambled that he was still speeding alongside me on a parallel course, three feet off my right fender. I swerved deliberately into the westbound lane and stamped on the brake.

The monster truck shot past. I felt his wake shake the battered chassis of my Scout. I might've experienced a split second of relief.

But my tires couldn't catch hold of the pavement. The pooled water lifted me up and carried me in an arc that seemed slow instead of fast. The front end turned until I was facing the way I'd just come, looking back with one headlight at the shredded remains of the guardrail. Instead of stopping, the Scout continued to hydroplane. The brakes were useless.

Now I was facing the field across the road from the river. I might have been all right. I might have slid off the sandy shoulder and come to rest in the softness of hay-scented ferns. I might have been fine if not for the damned ditch.

When the Scout encountered the flooded trench beyond the asphalt, the sudden loss of balance caused the vehicle to tilt and tumble. First I found myself looking down at the ceiling. Then I was jogged upright again. And then I was rolling sideways like a man on fire who's thrown himself to the ground.

The truck came to rest on the passenger side. I was suspended in midair, secured only by the seat belt, while gravity pulled me into the next seat. I looked to my right and saw curling green fronds where the window should have been.

Those first seconds of hanging in midair motionless were excruciating. My hands shook as I raised them before my face. My mouth tasted bitter from the iron in my bloody mouth.

Dumbly, I examined my body—my waxed canvas jacket shimmered with broken glass—expecting to find myself missing limbs or impaled upon the stick shift. One tingling hand reached upward for the door handle, but I lacked the strength to pop it open. I tried rolling down the window and got it three-quarters of the way before the handle came loose.

I reached to unbuckle my seat belt. Bad move. The second the strap slid back, I dropped across the passenger seat, plummeted down to earth.

Now I was upside down with my face in the ferns. I brought my knees to my chin in an attempt to rearrange myself, but my ligaments had hardened to steel cables.

Just then, the driver door above me opened. It swung upward, and then a leathery arm was reaching in and, behind it, the rest of the old man. He was crouched atop the side-resting vehicle. He had a bald head, lighter than his deeply tanned face. His eyes were as clear blue as the sky when you climb above the highest clouds.

"Mike?"

"Charley?"

"I thought you were dead for sure."

My larynx had a catch in it. "Almost."

"I never would have forgiven myself if something happened to you, son."

He took my wrists with his two callused hands and pulled with the strength of a man half his age. And just like that, I was free.

34

Breathing hard, I stretched out in the crushed ferns, the sweetness of them overpowering, while Charley crouched beside me. With his knobby fingers, he checked my body for injuries. He was dressed in a mechanic's faded blue coveralls and combat boots, neither of which I'd ever seen him wear. Rain streamed down his pale shaved skull. From this angle, I never would have recognized him.

"You're going to have a honey of a bruise from the seat belt, and I expect you'll wake up with a crick in your neck, but I don't see any serious injuries. That's as close to proof of God's grace as you're likely to experience today."

Panting, I said, "How about you tell me where you've been?"

"Following you," he said, lifting his head. There was that warm, wide grin, those deep-etched laugh lines, that comically oversized chin. "I should have been closer, but I knew you were onto the Jeep."

He made a hitchhiking motion with his thumb toward the idling silver Wrangler fifty feet down the road. Rain spun in its headlights.

"Is Nick Francis driving your truck? Why did he tell Kellam I was coming? What are you two up to?"

I sensed he was struggling not to answer. "I can't explain, Mike. I need to leave before anyone else arrives."

"Why?"

"Certain people can't know where I am."

"Which people? Kellam?"

"I told you not to follow me, son."

I had regained my breath. "You knew I would try to track you. You counted on it. And today was the second time it nearly got me killed. You've been using me as bait, Charley. Because you can't ask certain questions, you've let me do it for you, and it's put me in harm's way."

"I've always been nearby," he said, trying to reassure me with a fatherly tone. "I've always been watching."

"Like at Moccasin Pond? You were the man in the hat."

"It's one of Nick's."

"And it was you who called Chasse Lamontaine and tricked him into visiting Kellam."

"I did."

"And now you're just going to disappear again? Without any explanation? You owe me answers, Charley. Starting with who was behind the wheel of that truck."

"I can't tell you."

"Does that mean you don't know, or you know but refuse to say?"

"I understand how frustrated you are. Trust me when I say we're getting close." The old pilot rose to his full height. At five and a half feet, it would be a mistake to say he loomed over me. With his shaved head, he was nearly unrecognizable. "We owe it all to you, Mike. You've flushed them for us."

"I've been your bird dog, you mean? And by 'us,' you mean you and Nick Francis? Why do you trust him, but not me?"

He glanced up and down the darkened road without answering.

I was tired of his game. "Stacey's on her way here."

Now it was his turn to go gray. "When?"

"She has a flight from Florida tonight, and then she's flying your Cessna up here."

"You told her about me?"

"I didn't have to. She sensed something was wrong when she

reached out to you and got no answer. Ora wasn't going to lie when Stacey asked her what was happening."

"You can't let her come here. They're not going to stop now— not after what just happened. All we need is another day. We're so close to the truth, and they're getting sloppy."

"Who's 'they'? At least tell me that."

Two pinpoints of light appeared in the darkness: a vehicle following the river road from Fort Kent. Charley took a step toward the Jeep.

"You can't tell anyone you saw me," he said over his shoulder. "You have to trust me, son. I'll find you again soon."

Before I could say another word, he sprinted off toward the idling Wrangler.

Seconds later, it roared by, passing the oncoming vehicle. I watched the taillights grow smaller and smaller in the rain. Part of me felt relieved, even thrilled, to see the old man. Another part burned with resentment as if I'd swallowed acid.

Whatever Charley might have said, he had placed me in harm's way without my consent.

I shifted position amid the ferns. They were prehistoric plants, glad for the return of primordial heat. I tried to raise my left arm and could only lift it past my shoulder with considerable pain.

But nothing matched the agony of seeing the injuries done to my Scout. As it was perched on its side, I found it impossible to assess the full damage. The frame looked intact, and the tires were not hissing air, but the exterior was dented, scraped, mangled.

The oncoming vehicle turned out to be yet another pickup. For an instant, I wondered if the monster truck had returned, but this one was ghost white. I experienced a crazy vision of Joe Fixico, having driven two thousand miles from the Everglades to my rescue.

Instead of stopping along the shoulder, the pale vehicle drove straight across the ditch and out into the field with barely a bounce. It was a Dodge Laramie, recently washed and waxed; then rinsed clean again by the rain.

I raised a forearm to block its headlights. The diesel engine chugged as it idled. I heard a door open and slam shut.

"Bowditch?"

I squinted into the light. "Who's that?"

"Jesus, man," said Stan Kellam. "What happened to you?"

What were the odds of Kellam being the first person to come upon the crash scene?

"I hydroplaned off the road."

"And tumbled all the way here? It's a miracle you survived. I'm going to recommend to your colonel that you take a remedial driving class."

"With all due respect, Stan, go fuck yourself."

The retired warden wore a hooded olive-green raincoat, safari shorts, and leather sandals that reminded me of something Ernest Hemingway might have worn in his Key West days. "Did you just come from St. Ignace?"

"I was headed back into Fort Kent to assist in the interviews. Nico Zanadakis is running the investigation."

"He's the one who called me. You lied to me about what you were up to."

"I withheld information."

"Don't get Jesuitical with me, you little shit."

"Do you want me to apologize?"

When he opened his mouth to laugh, his breath smelled of beer. "Are you genuinely regretful?"

"Not particularly."

"Then it would be another lie."

He circled my side-swiped Scout. He crouched and ran a hand along the bumper. "It looks like you were rammed from behind."

I tried lifting my left arm again with the same results. "The whole thing was a freak accident."

"No one else was involved?"

"No."

Maybe he believed me. Maybe he didn't.

"I think I can winch you over onto your wheels. Whether this piteous deformity is still roadworthy is another story. But here comes the cavalry."

Blue lights flashed in the darkness. Stan and I didn't exchange another word until the cruiser arrived. The trooper turned his spotlight on us: a shaft of light across the field in which every raindrop became visible for a split second before it continued earthward.

"Is everybody OK there?" a voice shouted from the road.

"Peachy," said Kellam.

The trooper waded through the curling ferns toward us. He was dressed in a long black raincoat and a covered campaign hat secured by a strap around his chin. He and Kellam shook hands as if they were old friends. Maybe they were. Stan didn't need to worry about the alcohol on his breath—not from this chummy cop, at least.

The trooper asked me the same questions Kellam had, and I repeated my lies.

They discussed my predicament.

My skull was ringing like the inside of a church bell. The echoes made it hard to form a coherent thought.

Someone had just tried to kill me.

Roland Michaud had seen my Scout parked outside Angie's house. But surely there were other people who knew of their relationship, and he must have realized I'd already spoken with the detective if I'd come from the crime scene. He had no reason to murder me.

Maybe he wasn't that smart. Criminals rarely are.

Then again, Roland Michaud had kept quiet for fifteen years. He had held up to interrogations and resisted offers of leniency from prosecutors grasping at straws.

Another trooper appeared and focused his spotlight on the underside of my Scout. I watched Kellam stretch a cable from the front of his Ram. At the end was a hook, which he secured to the frame. Kellam engaged the winch, the steel hawser tightened, and my Scout began to tilt. I clenched my teeth as it teetered and then fell, hard, back onto its four wheels. It bounced once and came to rest.

In my time, I had visited plenty of automobile graveyards. Most of the junkers I had seen in those lots, being slowly scavenged for parts, looked like showroom models by comparison.

When I thought how much I'd spent restoring that vehicle—

But the insurance adjuster was the least of my worries.

Charley had told me not to trust anyone with the truth. But why should I trust him after the events of the past seventy-two hours?

Because, ultimately, he was my friend.

I shrugged off the assistance of the troopers and slid behind the wheel. The inside upholstery was slick and had acquired a vegetal smell. I put the transmission back into park and turned the key, still in the ignition. The engine purred as if it had just been tuned up.

"There's a stroke of luck," said Kellam through the shattered window.

"It's my lucky day, all right."

"You're alive, aren't you?"

For now.

35

The troopers followed me back to civilization. They were probably taking bets on how far my wrecked Scout could make it.

But twenty minutes later, I passed the sign welcoming me to the city of Fort Kent. The low clouds were lit from below by the radioactive glow of the international bridge. Border checkpoints are more brightly lighted than baseball stadiums.

I turned into the lot of the Fort Kent municipal center, drove around the brown building to the wing that housed the police station, and turned off the ignition, wondering if it would start again.

I had waited to arrive at my destination before making the call. I needed time to collect myself. Now I could feel the adrenaline dissipating in my bloodstream. I dreaded the inevitable moment when the damage my body had sustained would announce itself in pain.

"They've got her in the ICU," said Kathy Frost on the other end.

"Do the docs know what's wrong with her?" I asked in a voice that I hoped sounded normal.

"Not yet," she said, sounding increasingly impatient. "What's your ETA?"

"I don't have one."

"Don't give me excuses."

"Kathy, someone just tried to kill me."

On the long, slow drive into town, I had concluded that the time had come to take Kathy into my confidence. She was my friend, as much as Charley, and she deserved my trust. It wasn't just that I needed her to understand why I was being delayed. I also required input from one of the best law enforcement officers I had ever known.

When I'd finished my story, she had only one question.

"Are you sure you're OK?"

"My Scout took the brunt of the attack."

"I'm not kidding, Mike. You should get checked out by a doctor. You might have internal injuries."

I don't think I ever loved that woman more. "I'll take it under advisement. Kathy, you told me you came up here after the raid with the other K-9 teams to search for Pellerin's body. Did you ever meet Roland Michaud or Jon Egan?"

"I met them both," she said. "Roland's too smart to attempt that stunt. *Smart*'s the wrong word. He has this animal cunning."

"That's my sense of him as well. What about Egan?"

"Maybe. He struck me as the panicky type. I was surprised that he didn't crack. With Pierre gone, who was left for him to be scared of?"

I finally spoke the name: "Kellam."

"I can't be objective about that man. Stan and I have too much history."

"Dani told me."

"The man has always been brilliant—and controlling. I'm sure that Pellerin didn't make a move without his say-so. That's why everyone came down so hard on Kellam. Because we knew it was his failure that led to that shit show."

"Maybe he's been covering something up all this time—some act of negligence that led to Scott Pellerin's disappearance?"

"I can't imagine what it could have been. Besides, you said it was impossible for him to have killed Emmeline Bouchard's daughter. I want to get back to what Charley told you. It sounded as if he has someone helping him."

"All the signs point to Nick Francis."

"That makes sense, considering they were together the night Pierre Michaud drowned."

"What?"

"Nick was there, on Beau Lac, with Charley when it happened."

"He told me he was back in Indian Township dealing with tribal stuff."

"Police from all over the state came up to the St. John Valley to assist. Both the Penobscots and the Passamaquoddy sent officers to help. Nick certainly wasn't going to let Charley search alone. They were flying together in Charley's old Super Cub when they saw a canoe trying to slip across Beau Lac. Anyway, they lit up the canoe, and there was Pierre Michaud. He opened fire on them, and Charley returned fire, hitting him in the collarbone and knocking him out of the boat. He tried to swim for it, but he went under before he reached the shore."

"What was the official cause of death given by the medical examiner?"

"Drowning. Michaud's lungs were full of water."

"Is there any chance that was a lie?"

"Why would it be?"

"To quell some of the political fallout. I heard there were legislative hearings. The whole Valley was already in an uproar. If the ME gave the cause of death as drowning, as opposed to death by gunshot, it shifted the blame back on Pierre Michaud and off Charley and the Warden Service."

"Except it didn't shift the blame. And do you honestly believe Charley Stevens would have participated in a cover-up?"

"No."

"I thought he was too old for this reckless shit."

"Evidently not."

"It sure sounds like he's been using you to get information out of people he knows would never have talked to him. If I were you, I'd be pissed about it."

"I am, but . . ."

"You love the old fart, I know." She raised her voice to be heard over the hospital noises. "So when is Nico Zanadakis going to interview you?"

"Soon, I hope."

"Does he still dress like a *GQ* model?"

"I've never read *GQ*."

"My heart swells with pride to hear you say that, Grasshopper."

"As soon as I finish my interview with Zanadakis, I am going to find a plane and get down to Portland."

"No, you most certainly are not—not unless she takes a turn for the worse."

"You just said I had to."

"That was before you told me about being run off the road! How's Dani going to feel when she wakes up and learns you left a murder investigation to sit by her bed? I expect you already know the answer to that question."

"But what if she—?"

"I'm not superstitious, but I'd prefer you not finish that sentence. I'll be here for the duration. She stood vigil for me after I'd been shot. It's time for me to return the favor. Give me a call after Zanadakis is done raking you over the coals."

"Deal."

"And, Grasshopper? Watch your back. You might know more than you think you do—and that makes you a threat. Someone already believes you're a danger to them. And one last thing. When you see Charley again, please pop him in the nose for me. That geezer had no business dragging you into this."

—

Like many small-town police stations, this one had a locked vestibule that required someone behind the bulletproof glass to buzz you inside. A pudgy, bright-eyed patrolman by the name of MacLoon did the honors.

Beyond the door, there were a handful of offices, a kitchenette with a coffee maker, an interrogation room, a holding cell, and a garage, where the five officers on the force could maintain their black Ford Interceptor SUVs. If I had to guess, I would have said the Fort Kent cops dealt mostly with moving violations, property crimes, and drunk students from the college campus across town. Anything bigger and badder got kicked to the sheriff's office or the state police.

MacLoon provided me with a first aid kit and escorted me to the bathroom so I could attend to my cuts and scrapes. For once in my life, my injuries looked worse than they were. A fistful of ibuprofen, a tube of antibiotic ointment, and a few Band-Aids and I was good to go. My host told me to have a seat in the conference room while he fetched coffee.

"This is Tim Horton's," he said with the pride of a barista offering me some shade-grown varietal from the island of East Timor. "Chief sends me twice a week to fuckin' Edmundston for the stuff, but it's good, aye?"

I nodded, but I had never been a connoisseur of the bean.

"Can I ask you a personal question, MacLoon?"

"Depends what it's about." He rhymed the last word with *a boot.*

"Where are you from originally?"

"Allagash! Scots Irish through and through. Why are you asking that question?"

"I couldn't place your accent."

I hadn't realized that some English speakers on the Maine side of the border had picked up the pronunciations of their neighbors to the north. Given that the TV set in the break room was turned to the Canadian Broadcasting Corporation (Harry and Meghan's new digs), it made sense.

"So this strangulation?" MacLoon began. "Got to be the boyfriend. Don't you think? Always is in these cases."

"Not always."

"You'll change your tune when you meet Roland. They're bringing him in now, the greasy fuck."

A state trooper brought in Roland Michaud fifteen minutes later. There was a stir in the building when he arrived. I made sure to slip into the hallway to have a second look at the bear-faced man.

He wasn't wearing cuffs, which meant he wasn't under arrest, which meant he had agreed to undergo the interview voluntarily. That worried me. He was dressed in a corduroy trucker's jacket over a black T-shirt and the reinforced canvas pants preferred by loggers. He looked like he'd showered for the occasion, the way his beard glistened under the overhead lights.

"Here you are again," he said when he saw me in the hallway.

"I'm sorry about Angie."

"No, you're not."

One thing I have learned about criminals is that a life of compulsive lying and manipulation makes it almost impossible for them to accept any expression of sympathy as genuine. They assume the rest of us are just as cold and self-centered as they are.

MacLoon seated Roland Michaud in an interrogation room about the size of a phone booth. It contained two chairs separated by a small table with a one-way mirror on the wall through which we could observe the conversation and listen via intercom.

The suspect asked for a Pepsi. When MacLoon returned with a Coke, Roland complained.

While we waited for Zanadakis, I watched Roland through the mirror with the state trooper who'd brought him in. Michaud extended his thickly muscled legs under the table. Every once in a while, he smiled at his bearded reflection, knowing we were hiding behind it.

"Where did you find him?" I asked the trooper.

"At his trailer. He keeps it on a lot on Falls Pond in Dickey. We've been over there more than once. He's a fan of fireworks at all hours of the night. His neighbors love him to death."

I should have realized he had a local residence since he damn well wasn't living in the rubble of his former home. "He came willingly, then?"

"Didn't even argue."

"Shit," I said.

"Why?"

"What about a lawyer? Did he ask for one?"

"No."

"Shit," I said again.

Roland had an alibi. And the odds were that it was solid.

Zanadakis arrived, soaked to the skin. He removed his dripping trench coat and handed it to a trooper to hang somewhere to dry. Then he excused himself to use the bathroom to towel off. He returned five minutes later looking no less waterlogged, but having washed off the bug spray.

MacLoon brought him a mug of Tim Horton's finest.

"Before you get started," I said, "you need to know that Roland Michaud was positively the man I saw at Angie's house two days ago."

"Did they argue?"

"No."

He ran a hand through his still-damp hair and went into the interrogation room.

Zanadakis introduced himself and took his seat. There were a few minutes of chitchat. We listened through the speaker that piped the conversation into the sweltering room.

"Do you know why we asked you to come in?" the detective asked.

"I'll take a wild guess. It has something to do with a dead girl at the Valley View?"

His French accent seemed more pronounced than I'd remembered. Maybe it was being back in the Valley.

"Evangeline Bouchard was your girlfriend, I understand."

"Your word, not mine. We drank and smoked together, and we had sex."

"You don't seem broken up over her death."

"I'm grieving on the inside."

"This is going to go faster if you don't act cute."

Roland winked at the mirror. "Gee, Detective, I think you're cute, too."

The door to our little room opened, and it was Stan Kellam. He said nothing as he squeezed in. We had already been standing shoulder to shoulder. Now we were packed together as if testing the approved load limit of an elevator.

Zanadakis's voice came over the speaker: "For the record, I want to state that you have waived your rights to have an attorney present. Is that correct?"

"*Oui.*"

"When was the last time you saw Angie Bouchard?"

"Yesterday in Presque Isle. We had plans to go to Edmundston. Guy I know just opened a bar there. Le Cyclope. Angie told me she couldn't come. She wanted to check on the motel. She thought someone might buy it someday. What a joke that was!"

"And you didn't offer to go with her?"

"No."

"And you got back home when?"

"Two hours ago. More or less."

"Where did you stay when you were in Edmundston?"

"I didn't get her name."

"That might be a problem for you."

"Fuck no, it won't."

"And why's that?"

"Because I was in Canada. Get it? I went through customs two nights ago in Edmundston. And I came back through Fort Kent today. Talk to the agents. Check their video. I'm not your killer, Detective."

"Thank you for clearing that up."

"My pleasure."

Roland removed his jacket to reveal that his black T-shirt was sleeveless. I could see his bare arms all the way to the shoulders. Once again, I saw the raised scar that reminded me of a cattle brand.

"How does it feel being back in this room?" Zanadakis asked.

"This is actually my first time here. If you're referring to the shit that went down when my old man was murdered, those interviews took place in Houlton. You weren't there then, or I would have remembered you, as handsome as you are."

"You're quite the charmer, Roland."

"I have a gift."

"Did Angie mention being scared of anyone or anything when you last saw her?"

"There was a creep who showed up at her place. Stupid-looking son of a bitch. He claimed to be a game warden, but he wasn't dressed like one. I think he might have been an impostor. You should check on him."

"We'll do that. Anyone else bothering her?"

"Nope."

"The Valley View has been closed for two years and is in rough shape. What made Angie decide she needed to cancel her plans in Edmundston and rush back there?"

"She didn't say."

"And you didn't ask?"

"We had an agreement. She didn't butt into my life, and I didn't butt into hers."

I pressed a button on the intercom so that I could be heard in the interrogation room. "Ask him about the brand on his arm."

Zanadakis glared into the mirror with obvious disapproval.

"This thing," Roland said, fingering the circle of raised scar tissue below the shoulder bone. "I got this when I was a kid. It was kind of an initiation ritual. Everyone had to get one if you wanted to be in the club."

I pushed the button again. "What club was that?"

He had recognized my voice. "The Fuck You Club."

"Calm down, Mr. Michaud," said the detective.

When Roland rose to his feet, it was like a bear rearing up on his hind legs. In spite of himself, Zanadakis gave a start and pushed himself from the table.

"That's him, isn't it? The warden investigator?"

"Never mind that."

"I want to leave now," the big man said. "Is that OK, or do you need permission from the man in the mirror?"

36

Zanadakis had no grounds to hold Roland Michaud, not even as a material witness. The border had hardened in the past decade with the arrival of surveillance drones and undetectable sensors. On occasion, people still managed to slip back and forth over "the slash"—the cleared strip in the woods between the United States and Canada—but most of them triggered an alarm in the process that brought hard-assed Border Patrol agents swarming.

In other words, it was just about impossible that Roland Michaud could have strangled Angie Bouchard if his Canadian alibi checked out.

The next interviewee came in with none of the same cocky confidence.

Jon Egan had been another member of Pierre Michaud's poaching crew. Unlike Roland, though, he hadn't escaped a term in prison. Pellerin had observed him selling drugs to teenagers. It was his second stay in the joint. He'd only gotten out, Kellam told me, three years ago.

"He never talked, though," said Stan as we stood together behind the mirror. "You've got to admire that."

"Why?"

"Because he didn't break and give up his friends."

"That isn't a code of honor," I said. "It's a code of stupidity."

Before Kellam could respond, Zanadakis ushered Egan into the interrogation room.

The first thing that struck me about Jon Egan, aside from his diminutive height and the shock of red hair, was how many layers of clothing he was wearing. In this heat, he wore a green chamois shirt over a hooded sweatshirt over a tee. His baggy work pants hinted at long johns underneath. And his boots were tall neoprene LaCrosses. For all the padding, his stomach remained perfectly flat. Jon Egan had a lower body fat percentage than a marathon champion from the Horn of Africa.

"How is he not sweating?" I said to no one in particular.

The little man didn't sprawl in his seat, as Roland had done, but perched on the edge, his hands on his knees under the table. Almost at once, he began rocking back and forth.

"Can I get you something to drink, Jon?" asked Zanadakis.

"Milk maybe." His voice was deeper than I had expected.

The request amused Kellam. "Milk! That's a new one."

The detective said that there was, alas, no milk to be had, at which point he launched directly into his interview.

"Why did you decide to stop at the Valley View?"

"I used to plow the lot for Emmeline and do odd jobs and stuff. I have to pass the motel to go anywhere since I live at the end of the road in Allagash. I got in the habit of checking on the place even after Emmeline died."

"Why?"

"I knew it was Angie's legacy. That's the wrong word. I knew it was her inheritance. She hoped to sell it, and I didn't want kids accidentally burning it down."

"That's very generous of you."

"I don't know about that."

With his rust-red hair, his small stature, and his restlessness, I understood why he reminded Kellam of a red squirrel, but I had expected him to be feistier, more combative. This nervous man seemed one harsh word away from breaking into tears.

"Maybe you had a crush on Angie?" said the detective.

"She's just a kid!"

"She was past the age of consent."

"I've got a new family. I've got a baby boy."

Zanadakis opened a folder on the desk between them. "I'd like to believe you, Jon. I really would. Unfortunately, I have your criminal records. I have the transcript from your first trial—the one that sent you to prison when you were twenty."

"I was drunk," said the jittery man. "It was an accident."

"You *accidentally* removed your erect penis from your jeans in Riverside Park while a troop of Girl Scouts just happened to be there picking up trash."

"I had to piss. I get hard if I hold it too long."

"You couldn't have waited to use the port-o-potty?"

"That's all ancient history," he said.

"Those who forget the past are condemned to repeat it. That's a quote from Santayana."

"I don't listen to that kind of music. I prefer country."

"Getting back to this morning. Who knows that you have a habit of checking the motel parking lot?"

"My wife. Maybe some of the guys at Two Rivers."

"That's the diner in Allagash?"

"Yeah."

"Does Roland Michaud eat there?"

"Sometimes. When he's around. Lots of people do. The food is good." He brought a hand out from under the table to gnaw at his cuticles. "Why would I have reported the body if I'd been the one who'd strangled her? Especially when people know my history with the motel."

"That's an excellent point," said the detective. "One answer might be that you were counting on your connection to the Valley View to exculpate you. You counted on the police saying, 'Who could possibly be so dumb as to do that? It couldn't have been Egan.'"

"I ain't dumb," he said.

"So we *should* consider you as a suspect, you mean?"

"Now you're just trying to confuse me." He lifted the other hand from under the table and began to rub his shoulder as if he had a knot in the muscle.

"Where were you last night, Jon?"

"I went into Fort Kent to pick up a prescription and some Cadbury eggs for Dorothy, my wife. I got the receipts somewhere in my truck. I can prove I ain't lying."

"So you passed the motel on your way back home?"

He hadn't stopped massaging his shoulder. People under stress engage in what are known as self-soothing behaviors. We stroke the backs of our necks. We absently knead our legs.

"That's right."

"Did you check the parking lot?"

A light came into his eyes. He looked like a drowning man being thrown a life ring. "I did!"

"And Angie's car wasn't there?"

"No."

"What time was this?" asked Zanadakis.

"Eight o'clock, thereabouts. Not quite dark but close enough that I watched for deer and moose the whole way. They come out of the woods this time of year to get away from the bugs."

I pressed the intercom. "What kind of truck do you drive, Mr. Egan?"

The man nearly leaped out of his skin. He seemed to have been utterly unaware of being watched through the mirror. He actually pivoted both ways in his seat, not knowing where the voice had come from.

"Toyota Tacoma."

Too small to have been my monster.

The detective paused before forging ahead again. "Did Angie call you yesterday to tell you she was coming back to St. Ignace?"

"Why would she?"

"So you were surprised this morning to find her car there. Did you recognize it as hers?"

"I never seen it before. Last time I seen her, she was driving a Honda Civic."

"Tell us what you did next."

"I parked and got out and came around to the driver's side. I saw the window was down and there was a girl inside, and

I figured she was passed out, because a normal sleeping person would have reclined in her seat, you know? She had to be drunk or high was what I thought. Because the rain had come in through the window, too."

"Did you touch her?"

"Not at first. I tried speaking. Then shouting. But she didn't budge. I thought, too, maybe I recognized her—the back of her head. Angie has her mom's hair. So I touched her and nothing happened, and then I saw the marks on her neck."

"What did you do then?"

"Ran back to my truck and called 911."

"Did you approach her car again?"

"No, sir."

"So the only thing you touched in the vehicle was Angie herself?"

"Yes," he said. "Maybe. I don't know."

"Think carefully."

"My memory ain't great to begin with. Dorothy can vouch for that. My wife."

He turned to the mirror then. It must have finally dawned on him that he had audience.

"I been in prison twice in my life," he said. "When I got out the last time, I told Dorothy I'd die before I went back inside again. I ain't the man I was. She's got me reading the Bible. I never should have been in that park with that bottle of whiskey when those girls were there. And I never should have gotten tangled up with the Michauds. I can see as how you wouldn't believe an individual with my past history, but I wouldn't have harmed that girl even if I'd been tempted. I'm a coward is the reason. If I see blue lights in my rearview mirror, I just about shit my pants. I'm that afraid of going back to prison. I've done things I ain't proud of—wicked things. But the Bible says all who seek for redemption will find it. Even the thief on the cross was forgiven."

It was proof of Egan's timidity that he sat there another twenty minutes, enduring Zanadakis's questions, without once asking for a lawyer. As a felon, he had gone through this drill many times before. He knew his rights. With Roland, the refusal to ask for counsel had been an act of bravado. But Egan seemed afraid of provoking the ire of the police.

I found myself pitying him until I remembered the role he had surely played in the death of Warden Investigator Scott Pellerin.

When the redheaded man was finally told he was free to leave, I mumbled something about needing to use the bathroom. Instead I snuck out the front door of the station and waited for Egan to emerge.

The rain had eased up while I'd been inside, but the air was so saturated with moisture it felt like a downpour could occur at any moment. A rusty blackbird landed on the asphalt, almost at my feet, to gobble a drowned earthworm.

I made a point of inspecting the only Toyota Tacoma in the lot. It had a Meyer plow mount on the front and a rack of amber lights on the roof. There were rust holes around the wheel wells wide enough to stick a finger through. But it wasn't the truck that had tried to force me off the cliff into the St. John River. I peeked into the bed and saw the usual items: empty beer and soda cans, cable ties, candy bar wrappers, and a single shotgun shell casing.

It was the last item that engaged my interest. I found a discarded pen on the ground and slid the tip inside the shotshell.

Finding Egan's fingerprints on the crimped plastic might not be enough to gain a warrant to search the felon's house for another firearm, but the hull alone was sufficient for my purposes.

I hid it behind my back until Egan stepped out into the weak, wet light.

He came to a startled stop when he saw me. The badge on my belt announced my identity as a law enforcement officer. He approached warily.

"You must be happy to be out of there," I said.

He fumbled for a pack of Gold Crests in one of his many pockets. "I'll be happier to get home."

"I was one of the guys watching you through the mirror. I'm a warden investigator. My name is Mike Bowditch."

"Yeah?"

I removed the shell, balanced on the pen, from behind my back. "I found this in your truck bed, Mr. Egan. It suggests you might have a shotgun at home in violation of the law."

He couldn't have spit out the words any faster. "It ain't mine."

"So if I have it dusted for prints—?"

"If you heard me, you know I ain't stupid enough to risk going back to prison. I got a new life now."

"I'm not looking to put the squeeze on you, Egan. I'm just hoping you'll do me a favor."

He shook a cigarette from the pack, stuck it on his lip, and now endeavored to locate a lighter. "What favor?"

"Show me your upper left arm?"

"What for?"

"I'll explain after you indulge me."

His hand trembled as he clicked the lighter. "And if I don't, what happens?"

I raised the pen with the shotgun hull on it.

"You want me to take off my shirts, right now, in the rain and the cold."

"It's not currently raining," I said. "And the temperature, the last I looked, was close to eighty degrees."

"I won't do it."

"Your choice. But I'm taking this with me." I opened a pocket on my rain jacket and maneuvered the shotshell so it dropped inside. "I'll give you the afternoon to change your mind. Here's my number."

I handed him a business card.

For an instant, I thought he would rip it up, but instead he slid it into his back pocket.

I watched him drive off, knowing that I'd found the weak link in the chain.

But if I knew Egan could break, others did, too. What was his life expectancy under these dangerous circumstances?

37

As I returned to the station, I met Kellam coming out. With him was the local chief of police: a stocky man with olive skin, silver hair, and luxuriant black eyebrows. He was resplendent in a bright blue shirt with epaulettes, ribbons, and medals. His navy pants had satin stripes down the sides.

"Mike," said Kellam. "Do you know Chief Plourde?"

"No, but I have heard of the investigator," said the police chief in heavily accented English. I'd met more than a few Francophones since I'd arrived in the Valley, but Chief Plourde was the first who struck me as someone who'd clung to his accent as a point of cultural pride. "Your exploits have made the news, even up here."

"We're headed over to the Swamp Buck," said Kellam with disconcerting friendliness. "How'd you like to tag along, Mike?"

The only thing I'd had to eat all day was a granola bar. I kept a box of them in my truck because I so often found myself in the woods, miles from the nearest store or restaurant.

"Why not?"

"Do you need a ride?" Kellam asked. "Mike flipped his vehicle out on Route 161."

"I was driving too fast in the rain." For the time being, I had decided to stick with my cover story.

"That's a treacherous road," agreed the chief.

"The Scout ran fine all the way here. Even if it looks like I stole it from a junkyard."

Kellam insisted on showing Plourde my vehicle up close. "Chief, you'd better give your boys a heads-up about Mike's truck so they don't pull him over for a busted taillight."

Plourde chuckled, but his good humor didn't seem to be at my expense.

The sight of my battered Scout hurt in more ways than one. It made me remember the physical aches and pains I'd managed to forget during the interrogations. The agony of knowing my trusty ride was likely headed for the scrap heap hurt worse.

At least the engine turned over. I might need to tape up the passenger window with some plastic sheeting to keep out the rain, but I was still mobile for the time being.

I found a new text from Kathy Frost waiting:

> Temperature down to 100 degrees and steady.
> Sleeping now.
> Her family's here wondering where you are.
> What should I say?

Kathy would have done her best to explain, but an explanation is not an excuse, and Dani's mom and brothers had a right to question what kind of boyfriend I was.

In the past I had dated civilians who hadn't appreciated the demands of my job. With Dani Tate, I could take comfort knowing that, as a cop herself, she would understand.

Wouldn't she?

Fort Kent was a small town, and there was no missing the Swamp Buck. The restaurant, on Main Street, had the aura of a local institution. The first sound I heard, coming through the door, was boisterous laughter. True to the name, there were antler light fixtures hanging from the ceiling and moose horns mounted on the walls.

Plourde and Kellam had arrived before I did and been given a seat of honor near the window, where the chief could see and be seen. The older officers sat side by side, forcing me to face them across the table. Clearly they had questions.

Roland's and Egan's interrogations might have been over for the day, but mine was just beginning.

The young woman who came to our table greeted the chief in French, then switched automatically to unaccented English when she addressed Kellam and me. She looked to be all of fifteen years old and gawky as an egret.

The chief ordered a swamp burger with a side of poutine and a cup of King Cole tea.

Kellam ordered something called a *sour cream salad* and a twenty-ounce glass of Molson Golden.

I asked for a tuna sandwich and a cup of coffee. "And a side of ployes."

These were thin buckwheat pancakes, served with butter: the traditional accompaniment to any Acadian meal. My grandmother used to make them whenever I visited their humble mill worker's house. Both she and my grandfather had died of the blood cancer that seemed epidemic in Maine factory towns that had processed pulp into paper.

Our server couldn't have been more apologetic. "We don't serve ployes here. I'm sorry."

I had been looking forward to the French Canadian delicacy. I missed my barely remembered grandparents.

Chief Plourde registered my disappointment. "How can you have a restaurant in the Valley that doesn't serve ployes? I tell you, we are losing our culture. The children, they don't learn French at home. Families don't travel between countries like they used to."

"I thought ICE had made it easier for the locals to cross."

"In theory, yes. But there are always new agents who are strangers here—they have come from the south where there is the feeling of a war—and they do not appreciate the specialness of the Valley."

I wasn't sure about customs agents, but I knew that every Border Patrol agent in Maine had been trained in the no-man's-land of South Texas, Arizona, or California. There, they were taught to regard all foreigners as prospective—if not presumptive—criminals.

Before 9/11, Americans and Canadians had crossed back and forth over the international bridge, often several times a day, with nothing more than a wave at the officer in the customs booth. They might live in Madawaska but shop in Edmundston, buy their prescriptions in Clair but gas up in Fort Kent. The collapse of the World Trade Center towers had sent shock waves that rippled all the way to northernmost Maine. With a butcher's cleaver, the Department of Homeland Security had severed a unique and vibrant community older than the Constitution itself.

Our server returned with our drinks.

Chief Plourde emptied five packets of Splenda into his tea. "Stanley says you're a friend of my friend Charley Stevens."

"That's right."

"I thought I saw him in town last night. But the man I saw was bald."

"Charley's up here," said Kellam. "He's poking around."

I put down my coffee mug. "I wouldn't know."

"Give me a little credit, Mike. Pellerin was like a son to Stevens. I'm wise to the game you two are playing."

Chief Plourde stirred his tea, then licked the sweetener from the spoon. "Charley, he was never satisfied with the outcome of the investigation, I remember."

"It had to do with not finding Pellerin's remains," I said.

"He didn't trust the findings," said Plourde. "The official report. He returned here often to ask questions. Not so much anymore."

All that was left in Kellam's beer glass was foam. "As far as I'm concerned, Mike, the two of you have Angie Bouchard's blood on your hands."

"For Christ's sake, Stan," I said. "Why did you invite me here? Was it just to insult me?"

Three middle-aged women were seated in a nearby booth. Although it was only midday, all of them wore dresses suited for a fancy dinner out, were made up with lipstick and mascara, and smelled of three different perfumes. One had tinted hair that reminded me of sangria. The second had hair as red as an overripe tomato. The third's was solid platinum.

Tomato raised a painted finger. "The Lord's name. You should not take it in vain."

"But we will forgive him because he is very handsome," said Platinum with a smile.

"Your young friend is a detective, no?" said Sangria with the same flirtatiousness. "He is here to arrest the man who killed Evangeline Bouchard?"

"Ladies, if you'll excuse us," said Kellam. "This is a private conversation."

"*Affaires de police,*" added the chief in the honeyed tone of a born politician. "*Je suis sûr que vous comprenez.*"

"*Pfff!*" said Tomato, unsatisfied.

During the exchange, I dug out my phone and opened up the photos app. I thumbed through the dozens I had taken of files Kellam had given me until I found one of the autopsy shots taken of the late Zacharie Michaud after his suicide.

I held the screen out for Kellam to see. "What would you say that was on his upper arm?"

He squinted at the screen, refusing to reach for his reading glasses. "Looks like a burn. What do you think, Chief?"

"A burn, yes."

"To me, it looks like a brand," I said. "Like someone drove a heated piece of iron into the muscle and charred the flesh."

"That's why you asked Roland that question," said Kellam. He sounded almost impressed.

"Roland has the same mark on the same arm. He said he got it when he joined a club. Nowhere in Pellerin's reports did I find anything about Pierre Michaud and his associates all having brands. Can you remember if he ever mentioned these burns to you, Stan?"

"I have no memory of it," said Kellam, raising his beer glass so the server could see he needed a refill.

"What about Pierre Michaud? Did he have a scar like that, too?"

"No," said the chief. "I was there when they dragged his body from *le lac*. They pulled off his shirt to find the bullet hole. It had passed through the muscle here." He indicated his collarbone. "I would have remembered a burn like this."

Kellam leaned his thick forearms on the table. "What exactly are you suggesting, Mike? That these guys conducted some sort of midnight ritual before Pierre admitted them into his top-secret poaching society?"

"Wouldn't Egan have one as well, then?" said Chief Plourde, showing deductive powers I had doubted he possessed.

"Maybe we should chase him down, strip his clothes off him, and have a look," said Kellam, glancing again toward the server. Clearly he needed another beer.

"I'm serious about this, Stan."

"No, you're not," he said. "You can't even say what it means."

"If Roland, Zach, and Egan all have the same brand, and Pierre didn't, I find it suggestive."

"Of what?"

"Maybe old man Michaud gave it to them."

"And why would he do that?"

"I don't know."

I wasn't facing the door, but the two older men were, and I noticed the chief sit up as a bell rang behind me.

I twisted my neck and saw Chasse Lamontaine, still in uniform, enter the restaurant accompanied by a young man, early twenties, who could only have been his son. He had the same ash-blond hair and rugged jawline. But unlike his old man, he was dressed like a civilian in a logo T-shirt, jeans that were distressed almost to the point of disintegration, and mud-caked boots that made the host go in search of a broom to clean up the tracks he left behind.

Father and son approached our table.

"*Bonjour*, Chasse!" said one of the women at the next booth. They all joined in, as giggly as teens.

"Don't you three ladies look beautiful," said Chasse.

"*Pfff!*" said Tomato.

Sangria said, "Your son, he looks more and more like you. *Très beau.*"

The son had no apparent interest in older women; he didn't answer or give them a glance.

"Excuse us, ladies," said the father, turning toward our table. Chasse had good manners, I had to hand it to him.

I could read the words screen-printed on the younger Lamontaine's shirt:

> *MUDHOLES*
> *THE ONLY PLACE*
> *WHERE PULLING OUT*
> *IS ENJOYABLE*

Chasse smiled without opening his lips. "C. J., you haven't met Warden Investigator Bowditch."

I rose from my seat to shake the younger Lamontaine's hand. "Good to meet you."

He was one of those young men who need to show their toughness with a death grip.

"You men having lunch?" asked Kellam.

"We grabbed subs at Subway," said Chasse. "We just happened to see you in the window as we were driving by. We wanted to see if the detective has spoken with Roland yet."

"Why?" I asked, settling back down in my seat.

He lowered his voice so that the women wouldn't hear, but the gesture was futile; they had ceased speaking and were clumsily eavesdropping. "Who else could have killed her?"

"He has an alibi," I said. "He was across the border at the time."

"Bullshit," said C. J., who had inherited his father's good looks but none of his charm. "Angie was terrified of that asshole. I saw him hit her once. Roland definitely killed her."

His father put a hand on the young man's shoulder. "This isn't the place for this conversation, son."

From my seat, I looked up at him. "Maybe you should tell Detective Zanadakis about what you saw, C. J."

He reacted as if I'd challenged him to a fistfight. "Maybe I will."

Chief Plourde had trouble rising from the table—his stomach was in the way. "When are we going muskie fishing, Warden Lamontaine? You keep promising to take me, but you never do. Meanwhile, in Collins's store, I see the photos of the trophies people have been catching. There was one fish last week weighing forty pounds!"

"When things settle down, maybe."

The chief, grinning, held out his arms to their full wingspan. "You promised me a fish like this."

But Chasse had turned his attention back to Kellam. "What's this I hear about Charley Stevens being in town?"

"Ask Mike."

"Maybe he came here to catch one of your fabled muskellunges," I said.

Kellam broke in. "Shouldn't you be on patrol, Chasse?"

"You're not my lieutenant anymore, Stan," said Chasse.

"True, but I've got your sergeant's number on speed dial."

"Ha!"

The server arrived with our lunches (and Kellam's second beer), and the Lamontaines used that as an excuse to leave. The son gave us a scowl on the way out.

None of us spoke until the server had left our booth.

"What's the deal with Chasse's son?" I said, then took a bite into one of the best tuna sandwiches I'd ever eaten. "What's with the attitude?"

"C. J. wanted to be a game warden," said Kellam. "He applied for a job with the service last year. Chasse asked me to put in a word for the kid."

"Did you?"

"Actually I put in five words: *Don't fucking hire the cocksucker.*"

Chief Plourde counted off the words on his stubby fingers. "That's six."

"*Cocksucker* is one word," said Kellam with a leering grin. "You of all people should know that, Chief."

"*Dégage.*"

I was unfamiliar with the word but could guess the meaning.

The redheaded woman whom I had come to think of as Tomato cleared her throat. She had overheard the profanities and scowled at the three of us.

"*Désolé,*" said the chief.

But Tomato was having none of his apology. "*Pffft!*" she said again and returned to her salad.

38

As I made my way along the sidewalk, I thought about the brands on the arms of Roland and Zacherie Michaud. The burns were not identical—hadn't been made by an instrument forged to leave an identifying mark. It was more like the brothers had been jabbed with sizzling blacksmith's tongs.

I had no doubt Egan bore a similar scar. He would have been photographed during his intake to the county jail and later the Maine State Prison. Finding a picture of his upper arm would take me all of fifteen minutes' worth of phone calls.

Maybe the mark was just a rite of initiation: the necessary act before you were admitted into Pierre Michaud's confidence. The fact that the poacher king himself hadn't had the same raised scar strongly suggested he'd been the one who'd inflicted it. The man had hot irons aplenty at his smithy.

I was torn about what to do next.

I couldn't get past the guilt of not being at Dani's side. The fact that Kathy said her temperature had stabilized seemed like yet another rationalization. Her fever could always worsen again.

And yet I could hear Charley's cryptic message as clearly now as when he'd said it. "They're not going to stop now—not after what just happened. All we need is another day. We're so close to the truth, and they're getting sloppy."

Should I find a hardware store where I could buy supplies to patch up my truck? Maybe book a room for the night at the motel across the street from the border checkpoint?

I could begin asking around town who might own a monster truck customized for mudding expeditions. In a few hours, I should easily be able to narrow the list to fifty individuals—not counting the "jeep abusers" across the border.

In the end, I did none of these things because when I returned to my Scout, I found a note on my seat.

MEET ME AT 7 AT THE FORT

The note had been written on a brown paper towel of the kind you find in gas station restrooms. The writing was done in block letters. The ink was blue and didn't bleed into the paper. So probably a cheap ballpoint pen.

My first thought was that Charley had left it for me, but there was something about the note's terse anonymity that made me discard that possibility.

Who, then?

There was no lack of candidates.

It could have been Chasse Lamontaine or any of the law enforcement officers I'd dealt with that day (excepting Plourde, who, likewise, hadn't left the restaurant). It could have been Nick Francis, who seemed to be assisting Charley in this madcap investigation. It could have been Roland Michaud, for that matter, as he'd seen my vehicle outside Angie's house. Or maybe Egan had changed his mind about talking to me (had he seen me drive off in the Scout?). Last but not least, it could have been the son of a bitch who'd tried to run me off the road. Just because a trap is poorly set doesn't mean it's not a trap.

At least I didn't have to guess at the indicated location.

Fort Kent is named for a still-standing blockhouse made of rough-hewn timbers at the edge of the river. The structure commemorates the only bloodless war in American history.

Mere months after the Battle of Yorktown, Great Britain and the United States had begun quarreling over where to draw the new nation's northern border. The argument escalated over the decades to what became known as the Aroostook War of

1838–1839, when Congress authorized fifty thousand troops to march north, led by General Winfield Scott, later hero of the Mexican-American War.

For a year, American and British soldiers built fortifications and aimed cannons at each other across the St. John, but no shots were ever fired. The combatants chose negotiation over combat, and the international boundary between Maine and Canada was forever fixed by that agreement between Queen Victoria's canny emissary Lord Ashburton and the bedeviled Daniel Webster.

For a historic monument, the blockhouse couldn't have been more strangely situated. It was tucked behind a lumberyard at the edge of a residential neighborhood. Like the war it commemorated, Fort Kent seemed more of an afterthought than an important chapter in U.S. history.

I checked my watch and decided I had time to bandage up my Scout before my clandestine meeting. I paid a visit to a hardware store and filled a shopping cart with everything I would need to keep out the weather.

After I had taped up the window, I drove to the small wooded park that surrounded the fort and parked the Scout out of sight. Inside the vehicle, under the still-functioning dome light, I checked my Beretta, then dropped three fifteen-round magazines into the pockets of my Fjallraven jacket where I could grab them in a gunfight.

I tested the razor edge of my knife against the hair along the back of my hand. It was a Gerber 06 automatic that my friend Billy Cronk, Logan's dad, had carried with him in Iraq and Afghanistan. Occasionally when I was sharpening it, I would experience a disquieting sensation that made me think Billy had killed a man in combat with this blade.

The last weapon I took was the baton Maglite I had used as a patrol warden. The thing was as long as my forearm and required six D-cell batteries, but it could light up the eyes of a raccoon across a football field. As a last resort, the metal tube could serve as a makeshift club capable of shattering a nose.

At this latitude, there should have been two more hours of daylight, but the low ceiling of clouds meant that darkness would arrive before civil twilight. Shadows would be seeping from every tree at the time of the meeting.

While I waited, I sent an email to Ora telling her I had seen her husband, that he was alive and well, but he had slipped away again. I told her I hoped to find him again soon. I also asked that she alert me when her daughter arrived from Florida.

The thought of my ex-girlfriend returning to Maine disquieted me. Even from two thousand miles away, Stacey had cast a shadow over my relationship with Dani. She still made guest appearances in my dreams, often in risqué scenarios. Despite my best efforts, I found myself drawing comparisons. Dani came out on the better end of most of the pros and cons. But not all of them.

Dani's recent declaration that she would never have children had rattled me. I had always assumed I would be a father. I desperately wanted a son or daughter in fact. But I loved Dani. I wasn't sure what I would do if I believed she was resolute in her desire to remain childless.

As I had feared, my body had begun to stiffen and ache from the crash. My shoulder hurt especially. I tried to clear my head and rest, but my worries wouldn't leave me alone.

Eventually, I drew my hood over my head and left the shelter of my vehicle. Being outdoors was the only reliable way I knew to quiet my troubled mind.

The fort loomed in the failing light: a square, top-heavy structure, with a second floor that was greater in area than the first. The roof was shaped like a pyramid. The blockhouse might have looked like something out of *The Last of the Mohicans* if not for the lawn-mounted spotlights, shining up against the graffiti-carved, rough-hewn walls.

Beyond the fort, the land tumbled down to a lower parking lot with picnic tables and steel grills. Under the sheltering leaves of ancient maples, I wandered down the hill to the water's edge. There, I stood upon the banks of the Fish River as it rushed to join the St. John.

Both rivers must have recently flooded, because there was mud smeared ten feet up the tree trunks, and everything on the ground—the dead leaves, the severed branches, even the discarded bottles and cans—was gunky with grime.

I took up a position behind a sugar maple as old as the fort itself and waited.

At fifteen minutes to seven, I spotted headlights coming down the one-way drive. The car did not turn in to the parking lot. Instead it continued on to the adjacent lumberyard. I had no view of the higher ground. I could only listen. I heard a car door being closed with care. No voices.

The park had become a patchwork of light and shadows. Illumination from the fort and the lumberyard lit up swatches between the trees, but there were just as many dark places. I watched for a flashlight beam to spark to life, but the driver seemed comfortable moving in darkness.

Finally, a silhouette rose atop the hill: a person in a hooded poncho.

He or she stood there a minute, and I suspected they were debating whether to wait for me in the light or find their own nest of shadows in which to hide themselves. They chose the shadows.

I watched the person in the poncho begin to pick their way down the hill. The leaves were slick and muddy, but my mystery visitor seemed as sure-footed as a goat.

They were halfway down when I made my move.

"Hold it!"

Startled, they lost their balance. They waved their arms like a flightless bird, then plopped to the ground. They slid on their backside down the rest of the hill.

I was on them fast. One hand rested on the grip of my Beretta. The other brought up the Maglite to shine straight into their eyes.

A brown face squinted up at me from inside the hood of a green poncho.

"Vaneese?"

She covered her eyes with the back of her arm. "Mike? Is that you?"

"What are you doing here?"

"I left you a note. Can you turn off the light, please?"

After I clicked the switch, the darkness flowed back in like water welling from the river. I moved my right hand away from my gun and extended it in her direction.

"Hold out your arm."

She did, and I grabbed her thin wrist. She weighed next to nothing. When she had regained her footing, I guided her out from under the trees into a pool of misted light.

"What's this about, Vaneese? Why all the secrecy?"

"I needed to warn you. It's Stanley. I've never seen him like this before. I think he plans on hurting someone."

39

We sat in her car to get out of the weather. It was a Subaru Crosstrek, late model, low miles. The absence of dog hairs on the upholstery told me Ferox was not permitted rides. Although the interior was as clean-smelling as could be, a tree-shaped air freshener hung from the rearview mirror.

Vaneese kept digging the nails of her right hand into her thigh, leaving scratches in the denim. Every stray car that passed, its headlights sweeping the inside of the Subaru, made her catch her breath.

I tapped the fragrant triangle of cardboard dangling before us. "Do you know what cops used to call these?"

She shook her head.

"Felony forests."

"I don't understand the term."

"People carrying drugs think air fresheners mask the smell of narcotics in a car. All these things do is give the sniffer dogs sore sinuses. A person could write a thesis about criminals and their folklore. Maybe I should consider going back to school when I retire."

She had no response to this digression, but as I'd hoped, it worked to put her at ease.

"I almost didn't recognize your poor SUV," she said in her lovely accent. "Were you in an accident?"

"I slipped off the road in the rain," I said.

"Were you hurt?"

"Thank you for asking, but no, I'm uninjured—for once."
The windows began to fog. "What's this about, Vaneese? Why
do you think Stan is planning on hurting someone?

"After you and the other warden left," she said, "Stanley
went into the guest room and brought out the boxes of files. He
spread the papers on the dining room table. He was trying to
discover what you'd been looking for. It was early, but he had
begun to drink heavily. I went to take a shower. When I came
downstairs, I saw him outside, talking to Edouard. He seemed
very angry, very insistent. I saw him give my brother the keys to
the farm truck."

I had a vision of a pickup roaring up behind me along the river
road. I heard the crash of my bumper crumpling. "What does
this farm truck look like?"

"It's old and rusty. Edouard uses it to carry firewood when he
cuts a tree."

"Do you know what a monster truck is?"

"Like from a demolition derby?"

"Does the farm truck have big tires? Does it ride high off the
ground?"

"Yes, I suppose."

The thought of Kellam dispatching Edouard Delhomme to kill
me was absurd. That wasn't to say it was impossible.

"Where did Stan tell Edouard to go?" I asked.

"*Le trou du rat*. That's Edouard's name for the cabin. It's a
place he hides sometimes from the ICE agents. I have never been
there. I don't think Stanley wants me to know where it is in case
I'm ever interviewed by the Border Patrol."

"Did you believe him? Did you believe that's where Edouard
went?"

"At first, yes, but when I asked why Stan thought ICE was
coming, he wouldn't say. He went into his den and locked the
door, and I think he called someone. When he came out, he was
very red in the face. His safe is inside. It is where he locks up his
guns. He took a pistol but tried to hide it in his raincoat. I could
see the impression."

"Did he tell you he was driving up here?"

"He said he thought he might be able to help the police catch the man who killed the girl. I asked him if he knew this Evangeline, and he said he met her a long time ago when she was a child. He knew her mother, he said."

"Stan and I had lunch together this afternoon." I resisted the urge to take her hand lest she misunderstand the intent of the gesture. "I can't say he was in a good mood, but he didn't seem like he was hell-bent on murder."

"Stan is an expert at hiding his emotions."

Not in my experience.

"You must've heard or seen something to make you so worried. You need to tell me what it was."

She stared at the misted windshield.

"Vaneese?"

"When he was in his den, I put my ear to the door. He was trying not to be loud, but I heard him say, 'He's going to destroy me.' And then he didn't want me to see that he took a pistol. Stanley doesn't hide his guns, because he is proud of them. He takes me target shooting."

"You're sure about the pistol?"

"I have the combination to the safe. It is a series of numbers. In case I need to protect myself while he is away. After he left, I went into the den to check, and he had changed the combination."

"Might he have done that before and forgotten to tell you?"

"No, because he told me to get a pistol yesterday while you were out on the lake. He never explained why. It was as if he expected someone dangerous to come to the lodge while he was gone. It was the usual combination."

I didn't know what to make of this admission, that while we'd been fishing, Stan had told Vaneese to arm herself. It was hardly comforting.

"I have never seen him violent before," she said. "But I have seen men before they commit violent acts."

As a foundation upon which to build a theory—that Stanley Kellam had come to the St. John Valley to injure some unnamed person—I wouldn't have called it rock-solid. But that was me thinking like a police officer. Vaneese knew and loved Kellam and understood when he was acting out of his worst impulses.

"What has Stan told you about Scott Pellerin's disappearance?" I asked.

"That it was Scott's own fault. That he was cocky and gave himself away. Because Stan was the supervisor, though, everyone blamed him. They said he should have gotten Scott out of the situation sooner. Your friend, the pilot, was the worst, Stan says."

Kellam had expressed a similar sentiment to me. I couldn't be certain if what he regretted was his misjudgments concerning Pellerin or the damage that the affair had on his career aspirations. He might have felt both emotions at once.

Vaneese started clawing at her thigh again. "It was Stan's plan to send in all those men into town at night. The politicians and the newspapers called it a 'raid,' but Stan said it was a rescue mission. Michaud started the fire that burned those buildings. The wardens were not responsible. But still everyone blamed Stan. And he was mad at your friend for killing Michaud before they could find out where he'd hidden Scott's body."

That simmering resentment explained Charley's reluctance to confront Kellam himself.

She reached for a tissue and dabbed the wad at her eyes. "Stanley said that his career ended that night. Before Scott, he was going to be the colonel. But the politicians made sure he would rise no higher."

"I want to get back to the phone call you overheard. You don't have any idea who he could have been speaking with?"

"No."

"What about the person who wants to destroy him?"

"Your friend, I think. Is that true? Does your friend wish to destroy Stan?"

She had been honest with me, and I felt she deserved the respect of a truthful answer. "It's possible he does."

"Why?"

"I'm not sure I can give you an answer that makes sense. Stan doesn't know you are in Fort Kent, does he?"

"No."

"What might he do if he finds out you came here to tell me these things?"

She reacted to this question by tensing the muscles in her face. Her eyes seemed overlarge in the dimness of the car. It was as if I had insulted her virtue.

"Stan loves me."

"That doesn't mean—"

"He has never hit me. He is the first man I've been with I can say that about. He would never hurt me no matter what I did."

As a law enforcement officer, you meet many women who are certain that their boyfriend or husband will never hurt them, not in a million years—until he breaks their arm.

For her sake, I hoped Vaneese was right about Stan.

———

When I returned to the Scout, I saw that the rain had found the weak point in the plastic that I had taped up as a makeshift window. I tried to reattach the tape, but the water had ruined the adhesive. I let the wet air seep inside.

Kellam hadn't mentioned where he was going after lunch. I had assumed back to Moccasin Pond. What would he do when he found Vaneese gone?

It pained me not to talk this through with Charley. He had said he'd been watching me. I wondered if he—or his proxy, Nick Francis—might be doing so now.

I couldn't leave the Valley, not yet. I hoped Dani would understand my decision. But until I knew Charley was safe, I couldn't absolve myself of the promise I had made to Ora.

I drove directly to the nearest motel. It was the one with the mile zero marker in its lot. I recognized Zanadakis's unmarked cruiser parked at the far end. It was a two-hour drive back to the nearest state police barracks, and no doubt the detective was as aware of the danger posed by night-wandering moose as I was.

Except for a nook with coffee and a rack of pamphlets advertising local attractions, the lobby felt like the living room of someone's French-speaking great-aunt.

"Sorry, but we are full up," said the awkward teenage girl behind the desk.

"Your sign says 'Vacancy.'"

"We just sold the last room a few minutes ago. I haven't had a chance to change it. I can call around and see if I can find a place for you."

"Is something going on in town?"

"The muskie derby."

Back in the 1960s, biologists in Québec had introduced muskellunges into Lac Frontière at the urging of local sportsmen. The fish are relatives of northern pike but are much larger and more aggressive, reaching lengths of nearly five feet and weighing as much as sixty pounds. They can live as long as thirty years. Their teeth are long and sharp enough to snip off your thumb.

Inevitably the super-predators got into the St. John watershed and made their way downstream into Maine, devastating every native species along the way. But at least the locals had found a way to cash in on the alien invasion. Maybe the people in the Everglades, plagued by pythons, needed to get creative with their economic development efforts.

"I thought the derby was in August," I said.

"The chamber of commerce is doing two this summer because there are so many fish. Are you sure I can't help you find a room? Where will you sleep?"

"My truck," I said. "It won't be the first time."

But in the past, the Scout still had windows to keep out the mosquitoes and the rain.

I was just about to leave when a realization smacked me in the forehead. "You're the girl who waited on me this afternoon at the Swamp Buck."

Her smile told me she appreciated being recognized. "This is my night job."

"It must keep you busy."

"I like to work," she said brightly. "But it does get hard during the potato harvest. I have to get up before dawn to get my hours in on the farm, too."

"Three jobs is a lot," I said.

"It is?" She seemed genuinely baffled.

I remembered seeing a drive-in campsite on the map of the Allagash River, just upstream of where it flowed into the St. John. Chances were that muskie fishermen had already "hoseyed" it, already laid a claim. The Valley wasn't short of clearings in the woods where I could park my vehicle for the night.

Thinking about Allagash village made me recall Jon Egan. The red squirrel lived there, I remembered.

The deep-woods hamlet was the terminus of one of America's great canoe trips. The federally protected Allagash Wilderness Waterway was a ninety-eight-mile chain of lakes, streams, and rivers through the heart of the northern forest. Most paddlers took a week to complete the journey, camping along the way at some of the most scenic sites imaginable. The Allagash was a place people put on bucket lists. It attracted paddlers from around the world.

Stacey and I had done the trip in five days. Even though we were young and fit, the effort had exhausted us. When we'd reached Allagash, we'd slept twelve hours at McKinnon's Lodge. The charming redhead who owned the place said the record had been set by a paddler who didn't awaken for thirty-six hours. She had been tempted to call her cousin, the mortician.

I could claim that I had forgotten that Stacey was headed north, that she would presumably be arriving in the morning in her father's borrowed plane, but it would be more accurate to say I had tamped down the thought. Seeing her again—and so soon—was more than I could deal with.

I needed to refocus on the problem before me.

Egan had stood up to hours of questioning after Pellerin went missing. He had done his full sentence in the prison Mainers nicknamed "Shawshank" after the Stephen King story and movie. He had never given up his secrets.

But Egan's circumstances had changed. He had a family, a baby. He was out from under Pierre Michaud's thumb, if not Roland's.

And someone had brutally killed Angie Bouchard. Whatever alternate theories Zanadakis felt compelled to explore, I knew her death was a direct result of that telltale badge. She had been killed to shut her up. Her murderer would know that Egan was a potential squealer.

What would Charley do?

Wrong question: *What was Charley doing?*

My friend would have the same instinct about Egan that I had. He would be watching the redheaded man closely. He would be waiting for him to panic and reveal some long-held secret. He would be preparing for Angie's murderer to come looking for blood.

40

The rain had stopped, but the temperature had risen. The clamminess made me remember something my father had told me about the war. In Vietnam, he had said, your uniform got soaked from two directions: from the mist seeping in and from your perspiration unable to escape.

Welcome to the jungle.

The road west along the St. John River had grown narrower with the ground fog. My nervous foot kept hitting the brake pedal. My imagination saw a looming moose around every bend.

Twenty miles out of Fort Kent, I again came to the crossroads. I passed the overgrown ruins of the Michauds' burned houses. Then the haunted Valley View Motel with its sad bilingual sign, now and forever vacant. Police tape hung across the entrance to the parking lot: a reflective ribbon. And then St. Ignace was behind me. The hamlet was no longer a real place, just words on a map that would, in time, disappear, too.

Finally, a handsome wooden sign, adorned with painted oak leaves, appeared in my lone headlight.

> ENTERING
> *A Scots/Irish Community*
> *Settled in 1838*

I lost my cell signal long before I reached town.

—

The village center sat at the looping confluence of the Allagash and the St. John Rivers. I paused in front of the lone eatery, closed for the night, and shined my flashlight onto the water-stained pages of my atlas, spread across the passenger seat. I had no idea where Jon Egan lived.

I only knew that I would recognize his Toyota Tacoma, with its distinctive plow mount and safety lights, when I saw it again. Most people in the area, I guessed, lived close to the roads. The lumber company that owned 99 percent of the land outside town had kept residential development confined to maximize the extent of its tree-felling operations.

Twin lights in the mist behind me announced the arrival of another vehicle—a large pickup, from the height of the beams—but before I could reach for my handgun, the truck stopped in the road. It was too far for me to identify the color, especially with its high beams on. The driver hesitated, but not more than fifteen seconds, then turned left onto a woods road.

Maybe someone tailing me, maybe not, but I had better things to do than go chasing it.

I made a slow circuit of the village, sparking the interest of more than a handful of watchdogs. Porch lights snapped on as I idled outside trailers. If I had been an Allagasher, I would have grabbed my gun if a junked Scout stopped outside my door.

Having found no sign of Egan, I crossed the Dickey Bridge. The span, above the St. John, was where the pavement ended. One could go no farther north in Maine except on private property. A handful of houses stretched out along the north bank.

I didn't spot any Tacomas parked outside these residences, so I followed the road north, losing hope with every tick of my odometer. Soon I would come upon yet another gatehouse and be forced to turn back. I couldn't even call anyone for assistance, my phone being useless.

I had just about given up when I saw the snowplow.

It was beached in the dooryard of a modular home. Two

ATVs were parked out front, his and hers, along with a Toyota 4Runner SUV that had seen better days.

The reason the plow caught my attention was its color. It wasn't the golden yellow of the snowplows made by the Maine-based company, Fisher. It was black and yellow: a Meyer Home-Plow. The same maker of the mount on Egan's pickup.

When I pulled into the drive, a dog began to bark inside the house. It didn't sound as fierce as Ferox, but even smaller breeds can take a hunk of meat from your calf. A motion-sensitive light came on, flooding the entire yard, catching a thousand moths and mayflies in midflight. A woman, holding a baby in her arms, appeared in the door. She had close-cropped blond hair and was dressed in mismatched sweats. She was at least twenty years younger than Egan. Taller, too, by almost a foot. A curly-haired spaniel peeked between her long legs.

Given the condition of my Scout and my unkempt appearance, I wouldn't have been surprised if she'd come out shooting.

"Jon ain't here!" she called from the stoop, as if this were her usual response to late-night visitors.

I swung open the door and stood behind it. "My name is Mike Bowditch. I'm an investigator with the Maine Warden Service. You're Dorothy, right?"

"Yeah, Jon told me about you. Said you interrogated him. He ain't around."

"Where is he?"

"Why? So you can go arrest him again? The cops have already crawled all over our house."

"Your husband was never arrested."

"We have nothing to hide."

"Can I come up?"

"I can hear you fine from there, Mister."

"I think Jon is in danger," I said. "Because of what happened to Angie Bouchard. You need to tell me where he is."

Cops routinely feed people bullshit to get them to cooperate. Dorothy Egan struck me as someone who knew this. I raised my hands where she could see them to make myself less threatening.

The baby opened his or her throat and let loose with a piercing cry that started the spaniel barking again. "Jon can take care of himself. He wasn't scared when he left either. He just needed to help some fool out. Be back real quick, he said."

"What fool?"

"Jon rents boats. Canoes, kayaks, tubes. He works for someone who does, I mean. One of the clients is up a creek without a paddle."

"Um . . . ?"

"The funny thing is the guy's an Indian. You'd think he'd know how to paddle a damned canoe. But he flipped over going down Golden Rapids and lost his paddle and is stranded on Musket Island in the middle of the river."

There was no cell service in Dickey. "How did he manage to contact your husband, this stranded man?"

"He's got one of those CB radios."

"He lost his paddle but managed to hang on to a radio without it getting wet?"

"Look, I wasn't present for the event. I can't offer you the whys and wherefores. Now, you need to excuse me. This baby requires his dinner, and I ain't going to just pull out my titty and give you a free show."

"Thanks for your time, Mrs. Egan. Just one last question. Does your husband have a scar on his arm, here?"

I indicated my left shoulder.

"He's got a tattoo there. A flaming heart!"

"Really?"

"I mean, he got the tattoo to cover a scar, yeah. It was a burn he suffered from falling against a radiator back when he still drank. Jon's a God-fearing man now. He found Jesus in prison. We go to services over in Allagash village every Sunday. The pastor washed him clean of his sins in the river, right below the church. My husband's been born again into the family of God. Can you say the same for yourself, Mr. Warden? I didn't think so."

41

It was no accident that Nick Francis had contacted Egan via a two-way radio. To implement Charley's plan—the exact shape of which still eluded me—they needed the conversation to be overheard by someone with a combination police scanner and CB unit. In backwoods Maine, that category of persons included everybody.

But the old pilot needed a specific person to be listening.

Who?

Not just Egan, obviously.

Like most petty criminals, Roland Michaud almost certainly owned a radio to keep track of the movements of local law enforcement.

Kellam had a police scanner in his truck. I'd heard it squelch when he was righting my Scout.

First responders and law enforcement officers in the area all had them. Chief Plourde. Zanadakis. Lamontaine.

I had one, too. The problem was it had stopped working during the crash.

My waterlogged map showed Musket Island as a glorified sandbar downstream of St. Ignace. It probably spent half its year underwater. The river was running high at the moment from all the rain. I wondered how much of the little island was above the surface.

Charley and Nick had a purpose in choosing to summon Egan to this particular spot.

The atlas showed that a bridge had once crossed the river at Musket Island. Probably the structure had been washed out decades earlier during an especially damaging ice jam. But there were approaches on both sides and an icon indicating a boat launch on the north shore. No doubt some of the old pilings remained. From experience, I knew that bridge supports can be dangerous places to paddle, both as obstacles in your way but also because currents flow faster where they are squeezed together.

The logging road from Dickey to the boat launch above Musket Brook was surprisingly well maintained. Fresh gravel had been spread and graded, and there were periodic bumps where new culverts had been installed to channel spring freshets under the hard-packed surface. Fully loaded logging trucks can weigh up to eighty thousand pounds. As a consequence, timber companies were also forced into the road maintenance business.

I passed a few buildings, their lights shining hazily up through the trees from the riverside. The timber company had leased waterfront plots to people to build vacation cabins. This arrangement was commonplace in Maine although less common than it had once been.

I drove into the first unattended camp. As I'd expected, the owner had a canoe. He had secured it with a chain to the biggest hemlock on the property. Unfortunately for him, fortunately for me, I kept a pair of bolt cutters in my vehicle. This wasn't the first occasion I'd had to "borrow" a boat.

I wasted no time tying the stolen Old Town to my roof rack. From there, it took me fifteen minutes to cover five miles. In the backcountry of Maine, that is called making good time.

As I descended the hill to the St. John River, I saw the old bridge looming in my high beams. The timber company had bulldozed boulders at its base. The rocks were intended to stop some drunken fool from driving headlong into the channel. As I braked and turned, my headlights caught the reflectors on the back of Egan's Tacoma, parked in a patch of sweetfern. He had towed a boat with him and backed the trailer into the water to launch the craft.

When I opened the door of my Scout, I could hear the rapids downstream. My muscles had grown even stiffer from the rollover. Like an arthritic old man, I limped through the woods along the river. I crushed wintergreen beneath my boots, loosing a minty, medicinal scent from the leaves. There was no moon, no light from the sky beyond a pale cast, but I could feel the towering pilings of the old bridge looming above me like the coldness of a shadow.

I squinted at where the island should be and saw a light flickering. Definitely a campfire.

There it was: the bait in Charley's trap.

But had Egan taken it?

I cut the ropes I had used to tie the canoe to the top of the Scout and positioned myself to take the weight of the broad-beamed boat onto my sore shoulders. I walked the overturned canoe up the shoreline, my tendons burning, my boots slipping on the loose gravel.

The current was too strong for me to cut straight across. If I attempted the shortest route, I would find myself carried past the island before I could make three paddle strokes. I would need to launch from upstream, I realized. Fortunately, the hull was made of polyethylene, which is lighter than aluminum or white cedar.

The hill above me was steep, and I reached a drop-off that impeded my portage upriver. I had no choice but to flip over the canoe into the water and secure the painter to the branch of an overhanging birch while I went to fetch the paddle.

I strapped on a 500 Lumens headlamp, the most powerful light I had with me.

I took hold of the beavertail paddle and used it to steady myself as I sat down in the center of the canoe. When paddling solo, the middle is where you usually want to be. Then I leaned forward and gave a yank to the quick-release end of the rope. The knot, a highwayman's hitch, slipped free of the branch, and I was torn adrift in the stream.

I turned the canoe with a series of sweep strokes so that my bow was facing downriver.

I thought I'd carried the canoe a fair ways up from the bridge, but it was only seconds before the foundations reared up dead ahead. I sideswiped the white-water eddy in front of the nearest pier and let the current pull me to the inner channel.

Musket Island was shaped like a football, narrow at the top and bottom, fat in the middle. I aimed for the pointed end. I needed to paddle hard to keep from being swept back into the deep water. My shoulder ached.

I have decent balance for a normal human, but not for a North Woods waterman like Charley. I didn't dare stand up in the canoe. Instead I slid over the gunwale into the river, going in all the way to my waist. The early summer water was warm, but not so warm that I didn't feel a stabbing pain in my groin. Once I had found my footing, I turned off the headlamp.

In the dark, I walked the canoe up the shallows, feeling that strange sensation you get in moving water of unseen hands tugging at your ankles, until I heard the bottom scrape gravel. Then I lifted the bow and did my best to muscle the thing onto dry land, all while remaining hunched over. I had seen the campfire at the bottom end of the football and wanted to approach with as much stealth as possible, given that the only cover on the low-slung island was a ridge of alders and willows running down the spine.

I kept low, then went lower, and finally began to crawl on hands and knees. Leopard frogs sprang up ahead of me from the wet weeds. Some of the grass blades had serrated edges and cut my hands.

"Come on up, young feller. You've been spotted."

The son of a bitch.

I rose to my feet, swiped my palms on my pants legs to remove the muck, and waded through the sedges to the two men I now saw seated across a small woodfire from each other.

Jon Egan, wild-eyed in the firelight, sat upon a skinned log that could only have rolled into the river from the back of someone's truck. His arms were bound behind him, and a kerchief was knotted in his open mouth.

Charley sat opposite him on a small boulder, resting his old service revolver, a Smith & Wesson .357 Magnum, on one bouncing knee. His head was just as disconcertingly bald as I'd remembered, and he was dressed in the same faded coveralls. They appeared vintage, as if he'd scavenged them from Goodwill, but I could have sworn that the American flag sewn on the chest was new.

"What the fuck, Charley?"

"I'm sorry, Mike."

"What are you doing? Why's he tied up like this?"

"I felt bad about what you said—about me using you as bait. So I decided to switch to Mr. Egan here."

"Bait for who?"

"Roland Michaud, of course. He killed Scott, and he killed that poor girl Angie when he found out she'd sold off that badge. She didn't know that it linked her boyfriend back to what happened here fifteen years ago."

Egan screamed into his cloth gag, shook his head violently, and rocked back and forth on his log. The redheaded man nearly toppled over backward.

Charley's theory baffled me, it was so full of holes.

"Roland was in New Brunswick the night Angie was strangled, Charley. I was in the room for his interrogation. He has people who can vouch for him, including customs officials."

"I've spoken to one of his so-called witnesses. I haven't been as idle as you think. One of those impartial customs officials Roland mentioned just happens to be his Canadian cousin."

"Charley, it wasn't Roland."

"We'll find out soon enough."

"If you're convinced that you're right, why are you holding a gun on Egan?"

"Because I intend to kill him."

The word came out in one breath. "What?"

"If Mr. Egan here doesn't tell me where they disposed of Scott's body, I'm going to brain him with this pistol and toss his body into the St. John. The police will think he overturned in the rapids."

"You wouldn't do that."

"I know you believe that, son, but the last few days have tested me, and, well, I've learned I'm not the man I thought I was. I failed Scott. But I am going to avenge him tonight, so help me God."

I felt the first stirring of a breeze on my cheek, saw the woodsmoke shift direction, even begin to rise. How many days had this stagnant heat sat motionless over us?

"So what do you expect is going to happen—that Roland is going to come motoring out here?"

"That's the general plan. Yes."

"That's ludicrous."

In the flickering firelight Egan's face had turned nearly the same shade of red as his hair. I worried he was going to hyperventilate before Roland even arrived.

"You're not a murderer, Charley."

"I killed Pierre."

"You shot Pierre. He drowned, trying to get away."

"I tried to kill him, though. And how can you be sure Nick and I didn't just let him drown?"

I didn't believe this last statement, not remotely. "Where is Nick?"

"Not here. I didn't want to include him in this if things go wrong."

"But you included me."

"More than once, Mike, I told you to stay out of this."

"For Christ's sake, Charley!" I took a step toward him, but a pitiless look came into his eyes that stopped me cold. "This isn't you. At least take Egan's gag off so he can breathe."

"If I do, he'll call out and give us away."

The man on the log shook his head vigorously to indicate he wouldn't ruin our plans.

"How can you be certain Egan knows where they hid Pellerin's body? The Warden Service searched half the County for it."

"And the Mounties searched their side of the border, too. But I think you might've guessed why I suspect Mr. Egan here was a party to a conspiracy. It has to do with a certain identifying mark."

I pointed at the bound man. "Can I see for myself?"

"Just so long as you cut the cloth and not the ropes."

I removed my knife from my pocket and pressed the button that opened the automatic blade. With the razor-sharp tip, I cut a hole in the shoulder of Egan's shirt. The dancing light didn't reveal much of the tattoo beyond the greenish-black ink. But I didn't need to see the design. I only needed to run my fingers over the raised skin to feel the old scar.

"Pierre Michaud branded everyone who participated in the killing," I said. "That way, they couldn't lie and claim they weren't there for the murder."

"They could still rat him out, though," said Charley. "I have no doubt that Mr. Egan was tempted to do so. But the prosecutor would've had a problem getting a reduced sentence for a self-identified cop killer."

"Pierre Michaud was a shrewd man."

"One of the coldest and most ruthless men I've come up against."

"But not shrewd enough to escape."

"He underestimated the wrong person."

For the past few minutes, I had felt like I was having a conversation with a dangerous stranger, a man whose actions I couldn't predict, possibly someone capable of unprovoked violence. But I recognized something of the old Charley as he spoke those words.

He underestimated the wrong person.

He wasn't referring to himself. He was talking about the person who'd told him where to look for Pierre. It hadn't been a coincidence that he and Nick had spotted the poacher king crossing Beau Lac that night. They had been tipped off.

I understood now.

This trap hadn't been set for Roland Michaud.

42

As I processed this revelation, I listened to the rapids below us in the darkness, the steady rush of falling water. It was an ominous sound that spoke of dangers impossible to see or avoid.

"You're not going to kill Egan," I said.

"Scott was like a son to me," Charley said, his voice creaking. "More than you even."

It would have broken my heart if I didn't know better.

I knew what I had to do next. I hardened myself to do it.

"I'm cutting him loose. Then I'm taking him back to Fort Kent. He's going to give a full confession to Zanadakis. I won't tell anyone what you did to him, Charley. And Egan won't either, will you?"

Once more, the gagged man tried to signal his enthusiastic compliance.

"I can't let you arrest him, Mike. He has to pay the price for what he did."

"He will."

"Blood is the only currency that matters."

I knelt down on the hard-packed sand beside Egan with the knife in my grip. He was sweating hard. The odor coming off him was the uniquely sour smell that comes from fear.

Charley rose to his feet, bulky in those ridiculously loose coveralls. "Get away from him, son."

I rose to my feet, feeling the breeze again on my sweaty neck. "I won't do that."

Charley raised the revolver at me. The barrel was aimed at my kneecap. Those old Smith & Wessons were massive guns. A .357 Magnum round would have amputated my lower leg.

"Back away."

"No."

He cocked the hammer, curled his index finger around the trigger. "Please, Mike. I don't want to do this."

"You won't be able to live with yourself if you do."

"Don't test me!"

I pulled down the gag over Egan's chin. He coughed, gasped out a few ragged breaths, and then spoke a single tortured word. "Forge."

Of course. It was what the investigators had feared at the time, why they'd found no evidence. Why we never would. Pierre Michaud, trained blacksmith, had dismembered Pellerin and burned him, piece by piece, in his smithy.

Charley's lip curled with contempt. "You saw Pierre do it?"

Some of the capillaries in Egan's eyes had popped, giving him a hobgoblin gaze. "We all did."

"Who's 'we'?" I asked, unable to contain my contempt.

"Me, Roland, Zach."

Most killers would have wanted as few witnesses as possible, but Pierre Michaud had seen the wisdom of incriminating his entire crew. He knew the butchery would haunt the men who followed him. He was confident in his ability to intimidate them into lifelong silence.

"And then Pierre gave you those brands so you'd all be implicated?" I said.

Egan worked his jaw, sore from the rag he'd had stuffed between his teeth. "He said he'd do himself last, but he didn't. Never planned on doing it. What were we going to do, though? Pierre would've killed any of us who challenged him."

I snapped my head around at Charley. "Are we done?"

The old man's features remained stony. But he eased down the hammer, slid his finger from the trigger guard, and turned the barrel of the revolver back to the sand.

"Yes," said Charley in a voice softened by shame and grief.

"Please tell me that isn't loaded," I said.

"It isn't."

Egan spat and sputtered. "What?"

"You violated all four rules of safe gun-handling there," I said.

"Three of them, at least," the old man answered with a sad smile. The character he'd been playing—cruel, vengeful, crazed—had disappeared in the night. "I'm sorry, Mike. I had to be convincing. I could only hope that you would sense that I was acting and understand why."

Egan had begun to blink furiously, as if he had sand in his eyes.

"It didn't make it any more pleasant," I said. "Where's Roland really?"

Charley glanced at his wristwatch.

"If I had to guess," he said, rubbing his hand over his head, already fuzzed white with stubble, "he's in the custody of the Canada Border Services Agency for attempting to transport a pound of heroin into the city of Edmundston, New Brunswick."

Once again I found myself catching my breath. "You didn't plant drugs on him?"

"Yes—and no. That smack belonged to Roland, all right. I just happened to steal it from under the outhouse where he had it hidden and hide the bag in his gas tank. That was his usual MO. Dogs can't smell narcotics through petroleum. This time, though, the Canadians had an anonymous tip to prod around in the tank."

"So you're a vigilante, too? In addition to being a kidnapper?"

Charley glanced at Egan, still bound, but no longer blinking and breathing more regularly now. "Do you plan on accusing me of kidnapping, Mr. Egan?"

"No!"

I crossed my forearms across my chest. "The man's terrified. Wait till he's free and has a lawyer to advise him. You're in big trouble here, Charley."

"It's been a while. Truth is, I kind of miss the experience. Don't you?"

I didn't want to admit that I missed our unsanctioned escapades. "I hope you're done tormenting Egan, at least."

"I wish I was," said Charley. "But we're still waiting on someone to make his appearance."

The breeze was picking up. Stars appeared, first hazily and then sharply, in the gaps between the clouds overhead. I actually shivered from the chill of my wet pants.

I saw the boat that must have been Egan's, a square-sterned Grumman sport with a two-stroke engine mounted to the transom. Personally, I wouldn't have trusted the underpowered craft in the river at night and certainly nowhere near rapids.

It occurred to me that I hadn't seen another boat, canoe, or kayak on my short trip across the island. How had Charley gotten here? The question could wait.

"You picked a vulnerable spot to set a trap."

"Our man wouldn't come if he didn't think he had us at a disadvantage."

"A night scope and a hunting rifle are all he needs to end this once and for all."

"He won't shoot on sight, because he doesn't know what we've discovered or whom we've told."

"But he has to know this is a setup. The story about the Indian flipping his canoe. Come on."

"Your father was a trapper," the old man said. "Didn't he ever set two traps, one after the other? Mr. Fox would think he was smart avoiding the first, then catch himself in the second."

"Who's the fox in this story?"

But before he could answer, we heard the sound we'd been anticipating. It was the low roar of an outboard motor heading toward Musket Island from upstream. A handheld spotlight showed on the surface of the water, which was as black as crude oil where the channel deepened. The boatman must have launched back in Allagash.

"How are we going to play this?" I said to Charley. "I take it you don't have proof that will stand up in court."

"He'll give us what we need if he doesn't kill us first."

"You need to untie me," said Egan.

I put the knife back in my pocket and checked my Beretta. The pistol had gotten wet in the river, but it was the most dependable firearm I had ever owned.

Charley flipped open the chamber of his revolver and reached into his pocket for bullets. "I guess I should load this."

Egan nearly burst into tears again. "It was empty?"

"You wearing your vest?" Charley said, meaning the light-weight body armor that protected my torso beneath my shirt and rain jacket.

"Always," I said, tapping my sternum. "Ever since I got shot in that gravel pit."

He smiled and winked. "Maybe you stand in front of me, then."

"It's not much help if he aims at my head. If I remember right, he's a good shot."

Charley dropped a bullet. As he stooped to pick it up, I saw BIG AL'S AUTO sewn in reflective letters on the back of his cover-alls. They were two sizes too large on his wiry frame.

"You need to untie me!" said Egan again.

The boat was coming fast downstream. He knew the river, its channels and currents. He was unafraid of it. He kept the spot-light on our faces, blinding us the way a poacher does a deer, until he slipped alongside the island. The diminishing light of the campfire revealed him standing tall in the stern of the Grand Laker with his hand on the throttle. He let the river carry the boat past the island and then gave the outboard some gas and came straight back at us in the lee. He rammed the bow of the square-sterned canoe into the sand as if he'd done that maneuver a hundred times before.

He probably had.

As he was always quick to remind us, Chasse Lamontaine had grown up on this river.

43

The game warden we'd mocked as Dudley Do-Right was dressed in his fatigue-colored uniform, wearing his duty belt and his ballistic vest fortified with ceramic plates in the front and back. He had eschewed a personal flotation device. He kept his hand on the grip of his sidearm, a SIG P226 with a magazine holding twelve .357 rounds. He probably had a bullet in the chamber, too.

"Charley Stevens, you've lost your hair."

"Misplaced it is more like it."

"There must be a mistake. I heard a distress call about an Indian getting himself stranded on this island. But instead of finding Crazy Horse, all I see are three horses' asses."

Who was this man? Even his voice sounded different. Quick and confident.

"I never knew you were funny, Chasse," I said.

"One of many things you didn't know, I expect. Why's your hand on your sidearm, Mike? We're all fellow wardens here. No need to be jumpy."

I kept my hand where it was.

"So you've come to rescue us, then?" said Charley.

"Do you need rescuing? My first thought was that this was a prank you decided to play on me. I'm used to being the butt of jokes. I know wardens think I'm some naive Boy Scout."

"It must bother you," I said.

"The opposite," he said. "People are never so dumb as when they think they're putting something over on somebody smarter than they are. Charley, that shaved head of yours is freaking me out. Were you afraid to come back here except in disguise?"

"More like I wanted to keep a low profile."

"Too low, I think, given where we are." He cast a glance at Egan, who had gone as motionless as a fawn hoping not to be noticed by a predator in the tall grass. "You've looked better, Jon."

"Chasse."

"So, seriously," said Lamontaine, "what's this about?"

Charley tossed a small object into the light cast by the burning driftwood. It landed with a *clink* on the river-polished gravel. A miniature metal shield.

"I suppose you recognize this," said the pilot.

"Looks like a toy badge. You get it out of a gumball machine?"

"It's real enough. And you have no idea whose badge it is?"

Chasse let out a pretty convincing chuckle. "It's kind of hard to identify from twenty feet away."

"Come have a closer look," said Charley.

"I will when you gentlemen take your hands off your sidearms."

"The badge belonged to Scott Pellerin," I said.

"Pellerin was undercover," said Chasse, sounding genuinely mystified. "He wouldn't have had a badge with him."

"Actually, it belonged to Scott's grandfather," said Charley. "Emmeline Bouchard found it hidden in the room Scott was renting at the Valley View. No doubt Pierre had told her to search the place from time to time. Scott must've gotten careless hiding the thing."

"So that's how Pierre found out that Pellerin was a warden."

"You're acting like this is news to you," I said.

"Of course it is! Pierre never told anyone before he died, except Emmeline, of course. I'm surprised she didn't let that slip later—when I would visit her at the motel."

So Chasse had had an affair with Angie's mother, too. Emmeline Bouchard's taste in men couldn't have been worse.

"You remember what a cold-blooded bastard Pierre was," Lamontaine continued. "Killing that man was the best thing you've done. I know you're too 'honorable' to admit that. Or maybe that's another lie you tell yourself."

"I've told myself plenty, that's true."

"Maybe you don't like to remember what you did."

"Maybe," Charley said. "It's true my memory's gotten more selective. But I remember one thing from that manhunt as clear as last night. It concerns you, Chasse. I remember how it was you who kept asking to go with me in my plane to look for Pierre. You said you knew this land better than any outsider, even though you were just a deputy warden back then."

"It was the truth. I know every inch of this river and its tributaries."

"I hurt your pride when I refused. I told you there was only room in the Cub for two and I trusted Nick Francis."

He shrugged his broad shoulders. "It was your prerogative."

"What I didn't admit—to myself or to you—was that I already had a sneaking feeling about you."

"Why was that?"

"Because of how insistent you were that we fly over Beau Lac. You said Pierre kept an old canoe chained to a tree there. You said he would try to cross before the clouds cleared and the moon came out. Nick and I thought you were just trying to prove your own importance. We were surprised when we actually flew up that way and there was a man in a canoe trying to slip across. I'm not sure we gave you the credit, though."

"No," he said, sounding piqued. "You didn't."

"Not that you wanted it, I'm guessing. It wasn't the moment for you to call attention to yourself."

"Charley, are you accusing me of helping Pierre Michaud escape?" The suggestion seemed to amuse him.

"The opposite! You wanted to make sure Pierre *didn't* escape."

"And why would I do that? He deserved to die for what he did to Pellerin. I believed it then, and I believe it now. Why else did you shoot him if you didn't agree?"

"Nick and I did everything in our power to save that son of a bitch's life—despite his horrible crimes."

"Sure you did." The Boy Scout had turned out to be as cynical as a career criminal. "Suppose what you're saying is even half-true. Suppose I had a hunch where and when Pierre was going to try crossing the border. So what?"

"The word you're looking for is *complicity*," I said.

"Shut up, Bowditch," he said. "No one cares what you think."

"You stage-managed Pierre Michaud's death," I said.

"Prove it."

"We can't," said Charley.

He actually laughed at that. "So what are we all doing here?"

The gravel rustled as Charley shifted his weight. "I consider myself a pretty fair actor. I can play as dumb as Lieutenant Columbo when the situation calls for it. But you, Chasse, have a true gift for letting people believe you're a numbskull."

Lamontaine's voice hardened. "Did you come all the way up here to insult me, or are you accusing me of something? I had nothing to do with Scott Pellerin's death."

"I think you did," said Charley. "I think you went to work as a deputy warden with an agreement to cover for Pierre Michaud. You promised him protection in exchange for a cut of his profits. You've always boasted how you grew up here and know everyone in the Valley."

"I was just a deputy. I had no authority."

"But you had information about where the wardens would be laying their ambushes. You made it easy for the Michauds to stay one step ahead—and then you tried to use the situation to secure a full-time job where you would've been even better positioned to protect their illegal activities."

The accusation amused Chasse. "Are you accusing me of being Pierre's mole in the service?"

"Not a good one. He must have been pissed that you failed

to recognize Scott Pellerin when you met," I said, taking a shot in the dark.

Chasse's reaction—his refusal to rebut the statement—confirmed my guess.

"If you guys are accusing me of being a party to a criminal enterprise, let alone a cop killing," he said with a sneer, "then go ahead and prove it. You won't be able to."

"How about showing us your shoulder, then?" I said.

"My shoulder?"

"I suspect you have a brand on it from the hot iron that Pierre used to implicate the men in his crew."

"Fuck you, Bowditch."

"It had to be you, Chasse. When I showed up at Angie Bouchard's house, asking about the badge that linked her mom to Scott Pellerin's death, who did she seek out for advice?"

Somewhere out in the channel, a big fish thrashed in the water, chasing bait—it could only have been a muskellunge.

"You're the only warden she knew," I continued. "She wanted you to tell her that her mom had no connection to Pellerin's murder. Children hate to believe the worst about their parents."

"You know, Bowditch," Chasse said, "not all of us are as bloodthirsty as you are. How many lives do you have on your conscience now? I have never personally killed another human being in my life. Besides which, I have an alibi for the time of Angie's death."

"Does your son C. J. have one, too?" said Charley with some of the old menace. "I bet he doesn't."

"You sent C. J. to meet Angie at the motel," I said. "Maybe you just wanted him to get some information out of her, but he took matters into his own hands, so to speak. You've raised a fine boy, Chasse. You're the father of the year."

"You can't prove any of this."

There was a catch in Chasse's voice as he spoke these words. He had been so careful himself, but he knew what a hothead his son was.

"We can prove that C. J. was the one who ran me off the road the other day," I said.

"I was there," said Charley. "I was too late to intervene, but I passed his truck going the opposite direction and got a decent glance at the driver."

This, I happened to know, was a lie, since Charley had been following me, but Chasse wouldn't have known.

He seemed rattled now. "How are your eyes these days, old man? Sharp enough for a jury to believe you could ID someone speeding in a pickup on a rainy day?"

"I'm sure the paint on Mike's bumper matches your boy's bigfoot."

It was slang for a pickup modified for off-roading.

Some of Chasse's cockiness returned. "My son doesn't own a bigfoot."

"Oh," said Charley. "I am sure you ditched it in some bog where it won't be found. But when the state police start asking around about your son's recently disappeared pickup, I'm sure plenty of people will recall certain identifying details."

Now Chasse's smile became arrogant. "You've always been a talker, Charley. But you can't prove any of this. If you could, we'd be having this conversation in an interrogation room and not on a sandbar in the middle of nowhere."

"Let's have Detective Zanadakis take a shot at your son, then," I said. "How confident are you that C.J. won't slip up?"

I wasn't sure what I expected. I thought his self-confidence might waver for a split second. Instead Chasse Lamontaine somehow had his gun in his hand, pointed at Charley. He had the quickest draw I had ever seen outside a western.

My reflexes took over. I drew my own sidearm and leveled the barrel at his Adam's apple. There is a hollow at the throat left exposed by the ballistic vest. From this distance, I couldn't have missed the mark.

Charley kept his revolver aimed at the ground.

"Probably a good time for you two guys to drop your guns," said Lamontaine.

"Can't you count, Chasse?" I said. "You're outnumbered here."

"Am I?"

Suddenly, Charley collapsed beside me like a marionette whose strings have been cut. A split second later, I heard the rifle shot.

44

The night became electric with gunfire. It seemed to be coming from every direction, from places it couldn't possibly be coming.

Without a single conscious thought, I threw myself on top of the old man. I would take whatever bullet came next before I allowed him to be shot again. I landed pretty hard.

I raised my head and swung my gun around in an arc, trying to find Chasse Lamontaine. But he had disappeared. My thought was that he'd ducked down into the water behind his Grand Laker or possibly even Egan's boat.

Then came a cry from the bridge above. "I'm hit, Dad!"

Charley groaned in my ear. "Get off me, you damned fool."

I realized that his body, under the ill-fitting coveralls, felt as hard as a suit of armor.

"You're OK?"

"I'll be better if you let me breathe."

I rolled onto my backside and held my sidearm in a two-handed grip, trying to find a target in the water. Egan lay on the ground, his knees drawn up to his chest like a pill bug rolled up on itself.

Charley's leathery face was contorted with pain. I wasn't sure if it was from the rifle shot or how hard I had landed on him.

From my seat in the sand, I could see Egan's Grumman drifting downstream. In the confusion, Chasse must have pulled the boat off the sandbar. He wanted to deprive us of a means of escape or pursuit.

He had to be hiding in the water now behind his Grand Laker. I could have started firing at it—the cedar planks wouldn't have stopped the sixteen hollow-point bullets in my Beretta, although I would have preferred jacketed rounds. But I wasn't as blasé about murdering a man as Lamontaine had accused me of being.

"I know where you are, Chasse," I said.

Another burst of gunshots: suppressing fire, in the language of the military. When I dared raise my head again, I saw that the Grand Laker had also come unmoored. It was moving away in the river, pinwheeling in the current. As it drifted farther from the island and the glow of the campfire, I saw Chasse pull himself up from the water over one of the gunwales.

I fired three shots.

One of them must have struck, because he fell backward out of the boat before he could gain his balance.

He was at the mercy of the water now. He wasn't wearing a life vest. His gun belt weighed somewhere between fifteen and twenty pounds. His body armor, assuming he was carrying the full complement of steel-core plates, might have weighed forty pounds.

He was a strong man, but not stronger than the river.

Charley worked his shoulder in a rotation, but the movement only made him wince. "Where's Lamontaine?"

"In the river. I think I might have winged him. He's going to drown, Charley."

"Where's Egan's boat?"

"Gone," I said. "But there's one left."

Charley could have let Chasse Lamontaine die, just by hesitating. Instead he sprang to his feet like a man half his age. "Let's go."

We trotted back up the spine of the island.

"I had figured out he was smarter than he pretended to be," said the pilot, behind me. "I should have realized he'd set his son up as a sniper, the same as I did with Nick."

So it was Nick Francis up there on the ruined bridge, or wherever he'd made his nest, who had saved us from being picked off by C. J. Lamontaine.

I found the canoe in the light of my headlamp.

"That's not much of a watercraft," said Charley.

"And there's only one paddle."

"Better let me take it, then."

There was no argument. As old and injured as he was, Charley Stevens was one of the best boatmen I had ever known. I had seen him pole a canoe up Class III rapids: a feat I had believed impossible until he accomplished it.

I'd barely taken my seat in the bow before I lurched forward. Charley, running, pushed the boat along the sand. I heard the splashes of his boots and then the forward shove as the keel scraped free of the gravel and floated into the current. There was barely a wobble as the injured old man leaped into the stern.

He rarely sat in a canoe, preferring to stand (if he was poling) or kneel, like the Penobscots and Passamaquoddy did in their slender birchbark creations. Kneeling was an ancient way of paddling, and there was something holy about it beyond the churchly posture. It was how you demonstrated humility before the power of the river.

I fired up my headlamp. As we drifted past the south end of the island, I turned my illuminated gaze on the dying fire. Egan was wriggling around on the sand. I wished I'd thought to cut him free.

"You all right there, Jon?" I asked with real concern.

"Fuck you," was his reply.

—

As the bowman, it was my job to shout out the obstacles ahead and spotlight the water for signs of Chasse Lamontaine. I focused on the nearly phosphorescent froth.

Running water appears dark above channels and certain eddies but bubbles white where it gains speed in the narrows. Follow the waves and shoot the vees between the rocks and you should be fine. Steer even a little off course and you might crash against a boulder and flip over. If you're particularly unlucky, you might find yourself held beneath the surface by the hydraulics of a falls, doing endless somersaults. Or you might be pinned between the overturned canoe and a rock by the force of the river until your crushed lungs fill with water.

I saw no personal flotation devices in the canoe—a violation I used to cite paddlers for every day when I was a patrol warden. We'd be in the same tough spot as Chasse if we spilled in the rapids.

Spray, tasting of wet moss, exploded in my face. I kept watch for the missing boats.

Even before we came to the serious white water, the river had already begun to step down—I experienced the sensation of descending, the top half of my body tipping forward. The current guided us through the first of the real rapids and sucked us forward and faster into a white expanse of waves.

"On your left!" Charley said.

I swung the light around but not before the hull knocked against the submerged part of a boulder I had missed seeing. The impact might have been enough to turn us broadside if not for Charley's expertise. Somehow he made a series of strokes that centered us once more in the white water.

I wished I had a paddle to help him.

It wasn't just that we needed speed to find Chasse before an eddy sucked him under. Navigating the stepped falls without spilling required us to keep pace with the current.

I never even heard the crash.

But all at once we were upon the wrecked boat. The unmanned Grand Laker had failed to navigate two boulders—Scylla and Charybdis in miniature. The bow had gotten stuck, wedged between the rocks, while the hydrodynamics of the river had lifted the stern clean out of the water. Within seconds, the front had swamped, and now the upended boat loomed ahead of us, on the verge of breaking apart. Of Chasse, there was no sign at all.

To our immediate right was a ledge. Behind it was a protected eddy. Charley spun our canoe around into the calm water with a grace that seemed effortless.

"Do you see him?" I called above the thundering falls.

"Get out!"

"What?"

He gestured with his paddle at the boulder as we turned along-side it. I reached out with both hands and did my best to keep my center of gravity low to avoid upsetting the canoe. The next thing I knew, I was hanging from the rock with my legs dangling in the water. The surface was slick in places. I nearly lost my handhold as I began to climb. And my waterlogged boots were all but useless when I tried to involve them in my ascent.

I stood atop the ledge, squinting downstream. I saw some-thing pale. A hand perhaps.

I shouted down at Charley, still holding his position in the eddy, "I think I see him!"

"Run to shore."

"What?"

The ledge ended ten feet to my right. Beyond lay another, smaller ledge. Then a clump of bushes overhanging a dark, still stretch of stream. We'd cut across the river as we'd descended, and this was the far bank.

"I'll meet you below," the old man said.

I crept forward to the end of the ledge and found myself fac-ing a gap of at least five feet. Under normal conditions, it would have been an easy jump. But in the dark, leaping from a slippery bit of stone, with the landing place likely to be just as slick, I had no choice but to throw myself across the divide and hope for the best.

The opposite ledge was as mossy and as treacherous as I had feared. I fell hard but not into the water.

The next leap was even farther. Easily ten feet, which meant I would be swimming, carried by the current while I tried to grab hold of one of the frail alder branches overhanging the river.

Without pausing to remove my boots, I dove in. The impact pulled the headlamp off my head.

I came up spitting, already twenty feet down the river from where I'd gone under and not at all close to the shore. I kicked and crawled and continued to drift, seemingly making no progress.

Then I saw a branch protruding from the water. I lunged and grabbed hold of it, and my momentum swung me around until I was floating on my back, facing my boots downstream.

The dead tree had toppled from the shore when its roots had been eroded. It had lost most of its branches, but I was able to use the snags that remained to pull myself along until I was looking up a leafy willow. Soon I was clawing through the waterside puckerbrush, reopening cuts on my hands and skinning my shins on hidden logs.

The wind was up, and the sky was clearing fast. Hundreds of stars had come into focus. I caught a glimpse of the Milky Way.

Eventually, I broke free of the brush and found myself standing on an almost impossibly beautiful sandbar. Over the eons, the river had twisted and turned like a restless sleeper in its bed. I stood upon a low ridge and scanned downstream only to realize that my journey to shore had carried me past the place where I'd spotted Chasse's hand.

Just below the rapids where the Grand Laker had wrecked was another bar of gravel, almost an island, complete with a grassy crest and even a few wildflowers glowing white in the starlight. The river below was rippled but unbroken by obvious rocks. If Chasse had just made it through the last stretch, he might have washed up, alive, on this bar amid the orchids.

But there was no sign of him. Nor of Charley.

I waded out as far as I could, then plunged into the river again, using the lee of the island to avoid being caught in the current. I walked the length of the bar, following its weedy crest, my boots so full of water they squished. My movements startled a sleeping snake. It was dark, the length of my arm. I watched it take off across the surface of the water in a series of S-shaped motions. A northern water snake, native to this land.

"Mike!"

I looked up and saw Charley making his way toward me in my borrowed canoe. The sky had become luminous with constellations. My eyes had adjusted to the night. But my vision was anything but sharp. It took me a moment to realize that the old man had Chasse Lamontaine in the boat with him. The tall warden lay awkwardly, unmoving across the thwarts and the center seat.

"Is he—?"

"Alive, yes. Had a heck of a time pulling him aboard, though. The son of a bitch weighs as much as a moose calf."

45

We laid Chasse out on his side along the sandbar. The water had leeched the color from his skin. His fingers were icicles. Because he was still breathing, albeit shallowly, we didn't administer CPR. We stabilized his neck in case he'd sustained a spinal injury in the rapids.

I found three burn holes in the fabric of his uniform: a tight cluster over his heart. Every bullet I had fired had struck him and bounced off the armored plates. If I lived long enough, I might someday become a decent shot.

Then we waited.

Like a man with an itch, Charley tried unsuccessfully to reach for the one spot on his back his fingers couldn't touch. I turned him around and found the hole in his coveralls where the bullet had pierced the fabric. The projectile had flattened itself against the combat vest Charley had been wearing, concealed beneath his mechanic's disguise.

"Which letter did he hit?" he asked.

It took a moment for me to understand that he was referring to the reflective words on his black. "The *L* in AL's."

"He was a true marksman, then, Chasse's boy. I guess I'm lucky he didn't go for a head shot. But few gunmen can resist an easy target when it's offered."

The flag newly sewn on the chest and the slogan on the back of the coveralls made sense now—Charley had chosen the outlandish outfit to give a shooter something to aim at. While I watched, my friend slipped off his monkey suit to remove the armor he'd been wearing underneath. The steel carapace must have weighed a hundred pounds, but it had saved his life.

"C. J. called out that he'd been hit," I said.

"I told Nick not to hurt him bad if he could avoid it. That's better than he deserves for what he did to the Bouchard girl."

We'd landed on the south shore of the St. John. Above us, a steep hillside, nearly a bushy cliff, rose to Route 161, the lone road from Allagash to Fort Kent.

It must have been Nick Francis who'd called in the gunfight on his CB.

The first officers to arrive were Chief Plourde and one of his men from Fort Kent, followed by EMTs, sheriff's deputies, and Border Patrol agents outfitted in tactical gear and carrying Colt M4 carbines. The feds even sent a helicopter with a floodlight brighter than the noonday sun.

The last of the principals to arrive was Detective Zanadakis, who wore a suit but no tie and without any product in his hair. I had never seen him so casually dressed. Then again, it was the middle of the night.

"What happened to Egan?" the detective asked.

"Hopefully, he hasn't rolled himself into the river by now."

Zanadakis frowned. I explained that we had left him tied up on Musket Island.

The detective left to confer with his troopers.

Charley was sitting on a log, chewing on a hunk of jerky and drinking from a canvas-covered canteen.

"There's a lot about what you've been doing in the Valley that you need to explain," I said. "And not just to me."

"There'll be time for that."

"You beat John Smith to a pulp." My intonation was almost that of a question; I was still hopeful I might be wrong.

Instead Charley turned ornery. "I don't suppose he mentioned that he maced me first. I hadn't even raised my voice and he sprayed me in the eyes. The next thing I knew, I was half-blind and he was raining punches down on me. But no one taught the man to box. I defended myself."

A prosecutor might argue that he had defended himself with excessive enthusiasm, but Smith had fired a bullet at me, and I found it hard to fault my friend for cleaning his clock.

I was more concerned about the fallout from his subsequent actions. "You kidnapped Egan. That's a felony."

"I took a risk and am willing to live with the consequences."

"What will happen to Ora if you go to prison?"

The grim prospect made him fall silent.

"I could be charged as an accessory," I added.

"You tried to get me to let him go. You're in the clear."

"You're not worried?"

"Worry's for people who think blowing on the dice will change their luck."

I never even heard Nick Francis coming. He wasn't there. And then he was.

Most of my adult life, I had dismissed the romantic notion of Native Americans being able to move silently as a kind of reverse racism. But the fact remained that I was hyperalert, still pumped on adrenaline, and yet Nick Francis got past my personal perimeter without setting off any alarms.

The old Passamaquoddy wasn't wearing hunting camouflage or the pixelated pattern of greens and browns favored by the armed forces. He'd had no need of it, clearly. He was dressed from head to foot in denim: a western leisure suit. On a sling over his shoulder was the lever-action Winchester 94 rifle he had used to ambush C. J. Lamontaine. He'd done his shooting in the dark, without a night-vision scope, using only iron sights.

I was glad not to have the man as my enemy.

Charley had noticed how I'd jumped when his old friend appeared. "Nick's a stealthy son of a bitch, but it's not on account of him being a Native."

"I've just learned to be quiet around white people," said the former Passamaquoddy chief. "You folks are too unpredictable."

"Thanks for taking care of C. J." Charley offered his jerky to Nick who bit off a chunk.

"Stupid kid," he said, chewing.

"Murderous kid," I added.

Charley picked a piece of meat from between his teeth with a fingernail. "Where'd you shoot him anyway, Nick?"

"In the ass. It seemed the appropriate spot."

Seeing the two old men joking together made me think of Wheelwright and Fixico again. How many losses are greater than the loss of a good friend?

Nick explained that C. J. Lamontaine had made a sniper's nest for himself atop the broken bridge. He had come equipped for the ambush with a .30-06 Browning outfitted with a night-vision scope that showed heat signatures. And yet he'd still managed to miss seeing the septuagenarian Native crouched calmly in the bushes nearby.

C. J. wasn't the only one feeling ambushed.

"So you've been spying on me since Houlton," I said.

"Keeping tabs," said Nick.

"We took turns," said Charley. "I was flying by the seat of my pants. I realized no one up here would talk to me, even with this brilliant disguise." He ran a hand over his shaved head. "I knew word would get out who I really was eventually. People in the Valley remember what happened in St. Ignace and what I did to Pierre Michaud. The only way I was going to get information from certain parties was through a surrogate."

I turned to Nick. "Which was why you sent me to see Kellam."

"Don't blame me," the Passamaquoddy said, lighting a cigarette. "I'm not the Lone Ranger in this scenario. Or any scenarios."

"They're going to keep us here all night, answering questions," I said.

Nick exhaled smoke. "You have someplace to be?"

"As a matter of fact, yes. A person I care about is in the hospital. And I have been stuck up here instead of doing what I should have done and gone to see her."

Charley rose to his feet, looked me straight in the eyes, and rested one of his oversized hands on my shoulder. "Dani?"

"The last I heard, her temperature was through the roof."

"I'm sorry," he said. "The Border Patrol can patch you through if you can't get a signal."

"Good idea."

The Fort Kent Fire Department had lowered ropes for the first responders to use climbing up and down the incline. I refused the offer of being pulled up and made my way under my own power to the road above. Between the rollover and the river, my body felt as if it had been pounded between a mortar and a pestle.

I caught sight of Zanadakis standing outside an ambulance, talking to someone seated in the back. It had to be Chasse. The disgraced warden had revived quickly under our care. I was too far away to overhear the conversation, but the detective seemed barely able to contain his rage.

Another ambulance had already taken the son to the hospital for emergency ass surgery.

I glanced around for a familiar face among the Border Patrol guys. My phone showed no bars. The feds always get the best toys, including satellite phones for isolated backwaters like this one.

Then I saw the imposing form of Stanley Kellam, making his way through the scrum. His shoulders were hunched, his hands dug in the pockets of his GoreTex jacket. Despite the fact that he had given up his badge years earlier, not a single law enforcement officer stopped him. The aura of command surrounding the man was that overpowering.

When he caught sight of me, he came to an abrupt halt. We stared at each other through the kaleidoscope of emergency vehicle lights. I remembered Vaneese's warning. Instinctively, my right hand fell to my side where I had holstered my Beretta.

"Kellam!"

The lieutenant started forward again.

I realized where he was going.

There were cruisers of various kinds now between Kellam and me. Huge metal obstacles with groups of men between them, gabbing as cops do at scenes where there are too many of them assembled and not enough tasks to go around.

"Hey, Kellam!"

Two Border Patrol trucks were parked nose to tail, with less than a foot separating them. I stepped onto the bumper of one of the Tahoes, heard its driver shout an obscenity, then threw myself forward.

Kellam had reached the ambulance. Zanadakis had become aware of him. The detective turned toward the former warden with a questioning look on his face.

"Detective! Stop him!"

Zanadakis heard my voice but didn't catch my meaning. He stepped clear of the open doors, and I caught a glimpse of Chasse Lamontaine gazing out of the brightly lighted ambulance, handcuffed, and with a blanket around his broad shoulders.

The officers nearby must have thought me a madman. I threw myself at Stanley Kellam as he leaned inside the ambulance, pulling the Heckler & Koch pistol from his jacket. It was a point-blank shot with a .45-caliber bullet.

There was only one reason it missed. The second Kellam's finger curled around the trigger, I slammed his forehead against the door frame. His hand jerked, and the pistol fired into a defibrillator. The hollow point exploded the glass monitor.

By now, I had one hand on Kellam's thick wrist, trying to keep him from regaining his aim, while I snaked my other arm around his throat. I pulled with all my strength.

The second shot passed over Lamontaine's bent shoulders and careened off something metal.

The detective, having regained his wits, stomped on Kellam's Achilles tendon. The lieutenant staggered as I tightened my arm around his throat, but I wasn't in position to choke the breath out of him or cut the supply of blood flowing to his brain. The big old man kept fighting.

Zanadakis delivered a punch to the back of Kellam's thigh, to the nerve bundle between his hamstrings. The lieutenant should have crumpled, but he only dropped to one knee. He fired a third shot, this time into the air.

In the end, it took five officers to disarm Stanley Kellam and bring him to the ground. I was pinned atop him by the weight of bodies. One bonehead even punched me in the kidney by mistake.

The cops, local and federal, finally succeeded in cuffing the retired warden and standing him upright. His face was coated with mud from the roadside. He glared with blazing eyes out of the brown mask, his anger directed now at a single person. Me.

"Why?" he demanded.

"Because Chasse didn't kill Pellerin," I said.

"It doesn't matter!"

Stan Kellam had heard the call go out over the police radio. He had sped here to exact vengeance for his dead investigator. It never occurred to him that the person he really wanted to punish was himself.

46

The Border Patrol patched me through on a sat phone to Dani's hospital room, where my call was answered by her mother.

Nicole Tate was a widow whose husband, a laid-off mill worker, had died before his fiftieth birthday. She was a hairdresser and cosmetologist by trade, and one of the great sadnesses of her life was that her daughter had turned out to be a tomboy who didn't own a single tube of lipstick.

"How is she?" I asked.

"Asleep." Nicole was a kind woman by nature but made no effort to hide her frustration with me. "Her temperature is down. She doesn't remember how she got here and doesn't understand how sick she is. She keeps telling everyone she wants to go home."

"Have they figured out what's wrong?"

"Encephalitis."

The word might as well have stabbed me in the eardrum. "What?"

"They think it might have been from the tick that bit her."

"Dani has the Powassan virus?" Encephalitis was one of the diagnostic symptoms.

"They're not sure."

The disease was rare and often fatal, and many of the survivors suffered permanent neurological damage. Now it was my turn to gasp for breath.

I had been in Florida for a full week, where half a dozen "new" tropical diseases, from yellow fever to West Nile virus, were sending people to hospitals and graveyards. And yet I had emerged from the Everglades with mosquito bites that had already stopped itching.

Meanwhile in Maine, a state everyone assumed was safe from such insect-borne plagues, my girlfriend had seemingly contracted a rare illness that might yet kill her after a single tick bite.

The situation was simultaneously ironic and terrifying. What made it worse was the likelihood that Dani's case was a harbinger of American life as we would experience it in the coming decades, with death's emissaries breeding in every backyard birdbath and in every unmown plot of grass. If she even lived to see that dystopic future.

That disquieting sensation of not having escaped the swamps of South Florida returned. I felt nauseous. But the sickness might have been as much out of guilt and fear for Dani.

"I am so sorry for not being there, Nicole."

"She wouldn't have known if you were. Well, maybe she would have. She was delirious when I got here and thought one of the nurses, a young man, was you. She was mad at him. She said she knew he cheated on her. She was delirious, like I said. It didn't mean anything."

Like hell it didn't.

"I'm headed back in the morning. I'll catch a plane first thing."

"Did you find your friend, at least?"

"Yes."

"I hope it was worth it."

—

Afterward, I caught a ride with Chief Plourde to my Scout on the far side of the river. During the drive, he regaled me with the culture and tragic history of the Acadians in the St. John Valley.

"We are a displaced people," he told me.

Plourde might have made a good tour guide if my thoughts weren't so haunted.

I wondered if anyone had contacted the warden colonel yet

with the news about Chasse Lamontaine and Stanley Kellam. The duty was mine by all rights, but I found myself hoping that someone else had reached him first.

Tim Malcomb would be livid. Knowing the man's sense of honor, I imagined that he would feel it necessary to resign over the inevitable scandal. He had stayed too long in the colonel's job anyway, and it had eroded some of his better qualities.

I didn't envy the man who succeeded him. The Maine press would rake the Warden Service over the coals for what our two officers, Lamontaine and Kellam, had done.

Maybe Chasse was right; this valley had never been a good place for game wardens. Borders are always places of temptations. Drawing a line creates an open invitation for people to cross it. Not just men like the Michauds but Charley, too. I found myself impressed by his courage and ingenuity—everything he'd done had been for Scott Pellerin—but I was disappointed in him, as well.

In an odd way, he had paid me a compliment; he had respected my abilities to do what he lacked the capacity to accomplish himself. My love for the old man was close to unconditional. But this day signaled the end of my apprenticeship. I had no doubt that Charley Stevens would continue to teach me life lessons, but only small boys and fools worship other men. The point of life is to find heroism in yourself.

Plourde dropped me at my truck.

The police were still mopping up the crime scene when I returned. Too much had happened that needed to be recorded and collected. A trooper directing traffic told me that the attorney general himself was flying to Fort Kent to be debriefed. No doubt Colonel Malcomb would be accompanying him. For once I was glad not to have cell service.

I found Charley and Nick again by searching for the silver Jeep. They were seated side by side on a guardrail, waiting to be interviewed by Zanadakis. Nick held a cigarette pinched between his fingers.

"How's Dani?" Charley asked. "That tick virus is the real deal."

"How did you—?"

"I just got off the phone with Ora, who spoke with Kathy. You must've been worried sick."

"Not as worried as I should have been."

When a mosquito circled my head, I caught it in midair and gave it a squeeze. I opened my palm but found that it was too late. The insect had already drawn blood.

"Ora and I often say we're ashamed of the overheated world we are leaving our grandchildren."

"You're no more responsible for the dismal state of affairs than anyone else."

"No less responsible neither."

"You're never going to be able to make this up to Ora, you know. The fear you put her through the past few days. You'll need to clean out an entire flower shop."

"She's forgiven me for worse," he said, meaning the crash that had left her paralyzed. "But you're right that I have a lot to atone for."

"I need to catch a plane as soon as possible."

"Of course, but Zanadakis will need to interview us first."

"Do we have a story we're sticking to?"

"The truth."

"Which truth?"

He showed me that jack-o'-lantern grin. "That's always the question, isn't it? I'm sure we can get going by midmorning at the latest. Hopefully soon."

"I don't suppose you have a buddy with a plane, willing to give me a ride down to Portland."

"As a matter of fact, I do."

Then he rested a hand on my shoulder. Sometimes I forget the simple power of human touch to soothe one's anguish.

⁓

After our interviews, Nick Francis drove Charley and me to the grass airstrip outside Fort Kent. I had left my Scout in the care of Plourde. The chief said his nephew was a prodigy when it came to auto-body repairs. I would find my *véhicule* better than new when I returned to Fort Kent, Plourde proclaimed with characteristic grandiosity. I didn't dare hope.

Nick pulled to a stop outside the single hangar and long strip of grass that comprised the Fort Kent airport. An orange sock was filled with a cool breeze streaming to the rescue from Canada. The sky was crisp and blue with only a few sheeplike clouds bouncing along.

I'd turned off my phone before I'd gotten service again. My superiors could wait for my attention until I'd seen Dani.

Nick, however, had calls to make—something about his jailed son. He remained in the Jeep while Charley and I unloaded the gear we would be taking back home with us. I had waited for a private moment to discuss the events of the past days with him. Friend or not, he owed me a reckoning.

"That letter you left me? You must have suspected Chasse from the start. He was the patient man you warned me about."

"Yes and no," Charley said. He looked more himself dressed in green Dickies and a green tee. He was a wiry man whose forearm muscles still showed when he lifted the bags. "The truth is, I didn't know what to think when I saw that badge on Smith's table. I'd always assumed it had been buried—burned—with Scott's body. I couldn't believe my eyes at first."

"In your letter you said you'd been duped."

"If someone had the badge all this time, it meant everything I thought I knew about this case was wrong. I started to turn it over in my mind again, wondering who I'd misjudged. There was Roland, of course, still running wild. And Egan, I learned, was out of prison. Even Kellam has always been such a prickly pear—I was sure he had kept information from me. But it was to Chasse, yes, that my suspicions first went. It just seemed so unthinkable, though, given his sterling character. He would've had to have been a master manipulator . . ."

"He's a hell of an actor," I said. "I'll give him that much. I still don't believe he failed to recognize Scott when they crossed paths at the Valley View."

"He might be telling the truth about that," said Charley.

"There was something odd about Scott—he had a quality about him—he could seem like just another face in the crowd. Sometimes I can't fully recall his features, and my memory isn't that full of holes yet."

The sound of a plane passing overhead made us look up, but it was just the Border Patrol on another aerial reconnaissance mission.

"I think what happened," said Charley, "is that Kellam sent Scott here incognito. Probably he told the warden who'd hired Chasse as his deputy, but the information hadn't gone further than that."

"So the first time Lamontaine even learned there was an undercover investigator in the area was when Pierre confronted him with the screwup."

"Keep in mind that this all began with Chasse's ambition. He became a deputy warden with an arrangement already in place with the Michauds. But even with the money he was getting from Pierre, he wanted more. He realized he could improve his clout and his financial situation if he could become a full-time officer. It was Chasse who convinced the local warden to complain to Kellam about the Valley being overrun with poachers, not realizing the lieutenant would send in an undercover operative without his knowledge.

"After Emmeline found the badge and Scott's cover was blown, Chasse had a chance to tell the Warden Service. He could have saved Scott's life. But he was worried that the investigator had learned of his side deal with the Michauds, and so he stood aside as Pierre killed him. Chasse's shoulder doesn't have a burn scar, by the way—but it does show signs of plastic surgery, Zanadakis told me.

"Chasse's predicament, following the raid on St. Ignace, was that the Michauds could still turn on him and expose him as an accessory to murder. My theory is that he shepherded Pierre into that ambush. I think Chasse was the one who suggested the escape route across Beau Lac."

"Why would Pierre have believed him?"

"Desperation," Charley said. "Pierre couldn't be positive that someone in his gang wouldn't crack. He needed to get out of Dodge. Maybe he gambled that Chasse wasn't smart or ruthless enough to turn on him. Pierre Michaud wouldn't be the last man to underestimate Chasse Lamontaine."

"So let me get this straight," I said. "Chasse's plan was to go with you to Beau Lac and make sure Pierre died. Either he would shoot the fugitive or you would. If everything went like clockwork, he would eliminate the man who could link him to Pellerin's death and come out as the hero who took down a cop killer."

Charley nodded that big noggin of his. "The one flaw in his scheme was that he assumed there would be a seat for him in my Super Cub."

"So instead of being the man who shot Pierre Michaud, it was you who got the glory."

"That's an empty word for it, but yes, people congratulated me for what happened, even though it meant we never learned what Pierre had done to Scott. Emmeline had been kept in the dark about the details of the murder, I honestly believe. Michaud's sons refused to break, and I think Egan was terrified that if he revealed his part, he'd spend the rest of his life in a cell. Another tidbit I learned this week was that Egan suffered sexually during his first stint in the Maine State Prison—endured abuses I don't care to imagine.

"In the end, Chasse got his promotion even if he didn't get a medal for shooting Pierre Michaud. He went on to have an undistinguished career, probably because he's been on the take the whole time from assorted lowlifes on both sides of the border. Pellerin's death was safely in the past until I came across Dupree's badge on John Smith's table."

I glanced at Charley with dismay. "You forgot it! Back on the island."

Grinning, the old man reached into his pocket and produced the metal shield.

"I went back for it while you were disarming Stanley Kellam."

Amazingly, this was the first time I'd seen Duke Dupree's badge up close. It was smaller than mine, but it felt oddly heavy in my hand. It seemed like a malevolent artifact.

The badge had inspired young Pellerin to become the warden his grandfather never was and restore the family honor. And yet this same piece of metal had been Scott's undoing, too. It had given away his identity when Emmeline found it hidden in his motel room.

Truth be told, I was glad to give it back.

"I wish you and Scott could have known each other." Charley Stevens was not a man inclined to tears, but I could hear emotion in the sudden softness in his voice. "He'd be forty-two now, and maybe he could have taught you some things. You could have taught him, too. More is likely."

I understood that he had a story worth listening to, and so I stayed quiet.

"He showed me this badge, second or third time we met," Charley said. "Told me about his grandfather's disgrace. Of course I had heard all about Warden Duke Dupree, and there were some details I could've added to the tale, but I could see the young man needed to believe in his granddad's tragic fall. It wouldn't have helped to tell him what an ass Duke was. Scott carried the badge everywhere as a good-luck charm. I warned him against bringing it undercover, but he laughed at me and said, 'Charley, you worry too much.'

"After he went missing, I told the detectives to be on the lookout for it. I said it might be the most important clue they found to his whereabouts. But I figured Pierre wouldn't have risked its discovery. That's why I was so gobsmacked to see it on Smith's table in Machias.

"I felt that providence had placed the badge before me and presented me with a second chance to do right by Scott. We all assumed that the truth of what had happened had died with Pierre, but if someone had the badge all this time, maybe they knew the whereabouts of Scott's remains, too. They might even have taken this thing off his body as a souvenir. The way I figured it, the only person who could've had this badge was one of the coconspirators. They'd stayed quiet before—but not this time, by God. I am an old man, and what did I have to lose from leaning on them beyond the limits of what the law allows?"

"You could have lost your liberty," I said. "You could have gone to prison."

"I was so beset with anger, I wasn't thinking straight. I rushed up to confront Smith without even the ghost of a plan. You saw how that turned out."

"I saw it up close," I said.

"Afterward, I knew I needed help—someone calmer than me—so I asked Nick to be my second, so to speak. Not once in all the years we've known each other has that man let me down. The name Angie Bouchard connected us back to the Valley View. We hadn't heard Emmeline had passed. It seems we would've been better off following your lead and speaking with her daughter."

"You didn't need to," I said. "You only had to wait for me to show up."

"We knew that Roland was there—I was watching the house while you met with Nick—and figured your appearance on the scene might flush him into doing something careless. But when you left for Kellam's place, we had to make a decision. Nick followed Roland to Edmundston in my truck, and I followed you in his Jeep. It ended up costing Angie her life."

"I feel like I have her blood on my hands, Charley. If I hadn't knocked on her door—"

He squeezed my arm. "You can't take responsibility for C. J. Lamontaine's evil act. Guilt is a temptation. It's understandable, but in this case, don't fall prey to self-reproof. It won't make you a better man, I can tell you from hard experience."

The breeze blew puffs off the dandelions in the field, each seed a white parachute. I saw the shadow of a bird pass along the ground and, looking up, spotted a raven riding the wind, silent and watchful. Those intelligent black birds didn't miss a thing.

"You used me, Charley. You used me to flush out Roland, and then you used me to interrogate Kellam."

He was watching the raven as it made another reconnaissance of us.

"I hope I have a chance to make amends for that. It was just that we knew that Stanley knew something more than he was telling, and there was no way he would share his information with me after our falling-out. When you accuse a fellow warden of negligent homicide, by which I mean Scott's, he's unlikely to take you into his confidence again."

"As it turned out, Kellam wasn't keeping any dark secrets. My visit with him was a bust, looking back."

"Not so! You saved him from killing Chasse."

"Maybe that was another mistake."

"Take it from a POW, a quick death is a gift compared to life in prison. In C. J. Lamontaine's case, we're talking about a long time with nothing to think about except his bad decisions. And his father, too, is facing charges that might end up as a life sentence, hopefully will."

"When did you begin to suspect Chasse?"

"From the first. See, over the years, I had allowed myself to believe that I understood the whole story. The only mystery was Scott's final resting place. That's why seeing the badge shook me. I thought it was buried forever. But somehow it had gotten loose into the world and had ended up with this John Smith jackalope. How was that possible?

"The badge told me that I knew less than I'd thought. So I went back over everything again in my mind. And I remembered Chasse's 'suggestion' we take a ride up to Beau Lac. With the advantage of hindsight, it occurred to me that Warden Lamontaine had been the only one who'd come out of the tragedy better off than before. But there was nothing to connect Chasse to Scott's murder—and I didn't want to get ahead of my evidence."

"Do you think Chasse sent his son to kill Angie?"

"It's just as possible he only wanted to find out what she suspected. And so he dispatched C. J. to get the information. But the father should've known his son well enough to realize how violent he was."

"As long as he suffers for her death." I began to count off the charges that could be brought against Chasse Lamontaine on my fingers: "Accessory to homicide, criminal conspiracy, multiple counts of attempted murder—"

Charley reached out to close my hand. "They're both going to pay, Mike."

"But not for Chasse's original crime. He's going to get away with being a party to Scott's murder."

"I wouldn't be so sure," my friend said with a hint of the old mischief. "Roland is facing mandatory sentences on drug trafficking charges. He's likely to be more amenable to a plea than he was fifteen years ago, especially when he learns it was Chasse who betrayed his father."

"Speaking of which . . ." I found the waterlogged square of paper in my wallet. Pierre's bearded face had already begun to dissolve. "I'm afraid your photo got wet."

He pointed at a garbage can beside the fence. "Throw it in the trash where it belongs."

"I have a question about the inscription on the back."

The ink had run, but I was able to read the words to him: "'*In battle, in the forest, at the precipice in the mountains, on the dark great sea, in the midst of javelins and arrows, In sleep, in confusion, in the depths of shame, The good deeds a man has done before defend him.*' Ora says that's a quote from the Bhagavad Gita."

"I got it out of a biography on Robert J. Oppenheimer," he said, almost with embarrassment. "The head of the Manhattan Project. It was a favorite verse of his. I figured the man who brought the atom bomb into the world knew more about shame and self-doubt than most people. The picture was so I would remember what I had done, and the quote was so I would forget."

A flock of black-capped chickadees landed in the bushes at the edge of the dirt parking lot. Among them was a bird who sounded as if he had a sore throat.

"Hear that?" Charley said, whispering lest he scare them off. "There's a boreal chickadee in there with his black-capped cousins. You only get that species up north."

"I know, Charley. You taught me that a long time ago."

"Right."

He coughed and looked at the grass beneath his boots.

"Was it worth it?" I asked. "Angie Bouchard dying? Kellam facing prosecution? Edouard Delhomme staring at deportation, now that his protector is gone? Was it worth it for you to have closure?"

He raised his eyes to meet mine. "You've never had a son, Mike."

"Neither have you."

"That's not true. I have had two of them. Someday, when you're a father yourself, you'll understand."

47

When Stacey arrived in Charley's plane, I wasn't sure if she was going to punch him or hug him. She did both. The punch was playful but not light, delivered to the old man's sternum. It was the hug that caused him pain. He'd received a bruise in the back from the impact of C. J. Lamontaine's bullet against the steel plate in his body armor. It was a good thing his daughter didn't see the grimace when she tightened her arms around his torso.

"You scared Mom and me half to death—again," she said.

Charley groaned an apology.

"And your bald head!" She couldn't resist running a hand over her father's stubbled skull. "It's hideous."

"We never knew what a master of disguise your dad was," I said.

Stacey spun around at the sound of my voice. "And you!"

I wasn't sure what treatment I was going to receive, but I prepared myself for the punch. Instead she wrapped her arms around my waist and pressed her face against my neck so that I was looking down at the top of her head. Her thick brown hair smelled of the lavender shampoo I remembered having used in her shower.

"Thank you, Mike," she said in a voice close to choking. "Thank you for being here when he needed you."

I disengaged myself from her embrace.

"He's done the same for me," I said. "More times than I can count."

"Nick and I had it all in hand," said Charley. "But we appreciated the young man's help."

Nick, hoping to head off an embrace, had lit another American Spirit as a diversion. He held out his free hand for Stacey to shake. She took it in both of hers. Nick Francis was clearly not a hugger.

"I'm sorry to have brought you all the way up here from Florida," said Charley.

Stacey lifted her aviator sunglasses and positioned them on top of her head. In the strong morning light, her eyes were the palest shade of jade.

"Didn't Mike tell you? I'm applying for the position of chief warden pilot. I heard the lead candidate was forced to drop out. Who better for the job than the daughter of the best man ever to hold it?"

"Stacey!"

I hadn't seen Charley look that excited in years, not since he'd learned his daughter and I were dating.

She brought a hand to her mouth. "No, Dad."

"What?"

"I was joking. Me, a game warden? That's nobody's idea of a good idea. Besides which, the department fired me, remember?" Once more, she turned her green gaze on me. "They don't need another troublemaker on the state payroll, not when they have Bowditch here."

"I do my best," I said. "Is it true about Wheelwright being eliminated from consideration?"

"Mom heard it directly from the colonel."

Maybe Major Pat Shorey had had a moral awakening. More likely others had persuaded him that hiring the hotshot pilot wasn't worth the risk to the service's reputation.

Stacey hugged her dad again. "If it's any consolation, I'm thinking of sticking around for a while."

Her father couldn't suppress his eagerness. "How long?"

"Indefinitely."

She didn't look at me when she spoke the word. She seemed to make an effort to avoid doing so. But I felt as if she'd whispered it into my ears.

"What about the panthers?" Charley said.

"It's going to take more than one woman to save them." None of us had asked for an explanation, but she must have been preparing her speech on the flight up. "You know, I used to think I could win every battle if I fought hard enough. But Florida has made me realize how close I am to becoming a casualty of war. I guess I'm tired of fighting everything and everyone all the time."

I hadn't had to think about Stacey while she was in Florida. No decisions were required of me. Her returning to Maine didn't need to affect my relationship with Dani. I made a vow to myself that it wouldn't.

"How's Buster?" I asked.

Stacey grinned. "To be honest, I think his nose is going to be improved by the surgery."

"Her friend was bitten in the face by a python."

"Let's hear the story!" said Charley.

"I'll tell it on the flight." Stacey returned her aviators to the bridge of her nose. "We have to get you home to Mom. She's been waiting long enough."

"You need to drop me in Portland first," I said.

"What's in Portland?"

Charley leaned in close to his daughter and whispered something I couldn't hear.

———

Dani was awake when I arrived at her hospital room. I was in need of a shave and a shower, but I had purchased a bouquet of red roses from the shop downstairs.

She had tubes and wires attached to her arm, but she was sitting up in bed. Usually, she wore her shoulder-length hair in a ponytail, but now it was spread across the pillow. Her face looked like it would scorch my hand if I touched it.

The television mounted to the wall was tuned to one of those

Saturday bass fishing shows that I abhorred. Nicole was keeping vigil beside the bed, with a copy of *Us Weekly* magazine open on her lap. More Harry and Meghan.

"Hey, stranger," Dani said as if I had just returned from a quick trip to the cafeteria.

"Hay is for horses." It was one of our jokes.

I leaned down and kissed her on the forehead. The skin felt as hot as it looked.

"You just missed Kathy," she said. Her eyelids were heavy. Her throat sounded scratchy.

Nicole Tate rose to her feet as if in indignation, but it was only to take the inadequate bouquet from me. "Kathy Frost has been here a lot," she said, emphasizing the last word so the message was unmistakable.

I leaned over the bed again and looked into Dani's tired gray eyes. I had expected to see fear in them, but I didn't. In her place, I would have been terrified. "You look good."

"For someone whose brain was about to explode, you mean?"

"I'm sorry, Dani."

"Why?"

"For not getting here sooner. I should have—"

"Yes!" said Nicole.

"Mom, can you give us a few minutes?"

"They're going to be coming soon to take you for those scans, Danielle."

She exerted herself to raise the arm with the IV from the mattress. "I'm not going anywhere."

After Nicole had left, still clutching my flowers, I knelt down on one knee beside the bed and took Dani's hand. The bed, on its wheels, was quite high, making the gesture feel all the more ridiculous. We couldn't even make proper eye contact.

At least she smiled, revealing one of her secret dimples. "Get off your knee, Mike."

"I don't have an excuse, but I have an explanation."

"I don't want either of them. I know about what happened up there. Kathy told me. That son of a bitch Lamontaine. People can be so evil it makes me sick. I don't know how anyone can decide to bring children into this world, as fucked up as it is."

I let that one go. "I understand if you're not ready to forgive me."

"You were doing your job."

"But I *wasn't* doing my job. It was a personal thing."

I could see her forcing her mind to focus. "You want to feel guilty."

"I do feel guilty."

"That wasn't a question. Guilt is your go-to place. Always has been. Get over it."

"Move in with me," I said, reaching for her hand again.

She rolled her eyes. "No!"

"I'm serious. I thought about it on the flight down here. Apply for a transfer to Troop D."

"*You* apply for a transfer." When I didn't respond, she said, "See, that's just it. I don't have a problem with your not being here. I have a problem with your not knowing what you want."

When I had stood up, I felt stiff, sore, and light-headed from lack of sleep. Thirty-one was too young to be middle-aged. But it was too old to be having the conversation Dani and I were having.

"Consider it, at least," I said.

"No."

"Why not?"

She was beginning to flush and perspire. "Because I have plans. They might all be shot to shit, but I've worked my ass off to get to where I am, and I won't stop now, whatever the doctors say."

I had always admired her perseverance—she had the most grit of anyone I had known.

"You're right. I'll put in for a transfer. I'd even be willing to go back to patrol."

"I'm too tired for this conversation, Mike. You might think you're ready for happily ever after, but you aren't. Take care of your wolf first. See how that goes."

Two nurses arrived to wheel her to whatever imaging scanners they were going to use to map her brain. I hadn't detected a change in her mental process. If anything, I'd been taken aback by her lucidity. More than taken aback. Properly chastened. Danielle Tate had a constitution that made Rasputin look like a ninety-eight-pound weakling.

"I'll be here when you get back," I said with artificial-sounding good cheer.

"Feel free to change the channel."

After they took her away, I dropped into the chair vacated by her mother and found it still warm with body heat. I let my bloodshot eyes rest on the television set.

The host of the fishing show was a good old boy with an impressive tan. I watched him muscle a bass out from under a fallen cypress in a lake that looked a lot like Okeechobee.

"Hoo, baby! This one's a swamp donkey. Look at her kick!"

I hit the Mute button on the remote.

In the quiet my mind drifted back to the Fort Kent air strip, before Stacey had arrived in the Cessna.

Standing at the edge of the runway, Charley had held out an arm to indicate a faint path, more like an accumulation of footprints in the grass, crossing the landing strip. The prints led to a line of trees, lush and green in the morning sun.

"Follow that trail a short ways and there's a nice waterfall," the old man had said. "Used to be a sure place to catch salmon and trout. Then the muskies got into the watershed, and they cleaned out most of the native fish. They're apex predators, muskellunges. They're here to stay, like it or not."

"There's always someone bigger, someone hungrier," I had said.

"What's that?"

"I was remembering my visit to Florida. Before I left, you told me, 'Never trust a man without secrets.' What did you mean by that?"

"Are you still chewing on that chestnut?" He was back to being the folksy old woodsman I knew and loved. "Every human being has secrets. If a person doesn't seem to have any, it just means they're devious at covering them up. Your man Wheelwright, for example."

"Not just him."

"No," he'd said, catching my meaning. "Not just Wheelwright."

Both of us had fallen silent then. Across the strip of grass, the dry wind, gusting down from Canada, blew ripples in the treetops like waves across a green sea. The humidity had broken, but it would return soon enough. It was only June, after all, with the hottest months ahead.

Eventually, the Cessna appeared, no bigger than a fly in the southern sky.

I hadn't been thinking about Stacey before I saw the plane, hadn't been anticipating seeing her, hadn't felt excitement stirring inside me. Those were the lies I told myself.

AUTHOR'S NOTE

My connection to the St. John Valley is indirect. While the people of the Valley and I share a common heritage, I grew up at the southern extremity of the State of Maine, part of another community of displaced Acadians. However, my great uncle, the Reverend Romeo Doiron, served as the longtime parish priest at St. James in the town of St. Agatha, and is well remembered there. On every visit I have made to the Valley, I have been welcomed like family.

Thank you to my friends at the Long Lake Public Library in St. Agatha, especially the late Maude Marin, and to Lise Pelletier at the Acadian Archives of the University of Maine at Fort Kent. I learned much about the unique culture of the Valley from Don Cyr of the Musée culturel du Mont-Carmel in Lille.

To readers interested in the history of the Valley, I can recommend no better resource than *Imaginary Line: Life on an Unfinished Border* by Jacques Poitras.

As is the case with all of my novels, you will find most of the places mentioned here in your Maine atlas, but not all of them. (St. Ignace is a prime example.) In some cases a real location may appear under an assumed name. In others, an actual place—for instance, Moccasin Pond—won't be where it appears on maps; it has grown restless, gotten up, and moved while tripling in size along its journey. Consider this another reminder that *One Last Lie* is a work of fiction and should be read as such.

As always, I owe a debt to the staff of the Maine Department of Inland Fisheries and Wildlife, especially to Commissioner Judy Camuso. Thank you to the warden investigators I interviewed (and whose names I promised not to advertise) and to Corporal John MacDonald for answering my questions.

Thank you to my terrific team at Minotaur Books: Charles Spicer, Andy Martin, Sarah Melnyk, Paul Hochman, Kelley Ragland, Joe Brosnan, Holly Rice, and Sarah Grill.

Ann Rittenberg, I wish every author were as fortunate to have an agent with such well-honed editorial expertise.

As ever, my family's support means everything to me. Mom and Dad, thank you for being my self-appointed public relations team.

Kristen, you are my world.